8 Minutes to...

DIGITAL WINTER

MARK HITCHCOCK

ALTON GANSKY

HARVEST HOUSE PUBLISHERS
EUGENE, OREGON

Cover by *Left Coast Design, Portland, Oregon*

Cover photos © *idiz; isoga; Vereshchagin Dmitry, Dima Kalinin / Shutterstock*

Mark Hitchcock is represented by William K. Jensen Literary Agency, 119 Bampton Court, Eugene, Oregon 97404.

Alton Gansky is represented by MacGregor Literary, Inc. of Hillsboro, Oregon.

DIGITAL WINTER
Copyright © 2012 by Mark Hitchcock and Alton Gansky
Published by Harvest House Publishers
Eugene, Oregon 97402
www.harvesthousepublishers.com

Library of Congress Cataloging-in-Publication Data
   Hitchcock, Mark, 1959-
   Digital winter / Mark Hitchcock and Alton Gansky.
      p. cm.
   ISBN 978-0-7369-4912-5 (pbk.)
   ISBN 978-0-7369-4913-2 (eBook)
   1. Cyberterrorism—Fiction. 2. Psychological fiction. I. Gansky, Alton. II. Title.
   PS3608.I84D54 2012
   813'.6—dc23

2011048820

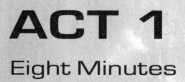

ACT 1

Eight Minutes

PROLOGUE:

Stanley Elton

JANUARY 20, 2014

> Shadow, shadow on my right,
> Shadow, shadow on my left,
> Shadow, shadow everywhere,
> Shadow has all the might.

Stanley Elton emerged from the bedroom at precisely 7:10 a.m., his favorite mug in his hand containing his favorite African blend of coffee. Truth was, he had seven favorite mugs, one for each day of the week. He had seven favorite blends of coffee as well, seven favorite dress shirts, seven chosen suits of varying shades of gray, and seven power ties.

The morning sunlight had already pushed back some of the thick clouds that covered the parts of San Diego closest to the Pacific. His part of San Diego was called Coronado Island, although it wasn't a true island. Situated on a stretch of land called the Strand, the small community rested on a jut of property that looked from the air like an arthritic thumb sticking into the blue waters.

Founded in 1860, the city of Coronado was home to the elite.

North Island Naval Air Station took much of the prime real estate, but there was still plenty of room for retired admirals, CEOs, and entrepreneurs who made sudden wealth in the digital age. A stroll through the city streets sometimes allowed tourists a glimpse of a celebrity.

Stanley Elton was no celebrity or entrepreneur; he wasn't a retired admiral or a man of old money. He was, however, the CEO of San Diego's largest CPA firm, a company whose client list included scores of the top companies in the country. He was on a first-name basis with people often mentioned in the *Wall Street Journal*. For thirty years he worked for OPM Accounting. Most people assumed OPM stood for the founders of the firm, people who died a generation ago. It didn't. Insiders knew OPM stood for Other People's Money. A bit tongue in cheek, but it drew hearty laughs for the few who knew the joke.

"Nice day." Stanley moved to the open kitchen and kissed his wife on the top of the ear.

"You know that gives me the shivers." Royce Elton pulled away and tried to rub her ear on her shoulder, her hands busy flipping eggs and turning bacon. A pot next to the frying pan cooked down some oatmeal. Instant oatmeal wasn't good enough for her son, Donny. At least he ate something close to healthy.

"My presence has always made you shiver." Elton slurped his coffee.

"Shudder is more like it." Her tone was playful.

"Shiver, shudder; potato, patahto." He moved from the kitchen and took his usual spot at the floor-to-ceiling window overlooking the rolling Pacific. The $3.5 million condo was on the top floor of one of the fifteen ten-story structures on the Strand. Built in the 1960s, the luxury buildings caused such a stir that a city ordinance was passed forbidding similar towering structures in Coronado. Too late and too little.

From the wide living room, Stanley could look to the left and see the Pacific Ocean or look right and see the calm waters of Glorietta Bay. "Water everywhere and not a drop to drink."

"Good thing we have plumbing and coffee." Royce dropped two pieces of bacon (well done) and two eggs (over hard) onto a scalloped-edged green plate. A moment later, she added two pieces of rye toast.

He stepped to the dining table. "Dining room" would be inaccurate. The only real rooms in the open floor plan were the bathrooms and bedrooms. Royce set the plate on the glass top. She sat next to him, sipping a chocolate diet shake.

"Eating real food while watching you suck on that stuff fills me with guilt." He stuck a piece of bacon in his mouth.

"You're a man. You're supposed to feel guilty. It goes with the Y chromosome."

"This is what I get for marrying a geneticist."

"Brains are sexy."

"Really? I hadn't heard."

Royce raised an eyebrow. "You know, I can poison your breakfast."

"That's why we have Rosa cook our other meals. Cuts down on your opportunity to cash in on the life insurance." He cut one egg in half and scooped it into his mouth. Stanley didn't like wasting time on trivial things like breakfast. "Busy day?"

"Usual classes at the university, and then I have about four hours in the lab. I'll be late. I have to grade test papers after that. Rosa has something planned for you and Donny."

"She's as good a cook as she is a nurse." Down went the second half of the egg.

"She's a jewel. We should pay her more."

It was Stanley's turn to raise an eyebrow. "Really? She makes good money now."

"I'm not sure it covers all she does. Dealing with Donny isn't easy."

Stanley contemplated the comment while gnawing on the bacon. "What do you mean? He sits in his room and doesn't cause any trouble. He's as passive as someone with his condition can be."

Royce frowned. She hated it when Stanley referred to Donny's challenges as *his condition*.

"Sorry," he said. "You know what I mean. Other people like him can be high maintenance."

Another frown. "He requires a lot of care, Stan. You know that."

"Of course. I do my share."

She touched his arm. "I know, dear. I didn't mean that. You do more than any other father would. You provide an income that allows us to get all the help we need. My professor's salary wouldn't pay for one room in this place. I'm just saying we should reward Rosa. She's been with us since Donny was ten. That's twelve years."

"She's a trooper. Did you have something in mind?"

"I thought of a paid vacation, but I don't think she'd leave Donny for more than a few days. She's so devoted to him. I know that her car is getting a little long in the tooth. She had to take it into the shop. Cost her a pretty bundle to get the transmission fixed."

"You want to pay for the repairs?"

"No, I want to buy her a car."

Stanley lowered his fork. "You're kidding, right?" He could see she wasn't. "You mean like a Porsche or Ferrari or—"

"Of course not. I was thinking of a Prius or some other hybrid. It would save her some gas money."

Stanley furrowed his brow, narrowed his eyes, and clinched

his jaw, but he couldn't maintain the pretense. He had never been angry at his wife and couldn't imagine starting now. The forced frown gave way to the upward pressure of a smile.

"You're working me, aren't you?"

"Yep."

"Okay, but it's going to cost you another cup of coffee. I'll let you make the arrangements. Take the money from the house account." He paused. "We are talking just one car, right?"

"For now." She rose, kissed him on the forehead, and took his cup to refill it. "Speaking of Rosa, she said something yesterday that seemed…"

"What?"

"I don't know what word to use. Unexpected." She filled the cup and returned to the table. "She said Donny spoke."

"Spoke? You mean more than one word?"

"She meant sentences."

"You're kidding. I've never heard him link words together. I thought it was beyond his ability."

"We don't know that." Royce the geneticist was talking now. "His condition is a mystery. There are only a handful of savants in the world. We don't know what goes on in his brain."

"What did he say?"

"She told me she couldn't make out all the words. He stopped when she entered the room. Something about shadows."

"Maybe she was hearing something from one of his computers."

"Maybe, but she didn't think so."

Stanley checked his watch. "Why didn't you tell me this last night?"

"Um, because you didn't come home until nearly midnight and you were half asleep."

"Oh, yeah." He rose. "Thanks for breakfast. Good as Rosa is, food cooked by my wife always tastes better."

"I manipulate the alleles in the eggs."

"That's more science talk, isn't it?"

"You going to say goodbye to him?"

"Just like every day for twenty-two years."

"Thanks."

Stanley started the most difficult task of his day. He loved his son, but he would rather face off against a bunch of IRS attorneys than turn the doorknob to his boy's bedroom.

As his hand touched the brass knob, he heard a voice from the other side of the door:

> Shadow, shadow on my right,
> Shadow, shadow on my left,
> Shadow, shadow everywhere,
> Shadow has all the might.

■■■■

Donny Elton sat in his chair as he did every hour he wasn't sleeping. The chair was an expensive, well-padded iBOT designed by inventor Dean Kamen. It was powered and could raise Donny to the eye level of any adult not playing in the NBA. A series of gyros and a robust computer program enabled it to climb stairs without tipping. The invention had been a boon to wheelchair-bound consumers.

But Donny wasn't bound to the wheelchair. He could walk if he wanted, jump if he desired, and even sprint if he had a mind to, but he never did. At least that was what the doctors said. Under heavy sedation, Donny had endured MRIs, CAT scans, X-rays, muscle conductivity studies, and other medical tests. All came back negative.

"The problem isn't with this body," the doctors said. "The problem is in his mind. He doesn't want to walk." That had been the end of their assessment. No one could offer any ideas of how to make a healthy twenty-two-year-old who was monosyllabic on his best day and mute on his worst and who possessed an IQ above 200 do what he didn't want to do. "You simply cannot make a man walk if he doesn't want to." They had been united in that assessment.

Stanley, in the few quiet moments he allowed himself, wondered why his son refused to walk or engage with humanity. Yes, his savant condition was probably due to autism, but research had yet to come to a consensus on that.

Stanley stood in the open door with a bowl of hot oatmeal in one hand and wondered if he had heard what he thought he heard.

"Hey, buddy. Mom whipped up some oatmeal for you." He moved to the long desk that took up all of one wall in the place they called Stanley's bedroom. It looked more like a NASA control center than a place to sleep. A series of four 27-inch monitors lined the table, and two computer towers sat nearby. They were never turned off. More than once, Stanley had awakened in the night to hear Donny's fingers tapping on the keyboard.

"Oatmeal. Food. Oatmeal. Good."

Stanley set the bowl and spoon on an unoccupied spot of the table. "Whatcha working on, pal?"

"Oatmeal. Good."

Stanley was thankful Donny could feed himself. He needed help dressing and using the bathroom, but at least he could manage to put a spoon in his mouth or hold a sandwich. *Small blessings.*

The large window of the bedroom overlooked the Pacific side of the Strand. The thinning cloud cover allowed the morning sun to paint sparkles on the gentle swells and surf. A short distance from the shore, surfers waited for the ocean to offer more waves. Although Stanley couldn't see them from this window, he knew that new Navy SEALs were training there. Such was Coronado: home to the wealthy, a mecca for sun worshippers, a training ground for the Navy, and a magnet for tourists.

Donny knew none of this. Stanley doubted his son had ever noticed the beauty outside his window, the kind of view that made the 1700-square-foot, three-bedroom, three-bath condo worth $3.5 million. The only things Donny seemed to notice were on the computer monitors. Stanley doubted the young man even knew him. The last thought brought pain, as it did a dozen times every day.

Line upon line of code filled the monitors. For a few moments, Stanley considered having a programmer look at it, but he dismissed the idea. What difference would it make?

"I'm headed to work, son. I'll be home late again, but I'll look in on you. Mom will be here until Rosa arrives."

"Rosa. Oatmeal. Good." Donny took a bite of the pasty meal.

Stanley ran his fingers through his son's hair. He loved the boy even if he had never caught a baseball or watched a football game. "Take it easy, champ."

"Bye. Later. Oatmeal."

Stanley turned when something appeared in the corner of his eye—something dark, indistinct. He snapped his head around but saw nothing.

Closing the door, Stanley paused and tried to push back the gloom that draped his mind. Then he heard Donny's voice again.

Shadow, shadow on my right,
Shadow, shadow on my left,
Shadow, shadow everywhere,
Shadow has all the might.

1

Roni

"There he is—tall, dark, and yummy."

Roni Matisse gazed down the first-floor hall of Harris Memorial Hospital. Like hospital halls everywhere, this one was wide with a floor as glossy as a sheet of water. A man, six feet two and trim from regular exercise, walked their direction.

"Square of jaw, broad of shoulder, brown of hair—"

Roni cut the head surgical nurse off. "You know that's my husband you're talking about."

Loren Grimm kept her eyes fixed on the approaching man. "Oh, yeah. I forgot."

"You'd better not forget, girl. I'm really handy with a scalpel."

"It's not my fault, it's his."

"How do you figure that?"

"That uniform. It's unfair. A good looking man *and* a military uniform. No court would convict me."

"He does look pretty good, doesn't he?" Roni started for the man walking their way. Loren started to follow. "Stay, girl. Stay."

"Don't make me bite you." Loren hung back.

Roni harbored no worries about Loren. She was quick with a

joke, an excellent nurse, and happily married to her husband of twenty years.

A few steps later Roni stood before the tall man. "Colonel Matisse."

"Dr. Matisse."

They hugged for a moment before she pulled back. "This is a surprise. To what do I owe the pleasure?"

"Do I need a reason to see my wife?"

"Nope. But what if I had been in surgery?"

"I would have barged in, taken you in my arms, and embarrassed the surgical team."

"That might break our sterile environment."

"I'm not scared." He grinned.

"I was thinking of the patient."

"Oh, yeah. That could be a problem. Anyway, I shortened my jog, and that left me enough time to swing by and have a cup of coffee with you before I head to Maryland."

"Okay, what's happened?"

"I told you."

"We had coffee together this morning, and you *never* cut your jog short."

"What? A man can't have another cup of coffee…Oh, all right. I'm going to have to spend the weekend."

Roni clenched her jaw. "I was looking forward to our trip to New York."

"Me too. I'm not happy about it, but you know the military. They tend to give orders, not make requests."

"Is there a problem?" A wave of worry rolled through her. Jeremy worked in the little-known USCYBERCOM in Fort Meade. While other soldiers wielded guns and bombs and drove tanks, Jeremy drove a computer. His only overseas duty had been to train cyber security officers.

"No. Well, yes, in a way. I have a bunch of Army shavetails coming in. They like nothing better than having an Air Force bird colonel briefing Army personnel."

"I think you're the one who enjoys it."

"You wound me. You're right, but you wound me. It's a privilege that comes with being the general's favorite officer."

"So much for Christian humility." Roni regretted the dig. She meant it in good humor, and his expression said he took it that way. Faith was the one area they differed: He had it, but she didn't want it.

"That's not pride talking, just me relating a few facts."

"I already knew about the briefing, but why do you have to stay over the weekend?"

"Unexpected congressional tour. Some politician wants to make sure we're not playing video games instead of protecting the country."

"On the weekend?"

"The Senate Armed Services Committee carries a lot of weight."

"I understand. You want me to get the date changed on the theater tickets?"

"If you would. I'm going to be out of commission for a while."

"I can keep myself busy here."

"Tell me about it over coffee. I only have about twenty minutes before I hit the road."

Just as Roni started to speak, she heard her name called over the hospital public-address system. "Hang on." She went to a phone on the wall, punched in a three-digit number, identified herself, and then listened.

She hung up and stared at the blank wall for a moment. Jeremy stepped to her side.

"Something wrong?"

She looked at him, forcing herself to breathe. "Commuter

train derailed. The injured are being divided among the hospitals. We have at least fifteen patients headed to ER, and some have serious injuries. I have a feeling it's going to be a long day."

His face lost a shade of color. "That's horrible. At least they have the best trauma surgeon in the country waiting for them."

"I'm not the best in the country—just the East Coast." She forced a smile but doubted its believability.

"I'll pray for you, babe."

The smile felt more genuine. "I've got to go assemble the surgical teams and call in off-duty doctors. I'm sorry."

"Don't be. You make me proud. We'll talk soon." He took her in his arms, and she wished he would never let go.

"Be careful."

"I always am."

....

Rosa caught a glimpse of herself in the reflection of one of the windows and hated it. She always had—face too round, hair too thin, skin too pockmarked, eyes too dark, body too heavy, worry lines too deep.

She looked through the reflection to gaze at the ocean. There were easier jobs, but none that paid so well or provided such a view. Her work would never make her famous, never fill her bank account with cash. She was a care-at-home nurse, caring for a person who barely acknowledged her existence. Still, she had grown fonder of Donny than she had any of her past patients. She had become attached to him, something a nurse shouldn't do.

Maybe she was getting too old for this work. Fifty-two wasn't old, but old was closing in fast. At times she looked forward to retirement, to spending the day with her truck-driving husband and spoiling her grandkids, but reality always set in. She doubted she would be able to retire at an age where she could enjoy free time. Barney made a trucker's salary. She made decent money but not enough to create a nest egg. Like so many people of her class, she would depend on Social Security for retirement income, and that wouldn't be much.

Too old? Maybe. Donny was a fully-grown man who, for whatever reason, refused to walk. At times she could get him to stand, but that was only to move him from the powered wheelchair to the toilet. Even then she had to add her strength to his to make the transition.

Rosa's primary job was to care for Donny during the day, when his parents were away. Often their schedules meant she had to stay late into the night. They always gave her a bonus for those times.

She had been doing this work for two decades. The nurse before her had taken to stealing jewelry from Mrs. Elton's case. When they hired Rosa, they made it clear that they would prosecute any theft. Rosa had no problem with that. She cared nothing for jewelry, fine clothing, or artwork. She loved her family and her work, and that summed up her existence.

Her biggest challenge was dealing with the boredom. Although Donny couldn't be left alone, he was not demanding. If his food was delivered on time and she was available when he needed to go to the bathroom, he was happy staring at all those computer monitors by the hour.

To pass the time, Rosa cleaned the condo. It wasn't part of her duties, but it gave her something to do, and it was another way to say thank you to the people who paid her generous salary.

After cleaning up the breakfast dishes and chatting with Donny, who never responded, she straightened the magazines on the rosewood coffee table in front of the tan leather sofa. It was an eclectic gathering of reading material: *Time*, *Newsweek*, *Forbes*, the *Wall Street Journal, Barron's,* and other business periodicals for Mr. Elton; *Science Review, Journal of Genetic Studies,* and *Nature* for Mrs. Elton. Smart people.

Next she moved to a small cabinet of cleaning supplies, gathered up a bottle of Windex and a soft cloth, and began touching up the windows. She tried to focus on the smudges and spots but allowed herself moments of wistful ocean gazing. She tried her best to avoid her own reflection.

A breeze had picked up over the ocean, decorating the surface with tiny whitecaps. California gulls, white as milk with long, yellow beaks, soared high and then turned into the wind, hovering as if filled with helium. Cormorants did aerobatic dive-bombing runs, dropping from the sky like spears, disappearing beneath the waves, and reappearing moments later. In the distance, a cruise ship plied the waters, headed to the Mexican Riviera.

What a wonderful world.

A motion caught her attention. Something in the window, a reflection of something behind her.

Not something. Someone.

Dark. Tall. Faceless.

Rosa's heart stuttered like a car engine deprived of fuel.

No eyes. No mouth. No face.

She released a tiny scream and spun, pointing the bottle of Windex as if it were a weapon, as if the intruder could be killed by glass cleaner.

Nothing.

No shape. Nor form. No dark being. Nothing.

She looked back at the window. The reflection was gone.

From behind her came the muted voice of Donny in his room, closed off from the world.

Shadow, shadow on my right,
Shadow, shadow on my left,

> Shadow, shadow everywhere,
> Shadow has all the might.

"Donny!" She sprinted to his door and flung it open. Donny was alone.

2

Jeremy

Colonel Jeremy Matisse, PhD, had added distance to his trip by going into DC to see his wife. Had he headed north to Fort Meade from their College Park home, he could have saved ten or fifteen minutes, but he harbored no regrets. Any time spent with Roni was an investment in his own happiness. Fortunately, the travel time to Fort Meade from the nation's capital was less than an hour if the traffic cooperated. This being a Thursday, traffic was only mildly annoying. It was just a little after 1300 hours. By 1800, DC would be clogged with people looking to escape the city, many of them on US 50 with him.

Leaving his wife behind was nothing new. Over the course of their twenty-year marriage, he had left her behind many times. On the other hand, she had left him cooling his heels while she did double shifts at the hospital or traveled to various symposia. Such was the life of professionals.

He drove his Jeep Cherokee in the right lane, in no hurry to click off the miles. He had an extra hour before the new Army officers showed up for their tour. He let that thought percolate for a moment. He would help General Holt with the senator as well. At least he assumed so.

He wondered if more was going on.

The sun reflected off the chrome and windows of the car in front of Jeremy, stabbing his eyes.

By the time he crossed under the I-95 cloverleaf, his mind returned to Roni. As promised, he prayed for her. He had spent the first ten minutes listening to the news. Investigators had not yet determined why the train derailed a few miles northeast of the Amtrak terminal on Massachusetts Avenue. The news reported thirty or forty injuries but no deaths. That last part was good. In 2008, twenty-five passengers were killed on a Los Angeles Metrolink that ran into a freight train because the engineer missed a signal. He had been texting.

Jeremy took time to pray for the injured and the families. He couldn't imagine the turmoil going on at Roni's hospital.

····

The woman on the surgical table looked like Amy.

····

Roni Matisse started her medical career wanting to be a pediatrician. After all, that's what women doctors did, wasn't it?

The idea was old and out of touch with twenty-first-century thinking. But then, Roni grew up in a family that was stuck in the 1950s. She was the youngest of three children. More than once she had overheard her father refer to her as an "oops." Such comments undermined her already shaky self-esteem. It had taken all her courage to tell her parents that she wanted to be something other than a housewife.

But being the youngest and the unexpected child also had some positive impact on her life. It made her shy, and shy girls often retreated to the world of books and long, lonely hours in their bedrooms dreaming of things they never expected to experience. Roni poured herself into schoolwork. What else did she have to do? By third grade, she proved to be the best student in the elementary school and the darling of several teachers. That also made her the butt of cruel comments from other kids, and she withdrew all the more.

By fourth grade she developed a love for science. When asked what she wanted to be when she grew up, she replied, "A scientist." When asked what kind of scientist, she froze. Did it matter? She liked it all. On some days, she saw herself as a sky-breaking astronomer; on others, as a biologist. She was in college before she felt the first calling to medicine. Biology came easy to her, and she aced chemistry, microbiology, zoology, botany, and other upper-division life-science courses. That was at Morehead State University in Kentucky, a four-year school that had a good biology department and that was just far enough away from her parents' home in Flemingsburg to keep them from dropping in uninvited.

Morehead was very different from her high school, but Roni hadn't changed. A good day was spent in classes and the library. She was addicted to study. It protected her from others and gave her a sense of accomplishment. Graduating with honors was never the goal, but it was a certainty.

During her junior year, she met another studious coed. Amy had frizzy hair, bad skin, pale eyes, a photographic memory, and a passion for knowledge. She also had an unwavering goal to be a medical doctor. At night, Roni would listen to Amy speak of the future, of the glories of being a physician. "The money is good, but that doesn't matter; I want to change the world one treatment at a time."

Like Roni, Amy was not part of the campus scene, and if that bothered her, she never showed it. Roni had many interests, but Amy had just one one—medicine.

Alone at night, staring at her ceiling, Roni would think of Amy's enthusiasm. She was an evangelist of Hippocrates, a siren of the noblest profession.

At first, Roni attributed Amy's comments to loneliness, but Amy never wavered, and over the course of the semester, Roni began thinking about a career in medicine. By the end of the semester, she had committed to the additional years of training. During their senior year they took the Medical College Admission Test, and both passed easily. Armed with impressive scores, they applied to thirty medical schools. One night, over a chocolate milkshake at a restaurant near the campus, they agreed to attend the same medical school if they could. What could be better than having a lab partner you already know and trust?

Both received scholarship offers from Stanford University in Palo Alto, California.

Two months later, Amy's Vespa scooter was hit by a drunk driver in a thirty-year-old Ford pickup. She lingered in the hospital for several hours as Roni sat in the waiting room. Amy's family lived across the country, and Roni was the closest thing she had to a sister, so she answered questions from the medical staff and then made the call to Amy's mother and father. That was by far the most difficult thing she had ever done—until three hours later, when she called again to say that Amy was no more.

The drunk driver went to jail. Amy went to the grave.

One memory of Roni's darkest night surfaced a thousand times during med school. Dr. Carrie Mayer, dressed in surgical greens, walked into the waiting room. She was a tall woman with ebony skin and moved with confident steps, but her shoulders were bent.

Her eyes scanned the room and settled on Roni. "I'm Dr. Mayer, are you…" She looked at a note on a small pad in her hand. "Roni?"

"Yes."

"Sorry for my confusion. They spelled your name R-o-n-n-y. I was looking for a guy."

"I get that a lot." She blinked with brimming eyelids. "You… you're…"

"I'm a trauma surgeon. I understand you're Amy's—sister?"

They looked nothing alike, but telling the truth at this point achieved nothing. She did her best to lie convincingly. She managed one word. "Yes."

"I see. Are you here alone? No other family?"

"Amy's parents—our parents live on the other side of the country. They're on their way." Roni thought she saw a glimmer of amusement in the doctor's eye. A moment later, it drowned in a flood of sadness.

The doctor sat and pulled the surgical cap from her head. Once in the chair, the woman seemed to deflate. She took two seconds to breathe and then sat straight. "I'm sorry, but your friend is gone."

Roni started to counter the "friend" comment, but the rest of the sentence took the air from her lungs.

"We did everything we could. We used everything at our disposal, but there was nothing we could do. The damage was too extreme, and time wasn't on our side."

Roni's lip quivered. Seeing tears in the surgeon's eyes only made controlling her grief more difficult. "You've said that a lot in your career, haven't you?"

Dr. Mayer nodded. "Far too many times."

"What was the cause of death?" Roni tried to maintain composure by giving reason to revelation.

"Let's just say it was from internal injuries."

"Amy and I were going to go to med school together. She would ask the same question if it had been me instead of her."

"What school?"

"Stanford."

Mayer nodded. "Good school. Okay…but it's not pleasant." She turned to Roni and gazed in her eyes as if searching for a clue about the young woman's strength. "Amy presented with severe trauma. Her left leg was crushed, multiple fractures to femur, fibula, and tibia. Two of the breaks were compound. The soft tissue injury was extensive. If she had lived, I'm sure we would have had to amputate. Her hip was broken in three places; three vertebrae were cracked, and I'm sure there was significant spinal damage."

She looked at the arm of the waiting room chair as if searching for her next sentence on the plastic arm rest. Roni figured Mayer was giving her time to digest the first bit of gruesome detail. When Roni didn't react, the doctor continued. "There was other damage too. Left lung punctured, left rib cage crushed, and her sternum was pressed back to her heart. It bruised the heart muscle and the xiphoid process. That's the—"

"The hard bit of cartilage at the end of the sternum."

"Exactly. Anyway, it put a gash in the liver. The liver is blood rich, so it bled profusely. There were other organs damaged. She had almost bled out by the time she reached the ER."

"So there was no chance to save her?"

"None. I wish I could have done more."

....

Why did the woman on the operating table have to look like Amy? Her hair was the same color and just as wild, though it was now hidden by a green sterile bonnet. Roni had examined the woman in the ER, lifting her eyelids to check pupil response—eyes the same shade as Amy's. The ER docs had done an admirable job stabilizing the woman considering the number of patients who waited their turn, some screaming and moaning.

The injured lined the halls. As always, the early estimates were wrong. This time emergency personnel underestimated the number of injured by half. According to the first report, Harris Memorial would receive fifteen to twenty patients. But that many arrived during the first hour, and more were en route.

The head of ER started triage, judging who needed attention first. Usually the screamers were left to the last. Screams meant they could draw a breath. Unless they were bleeding out, they would have to wait. Roni performed a secondary triage on those who would clearly need surgery. Victims with broken bones were sent to orthopedic surgeons; Roni and other trauma surgeons would be responsible for those with internal injuries. In the worse cases, more than one surgeon attended to a patient. Such was the case for this woman, who had two broken arms requiring pins and metal plates. Roni's job was to stem internal bleeding, remove the pancreas, and check for a perforated bowel.

Roni called for a scalpel from the surgical nurse, took it in a Palmar grip—her index finger resting on the top of the blade—and set it to the woman's bruised skin.

Amy would be proud.

3

Shavetails

Jeremy was a kind man, taught by his parents to be respectful and polite. He prided himself on his calm, nonconfrontational demeanor. It was the way he thought all humans should act—except in uniform. The military way of communication was different from that of polite society. Rank existed for a reason, and Jeremy admitted to enjoying the often formal and disciplined way warriors spoke.

Inside the USCYBERCOM wing of the National Security Agency—to most, *NSA* stood for No Such Agency—ten newly minted Army officers, fresh from cadet training, chatted and joked as they awaited the arrival of the man who would deliver their indoctrination lesson. Jeremy had no intention of teaching like a college professor or delivering a speech like a politician. As the head of operations of the joint military unit, he was concerned with focus and knowledge. His team had no room for men and women looking for coattails to ride.

He paused before stepping into the small, theater-style classroom. From his position he could see twelve soldiers—eight men and four women—dressed in Army combat uniforms, similar to his airman dress uniform. The biggest difference was the sewn grade insignia on the collars: Theirs were single bars, indicating second lieutenant; his was the eagle of a bird colonel. Mixed into the group were eight other newly graduated cadets, four from the Air Force and four from the Navy.

As he stepped into the room, one of the soldiers glanced his way, blinked once, then shot to his feet. "At-ten-tion."

Twelve junior officers came to attention.

Jeremy strode to the front of the room and approached a metal podium with an artificial wood top. He let the group stay at attention for a few moments as he gazed at each of their faces. All so young; so fresh-faced. "At ease. Sit."

As only former military cadets can do, they sat at attention. He fought a smile.

"I am Colonel Jeremy Matisse. I lead day-to-day operations of USCYBERCOM. Welcome to the world of digital defense…and digital warfare. I am told you are the best and brightest to come out of the academies. I am told each of you has distinguished yourself in this year's cyberwar games." Several smiles crossed young faces. "You shouldn't feel too bad that the Air Force took the Director's Cup."

The Cyber War Games were held annually with teams from the various military academies to see which group of cadets could best defend a military network. The competition met outside Las Vegas and lasted four days, as cadets faced off against NSA specialists and the 57th Information Aggressor Squadron from Nellis Air Force Base. It was a real-world simulation and was essential in training the newest and most-needed breed of military assets.

One of the former Army cadets started to raise his hand but thought better of it. Jeremy had no doubt that the man wanted to remind him that Army usually won. He would be in his rights. West Point recruited and produced some of the best cyber warriors.

A motion at the back door caught Jeremy's attention. Two men entered the room. One wore an expensive-looking dark gray business suit. The other wore an ADU like Jeremy's but with a noticeable difference—two stars on the collar. Major General Tom Holt was nearly sixty but looked a decade and a half younger. He was six feet two and had the narrow build of an Olympic swimmer. His gray hair clung close to his head, and his aquiline nose and straight spine gave him an aristocratic air. The general raised a hand and gave a quick nod to Jeremy without breaking eye contact. The act kept Jeremy from calling the group to attention.

Bringing a visitor into the session had not been part of the plan. Holt and the senator sat in the back row, their entrance unnoticed by the others.

The visitor was no mystery to Jeremy, who prided himself on being a news junkie. Senator Ryan O'Tool looked as Irish as his name sounded: reddish-brown hair, ruddy skin, and a square jaw. According to rumors, the new head of the Armed Services Committee had the stereotypical Irish temper. He wasn't supposed to be here until tomorrow. A surprise visit? Jeremy wouldn't put it past the ambitious man.

Jeremy returned his attention to his charges and placed his hands behind his back. "Operation Shady RAT." He gazed at the group. No one spoke.

He waited.

He raised an eyebrow.

"Operation Shady RAT. Anyone?"

A young man who looked too young to shave raised a hand. "It was a recent—"

"Stand up when you address the group, Lieutenant."

The thin man scrambled to his feet. "Yes, sir. Sorry, sir." Had this been a college class, snickers would have circulated, but this group knew better.

"Carry on."

"Yes, sir. Second Lieutenant Rabin, sir. Operation Shady RAT was a hacking effort discovered by McAfee a few years ago. It was a five-year-long hack that embedded software on hundreds of computers around the world."

"Define 'around the world.'"

"Well, the US was the worst hit, and there were others."

"Sit down, Rabin." Jeremy frowned, searched the group for signs of intelligence, and pointed at a female Navy ensign. "Can you do better?"

The woman stood. Her round face was pretty, even with almost no makeup. "Yes, sir, I believe I can. Ensign Jody Liddell. The lieutenant is correct in calling it a five-year hack. The US received the most attacks. Forty-nine to be exact. Canada discovered four compromise attempts. South Korea and Taiwan each suffered three compromises. Other countries include Japan, Denmark, Vietnam, Indonesia—"

"Areas of attack?"

"Government agencies mostly, from the federal level down to county. Thirteen defense organizations were also attacked, including those in electronics, computer security, and satellite communications."

"Who did it?" Jeremy stepped to the side of the lectern.

"I'm not privy to that information, sir, but my best guess is the Chinese government or a group sponsored by them."

"That's a serious accusation."

"Yes, sir, I agree. But some of the attacks had to do with international sports, and the earliest part of the attack occurred before the 2008 Summer Olympics in Beijing, so it is appropriate to suggest China as the state player."

Jeremy looked at General Holt, who was smiling. Jeremy fought not to smile. "Thank you, Ensign. I don't suppose you know what fell off the truck." Jeremy always liked that metaphor.

"Again, sir, I have no proprietary knowledge, but the news and scuttlebutt is that the computer of the secretary-general of the United Nations was compromised, although as far as the public knows, nothing was transferred. However, in its report, McAfee suggested that a great deal of material was copied and sent to the actors."

"Very good, Ensign. Please take your seat." He addressed the group. "Every day, computer systems around the world are attacked. As I stand before you now, the network of the NSA, the Pentagon, the White House, congress, and military bases around the world are under attack. Make no mistake. We've been compromised in the past. There's a good chance we will be compromised again. We are no longer facing off against pimply-faced geeks living in their parents' basement. We're matching wits with powerful and very rich countries, several of which have technology equal to our own."

He paused to let the information settle, although he was sure the new officers already knew this. The speech was for the man in the gray suit scowling in the back.

"Your job will be to help stop that and, if called upon to do so, reverse the attack." He wondered how many people in the country knew that the military and intelligence communities not only defend the technology networks of the country but also had taken the offensive on several occasions. The war against Iraq began at a computer terminal. "Some of you will work here or at one of the bases around the country. Some of you will deploy to foreign fields to set up and defend computer systems in combat zones.

"The world has changed," he continued. "We are moving from megatons to megabytes. You will take us to the next level. Who can tell me the formal USCYBERCOM mission?"

An Air Force man near the back stood. He looked older than the others. "Second Lieutenant Ogilvy, sir. I believe I can."

Jeremy motioned for him to try.

"USCYBERCOM plans, coordinates, integrates, synchronizes, and conducts activities to direct the operations and defense of specified Department of Defense information networks, and prepare for—and when directed, conduct—full-spectrum military cyberspace operations in order to enable actions in all domains, ensure US/Allied freedom of action in cyberspace, and deny the same to our adversaries. The command is charged with pulling together existing cyberspace resources, creating synergy, and synchronizing war-fighting effects to defend the information security environment. USCYBERCOM is tasked with centralizing command of cyberspace operations, strengthening DoD cyberspace capabilities, and integrating and bolstering DoD's cyber expertise."

"Word for word, Ogilvy. Homeland Security handles threats to commercial cyber security. We focus on military—"

The lights flickered and then went out.

"Remain seated." Jeremy ordered.

Darkness lasted thirty seconds before the lights came back on, slightly dimmer than before.

"Is this a simulation, sir?" someone in the group asked.

Jeremy didn't answer. His eyes were fixed on the general and on the tech sergeant who appeared almost magically at the door. The sergeant whispered in Holt's ear. The general nodded then rose.

"The base is now on lockdown." He looked to Jeremy. "Colonel, get someone to take these people to the cafeteria and join me in the sit room." He exited with the senator on his heels.

▪▪▪▪

Roni worked with feverish determination, clamping several bleeders around her patient's liver. She was determined to save the Amy look-alike, mostly because it was her job but partly because she had been unable to do anything for the real Amy so many years ago.

She kept her head down and her eyes directed into the abyss of blood and tissue that was the woman's abdomen. She called for surgical instruments with a soft but authority-laden tone. Each tool was quickly but carefully laid into her gloved hand. Med school had given her a new perspective on many things. One was that all people, regardless of age and ethnic background, looked pretty much the same on the inside. Women had a few organs men did not and vice versa, but everyone came equipped with one heart, one spleen, one stomach, one spine, and one liver. All of those had been damaged in this patient.

"She's still bleeding." Dr. Marc Middleton was assisting.

"I can see that, Marc. It's kinda hard to miss. Hang another unit of blood." The last comment was directed to a surgical nurse. "This girl's liver is a mess."

"She may be beyond hope," Middleton said. "We've got patients lining the walls in pre-op."

"I know that too. Clamp." The surgical nurse placed a vascular clamp in her hand. "Jan?" Roni cut her eyes to the anesthesiologist.

Jan's fifty-eight-year-old eyes took in the digital information on her monitors. "BP is 102 over 80. She's dropped another five points. Respiration is normal. Pulse is 123 and thready. That should come down as soon as we get the blood volume up. We may need to deepen her sleep to get the pulse down so she's not pumping herself dry faster than we can fill her up. Still—"

"Suction." Roni applied the clamp and searched for other bleeders. Things had gone south quickly. The woman seemed to be trying to die. Every time Roni clamped another oozing vein, a new one appeared, most likely from the increase in the pressure. The woman's BP rose and fell like a roller coaster.

The patient was beyond Roni's skill, beyond any surgeon's skill. Middleton was right. Other patients needed her, but Roni couldn't give up. Not now. Dr. Mayer's sad eyes played in her mind; her voice rang in her ears. *We did all we could*…She hated those words but had said them plenty of times herself. She didn't want to say them again, but she knew she would before this day was over.

The lights went out. One of the nurses gasped. A second later, the emergency battery-powered lights over the door marking the exit came on, casting the OR in harsh lights and stark shadows.

"Great. As if this weren't challenging enough." Roni kept her head down, eyes straining to distinguish one blood-covered organ from another.

"Monitors are off," Jan said. She placed gloved fingers to the side of the patient's neck. "If the generators don't kick in soon, we'll be doing this surgery old school." A second later, she added, "I'm gonna need a BVM."

"Someone help Dr. Barry with the Ambu bag." Roni stood still, her hands deep into the patient's abdomen. "Come on, come on. Someone kick the emergency generator."

Seconds passed like geological ages before the lights came back on. The sound of the respirator sounded like music.

"Resetting the monitors." Jan's fingers worked the electronic devices around her.

"Duration?"

"I make it to be about twenty or thirty seconds. Seemed longer, but I don't think things were down long." Middleton leaned over the surgical area. "We still have bleeders."

Roni didn't answer the observation. There was nothing to be said. She was losing the battle.

The phone in the surgical room sounded, and one of the nurses answered. "OR-3." She listened. "Understood." She hung up and turned to Roni. "Power is out in the city."

"The whole city?"

The nurse shrugged. "I assume so. That was the head of ER. He said we need to prep for an influx of trauma. There are likely to be accidents and the like."

"A train wreck wasn't enough—now we have to lose power?" Roni shook her head as she searched for the next bleeder.

"They'll have the power on soon," Middleton said. "It's not our first power outage."

"I hope you're right," Roni said. "DC has enough problems without trying to get by without electricity, especially in January—" The pit of her stomach dropped. "Suction!" She blinked as if doing so would remove the image of blood rising in the patient's abdominal cavity like water filling a sink.

"That's arterial," Dr. Middleton said.

"You think?" Roni pushed her hand deeper and behind the woman's organs, searching for what she didn't want to find. When she did, her heart came close to stopping. "There's a breach in the descending aorta. She's bleeding out. Hang another unit. I'm thinking endograft."

Her fingers traced the abdominal aorta. Middleton pushed the intestines to the side. Blood poured into the space with every beat of the woman's heart.

"Dr. Matisse—"

"Don't say it, Doctor. I'm not giving up."

"Doctor." He put a bloody hand on Roni's. "The descending aorta has been crushed in several spots. The moment you stop the flow there it will break loose elsewhere—if not from the aorta itself then in another dozen bleeders."

"I won't give up."

Middleton sighed and then called for several aortic stents.

"This will work, Marc."

He shook his head. "No it won't. I'll help you do whatever you call for. You know that. But it won't work. There's just too much damage."

A half hour later, the patient died.

Roni removed her soiled surgical gown and gloves and donned new ones. OR-5 had another patient waiting.

▪ ▪ ▪ ▪

"The IRS is always changing the rules. They have more than a hundred thousand employees to keep busy. A simple tax structure would put a bunch of them out of work." Stanley stepped into the elevator near his office on the twenty-fifth floor of the Mission Financial Building near the heart of San Diego. The elevator had one glass wall overlooking San Diego Bay, its waters bejeweled by sunlight. Stanley still loved the view and watched the man next to him. He tended to distrust anyone who didn't pause to notice beauty.

"Including you?" The man turned to the window, his eyes drawing in the scenic waterscape.

Stanley laughed and put a hand on Ben Joiners's shoulder. The man was wide and tall and waddled more than walked. His body was out of shape, but he was the intellectual equal of anyone Stanley had ever met, and Stanley moved among the intellectual elite of the business world—people who used their brains to make money by the truckload.

"There's more to my work than taxes, Ben. Businesses like yours need everything from investment advice to legal counsel. OPM has more than just accountants. We have attorneys and investment brokers. We do more than count your money—we help you make it."

"You sound like a television ad."

"I suppose I do. I love my work. I tend to get carried away. But that's attracted a lot of people to our firm. That and confidentiality. We never discuss your business with any of our other clients."

"Even if they pay more than I do?"

"It's a matter of principle, not money, Ben. A couple of times I've threatened to break ties with customers who have tried to use me or my firm for what amounts to industrial espionage. No one has ever pressed the issue. They need the same commitment to secrecy as you." He pressed the button for the first floor.

"But you do work for other people in industrial real-estate development."

Stanley nodded as the elevator began its descent. It was an executive car available only to certain people in his firm. "Yes. We have six of your competitors on our books."

"Which competitors?"

"I won't tell you that, Ben. That's my point. I don't talk to them about you, and I won't talk to you about them. That's the deal."

Ben narrowed his eyes. "There are other high-end accounting firms, you know."

Stanley nodded. "There are. I can have my executive assistant send you their contact info if you'd like."

This time Ben laughed. "Just testing you, Stanley."

"I know. I'll have contracts drawn and sent to you for review by day's end. Then—"

The elevator lurched and slowed.

"Wha...what's happening?" Ben placed a hand on the side of the cab to steady himself.

The elevator's emergency lights came on, dim in the bright of the day.

"I...I don't know. The elevator stopped moving."

"I figured that part out." Ben looked at the floor-indicator lights over the door. "Does this happen often?"

"No. Well, once before. In 2011, a power company employee working on the grid that feeds the city made a mistake and pulled the plug on San Diego. Lasted for better than a day."

"Anyone get stuck in elevators?" A bead of sweat appeared on Ben's forehead.

"Yes. It even happened here. No worries, though. This is a modern building, which means—"

The elevator lurched again and began a slow descent.

Ben pulled a handkerchief from his suit coat and dabbed at his brow. "That didn't take long. Power must be back on."

Stanley moved closer to the glass wall of the cab and looked down. "I don't think so. Traffic lights are still out."

"Then...?"

"Our elevators have emergency power. All the elevators in the building will be moving to the first floor. The power will probably be back on soon."

"How are you going to get back to your office?"

"I'm not going to climb twenty-five flights of stairs, I can tell you that. I'll just wait in the lobby for a while."

The elevator cab reached the first floor, and the doors opened slightly slower than usual. People in the lobby murmured. Some seemed amused; others were put out.

For Stanley, it was a bit of an adventure.

■■■■

Donny Elton piloted his power wheelchair out of his room and started doing laps about the condo.

"Donny? What are you doing?" Rosa didn't expect a response. She got one anyway. Donny laughed and clapped his hands. She couldn't recall him laughing before.

4

Lockdown

Senator Ryan O'Tool looked put out. The sudden interruption was an annoyance to him.

To Jeremy, it was potentially much more. He had to jog through the halls of the NSA building to catch up with the rapid pace of General Holt. O'Tool had already broken into a light sweat.

"What's the rush, General? It was probably just a fluctuation in the power grid."

Jeremy took a position two steps behind the men, close enough to hear without inserting himself into the conversation. Holt had a reputation for having a mind that worked like a bulldog's jaw: clamp and lock in place until the work was done. Holt took the same approach with important tasks. Focus on the issue, and don't let go until happy with the outcome. Jeremy had seen the man work eighteen-hour days for weeks on end.

"I hope you're right, Senator. I'll arrange a comfortable office for you to wait in until the lockdown is lifted."

"No way, General. I'm here to see what you and your team really do with the millions we send your way."

"It's hundreds of millions, but I guess you already know that." The general rounded a corner and stopped so abruptly that O'Tool ran into him. Despite the senator's mass, he failed to budge the general. "I think you would be more comfortable in one of the offices or in the cafeteria."

"I didn't come to be comfortable. I came on a fact-finding mission. This is probably a waste of time and effort, but the least I can do is watch you work."

"Very well, Senator, but please don't get in my way. You're right—this is probably nothing serious, but we get paid to take everything seriously, so until I know better, I'm going to assume we have a problem."

"Ah, the military mind."

How Holt kept from decking the senator was beyond Jeremy. They walked to a corner office and marched into the lobby. The Air Force captain at the desk came to his feet the moment Holt entered.

"As you were, Captain."

Jeremy had been in this office many times and heard Holt call the captain by his first name. The formality was for the senator's benefit.

"Report." Holt stopped at the wide, metal desk. The office foyer was the size of a living room and held not only the desk but also two sofas and two padded chairs for people waiting to see the general.

"Sir, the NSA director and his team are on alert and are monitoring news and intelligence sources. The base commander has the base locked down. No one in or out."

"Anything to indicate this is more than a downed power line?"

"Yes, sir. We have reports that power is out in several places along the Eastern seaboard, including DC."

Holt's eyes narrowed. "Anything from intel?"

"Not yet, sir. But it's been less than five minutes."

"Understood. The colonel and I will be in the sit room. I want all info piped in there. Make that happen, Captain."

"Yes, sir."

"I'm going to the sit room with you." Senator O'Tool made it sound like an order. When Holt hesitated, he added. "I'm the sitting chair of Armed Services. My security clearance is as high as it gets. Not that I need it for a power outage."

Jeremy caught the two emotions in Holt's eyes: fury and pity. "You will stay out of the way, Senator. I don't mind showing you around. I don't mind answering your questions, but you need to know that I take what I do very seriously. If this is a simple blackout, then well and good. It's a nice real-world drill for my people. If it's more than that, then I don't want to be caught with my pants down."

"Don't need to worry about me. I came to learn this stuff. Who knows, it might even save your budget."

Jeremy took a step back just in case the general decided to do a little boxing. He didn't. Instead, he spun on his heel and headed out the door and down a hall to a room situated in the center of the building.

The sit room was dim and had no windows. The walls were plain and covered in sound-deadening material. A table ran the length of the long room and could seat twenty people when necessary. Jeremy oversaw dozens of scenarios and drills from this room. Computer monitors lined the walls on each side of the table, and a bank of monitors made up the wall opposite the entrance.

The table was made of a light wood along the edges and dark panel down the middle. A phone with a digital screen was positioned within arm's reach of every seat. The thick, cobalt-blue carpet deadened ambient noise.

Before the door finished closing, an airman entered and went to a control center in one of the corners. A moment later the monitors came to life, adding their light to the dim space.

"I want CNN and FOX news. Get me a local DC station and one for this area."

"Yes, sir," the airman said.

"I want department heads on the Wall." The name referred to the segmented monitors that covered every inch of the far wall above three feet.

"Yes, sir."

Holt turned to Jeremy. "Colonel, bring the senator up to speed on this place."

"Yes, General. As you have probably guessed, this is one of our situation rooms—"

"One of? How many are there?"

Jeremy waited a second before answering. "Several. This is our primary room. Another one is on base, and a few others are in protected areas around the country. If Fort Meade were compromised, we could move to another facility."

"But that would take time. How do things get done while you're in transit?"

"Key personnel are able to control the work while on the move, much like the president does. He might go to Camp David, but he takes White House communications with him. There are also redundant teams. If we're knocked out, others can take over in short order."

"Who are these others?"

"I'm not at liberty to say, Senator."

"I've already said my clearance—"

"It's need-to-know, sir." Jeremy quickly moved on, hoping for no more interruptions. "This is the processing center, where decisions are made based on information fed to the general and his team. We can host twenty around the table, and there is room for aides to sit along the wall. Have you been in the White House situation room, sir?"

"Can't say that I have." O'Tool seemed embarrassed by the admission.

"It's similar to this. Both have state-of-the-art communications and satellite connections. We have a few more toys. From here we can videoconference with Homeland Security, the Office of the Director of National Intelligence, the CIA, the FBI, the National Reconnaissance Office, the National Geospatial-Intelligence Agency, and all the intel components of the military. Of course, that includes the NSA."

"I don't think your mandate includes intelligence work." O'Tool looked suspicious.

"It doesn't. We don't do direct intelligence, but we have to work with those agencies to protect the interests of the United States. We leave the spy work to the spies. Our job is to deal with cyber attacks."

The voice of a CNN newscaster filtered into the conversation. It took only a moment for Jeremy to know they had little information. Not surprising. Just over five minutes had passed since the power blinked out and the building went on auxiliary power.

"It's just a power outage," O'Tool said. "You didn't set this up just for me, did you?"

Holt's jaw tightened, and Jeremy thought he would soon hear teeth cracking. "You weren't supposed to be here until tomorrow. So, no, we didn't set it up for you. I doubt we could get CNN to cooperate."

"Just checking, General. That's all. Still, it seems a little overkill, don't you think?"

Jeremy thought it best to intervene. "Let me tell you why this is not an overreaction. Most likely, this will pass in an hour or two, but one of our greatest concerns is the safety of the power grid. More than 315 million people live within our borders, all of them in need of electricity. Unfortunately, our power grid is highly susceptible to attack."

Jeremy folded his arms. "More and more of the control systems for the three basic grid areas serving the lower forty-eight states are connected to the Internet. It has made many things more efficient and made monitoring systems instantaneous. It has also made it possible for hackers to bring down our system."

"Hackers? Really? A bunch of pimply-faced—" The phrase was similar to what Jeremy had used earlier.

"Excuse me, Senator, I'm thinking a little larger. We have discovered software programs sleeping in grid control systems. Not one malware, but several. The sophistication of these programs points to more than just mischievous kids. The Internet being what it is, we can't prove who the culprits are, but we do have our suspicions."

"Such as?"

"China and Russia. We know both countries have mapped our infrastructures. We also know that sophisticated software is designed to shut down the power grid, most likely in case of a war. You can imagine how hampered our intelligence and military operations would be without power."

The senator raised an eyebrow. "Aren't those organizations able to work off the grid? I was told they were."

Jeremy nodded. "They are, to an extent. Even so, imagine what happens in our country when 315 million people are suddenly without power. It wouldn't be pretty. Let's back up to the pimply-faced hackers you mentioned. When the hacking team known as Anonymous was arrested in 2011, only two or three fit the image most people have of hackers. Just to be clear, one person can do a lot of damage. In 2000, an Australian man—apparently angry with the company he worked for—rigged a computerized control system to dump 200,000 gallons of sewage into rivers, in parks, and on the property of a Hyatt hotel. It doesn't take much."

"Sir," the airman said.

"What is it?"

"The blackouts are spreading. I'm getting reports that New York has gone dark. So has much of New Jersey."

"Put it on the screen." The general took a seat at the head of the long table. Jeremy sat to his right. O'Tool, looking like a man who didn't want to stand alone, pulled out a chair a few spaces down the table.

A stylized map of the country showing the three power grid areas appeared. The map showed state lines and capital cities. It also indicated every military base. Most of the country was colored green, indicating unaffected areas. The areas without power were black.

The black was spreading like mold.

"Southern California, Arizona, and parts of New Mexico have been affected. There's no pattern to it."

Holt rubbed his chin, his eyes mere slits as he studied the image. "Put up the nuclear power plants." Yellow dots appeared. "Just like our scenarios."

"What?" O'Tool looked confused.

Jeremy answered. "Nuclear power plants are designed to shut down if there's a sudden loss of power. They need power to control the nuclear reaction. No power, and things go bad quick. Remember Japan after the 2011 earthquake and tsunami? The flood knocked out the diesel power generators used to control the cooling system. It went downhill from there. When a plant registers low voltage, backup systems kick in, and the plant is shut down for safety."

"They're a bear to start up again," Holt said. "Gravel Neck in

Virginia is shut down. Mineral, near Richmond. Calvert Cliffs and Douglas Point here in Maryland. This isn't good."

Jeremy focused on the West Coast. "San Onofre in California is out."

"How many do you think will be affected by this?" The abrasiveness had left O'Tool's voice.

Jeremy couldn't tear his eyes away from the image on the large screen. "We don't know. I've never seen so many blackouts and in different zones. What happens in California shouldn't affect anything in this half of the country." He rubbed his forehead. "There are 104 nuclear plants in 31 states, Senator. I don't know how many will shut down."

"Shouldn't you be doing something?" O'Tool sounded angry.

The general pinned the man with his eyes. "Just because you don't see it doesn't mean nothing is being done." He turned to Jeremy. "Get the department heads in here. I'll call the president."

Jeremy rose without hesitation and marched from the room. He had trained for this and hundreds of other scenarios. He was prepared.

So why did he feel like vomiting?

5

Stanley

Stanley moved through the crowds on the sidewalks. They grew as employees in various buildings used the sudden loss of power as an excuse to leave their desks for an unplanned break. People laughed, and strangers struck up conversations. Stanley thought it odd that something as inane as a power outage could garner such attention. He had no doubt that the power would be back on soon.

He let his eyes drift up the tall buildings that made up San Diego's iconic skyline. Most were shaded or reflective, but he could see people standing on the other side of the glass, watching the growing hubbub below.

Traffic on Kettner had slowed to a crawl, and Stanley could only imagine the confusion at Kettner and West Broadway and other intersections. The outage was costing him time, but he didn't care. He had reached the point in business where worry was a distraction. He had made enough money to retire comfortably. Still he worked because it defined him. What else could he do? Traveling with Donny was almost impossible. Donny didn't enjoy it, and that meant Stanley didn't enjoy it.

He chastised himself for the bitter thought. Having a special-needs child came with a price tag other parents didn't have to pay. The few times he and Royce had traveled alone required a crew of nurses and caregivers. Donny didn't like new faces. That meant Rosa had to move in while they were gone. It worked, but she had to ignore her family for the duration of the trip—something that made Royce extremely uncomfortable.

So this was his life—a wealthy and esteemed San Diego CEO with a trophy wife who was as beautiful as she was smart, respected by a hundred and fifty employees…and yet he still felt confined, held back.

He pushed the thoughts from his mind. Like many high achievers, he was prone to small bouts of depression, but they seldom lasted long. When the blues arrived, he treated them with extra caffeine and work. He also counted his blessings, including this unplanned break in the morning.

Stanley walked half a block to his favorite coffee shop. Beanies was casual and well lit and played music from the seventies. Always a plus. Of course, they wouldn't be able to whip up his usual latte without power, but they always had dispensers full of the coffee of the day.

"Hey, Burt," Stanley said. "You got anything hot?" The store was empty. Paper cups rested on tables where patrons sat before the lights went out.

Burt was a college graduate with a degree in philosophy. The kid was bright—he just needed to find himself. In some ways, he reminded Stanley of Donny.

"Oh, hey, Mr. Elton. Still got a couple of pots of Kenyan. Brewed them right before everything went dark."

"Pour a large cup, will ya?"

"Sure, but I can't ring it up. Register isn't worth anything without juice, so we'll just make this one on the house."

Light poured through the glass storefront. A battery-powered emergency light cast an eye-stinging glow. "Thanks. Your customers desert you?"

"There's more excitement out there than in here."

"They'll be back. We're all coffee addicts now."

"The beans have been modified to affect your brain that way. It assures our continued success." Burt had already poured a generous amount of half-and-half into the cup. "You taking a break?"

"I was in the elevator when things went dark."

Burt's eyebrows shot up. "You were stuck in the elevator?"

"Not really." Stanley explained about the new safety mechanisms that allowed the elevators to descend to the first floor. "Of course, not every building has that. I imagine hundreds of people are cooling their heels in the older buildings. It's happened before."

"I hope things get back to normal soon. I have a daily quota to meet."

"I'm sure they will." Stanley moved to a table and removed his cell phone. He dialed his wife but got a fast busy signal. That didn't surprise him.

"I can't get out on my cell either." Burt moved into the service area and gathered abandoned cups. "I imagine the cell network is a little stressed. You might try texting. Sometimes that gets through when a voice call won't."

"I hate texting. I remember when people used phones to talk to each other, not send them cryptic messages." He paused. "I guess that makes me sound old."

"I would never say that, Mr. Elton."

"I bet you'd think it."

Burt avoided the comment. "The landline works. The phone company provides its own power to wired phones. Something to do with FCC regulations."

"Thanks, Burt. I need to call the office and let them know

I'm okay and that I won't be walking up twenty-five flights of stairs." Stanley rose and moved to the phone behind the counter and placed his call. He then called his wife's cell but couldn't get through. He tried her office phone. She answered on the first ring. "Hey, you."

"Hey yourself. Are you okay?" Royce sounded stressed.

"Just peachy. Got stuck in the elevator for a few moments, but twenty-first-century engineering saved me. How about you?"

"Everything on campus is down. Emergency generators are running essential stuff like the bio labs. Everything else is dark."

"So this extends to La Jolla. Interesting. It must be more widespread than I realized."

"Well, it's not everywhere. I just got off the phone with Rosa. She said they still have power."

"Really?" A twinge of guilt stabbed Stanley. He hadn't thought to call home. "That's good. Donny wouldn't understand why his computers weren't working."

"That's another thing. Rosa said Donny was motoring around the condo and laughing. Something has made him happy."

"At least he's happy. We've seen the other side, and it isn't pretty."

The comment was met with silence. Stanley decided to push on. "I wonder why Coronado still has power." He watched Burt wipe down the tables. Outside, people milled along the walkway. Men in suits stood shoulder to shoulder with the homeless.

"I don't know. We have an old boom box in the lab. Normally we have it plugged in, but it still had some juice in the batteries. The blackout is happening up and down the coast and even in Washington DC."

"No way."

Burt looked at Stanley.

"I didn't hear the newscast myself, but several others did."

"Okay. Wow. I don't see how that can be. How can DC be

having an outage at the same time? It doesn't make sense. I'm no expert, but I know we're on separate power grids." Stanley was an avid reader, devouring two newspapers a day and a dozen magazines a month. There had been several articles written about the US power grid after Southern California's last major outage, and each one had a map of the country's power grid. East and West did not meet.

"I'm just telling you what I was told."

"I know, hon. I'm just trying to process things. Look, if this thing lasts long, getting home might take a while. I don't have that far to go. As long as things don't back up over the bridge, I can get home fairly quick. Let's keep in touch—" The connection crackled. "Royce? Baby?"

Nothing. The line went dead.

"Great. Just great."

"What's wrong, Mr. Elton?" Burt walked his way.

"Stupid phone quit on me. I don't suppose you have a battery-powered radio."

"Sorry. I get all my tunes on my iPhone. The music system for the shop doesn't run on batteries."

Stanley smiled. "Not your fault, Burt." He looked at his coffee. "Can I get that in a to-go cup?"

"Headed back, sir?"

"I'm going to the car. Maybe I can get something on the radio."

A few moments later, Stanley began to work his way through the crowd. In the distance, he could hear car horns honking and the mournful sound of sirens.

■ ■ ■ ■

Roni moved through her second surgery quickly: a young man with a ruptured spleen. It was still a lengthy operation, and she couldn't cut corners. She couldn't waste time either.

The door to the surgical theater opened, and a man clad in a green surgical gown entered. He was gloved and masked, but his broad shoulders and short neck gave away his identity. Dr. Peter Court was chief surgeon for the hospital. Much of his day was spent in administration and dealing with doctors' egos, but he maintained a consistent presence in the OR.

"How we doing, Doctor?" His voice was a half-octave too high for a man his size and age. He approached, his kind gray eyes watching the orchestrated movements of modern surgery. Roni glanced up again and then returned her attention to the work before her.

"So far so good, Doctor. I was unable to save any of the spleen, and there's some additional injury, but none life threatening."

"Good to hear. How are you holding up?"

The question worried her. "Fine. A little tired but we all are. I'm good for more surgery."

"That's good. That's good…"

"Is there something you want to tell us, Dr. Court?"

"There are more on the way. The day and night might be longer than we assumed."

"From the train wreck?"

"Most of those are in, but we're taking West Regional's share."

Roni looked up. "You're kidding, right?"

"I wish I were. Their backup power system failed. I don't know why, but my guess is that they didn't maintain the generators. It happens in a tight economy."

"How many?"

"Another thirty patients from the train, but most don't need immediate surgery. Maybe fifteen high-priority surgeries. Orthopedics and otolaryngology have their work cut out for them. West had several people in the OR when the power went out. They've been stabilized and are being transported here. We're also taking CICU and ICU patients."

This is a nightmare. She glanced at her team. "Are we getting help?"

"I've called in everyone I can, but it's taking longer to get in. Traffic is a mess."

"DC traffic is always a mess."

Court nodded. "Especially when the traffic lights don't work." He took a breath. "I'm afraid you'll be shouldering more than your fair share."

"Understood. We're up to the task. I recommend a rotation system for the surgical nurses."

"I've already set something up. Of course, off-duty nurses are having the same problem getting in as the doctors. West Regional is sending staff with patients. They'll be around to help us. We'll get some surgeons and OR docs too."

Roni couldn't imagine the nightmare going on at West Regional. She made a mental note to thank the hospital administrator for keeping the backup systems up to date.

Court remained in place.

"Is there more, Doctor?"

"The blackout isn't just in DC. It's hit most of the East Coast and other states. The phones went down a few minutes ago. The cell system is jammed."

"Life just gets better and better."

"Could be worse," Court said.

"Really? How?"

"You should see ER. At least it's quiet in here."

■ ■ ■ ■

"Are you sure you're not hurt?" The man in a blue lab coat leaned over Cody.

"I'm okay. Where's my mother?"

"She's behind those doors." The man pointed to a pair of white doors on the far wall. Cody had watched people being taken back there. None ever came out. "That's where the ER doctors work. Do you know what ER means?"

Cody shook his head.

"Well, it means 'emergency room.' The doctors here are trained to help people like your mother."

"Are you a doctor?"

"No, I'm a triage nurse."

Cody didn't know what *triage* meant, and he didn't know men could be nurses.

"Where is your father? Is he at work?"

"He's dead."

The man-nurse looked down and then made eye contact again. "I'm sorry. Did he die in the accident?"

"No. He was a policeman and a bad guy shot him. That's when I was eight."

"How old are you now?"

"Ten. My birthday was last month."

"Happy birthday. My name is Alan. What's yours?"

"Cody Broadway."

"Okay, Cody. Do you have any other family in town?"

"No. It's just me and my mom."

"I see. I have to get back to helping these other people, Cody, so you stay right here. If you need anything, you go to that window over there." He pointed at a window near the ER doors he indicated earlier. A woman in a uniform sat behind the glass. "You tell her you want to see Nurse Alan. Okay?"

"Okay."

"One other thing, Cody. As you can see, there are a lot of people here. So it might be a while before I can check on you again. You can be brave, right?"

Cody nodded.

"Are you hungry?" He pulled several one-dollar bills from his wallet. "There are vending machines down the hall. You can get a soda and some chips." He held out the bills, and Cody took them. He was hungry, and a soda sounded wonderful.

The man walked away, and Cody wondered about the train wreck. He hadn't been on a train. He was in the car with his mother when a pickup ran into their car.

It was a bad day.

6

Mr. President

When the lights went out, President Nathan Barlow was having an early lunch with his wife, Katey, something he tried to do at least three times a week. During the first two years of his administration, he had averaged one and a half times a week. Fifty-percent wasn't bad for a man whose schedule was timed to the minute and whose average day included at least one crisis. When push came to shove, personal time always took a backseat to state business. Especially these days. Six years of recession teetering on depression had created issues few presidents had faced.

The lights in the residence wing of the White House dimmed, brightened, and then failed. In seconds, the emergency power came on—and the Secret Service locked down the White House.

Barlow had been tempted to approach one of the windows of the second floor and see the effects of the power outage. The family dining room overlooked the north lawn and Pennsylvania Avenue, but he knew the drill. Although the windows were bulletproof, he was to stay away. "No need to broadcast which room you're in." The Secret Service was paranoid about paranoids and just about everyone else.

He didn't have to get up to know what was happening around the building. They went on lockdown at least once a month because of potential threats. West Wing staff were moved to offices without windows, all doors into the building were locked, and the Marine guards who stood around the perimeter became more than sharp-looking ornaments. Agents dressed in black uniforms and looking more like special ops than Secret Service walked the roof, automatic rifles in hand.

Five minutes later, the phone in the dining room chimed. Barlow answered, listened, and then hung up. He returned to the table and sipped his coffee. He admitted to being addicted to caffeine and had no intention to give it up.

"End of the world?" Katey sipped her tea. She was the most unflappable person Barlow knew.

"Nah, just a power outage in the city. Probably a squirrel in some relay station. That's one mistake the critter will never make again."

"Don't be cruel, Nathan. Squirrels are cute."

"I'm not being cruel. Besides, he might have been a terrorist squirrel. His demise was quick. Okay, I don't know that it was a squirrel. Just an outage. No doubt the power will be back on soon. I'm just glad I don't have to commute to work."

The phone rang again. Again the president listened and thanked the caller.

"Don't tell me—the squirrel was a Republican."

Barlow sat at the table again but didn't respond.

"Nathan?"

"What?"

"You okay?"

He smiled. "Sure. I'm fine."

"You look concerned."

He rubbed his chin. "That was Frank. The problem is a little more widespread."

"A little more?" Katey set her glass down and spooned some vegetable soup into her mouth. After two years of living with the head of the world's most powerful nation, she had grown used to the constant intrusion of problems. Still, the chief of staff was not prone to exaggeration. "More than a few blocks? The whole city?"

"Much of the East Coast."

Katey set the spoon down.

. . . .

By the time Barlow reached the Oval Office, Frank Grundy had a fresh report for him. The chief of staff was a tall, attractive man with dark hair and a square jaw who once admitted that he longed to be president. He served two terms in congress before realizing that he didn't have the political drive to seek the nation's highest position, but he did have the smarts to help someone else get there. He was most effective and most comfortable behind the scenes.

They exchanged greetings and got down to business. "We don't have details yet, but DHS is getting reports from the field that the power grid is in serious trouble."

"Terrorism?"

"We can't prove it, but that's my suspicion. This isn't confined to one segment of the grid. It's hopscotching around the country."

"How long before the utility companies have things back up and running?"

"Unknown, Mr. President. That would depend on the actual cause. Secretary McKie asked to see you. I've bumped the afternoon meetings. Traffic is at a standstill, so most people were happy to reschedule."

"She didn't want to do this on the phone? If the traffic is as bad as you suggest, Monica is going to have a tough time getting here."

"She wants to do this in person. Police will do what they can to get her here. There's one more thing—she thinks we need to set up a videoconference in the sit room."

"With whom?"

"Several people, including USCYBERCOM."

Barlow thought for a moment. "She knows something."

"Yeah, that's my take."

"Let me know when she's here."

■ ■ ■ ■

Stanley listened to the radio in his Audi Q8. The car was as comfortable as his living room, and the stereo system would be the envy of any audiophile. Despite the eight grand he had spent to upgrade the audio, the sound was scratchy and muddled. The concrete and steel in the basement parking and the twenty-five story building above him didn't help, but he knew the audio shouldn't be that bad. He attributed it to radio stations being on backup power.

He marveled that technology was unwilling to yield to setbacks. A series of national disasters over the decades had pushed the country to make sure that communications continued. The Cold War had been a pretty good motivator too.

Stanley shifted from the San Diego news station to one in Los Angeles. The news was the same: Power was out in San Diego, Los Angeles, and points in between. The lights went out in central California shortly after power was lost here. The radio announcer mentioned how odd that was. In 2011, power loss was felt as far north as Orange County but no more—at least in California. Other states were affected, but he knew more about what his own state experienced than he did about the others.

Stanley switched back to the San Diego announcer just in time to hear him pass on some messages from the mayor's office.

The last outage in San Diego lasted eleven hours in some areas.

Traffic was currently jammed on all major freeways and streets. Estimated time to travel from center city to North County was four hours.

People were asked not to drive if they had less than a quarter of a tank of gas. Gas stations were shut down and unable to pump fuel. Stanley assumed this bit of advice was meant to keep cars from running out of gas while idling on I-5.

The traffic lights at some major intersections had battery backup and would most likely continue working through the night if need be.

San Onofre nuclear power plant had gone off-line as a security precaution.

When power came back online, it would do so in stages. The announcer explained that it wasn't like throwing a switch. It had to be done in stages or the sudden flow of power would activate other safety protocols.

Raw sewage was beginning to spill into San Diego Bay and could begin to pour into the streets. In 2011, more than two million gallons of sewage polluted the coast.

The newsman said something else that caught Stanley's attention. "The blackout covers all of San Diego County and east to New Mexico…"

He had almost missed it. The man had to be wrong. Didn't Royce say the power was still on in the condo? Rosa had said so. That couldn't be right. He tried to remember if the ten buildings that made up the condo complex had emergency power. They didn't in 2011, and he had received no word of an update to the buildings that could explain why his lights were on.

It didn't make sense. Royce must have misunderstood.

■■■■

Rosa stood at the window facing the Glorietta Cove and gazed at the blue ribbon of the San Diego–Coronado Bridge. Since 1969 it had been one of the gems of San Diego. At night it appeared bejeweled, magical, with blue light that painted the tall concrete columns that held it 200 feet above the calm waters of the bay. A Navy ship moved beneath the span on its way to open ocean.

A thirty-four-inch-high concrete side rail allowed motorists an unobstructed view of the bay. It also made it easy for those weary of life to slip over the edge. Hundreds had done so. From the tenth floor, Rosa could usually see what few could: cars moving across the five-lane road. At night, the red taillights made an image begging to be photographed.

But today, the cars weren't running as normal. Traffic had come to a standstill. Cars sat on the two-mile span. Getting home tonight was going to be difficult. Her husband was on a long haul, guiding his truck through the Southern states for a delivery in Atlanta. He wouldn't be home for days. Maybe the Eltons would let her stay over if things didn't get back to normal soon.

Donny continued his bizarre behavior. He zipped his wheelchair into his room, looked at his computer monitors, and then zipped back into the living room, stopping a few inches from the large windows. Clap. Giggle. Repeat—again and again.

At least he was happy.

■■■■

Cody Broadway fought tears. Tears were for kids, and he was ten. More than once his mother had told him he was now the man of the house. He took that seriously although he didn't fully understand what the words meant.

More people came into the waiting room. Some were crying.

Others were hurt. Outside he could see ambulance after ambulance drive by the window and stop at the rear doors. His mother had passed through those doors while a nurse examined him briefly and then led him to the waiting room. She wasn't as friendly as Alan.

Cody took another bite of a Snickers and then a sip of orange soda. He didn't feel well. For a time, he thought the mix of candy and soda might be upsetting his stomach, but then realized it was something worse—fear.

The tears began to rise again, but he pushed them back. Crying would do no good. Nobody in the full room knew him. He doubted any cared. They had their own problems.

He wished his dad were still alive.

●●●●

When President Barlow strode into the White House sit room on the ground floor, everyone stood. The Woodshed was a complex of rooms covering 5000 square feet and included offices for National Security Council watch officers and a president's briefing room, a smaller version of the main conference. Renovations began in 2007 and were completed in 2009, but they had begun again, utilizing the latest in communications. Keeping up with technology was an unending task.

"Be seated," the president said as he took a seat at the head of the long wooden table surrounded by thirteen padded black chairs. Most of them were filled.

The south wall featured a large monitor to facilitate videoconferencing with other heads of state. The sit room was manned every minute of every day by watch teams. More than thirty personnel kept things flowing smoothly.

Contrary to what most believed, the room was used often and

not just for emergencies. This was especially true during Nathan Barlow's administration. He loved to pull information from around the world and discuss it face-to-face with his advisors.

The long, dark, wood conference table dominated the tunnel-like room. The walls had once been covered in mahogany, but now WhisperWall treatments had replaced the wood. Several smaller monitors lined the east and west walls.

"First question: Is this a terrorist attack?" Barlow leaned back in his chair as if he asked the question every day. He didn't, but he did think about such things frequently. Such was the life of the commander in chief. He looked at the secretary of Homeland Security.

Secretary Monica McKie pressed her lips. "Mr. President, I've received reports from around the country, and there is no indication of a physical attack. No bombs in substations or that sort of thing, but something is afoot."

She started to say something else when Barlow snapped his head around to Leon Sampson, a small man who looked like someone who was picked on in school. That was an illusion. Only five feet eight, he proved himself tough through a long and decorated career in the Army. He retired from the military with three stars on his uniform. Barlow insisted on calling him by rank. "General?"

"CIA has nothing to indicate this is a terrorist attack. By that I mean we have nothing new. We are all aware of cyber infiltration into power systems of several countries."

Barlow turned back to McKie. "What do you think is afoot?"

"Leon has it on the money. I suspect a cyber attack, but it's too soon to say with certainty. What we do know is that there is no mechanical problem. I've also checked with NASA and NOAA, and no coronal mass ejections are reported."

"Could a CME be responsible for outages on both sides of the country?" Barlow leaned into the desk.

"If it was big enough, yes." McKie didn't flinch under Barlow's gaze. She never flinched. "It wouldn't be the first time."

"But you don't believe that's the case now."

McKie shook her head. "No, sir. A CME would impact the world's satellites, and we have no indications of that. More to the point, NASA's Solar Dynamics Observatory satellites are orbiting the sun. We know every burp the star makes, and nothing has been noted."

The president looked at his hands as if they held the answers to his questions. "So if you're right, some actor has planted programs in our power grid just like before—or did we fail to clean out the Chinese viruses?"

McKie took the question. "Our cyber experts are certain that the previous incursion was adequately dealt with. That was under a different administration, but they did a good job dealing with it. There are thousands of attempts every week to compromise sensitive computers. So far, we at Homeland and USCYBERCOM have kept domestic and military networks clean. Still, we have lost material. Everyone has lost data."

The large panel monitor on the south wall came to life. "General Holt," the president said. "Glad you could join us." A solid-looking man stood next to the general.

"Thank you, sir. Sorry to be late, but I wanted to have the latest report for you." He glanced at the man by his side. "For those who might not know, this is Colonel Jeremy Matisse. He oversees the day-to-day at USCYBERCOM."

Barlow leaned on the end of the table. "We've already decided that the blackouts on the East Coast and West Coast are not caused by something natural. We're thinking a cyber attack of some kind. Do you concur?"

"I think it is wise to assume so, at least for now. Early diagnostics haven't found anything in the military networks. If a hostile is involved, the perpetuator appears to have targeted civilian sites."

"That's bad enough, isn't it?" Barlow asked.

"Yes, sir. Military bases can run on backup power for some time, but all American bases depend on local power."

A watch officer stepped into the room and handed a note to Frank Grundy, who read it, folded the paper, and set it on the table. "The grid is coming back online. DC will be one of the first areas to get power. It looks like this has been a tempest in a teapot."

There were smiles around the table.

"Good to hear, Frank. Okay then, so we'll be back to normal soon. Is that right?"

"It appears so, Mr. President." Frank looked relieved.

Barlow stood. "Thanks for all the good work, folks. Someone get me answers when they become available. Frank, make sure Des is up to speed and has something good to say to the press."

"Yes, sir."

Barlow exited the room. As he did, the lights in DC came back on.

7

O'Tool

"Tell me the truth, General. Was all this done for my benefit?"

Jeremy exchanged a glance with Holt. The man's expression didn't change, but something in the commander's eyes said he couldn't believe the insufferable arrogance of the Senator.

"As I said earlier, Senator, this was not arranged for you. If you'll recall, you arrived early." Holt's voice remained calm and carried no irritation. Jeremy had no idea how the man could do that.

"But you knew I was coming. You could have had things in place and then executed your plan." They walked from the situation room back to the general's office. Holt took a seat behind his desk as the senator grabbed one of the two guest chairs. Jeremy decided to remain on his feet.

"Senator, you can't believe that I or anyone in the service would cause millions of people to go without power. No doubt there has been loss of life. Second, if I were to arrange a dog-and-pony show for you, it would be one that made us look like heroes. All we did was kick in a few protocols."

"You know I'm just giving you a bad time, don't you General?"

"No, Senator, I don't." He leaned back in his chair and looked a year older than he did this morning.

Jeremy decided to run interference for his immediate superior. "Imagine if things had not resolved themselves so quickly, Senator. I can imagine the computer jockies over at Homeland are rejoicing."

"Do you exchange information? With DHS, I mean." In Jeremy's opinion, this was O'Tool's first reasonable question.

Jeremy looked at Holt, who motioned for him to carry on. Holt was brilliant, determined, and a genius at organization. One thing he wasn't was patient. "Yes, Senator, we do. We even drill together. One thing 9/11 taught this country was that the first victim of an attack is communication. Today, everyone who needs to be connected, is connected."

"That's the way it should be." O'Tool steepled his fingers. "I look forward to continuing the tour—"

The phone on Holt's desk rang, and the general snapped it up. He listened and then nodded as if the caller could see him. "Good." He set the phone back in the cradle. "Power is back on in our portion of Delaware."

The news was good.

. . . .

Backup generators had kept the power going in Harris Memorial Hospital, but the lighting remained muted. Roni was well into her third surgery when things brightened.

"That's an improvement." Surgical nurse Loren Grimm looked up from her tray of instruments just long enough to make the comment. "My eyes are killing me."

"Me too," Roni said. "I'm getting a bit of a headache."

"Need some ibuprofen?"

"I was thinking of morphine." Roni didn't move her eyes from the patient with a rib sticking into his lung. "Someone get me an update on pending surgeries. Who have we got in the halls?"

One of the other nurses stepped to the phone on the OR wall. She hung up a moment later. "It's official—power is back on."

"And the surgeries?"

"There are eight more waiting for ORs to open. Admitting says Dr. Hall lost a patient about half an hour ago. He took the next one in line, which was yours. You have one less on your list."

"Remind me to kiss the man." Ronni called for another instrument. "So that means—what, three more?"

"Yes," the nurse said.

"And here I thought it was going to be a tough day."

Loren grumbled. "The day ain't over yet."

"No wonder people call you a ray of sunshine." Roni stopped long enough to stretch her back and move her head side to side, trying to untie the knots in her neck.

She allowed herself to relax for a moment. Things were looking up. She might even get to go home tonight.

••••

Stanley sat in his car, letting time and the world pass by. In some ways he was a prisoner. His office was twenty-five floors above, a long trek in a stairwell lit only by battery-powered emergency lights. His home was across the bay, near but made far by traffic that had turned roads into parking lots. His wife was in La Jolla at UCSD. He had little to do but listen to the car radio.

Hope surfaced when the news announced that some power had returned to the East Coast. Washington DC now had power, as did parts of Virginia and Delaware. Upstate New York had electricity flowing, as did Albany. Soon the lights of Broadway would be blazing in the Big Apple again.

He smiled. This would be the talk of friends and family for weeks.

▪▪▪▪

A few people near Cody Broadway cheered as word spread about the return of power. Most, however, seemed lost in their own pain. Cody couldn't blame them. All he could think about was his mother.

More people arrived in the ER, but the stream seemed to have slowed. Maybe he would be able to see his mother soon.

▪▪▪▪

Rosa had the radio on in the condo and had been following reports closely. The San Diego news station had kept up a constant flow of conversation, most of it repetitious, about the outage. When they reported that parts of the city had power again, she felt a flood of relief. Rosa liked things orderly and consistent. Change made her nervous.

Donny wheeled out of his room, stopped a foot short of the window, and fixed his gaze on downtown San Diego. He seemed content but was no longer laughing.

He didn't move. He just stared.

Rosa stepped to him and placed a hand on the young man's shoulder. "Quite a day, Donny. Quite a day." When she turned to walk away she caught a glimpse of Donny's reflection. It didn't look right, didn't look like him.

She did a double take.

The reflection turned and looked at her.

▪▪▪▪

President Nathan Barlow returned to his schedule. Several meetings had to be canceled because of road congestion, which was fine with him. He had a mountain of information to read. He might even set aside thirty minutes to read something other than government documents.

He was tired. He, like anyone who followed the presidency, knew that presidents aged at twice their normal rate. The weight of responsibility, the long days, the overflowing schedule, and the inability to please everyone—sometimes anyone—pressed him down.

Still, he loved the job. It had been the only thing he truly desired. As a boy, his great-grandmother had said what grandmothers had been saying for generations: "In this country, a boy like you could grow up to be president." Barlow had taken those words to heart, and politics became his only passion.

Born to wealthy parents who made their money in banking, Barlow attended the best schools in Massachusetts, including Harvard. After his undergrad work, he studied at the London School of Economics, where he excelled. His father set him up in banking, and he spent the next ten years earning a fortune as an expert in international finance. Even then, his mind ran to the halls of congress, and on those days when he felt especially resourceful, the Oval Office.

It had all worked out, and at times he thought some higher power had scripted his life for him. As if he were in a dance class that painted footprints on the floor to teach the waltz, all he had to do was step where guided.

Part of his daily routine was to allow time for reflection and reminder. Each day, he sat in the Oval Office, or the private study next to it, or on Air Force One and said, "I am the president of the United States."

Most days, he didn't believe it, but then some crisis would

arise, and everyone in the country looked to him as if he had answers at the ready. It was the only thing he hated about the job—the way people looked at him when things went wrong.

Troops in Afghanistan had been reduced to a handful, but the Middle East was still a mess. Iran and North Korea seemed to be in a contest to see which government was most loony. The economy was better but not great, and the mountain of impossible-to-pay debt threatened to send the economy spiraling back down. Greed was still normal in the institutions that nearly bankrupted a dozen industries. The two-party system continued to be more obsessed with who got the last word in than achieving meaningful legislation. The country that once demanded the world's respect was slowly becoming a joke. He wouldn't allow that.

Or so he had said.

He knew enough history to know that the bigger the country, the harder the fall. Historians noted that ancient Egypt and Rome supposedly could not fail but did anyway. The Soviet Union had been a force to reckon with but then fell apart. The British Empire had been an empire for a long time. Even mighty China was marching toward history's banana peel.

At least the US had some moral sense. Not much, but some. In his dark hours, he wondered if the best days of the country were behind it.

He pushed those thoughts away. Negative thinking never achieved anything in his life. Focus did. Dedication did. Determination did. Optimism—well, that just made life a little more pleasant. But the dark cloud that hung near the ceiling of the Oval Office couldn't be blown away by the winds of positive thinking. It was nearly impossible to be an optimist in this city, in this building, in this famous office. At least one problem was off his plate. He had never been so happy to see the lights come back on. To prove the point, he pulled the chain on the green-canopied banker's light at the edge of his desk. The lamp was a cheap knockoff of the old lights popular decades ago, but his daughter had given it to him when she was twelve and he had won his first term in congress. She had saved her allowance to buy it, and the lamp had sat on his desk ever since. When he took the White House, he saw no reason to change the tradition.

The 60-watt bulb glowed beneath the curved green diffuser. Larger 100-watt light bulbs became illegal to sell in 2012, and 60-watt incandescents followed suit earlier this year. He wondered what the political repercussions would be if the country learned their commander in chief harbored an illegal product right on his desk. The thought made him smile.

Then the light went out. All the lights went out.

The door to the office opened, and Frank Grundy poked his head in. "Mr. President—"

"I know, Frank. We're on lockdown."

Three Secret Service agents poured into the room. Barlow had a bad feeling.

8

Descent of Darkness

NEW YORK CITY
POPULATION 8.5 MILLION

Rudy Watt was one in a million. Maybe one in a hundred million. He spent his life in what his grandparents would have called an iron lung. But there was no iron in his cocoon. He was in a clear acrylic cylinder with a suitcase-sized ventilator resting on the floor.

Rudy had spent the last two years in the device—a small amount of time compared to those who lived during the days of polio. Some, he had been told, had lived for years on devices that did their breathing for them. *Negative pressure breathing* they called it.

He called it prison.

His mother and father reminded him daily how lucky he was to be alive. He didn't feel lucky. Instead he cursed fate for not letting him die in the gutter where his head hit the curb after he fell from his motorcycle. Back of the head, above the Atlas vertebrae. His spinal cord remained intact but not the portion of his brain that governed autonomic respiration. The fall killed the medullary respiratory center but left the rest of his brain alive.

Most people in his condition would be attached to devices that forced air into their lungs. He had been on a ventilator like that for a while, but it failed to do the job. This was his only other choice.

Yep. Lucky.

When the lights went out for the second time that day, Rudy prayed they would stay off just long enough for the battery backup in his respirator to die. A thirty-year-old man shouldn't have to live with his parents and be cared for day and night.

The backup generator kicked in again, and Rudy cursed his luck.

■■■■

LOS ANGELES
POPULATION 4 MILLION

Harold Dack was unlike his peers. He loved driving a school bus. The noisy children made him feel young again. Sure, they could be nuisances, but those nuisances would one day run this world. The burdens of work and family would settle on them soon enough. Let them make noise as long as they didn't fight.

The elementary students had been stuck in school for hours while teachers waited for the power to come on. Finally, school had been canceled and the bus summoned early. Those who had adults waiting for them were released, and those who didn't were allowed to stay at the school until parents or guardians could retrieve them. That meant Harold's bus was only half full.

Traffic on the side streets was still light, but the major roads were still slow—a slight improvement over the gridlock of an hour ago. Fortunately, Harold's route avoided those areas and focused on larger streets through residential areas. Still, he had a few intersections to get through. With traffic lights working again, the jam at those junctures had thinned.

He had just missed making it through one intersection when he had to stop for a red light.

Children clamored. Harold looked in his review mirror. Two girls sat in the back, singing something they heard on the radio. Three children looked at cell phones, texting the world at an unbelievable pace. Four children listened to iPods. It made Harold shake his head. The digital world had created digital kids.

He looked up at the traffic light just in time to see it turn green. He pressed the accelerator and moved into the intersection.

Halfway through he noticed the green light blink out. Then he heard the rumble. The squeal of tires. The scream of a young girl.

The grill of a large panel delivery truck entered the intersection. Harold caught a glimpse of the driver looking at an electronic device in his hand.

It was Harold's final image.

■■■■

CHICAGO
POPULATION 2.8 MILLION

Chi-Town was known for many things: Chicago dogs, the Cubs, and interesting politics. Little known was the city's other claim to fame: It sported more movable bridges than any other city in the country. Tom Silcox was a native, born and reared in Chicago proper, as had been his parents and grandparents and several more generations of ancestors. His family tree included relatives who had seen the Great Chicago Fire of 1871 destroy their homes and businesses.

He didn't know if it was proper, but he felt proud about that. Unlike his distant relatives who made their living selling dry goods, Tom was no businessman. He never developed a taste for it, which was the reason he had spent the past twenty-two years in the Chicago Department of Transportation. He started as a laborer and became a mechanic, working on the city's forty-plus mechanical bridges. It was another point of pride for him. Not many men could claim to work on drawbridges.

Chicago's extensive river system required a creative approach to bridge building. In the warmer months, hundreds of boats moved along the 156-mile river system. Larger boats required more clearance than fixed bridges could provide. Since the 1800s, Chicago bridges had been rising and lowering or pivoting to allow watercraft safe passage.

During his years of service, Tom's interest in the city's bridge system had grown. He even entertained thoughts of writing a book once he retired. "There is a lot of interesting stuff about them bridges," he said to anyone who would listen. Over the years, fewer people had shown interest. The world had become enamored with digital phones and portable computers. People shuffled through life with earbuds crammed into their heads or phones pressed to their ears. They had no interest in such things as movable bridges.

Silcox pulled his car to the first of five drawbridges that spanned the Calumet River. Altogether they opened 30,000 times a year, yet he still loved watching their graceful rise and fall. Precision counterbalances made it all possible.

Most of the bridges along the Calumet were not manned full-time. Employees drove from bridge to bridge, opening them as needed. Silcox entered the operations building, shaking off the cold from his short walk from his vehicle.

A large yacht with a tall mast motored slowly down the river.

It was art on water. Silcox had learned to admire boats from a distance. Even if he had saved every penny he earned since leaving high school, he wouldn't have been able to buy such a craft. But he was good with that.

On the panel before him was a large red button. He pressed it and heard the warning horn blaring outside. Another button lowered the traffic barricades with their flashing red lights. Silcox fixed his eyes on the vehicles already on the bridge and waited for the last to clear the span. Then he activated the motors that added the power to move the large counterweight down. The counterweight did almost all the work—the motors just controlled the rise and fall.

Each half of the span began its slow rise. The dance had begun. He turned his attention back to the yacht. The skipper must be in a hurry. Silcox was seeing more wake behind the vessel. Several smaller boats motored past it, not needing to wait for the bridge to rise.

Suddenly, the sound of the railroad-like clang at the barricades fell silent. The lights in the control room that had been driving back the gloom of the January sky went dark.

Silcox snapped his head back around. The bridge was closing again. He snapped up a pair of binoculars and trained them on the approaching craft. He focused on the boat's bridge. No one was manning the helm. A man dressed in white had his back turned to the bow and was listening to another as he motioned energetically with one hand and held a drink in the other. The man in white, whom Silcox assumed was the hired captain, seemed uncomfortable. The other man was a "toucher," frequently touching the skipper's arm to keep his attention.

Another glance at the self-closing bridge sent Silcox's stomach to the basement. Without a thought, he slammed his hand on the emergency siren.

Nothing.

He sprinted from the enclosure, shouting as loud as his fifty-six-year-old lungs would allow.

Too late. The towering mast approached its doom.

Silcox screamed again, this time catching the crewman's attention. The man followed Silcox's outstretched arm. A moment later, Silcox heard the inboard engines throttle down, go silent, and then roar as the captain reversed the propellers.

The mast hit the bottom beams of the bridge, and the bow of the yacht pitched up. The man with the drink fell backward and down the companionway to the lower deck.

The top of the carbon mast shattered, falling aft of the bridge and onto the deck. Silcox sprinted back to the control and picked up the phone—at least that was working—and made two calls, one to 911 (it was busy) and the other to his supervisor.

On the yacht, the captain had regained control and held a microphone to his mouth. On the aft deck, passengers surrounded the fallen talker.

No one touched him. He didn't move. His drink glass rolled along the deck.

■ ■ ■ ■

Monica McKie had just begun to unwind. The morning had been filled with tension, something she thought she would have grown used to by now. She hadn't. Over the past two years she had carefully cultivated a public image befitting a woman in charge of Homeland Security. Always calm, visibly determined, unflappable, and focused. Her husband once quipped, "Monica talks at a 150 words a minute with gusts to 200." It always got a laugh. These days she had to think before speaking, choosing her words more carefully because the wrong choice could explode in her face.

She had followed the advice of consultants brought in to make her more appealing to the media and the public. She had held elected office at the congressional level and served as Idaho's governor for two terms before being appointed by President Barlow to head the DHS. She had the legal training for the work and had helped lower crime in her state by a healthy 12 percent.

Being the director of Homeland Security involved more work than all her previous public offices combined. And the fragmentation—oh, the fragmentation. So many things to watch, so many groups to track, so many congressional leaders and senators to appease. Add to that the number of governors who wanted her ear and money to secure their borders. To look at her, McKie was a professional woman with short, graying hair, clear blue eyes, and a thin frame. She could look like a grandmother, which she was, or a high-powered exec, which she also was.

When she returned to her office on Nebraska Avenue, she spent a few moments wallowing in the mixed waters of relief and embarrassment. No one would say she overreacted. After all, USCYBERCOM kicked their people into high gear. The problem warranted it. She was glad it was over. The thought of massive power outages was the stuff of her nightmares.

On her desk were dispatches from field personnel. DHS had offices all over the United States and oversaw the work of the US Coast Guard, FEMA, TSA, customs, and many others. The many heads of Hydra, each with its own appetite.

When she accepted the job, she knew it would be difficult and unwieldy. Two years later she still loved it. Most of the time. At the moment, she wished she were spending her days being Nanna to three grandkids—something that would hold her interest for a week. She loved her family, but she was wired to lead. Most likely she would be buried with her desk.

She rose and moved from her office to the large conference

room to meet with department heads. She hoped to get a complete picture of all that happened.

She was three steps down the hall when the lights died. So did McKie's patience.

9

Eight Minutes

Eight minutes. Jeremy Matisse couldn't wrap his brain around the thought. He read the hastily written report. He had sat in on the videoconference meeting with Secretary Monica McKie at Homeland Security and another that afternoon with the president and his advisors. Everyone wanted answers. No one had any. Not the NSA, CIA, FBI, Homeland Security; not the Joint Chiefs of Staff; and not the North American Electric Reliability Corporation, a congressionally directed company that regulates the 500 power companies in the US. The Department of Energy was clueless as well. USCYBER-COM had no answers, and it was their job to know such things. Between them and DHS, cyber attacks should never reach this extreme, yet Jeremy and his boss sat in light provided by generators.

General Holt rubbed his face. "I should have retired last year when I had the chance."

Jeremy shrugged. "I guess you could still play golf during the daylight hours."

"You're not trying to be cute, are you, Colonel?"

"I've never been very good at cute, sir. I assume I've failed at it again."

"Eight minutes, Jeremy. How does the North American continent go dark in eight minutes? It's not possible. For years we've run scenarios, Homeland's cyber unit has done the same, and so have the various associations of power producers. Sure, we could create scenarios that led to massive blackouts, but not the whole country. Not that fast. Not all at once."

The same frustration ate at Jeremy. Outages occurred all the time, leaving an average of 500,000 Americans without power but only for a short time. And such outages were regional—a city here, a part of a county there. A nationwide outage was thought impossible. Jeremy had said so himself many times.

He hated to be wrong. Especially this wrong.

Jeremy stood at the back of a large room manned by scores of uniformed workers—Air Force, Army, Navy, Coast Guard, and Marines. Each cyber warrior's attention was fixed on computer monitors or on the huge operations monitor on the far wall. The room was dark and smelled of warm electronics.

"I've been thinking about 2007," Holt said as he stared over the rows of workstations, each with several glowing monitors.

Jeremy needed no additional references. He was a major at the time, running security checks on Air Force computers. The event was little known, mostly because the DHS had requested it be kept secret. That year, Department of Energy researchers tested the vulnerability of the grid by mounting its own attack. It succeeded in bringing down a power generator. More specifically, it made the generator self-destruct.

Not good news. Still, that had been a small "success." Something like this was too large, too far beyond current technology, wasn't it? Then again…who was he kidding? That was the kind of thought one voiced to a senate subcommittee.

"I lost track of you." Senator O'Tool approached. He had gone off to the restroom. Jeremy and the general used the time to talk out of his presence. "What have you learned?"

"In the time since you went to the bathroom?" Holt said, "Not much."

"I must admit, I'm surprised you don't have a handle on this."

Holt turned to the senator and for a moment, Jeremy was sure a fist would precede the response. Instead Holt cocked his head. "I'll admit that I'm a little surprised myself."

"So you never planned for this kind of thing?"

"Again, Senator, USCYBERCOM deals with attacks on military and government computers. DHS handles the civil stuff."

"They seem to be off their game."

"It's a different world, Senator," Jeremy said without looking at the man. "Our country has been moving to a smart grid system, a system based on computers that control operations and communicate with each other. The technology is brilliant, and the move makes sense in so many ways."

"But…?"

"But every advance in technology brings new exposure to attack. We have the most robust security system in the world. Even so, it is a fragile thing."

"So you just sit around and wait to see what happens?"

Jeremy was a patient man, but O'Tool was working his last nerve. "No, Senator. There are hundreds of people working on the problem. We're verifying the safety of the military net and heading off any additional attacks. DHS is doing their part. Private security companies are weighing in. The United States Computer Emergency Readiness Team is active. More is being done than can be seen. There's one good thing about the power outage. No DoS or DDoS."

O'Tool blinked as if Jeremy had just started speaking Swahili.

"Denial of service attack, Senator. You've heard of it?"

"Of course. What's your point?"

"A denial of service attack is fairly common in cyberspace. One form of DoS is called DDoS—distributed denial of service. A virus infects thousands of computers, making them slaves that operate without the owners' knowledge. There are several methods of attack, but basically the attack tries to overpower a server with too much traffic, too much information. The target system is overrun with more data than it can handle."

"Drinking from a fire hose," O'Tool said.

"Yes. Such attacks take place around the world. Targets have included Google, PayPal, MasterCard, banks, and government offices. It can bring a whole system down quickly. Most companies and governments have procedures in place to deal with DDoS attacks."

"But that's not the problem here," Holt added. "Unless…"

"Unless what?" O'Tool looked like an art major in a calculus class.

"Unless the attack comes from outside our country. North Korea. China, Iran."

"Seems a stretch."

Holt turned to O'Tool. "Has it not occurred to you that we might be at war?"

The words seemed to shake O'Tool.

"Until we know different, Senator, I'm treating this like a digital Pearl Harbor." Holt inhaled deeply. He looked older and grayer than when this day started. "You'll have to excuse us, Senator. The colonel and I have another videoconference with the president."

"I would like to attend that."

"I'm sure you would," Holt said as he turned and strode away.

Jeremy followed on his heels. He heard Senator O'Tool curse.

■■■■

Secretary Monica McKie sat in the DHS teleconference room, not wanting to waste time driving from Nebraska Avenue to Pennsylvania Avenue. With her was Dr. Tasha Young, head of US-CERT, the DHS arm dealing with cyber security. Tasha looked ten years younger than her forty-two years, and her blue eyes sparkled with intelligence. Very few people in the world intimidated Monica. She had always prided herself on her intelligence and wit, but when she was with Tasha she felt just a short step up from ignorant even though Tasha never paraded her intelligence. The five-feet-eight, raven-haired MIT standout had every right to do so. Soft-spoken, the computer science expert was also a musical prodigy. Monica had never been able to understand why mathematicians and computer specialists were often blessed with such musical skill. The only thing Monica could play was the radio.

They entered the telecon room and waited for the large monitor to come to life.

"Ready?" Monica asked.

"No, ma'am. Not in the least." Tasha's voice had an Asian lilt to it, something Monica attributed to the woman's Japanese grandfather. Tasha would never be confused with an Asian, especially with her blue eyes, but those in the know could see a hint of the ancestry around her eyes and nose and in her dark hair.

"You know you're undermining my confidence."

"Sorry, ma'am." The corners of her mouth inched up before morphing back to the concerned straight line it had been a moment before.

A chirp indicated that one of the encrypted STU-III/CT phones had come to life. Monica checked hers and felt a moment of guilty relief to see it was still dormant. Tasha raised her unit to her ear.

The STU-III/CT was a secure, encrypted phone that operated

on a shadow cell system used only by the government. The secure system piggybacked on the public cell system and received priority incoming calls. It was the only way a call could be made over a flooded system.

"Dr. Young." She listened. A moment later, her olive skin paled. "I see. Keep me posted, and I want as much info as possible." She fell silent for a moment. "No, the secretary is with me. I'll let her know." She ended the call.

"More bad news?" Monica asked.

"Yes. Big-time." She started to speak again, but the videoconference monitor suddenly filled the room. A roomful of faces looked at them.

Monica took the initiative. "Mr. President, I think there's been a development."

"You *think* there's been a development?" The president's voice poured into the room from overhead speakers.

The image split, and the faces of General Holt and Colonel Matisse appeared alongside the image of the White House situation room.

"Yes, sir. Dr. Young just now received a call and she was about to fill me in."

"Well, she might as well fill us all in." The president shifted in his chair.

Tasha sat, setting her laptop on the table in front of her. "Yes, sir. Mr. President, there seems to be a problem at the Hoover Dam power station." She paused. "A big problem."

■ ■ ■ ■

Jeremy couldn't believe the words coming over the videocon. He did what military men are trained to do: stuff emotion and focus on the task at hand.

"The generators are running out of control," Tasha said.

Jeremy knew all the key players in cyber security, and Tasha Young was the discipline's equivalent of a rock star—pretty, knowledgeable, dedicated, and able to think faster than the computers she monitored.

"Exactly what does that mean?" Barlow narrowed his eyes.

"Sir, the US Bureau of Reclamation runs the power station at Hoover Dam. They're reporting that their turbines are—well, they're running out of control. All seventeen of them." Tasha glanced at her boss and then back to the camera in the monitor. Jeremy could see the entire room from the USCYBERCOM communications room. He stole a glance at General Holt. The color had drained from the man's face.

"How can that be?" Barlow's voice remained low but the words carried sharp edges.

"Like all power generators in the country, they're running on the power they produce. They're on the front end of the grid and don't depend on power coming in. That means their computers are still powered."

"The ones that run the turbines?" Barlow asked.

"Yes, sir. Well, all of the computers, just like ours, except we don't produce our own power like they do. We're running on backup generators…Okay, I'm telling you what you already know. Here's the concern: Whatever has affected the power grid has another level. Maybe more."

"Stuxnet." General Holt mumbled the word.

"What's that, General?" the president said. "We didn't get that over here."

"Sorry, sir. I made a reference to the Stuxnet worm of 2010."

"The one against Iran? You see a connection?"

"Too early to tell, but it sounds like the same kind of attack."

Jeremy's mind ran to the most sophisticated and effective

cyber attack to date. A complicated worm was unleashed into the wild. Unlike most computer worms and viruses, Stuxnet was a large bit of code with a mission: to find a specific type of PLC, or programmable logic controller. More and more PLCs were controlling such devices as assembly-line robots and even doors to prison cells. They were efficient and untiring. They are essentially computers, so they are vulnerable to hacking. Stuxnet targeted centrifuges made by Siemens, a German conglomerate. The centrifuges were used to make high-grade uranium. The worm circulated through the Internet, searching for just the right target.

It eventually reached the refining center in Iran's growing nuclear program in Natanz. The nuclear enrichment process used centrifuges to increase the amount of usable uranium. Stuxnet entered the system in June of 2009 and began sending Iranian centrifuges out of control, damaging many of the estimated 2000 such devices in Natanz.

"You're saying that the power generating plant at Hoover Dam was targeted?" Frank Grundy asked.

Holt nodded. "It appears so."

Israel was the primary target of blame for Stuxnet. Indeed, the code contained what some interpreted as a reference to Queen Esther, whose action saved the lives of countless Jews from Persian leaders 500 years before Christ. The reference might not be what it seemed, but it was enough to set accusations in motion.

The United States was also a target in the blame game. Some believed that Israeli and US operatives designed, coded, and released the malware.

What made Stuxnet so unique was its target. Instead of infecting the computers it used to move along the Internet, it simply multiplied itself and moved on until it found the centrifuges. And not just any centrifuges. No other uranium enrichment facilities were affected. The program was looking for specific centrifuges made by Siemens and operating in Iran.

"Mr. President," Holt said, "we've known for a long time that the US would be targeted for such an attack sooner or later."

Barlow sighed. "Do we have any other reports of such problems?"

No one spoke, but Jeremy expected someone to walk into the Woodshed and hand Barlow a note. He had no doubt that new reports would pour in.

"What's the purpose?" Barlow pushed himself back in his chair. Jeremy couldn't imagine the pressure on the leader.

"If I may, sir." Jeremy kept his voice steady. "I have a few speculations."

"Go ahead, Colonel."

Jeremy folded his hands and laid them on the table. "We have to assume that this is an attack and not the failure of a weakening, overused infrastructure. That might be the case, but it would be prudent to assume the worse and hope for the best. There is a good chance the first outage was just level one of the attack. It reset millions of computers, which I assume have been infected with this malware.

"This later incident reveals that the attackers have a bigger goal in mind. Whoever they are, they aren't satisfied with knocking the power grid off-line for a few hours. They want something closer to permanent. To do that, they have to attack power generation stations. When the power goes off, all nuclear power plants shut down as they're designed to do. I think we can expect similar problems from other power producers."

The president pinched the bridge of his nose as if the conversation were giving him a migraine. "So we're at war, and we don't know who the enemy is."

CIA director Leon Sampson spoke up. "Mr. President, I think

we can assume the attack has come from China, North Korea, or Iran."

"You think the Iranians are trying to get even?"

Jeremy wondered if Barlow just admitted to US involvement in Stuxnet.

Sampson nodded. "Perhaps. I wouldn't be surprised."

"So what do we do? Do we launch our own attack on three or four nations on the assumption that one of them has done this?"

No one answered. President Barlow looked into the camera, and Jeremy felt the gaze. "General Holt, do we have a like-response to an attack like this?"

Holt straightened. "Yes, sir. Slipper Net is still up and running on backup power, so we can send out a digital response, but it might not be effective." The general used the nickname for SIPRNet—the Secret Internet Protocol Router Network.

"Why not?"

"Sir, we can use cyber warfare against almost any technologically advanced country, but the offending party will be expecting that. I'm afraid it's a little more difficult than what we did to Iraq when we invaded in 2003. Our biggest problem is we don't know who to hit."

"Well," the president said, "I'm itching to hit someone. Get me a target."

The phone in the sit room sounded, and Frank Grundy answered. He listened and then rubbed his forehead. "Understood." He hung up. "Mr. President, London has just gone dark."

10

Husbands, Wives, and Mothers

Night had settled on DC, but Roni hadn't noticed because she had been confined in one operating room after another. The artificial light tended to skew a person's sense of time. Each operating theater had a twenty-four-hour clock, but she seldom focused on the time of day. She was more concerned about the length of each surgery.

She was losing track of other things. If asked and given a little time, she might be able to count the number of surgeries she had performed since the morning and the arrival of the first injuries from the train wreck. After six surgeries, she quit counting. Fortunately, some of the surgeries were simple. Of course, *simple* was relative. The person on the surgical table might describe it differently.

Every operating room had been pressed into service. Surgical teams rotated in and out, doing their work as quickly as professional responsibility would allow. Triage doctors in the ER had done an admirable job of caring for the most critical cases first.

What remained were nonthreatening injuries. *Nonthreatening* didn't mean unimportant. Scores of serious injuries still required surgery. Her long day was about to become a long night.

A conversation with an ER doc taking a ten-minute break wasn't encouraging. Roni had gone outside to get some fresh air. She needed to see something other than hospital walls.

"I thought you gave up smoking," Roni said as she stepped toward the thin, dark-haired man. The January air was cold, and a wind cut through Roni's scrubs.

"I did quit." Tony Rasmussen reminded Roni of a zombie looking for fresh brains to consume. His eyelids drooped, and his skin looked pale in the limited exterior lights running on reserve power. "I've quit three times. It's a hobby with me." He inhaled another lungful of tobacco smoke.

"You know smoking is bad for a doctor's image." Roni wished for a habit that would help her relax.

"Rumor has it that it's bad for the lungs and heart too, but I'm pretty sure that's just propaganda from the medical industry."

"You're part of the medical business." Roni did her best not to wave off the smoke. She knew the pressure the man had been under.

"Oh, yeah. I forgot."

Roni chuckled. "How you doing?"

"Hanging in there. I haven't been this tired since med school, and I haven't felt this much pressure since…I've never felt this much pressure." He dropped the half-smoked cigarette to the asphalt parking lot. They were standing twenty feet from the ambulance entrance to the ER. She guessed he snubbed out the butt for her benefit. "At least things have slowed."

"That's good to hear. Have you eaten?"

"Had a bag of potato chips about ten minutes ago. Carbing up. You?"

"Granola bar for lunch. I've got half an hour. I'm thinking about heading down to the cafeteria. Wanna go?"

"Nah, more patients are on their way in. Cardio. The old people are stressing. Especially since word got out."

"What word?"

"You haven't heard?"

Roni shrugged. "Of course I have. I just like hearing it again."

"Hmm, sarcasm." He turned to her, and his weary eyes grew serious. "The whole country has lost power."

"Yeah, right." She looked to the sky, seeing stars that were normally washed out by city lights.

"I'm serious. The whole country is in the dark."

"Not possible." Roni studied Tony's face, looking for proof that he was making a joke. She didn't find it.

"Apparently it is."

An ambulance pulled through the lot and beneath the canopy covering the ER entrance, its red and blue lights splashing color on the walls and seeming brighter than she had ever seen them.

Tony took a deep breath. "Duty calls." He walked to the entrance with his shoulders rounded and his head down. He had a wife and two young children at home. Roni knew where his mind was.

Again she stared at the sky. The stars and a three-quarter moon seemed unconcerned by the happenings below. If Tony was right, Jeremy must be up to his ears with work. A shiver of concern ran through her.

Turning her back on the dark, Roni reentered the hospital.

The ER waiting room was still full but orderly. Alan Morton, one of the triage nurses, sat next to a young blond boy. Roni glanced their way and started to continue on, but something made her take a longer look. She judged the boy to be about ten.

He drew a hand across his face, wiping away tears. Alan did the same.

As a trauma surgeon, she had regular dealings with Alan Morton and knew him to be dedicated and insightful—even intuitive. Several times she thought he should have gone to medical school. He had the smarts and the heart, but somehow the opportunity got by him. She never asked why.

Alan glanced her way and then let his gaze linger. He did nothing to ask for her help—no motion, no mouthed words. He just looked at her. Roni knew he wouldn't ask for help. ER was his world, and OR was hers. He wasn't the kind of man to pass a problem to someone else.

Your time is limited, girl. Get going. She moved, but not down the hall as she intended. Instead, she stepped to the corner of the ER where Alan and the boy sat.

"Hey," Roni said.

"Hi, Doc." Alan's voice came out weaker than normal.

"Who's your friend?"

Alan looked at the boy. "This is Cody. He's been here all day. Cody, this is Dr. Roni Matisse. She's a surgeon."

"Did you operate on my mother?" More tears. This time Cody let them flow.

"I…" Roni didn't know. "What is your mother's name?"

Alan answered when the boy hesitated. "April Broadway."

"I don't recognize the name, son. It must have been another doctor." She looked at Alan, who shook his head. He didn't know either. Any other day, he would have known which patient went to what doctor. This wasn't any day.

"Just got word. She passed on the table."

Roni's first instinct was to ask what happened and get medical details, but she reined in the impulse. "I see. I'm so sorry." There was no place for Roni to sit—patients took up every seat. Roni dropped to a knee so she could be eye-level with the boy. He was doing his best to be brave, to be strong, to hold it together for the adults. Roni admired his courage.

"Father?" She looked to Alan with the one word question.

"No. His father was a policeman. Slain on the job."

Roni's weariness turned to profound sadness. She had seen the worst that life could deliver. People's evil recklessness sent innocent people to her surgical table every week. Gunshot wounds were common in DC hospitals, as were stabbings and blunt-force traumas. Several times she had tried to piece back the insides of police officers whose organs had been damaged by high-caliber cop-killer bullets. A few times she had failed.

Returning her gaze to the boy, she asked the next logical question. "Grandparents? Aunts?"

Again, Alan shook his head. "Grandparents are long gone. Neither Mom or Dad had siblings."

Alone. The kid was alone in a big city in a strange time.

Alan anticipated the next question. "Social services are overwhelmed, as you might imagine. It will be a while before anyone gets here."

The kid looked fragile, a crystal vase teetering on the edge of a rock quarry. The thought of sending the youngster to a foster home chilled her, but what could she do?

His lower lip quivered. He lowered his gaze to the shiny lobby floor.

Roni touched the side Cody's head, pushing back a few strands of hair, and searched for words to say. None came to mind. No amount of talking would help. The kid's world had been shattered, and he had no idea what the future held. Soon, social services would put him in a home with strangers who might keep him safe, warm, and fed, but he would still walk the dark paths of grief very much alone.

Cody sprung from his chair and threw his arms around Roni's neck. A sniff, a whine, a sob...and then a flood of tears.

Roni held him close and fought the rising tide of pity in her, a tide determined to erode her professional detachment. Her eyes burned with tears as she held the convulsing boy. A glance at Alan showed flooded eyes. Why did the world have to be so cruel?

Roni let the boy cry, determined to hold him as long as necessary.

Then she heard her name called over the public-address system.

■ ■ ■ ■

Nathan Barlow slipped into the residence wing. Night, darker than usual, blackened the windows. The night had never frightened him, not even as a child. He found something comfortable in the lack of light. This dark, however, was different. It seemed to have a life of its own, like something from a Stephen King novel. He shook off the thought.

Katey sat at the dining table, a selection of cold cuts spread out on a platter. She rose to greet him, taking him in her arms and holding him a few seconds longer than normal. She was frightened. She'd never say so. She wasn't that kind of woman. His plate was filled with problems, she had once told him, and she saw no benefit in adding on.

"In for the night?" Katey avoided his eyes, another sign of the fear roiling in her.

"Sorry, no. Just a break. I told them I need to hit the head."

"There are bathrooms all over the White House." She returned to the table and poured coffee into a cup that bore the presidential seal of the United States and positioned it at his spot.

"I know that, but I need a few minutes away. Besides, you

haven't seen me since lunch, and I know how that makes you pine."

"It's true, I've been known to think about you two or three times a day." She returned to her seat. The humor lacked its usual snap.

Barlow sipped the coffee. He drank more coffee than he should, not because of an addiction to caffeine but because he truly loved the taste. The caffeine didn't hurt.

"I had the kitchen send up a few things. I didn't know when I'd see you, so I just went with lunch meat and cheeses. I can ask for something else."

Barlow raised a hand. "No, this is fine. It's going to be a long night, and too much food would just slow the gears in my head. Besides, I only have about ten minutes."

"Then back to the Woodshed?"

"Yes. The advisors are getting more information."

Katey nodded and picked up a bite-sized slice of cheddar and set it on a rye cracker. "How bad is it?"

He shrugged in an unconvincing manner. He sighed. He had been a politician so long, he could lie to a priest and not think twice about it, but he could never pull the wool over Katey's eyes. Protocols of secrecy meant that he couldn't tell his wife some things. In those times, he would just say he couldn't talk about it.

"That bad, eh?"

"The whole country is dark, and so is most of Europe. London lost power a few hours ago, and the rest of UK followed. Australia went out like a light...sorry. I wasn't trying to be funny. Their grids went down faster than I thought possible. Italy. Central Europe. It's like watching dominoes fall. Egypt. Saudi Arabia. You name it, and it's either dark or going dark."

"This has to be terrorism." Katey's face paled.

"We're still hoping that it's something else, but we're proceeding as if the country is under attack."

"How can this happen?"

"A digital worm, a virus, or something like it. USCYBER-COM is working with DHS to narrow it down."

"Someone infected our power grid?"

Barlow rolled a slice of ham lunch meat into a tube and took a bite. "Most likely."

"What else could it be?"

He frowned. He was tired of talking about it, but Katey had a right to know. "There's a slim chance we did it to ourselves."

"What? How?"

He sighed. "Military action in the twenty-first century is different than it was just a decade or two ago. Our country is digitally attacked every day. So are other countries. We know about them because we've done a little attacking of our own. The Chinese planted hidden programs in some of our key infrastructures, including the power grid. Truth is, we've done the same to them. These days, the first act of war is to take out the computers, a country's Internet access, communications, and…well, you get the idea."

"Are you saying one of the worm thingies went out of control? We attacked ourselves?"

"Not likely, but we have to look at the possibility."

She leaned back in the chair. "If that's true and we caused power outages around the world…Oh my, that's going to be hard to explain."

"I don't even want to think about it. People are dying because of this."

"Will the power come back on?"

Barlow took her hand. "Yes. I can't tell you when, but the problem can be fixed, and we have the world's best people working on it. For now, we're on a full military alert and trying to deal with the problems as they arise."

"What happens if we don't get the power back on?"

"There's no need to talk about that now." He reached for a cheese spread and a few crackers. "Have you talked to the kids?"

"Yes, but I had to get help from Communications. The phones are still working, but the circuits are maxed out." She rubbed her forehead. "Cell phones are almost useless. It takes hours for a simple text to go through."

"I'll have someone bring up a special phone. It uses the military cell technology and has priority in the system. You say you got through?"

"Yes. Teddy is home with the family. He left the office early today. He said it took hours to get home."

"But he and the grandbuddies are doing okay?"

"Everyone's fine. So are Abigail and her husband."

Barlow looked at his plate as if a message were magically appearing in the cracker crumbs. He looked up. "Katey, I need you to pull a few things together."

She stiffened. "We're leaving?"

He nodded. "We have to assume the worst, and the White House may be a target. Security is at its highest. The airspace around DC has been closed. Most commercial planes have landed at the closest airports anyway, so anything up there will be police or military. The military has cordoned off the area around the building. We're good for now, but we have to vacate to a continuation-of-government location."

"Mount Weather?"

He nodded.

"When?"

"Soon. We'll ride on Marine One. I need you to be ready as soon as you can be."

"Teddy and Abigail?"

"Secret Service is taking care of them. They will be moved to another site at first and then brought to Mount Weather if it looks like we're going to be there more than a couple of days."

Katey raised a hand to her mouth. Not being one to show shock, the response troubled Barlow. He hated upsetting his wife. Her welfare had been his primary concern since the day they married. For a time he had given up any thought of running for president because the position put this private woman in the public crosshairs unlike any other political position. She had given him the freedom to run. "I could never be comfortable knowing you made such a sacrifice. The country needs you. I'll be fine."

She had been fine and had even warmed up to the job of being first lady.

Barlow rubbed the center of his chest. "We're going to be fine, babe. This will all blow over soon enough. We're just going to Mount Weather as a precaution. Besides, the Secret Service and the military need the practice." He forced a smile, which dropped to a grimace a moment later.

"Are you feeling all right?"

Barlow waved her off. "Yes, I'm fine. A little indigestion. Lunch meat does that to me sometimes. That and coffee this late at night."

"I don't recall that happening before."

"I don't tell you everything, dear. I have to keep up my international man of mystery image."

"Man of mystery, eh? I think you should let the doctor look at you."

He shook his head. "No need. I know indigestion when I feel it. Besides, it would take some time for him to make it over here. DC has the worst traffic in the nation. Imagine what it's like without traffic lights. I'm fine, dear. Really." He stood. There was a tightening in his chest. "Pull those things together, will you? Pack a few books too just in case I get bored." He grinned.

He moved from the table to the door, hoping he had down-played everything sufficiently. There was no need for her to be as alarmed as he was.

11

Moriarty

As the night wore on, Jeremy wished for bed although he would not be able to sleep. His mind ran like the engine of an Indy car, but his body, while appearing relaxed, had become taut, unable to fully relax. His mind processed information like the computers he spent his life with. Jeremy was one of those people who saw code when others saw programs. It was a second language to him. Once, while working on a project at home, Roni had come in and seen a screen of "gibberish."

"Gibberish? You gotta be kidding me. This is poetry. This is highbrow composition."

"I don't see it." She had brought him a cup of green tea.

He took a sip. "Scholars say Mozart could compose long, complicated pieces of music without mistakes. He and Vivaldi could hear music in their heads and transcribe it note for note, part by part. That's what code is to some of us. This gibberish paints pictures on my mind, creates words and lines. It's like reading a novel."

"If you say so."

"When a patient is on your surgical table, what do you see? Just a person, or do you see the components?"

She paused before answering, and he knew he had her. "Okay, I get the point. I see a biological system in need of repair."

"When I see a computer program, I see the same thing. I see its parts, and I also see the fingerprints of the coder."

"Really?" There was a flicker of interest.

"It's the same as reading novels by different authors or poetry by different poets. They follow certain rules, but their personality slips in." He turned back to the computer monitor. "I do the same thing as epidemiologists at the CDC. They track down biological viruses; I track down the digital version."

"You know I've heard all this before."

He shrugged. "You know how men like to talk about their work."

"You got that right." She kissed the top of his head. "Back to it, Sherlock. Track your Moriarty."

It was that personality that Jeremy searched for now. Teams of USCYBERCOM personnel were doing the same. Time had become crucial. The country had been attacked, and the sooner they found the facts and the coder, the better.

Jeremy's office was next to General Holt's. Holt walked in every thirty minutes or so and updated Jeremy on what the president was doing, what DHS was up to, and what part of the world had just gone dark. His last report had been brief.

"England is down, so is France. Most of Western Europe has lost power. At least it's daytime over there. For now."

Jeremy rubbed his weary eyes and hoped he didn't look as worn as Holt. "You know this is impossible, right?"

"I do, Colonel. It can't be happening, but unless we've all been chewing on the same magic mushroom, it is. Possible or not, it's happening. A blackout is rolling around the world."

"Yes, sir. I was hoping you were going to tell me that I had lost my grip on reality."

"I order you to stay sane, Jeremy. The country needs you." He paused.

"There's more?" Jeremy didn't like the look on Holt's face.

"We're going to Mount Weather. Order came down from the C in C."

Commander in chief. The president. In general, that job didn't pay enough, and Jeremy wouldn't trade chairs with the man for all the world's gold. "When?"

"We depart in twenty. Lieutenant Colonel Carpenter will be our man on the ground here, but we'll still be running things from there."

Jeremy already knew this. Over the past few years they had run drills from Mount Weather. The agricultural age had given way to the industrial, which had been subsumed by the digital. Now the world was digital dependent. Modern society couldn't last long without power.

"Understood, sir."

"There is no need for me to say this, but it's required. I'm afraid you can't inform your wife."

"Yes, sir." Although he knew the words were coming, they still landed like a prizefighter's punch. "She knows how it works."

Holt studied the floor for a few moments. "She's going to be okay, Jeremy. Roni is a smart woman. She's resourceful."

"Thank you, sir. Your wife, sir?"

"We signed up for this, son, but that doesn't mean we have to like it. She's in Oregon, spoiling grandkids and spending my hard-earned money."

Jeremy chuckled. "Not anymore. The ATMs are down."

"Ah, the silver lining." He nodded at Jeremy's bank of computer monitors. "Any headway?"

"Not enough. About an hour ago, we determined that the code that hit the Hoover power station is a worm and not a virus. We've just confirmed it."

Holt took the news in, chewing it like a man masticating a bite of steak. Holt was one of most computer-literate people in the military. He didn't need Jeremy to tell him the difference, but the president would certainly need a brief definition.

"We guessed from the beginning. A virus might bring down a computer and spread to other computers through shared files, e-mail, or one of a dozen other delivery systems. But a worm…" His jaw tightened as if fighting a twenty-second bout of lockjaw. Worms self-replicated and spread from one computer system to another without users doing anything or even knowing. They were malware that could spread itself.

"I'll pass that on to the president. Anything else I should use to ruin his day?"

"Well, you can tell him that it looks an awful lot like Stuxnet. That might finish his day off."

"How similar?"

The question contained several unspoken queries. Jeremy had been asking the same questions. "Place the digital DNA side by side and there's about a seventy-five percent similarity. That's ballpark. Stuxnet was—is—a big file. It will take more time to get an accurate number. I wouldn't be surprised if it's more."

"Still, there's about a twenty-five percent difference. That means someone is messing with the thing. We have an actor."

"I'm sure we do, but…"

"Say it."

"We've also compared the version of Moriarty found in the Hoover Dam system with what we got off the power grid for the West Coast. There are differences."

"Moriarty. You've named the beast?"

"Something my wife said sometime back. It seems appropriate. Viruses and worms get names. Moriarty is—"

"The archenemy of Sherlock Holmes."

"Yes, sir, the guy who was always one step ahead. The worm that struck the region-two grid is slightly different from the one that hit region four in the west."

"A different worm for each region of the power grid?"

"Even worse. When we compare the nature of Moriarty that took down a portion of the east grid and the west grid to the second outage, we see even more changes. I think it's mutating."

"Tied to reboot?"

Jeremy nodded. "Only part of the country lost power in the first wave of outages. Systems were shut down and then rebooted. Shortly after that, Moriarty became a stronger worm. This time it took out all regions of the power grid and started doing the same around the planet."

"You know you're depressing me."

"Sorry, sir. I could do a jig if that would cheer up the general."

"Nah, it would only depress me more." Holt rubbed his chin but didn't offer his thoughts. "Be ready in…" he looked at his watch. "Fifteen."

"Yes, sir."

Jeremy comforted himself with the knowledge that in his line of work, discovering the enemy meant the war was almost over. Moriarty had been identified in several variations, but eradication software could be modified to find and destroy the lines of code. If things went well, power could be up in a couple of days at most.

■ ■ ■ ■

Roni's watch revealed that it was after ten. She had been working with minimal breaks and food for close to fourteen hours. She longed for a hot meal, a cold drink, and a warm bed. Just thinking of her bed with the thick quilt and fresh sheets made her long for home.

The trauma surgery needs of the night had slowed enough for several of the surgeons to slip away from the ORs. That was the good news. The bad news was that almost all the knife jockeys and some of the ER crews were in the doctors' lounge trying to sleep. If the hospital had not been dealing with a train wreck and injuries sustained from auto accidents clogging the intersections of the city, she might be able to find an empty hospital room and camp out for a couple hours. As it was, she couldn't find an empty gurney in a hallway.

A one-time smoker, Roni fought the desire to bum a cigarette off someone and puff away a few minutes in the black that covered the city, but she had given up the habit before entering med school. Cigarettes had taken the lives of her mother, father, and brother, and it had caused her premature birth and a childhood of asthma. She had no love for the tobacco industry, especially after her gross anatomy class, when she and a few other students cut open a cadaver as part of the class work. Where lungs should have been were two black bags of tissue. The cadaver had once been a middle-aged woman, too young to be a grandmother but old enough to leave a grieving family.

She had been able to give up the addiction, but the urge occasionally came back, usually when under great stress. Tonight qualified. Still, she could enjoy the night air again. Maybe the January chill would revive her.

She followed her previous course from the OR to the ER and out the public entrance. The crowd had thinned—a good sign. Maybe there was life after a power outage. She stepped around several gurneys in the hall, each loaded with someone in need but not with injuries severe enough to move them to the top of the list.

Three steps into the ER lobby, Roni caught sight of the boy who had previously dissolved into tears and wrapped his arms around her neck as if she were his mother. Cody? Yes, Cody. That was the name. He sat in the same chair next to the window, staring into the ebony night. The kid should be home in bed, but he no longer had a mother to tuck him in. Apparently social services hadn't made it by yet.

She looked at the others in the ER. One gaunt man, his thin beard stained with things Roni didn't want to know about, stared at Cody. He didn't blink, didn't look around. He wore a smile no boy should have to see. The man's clothes were as filthy as his beard. He rose and started for Cody.

"Hey, sport." His voice was loud for the circumstance. Either the man was close to deaf or possessed no situational awareness. "You look lonely."

Roni didn't weigh her options. She stepped forward, arriving at the man's side just as he touched Cody's knee.

"Excuse me." Her voice came out half an octave deeper than usual, and both words had edges. One step more and she had interposed her body between the lecher and Cody. She could smell the man. Booze. Stale cigarettes. Week-old perspiration.

"Hey."

Roni turned to face the man. "What?" The word was ice.

"Nuthin'."

She reached for Cody's hand. "Hey, you. Let's take a walk."

Cody didn't speak, but his face said he was glad to see her.

She led him down the hall and stopped at the first hospital phone she came to and placed a call to security.

"Where we goin'?"

"To a better place. You've been in that chair all night. Those fiberglass seats aren't all that comfortable."

"They're okay. They're kinda like the chairs in school."

She mussed his hair. "I hate those things. They make my fanny itch."

He smiled. The grin lacked conviction.

Roni tested the elevator. The call button lit when she pressed it. The hospital had only four floors, so the elevators were hydraulic and not driven by large electrical motors. She knew this only because the hospital held annual disaster drills. Hydraulic elevators were the choice of building engineers for low-rise buildings. The cabs rode on large metal pistons moved by hydraulic pressure. It took less electricity to run a pump than to operate a voltage-hungry electrical motor large enough to raise and lower a full elevator cab. Still, she felt apprehension when she and Cody stepped into the elevator car. She punched the button for the fourth floor.

The elevator began its ascent, but it seemed slower than Roni remembered. She wondered if the generators were being taxed beyond their limits. She couldn't imagine it being otherwise.

The door parted, and Roni looked into the small lobby and the hall that led to ICU. "This way, kiddo."

"Why are we here?" He trotted alongside, causing Roni to slow her steps. She had a tendency to walk fast when on a mission.

"There are too many people down there. You can have a little more room up here and maybe even a bed. The people here are the best."

"Where are we?" His voice was shaky. She couldn't blame him.

"This wing of the hospital has the CCU and ICU departments." He looked puzzled. "CCU stands for Coronary Care Unit. When people have heart surgery, they come here to get better. ICU means Intensive Care Unit. It's where patients who need special care stay. The doctors and nurses are the best. Wonderful people. You'll like them."

"Am I gonna live here?"

Roni stopped, turned, and bent so she could face the boy

eye-to-eye. "No way, Cody. This is just until things settle down. The hospital is a little crazy right now. I just want to make sure you're—" She decided not to say *safe*. "You'll be more comfortable here. Maybe even get a little sleep. If you want, I'll have some food sent up or even some ice cream. Do you like ice cream?"

"Yeah."

"What kind?"

"'Nilla."

"Vanilla it is. And a sandwich. You like tuna?"

"It's okay. Chips?"

"Sure."

Roni admired the kid. He was holding together better than a child his age should. She attributed it to emotional shock. He also had experience losing a parent. Of course, it was an act. He was trying to be brave for her. The thought ripped away a piece of her heart.

They stopped at a pair of wide doors. A white phone hung on a wall to their left. An engraved sign read "INTENSIVE CARE— DIAL 0." Roni did, and one of the nurses answered.

"Dr. Matisse" was all she said. The doors opened, and Roni led Cody into the dim medical area. A circular nurses' station dominated the space, and rooms with glass walls faced the area. Nurses, some in scrubs and some in lab coats, mingled with doctors. She glanced at the rooms and saw what she hoped to find.

"Hi, Dr. Matisse." The speaker was a nurse of East Indian descent. Her words rode on a lilting accent. "Checking on your patients?"

"Partly—"

"They're doing fine. Let me get their charts."

"Hang on, Padma. I wonder if you could do me favor." The thirty-something RN turned her brown face to Roni. Roni considered her one of the most exotic beauties she had seen. She also had a heart of 24-karat gold. She knew Padma better than the other nurses because Roni had been the surgeon who saved her husband's life three years ago after a car knocked him from his touring bike. Three surgeries later, Padma's husband was on the mend with only a slight limp to remind him of all of his injuries.

"Sure. What can I do for you?" Padma noticed Cody. "And who is this handsome young man?"

"His name is Cody. He's had a rough time." She spoke in medical code. "Vehicular trauma. Surgery. Heroics failed." She explained about Cody's father. "No relatives. As you can imagine, ER is a zoo, and they have a few undesirables in the waiting room." She made eye-contact that carried the unspoken words. "I doubt SS will show anytime soon. Can we find a cot for him?"

"We have two empty beds, but we may lose those soon." Padma thought for a moment. "Let's do this. I'll set him up in an empty room and let the staff know. CCU can take overflow. If we get too crowded, I'll set up a gurney in the lounge. We'll take care of him."

"You're the best, Padma."

"Yes, I know." She followed the words with a grin. Roni could see the weariness in her eyes. "Are you getting any word from the outside?"

Roni shook her head. "Not much. I've been in and out of OR all day and night. In fact, I've got to be back in about fifteen minutes."

"I've heard that power is down across the country."

"Maybe. I don't know how that can be true, but I haven't had time to think about it." Roni dropped to a knee as she had done in the ER hours before and faced Cody. "Okay, kiddo. This is Nurse Padma. She's the nicest person in the world."

"Nice as you?"

"Okay, she's the *second* nicest person in the world." Roni conjured up a smile. "She's gonna keep an eye on you for a while. Try to get some sleep. I know it's going to be hard, but try anyway. Will you do that for me?"

"I guess." Tears rose.

Roni's eyes followed suit.

Cody threw his arms around her neck again, and Roni embraced him and let the child cry. It took all of Roni's will not to join the weeping.

A few moments later, Padma laid a hand on Cody's shoulder. "Come on, handsome. Let's get you set up. I have an iPad with some games on it. You can use it if you want."

Roni rose. "I promised him some food."

"I'll take care of it, Doctor."

"Also—"

"We've got this, Doctor. He's in good hands. I'll make sure he's well taken care of."

Roni had no doubts.

12

Mount Weather

The VH-60N Whitehawk helicopter landed on the helo pad a short distance from the West Wing. President Nathan Barlow, his wife Katey, the secretary of state, and Chief of Staff Frank Grundy were moving toward it before the craft fully settled. Secret Service agents accompanied them. The helicopter pilot, a Marine colonel dressed in the Marine's Blue Dress Charlie/Delta uniform, met the president with a salute. Barlow returned it and followed Katey into the craft. Three minutes later, the aircraft was airborne and thundering over DC.

Barlow gave no indication of tension. He sat in his chair, his wife in the swivel seat opposite his own. He smiled and patted her hand. They had followed this procedure once a year. Even the president of the United States had to practice, although there was little for him to do except walk where he was told to. The military and Secret Service took care of the rest.

The flight would be short. Mount Weather was less than fifty miles from DC. By air, the trip would take less than thirty minutes even using an indirect course.

Out his window scrolled a scene he never imagined—DC

in the dark. Like all cities, DC had its share of temporary power outages, but never the entire city. He might even have found that acceptable if DC had been the only city affected. The whole country was dark except for those buildings that had auxiliary power. Lights blazed inside the White House, but out here only hospitals, airports, and a few other buildings glowed with power. The streets were dark except for the headlights of the mass of cars bound in traffic. Red and blue lights of emergency vehicles flashed in the blackness.

"What a mess." Katey's voice had a tremor. "It looks like a scene from a science-fiction movie."

"If only it were." Barlow closed his eyes, completing the blackness. What lay ahead of him was a situation no president had ever faced before. The government made plans for almost every kind of contingency, even the loss of power along the Eastern seaboard. He knew of no simulation that had lights going out everywhere.

The moment Barlow stepped into the VH-60N, the helicopter's call sign changed. It was now Marine One, a craft run by the Marine Helicopter Squadron 1—HMX-1. This craft and another like it had been equipped with specialized communications gear and defensive weapons. It was an amazing piece of equipment and one of Barlow's favorite ways to travel.

"Marine Two is airborne and five minutes behind us," Frank said. He had received the news over his specialized government cell phone. "The VP and his wife and COS are aboard."

"Cabinet members?"

"All due to depart within minutes." Frank spoke like a man used to trouble.

Barlow just nodded and thought about the place he would be spending the night. Mount Weather was nestled into the Blue Ridge Mountains not far from Bluemont, Virginia. In the 1800s it had been used as a military weather station. Over the years it had grown into something much more. Other continuation-of-government sites were scattered around the country, places where leaders could continue to govern the US during times of crisis. Over the decades the places and roles of these sites changed.

Mount Weather was one of the best-known secrets in the world. Technically, it was the emergency headquarters for FEMA, and it appeared in the US budget as such, but conspiracy theorists believed it to be much more—and they were right about many things.

The Mount Weather facility had two faces, one aboveground and one below. Below the buildings and large antennas, behind the ten-foot-high chain-link fence with its crown of razor wire, under the watchful eye of the best security teams the country could produce was a facility few ever saw and no one talked about.

FEMA's national radio system, a communications network linking key federal public-safety agencies and the military, was located there. The buildings on the surface were designated Area A and covered 434 acres. Below grade, dug first in 1936 by the US Bureau of Mines with work that continues to the present day, was Area B, an underground city with 600,000 square feet of habitable space. Deep beneath the Virginia soil, not far from Virginia State Route 601, it was a complex that included apartments, dormitories, cafeterias, a hospital, a water and sewer system, and even a transit system. Hundreds could live here for several months without concern about food and water.

Power wasn't a problem. It could produce its own electricity with generators and kept enough fuel on hand to keep them running for months. The government also had access to large amounts of diesel and gas reserved for the continuation of leadership.

It was remarkable in every way. Nonetheless, it wasn't the

place Barlow wanted to end his presidency. He rubbed the center of his chest and then his left shoulder.

"Are you okay, sir?" Frank leaned close.

"Sure. Why?"

"You were massaging your shoulder and chest."

Barlow waved him off. "A little indigestion. I get it from time to time. Stress and food don't go together well."

"We'll have the doctor look at you after we land."

"No 'we' won't, Frank. I'm fine. I know my own body. I get indigestion now and again. I know what it feels like. I'm good. However, should I decide to have a heart attack, you'll be the first to know."

"Excuse me," Katey said.

Barlow winked at her. "*After my wife*, you'll be the first to know. She outranks us both, you know."

"I can live with that." Frank tightened his lap belt.

"Still the nervous flier, Frank?" The president grinned. "We'll have the doctor look at you when we land."

"If God meant for men to fly, we would have been born with parachutes." He leaned back. "When we leave the West Wing, I will give up my days of flying."

As if offended, the helicopter bounced in the air.

Barlow looked out the window again. "I don't think the city has been this dark since Jefferson was president."

"It doesn't look right," Katey said. "It looks all wrong somehow."

Barlow lifted his eyes. "At least there's less light pollution. The astronomers should be happy."

"They need power too, Mr. President. Telescopes are moved by electric motors, photos are all digital, and—"

"I got it, Frank."

The thrum of the two General Electric T700-GE-701C turboshaft engines driving rotors with a fifty-three-foot diameter vibrated through the craft. Within five minutes of liftoff, the helicopter reached its cruising speed of 150 knots. Barlow watched the dark terrain scroll beneath them as they flew northwest from DC. Dark.

DC, dark.

Silver Spring, dark. McLean, Reston, Ashburn, Purcellville—all dark.

Scenarios ran through Barlow's brain, not one of them good. He longed for a message that read, "Oops, our bad. Blew a fuse. World will be up and running in fifteen minutes." Barlow was too much of a realist to hope for very long, and he had been in politics too long to be an optimist. Something bad had happened. This was no accident. It was an attack by an unknown individual or group.

He tried to imagine what the people below were doing. Most were probably at home in bed, expecting power to return by morning. The media had gotten word about the extent of the blackouts, but only people with battery powered radios or who listened to the news in their cars would have heard. Most, he assumed, were still in the dark about the extent of problem. He paused to smile at his pun. Humor, even if it lasted only a second, was appreciated.

Barlow had flown here only a few times, once to see the new improvements to the FEMA operations and twice as practice for a day like this. The compound had several areas for helicopters to land. They would set down on pad M4 near the center of the aboveground complex. The other pads were associated with parking lots and were farther from their target building.

"Please prepare for landing." The pilot's voice came over the cabin speakers. "We've been cleared for final approach." Of course they had. One didn't keep POTUS circling a government facility, waiting for permission to touch down.

The chopper slowed and began its descent to the compound. It rocked in a stiff breeze, but the pilots kept the craft steady. They were the best the Marines had to offer and had special training and skill to fly this and other helicopters kept at the ready of the president and key government officials.

Another glance out the window showed several buildings with lights on. Most of the others, especially the older ones, sat in darkness. The surrounding Virginia forest, lit only by the silver light of a three-quarter-moon, appeared menacing, an amorphous monster ready to dine on the emergency center.

"What's that?" Katey had her face close to the window by her seat. At first, Barlow looked down and saw nothing unusual. "What's what?" She was looking up.

"In the sky. I saw a light. I can still see it, but it's not as bright."

The others in the cabin tried to catch a glimpse out the window. "I see it. Odd, it's like a large, dim star."

Katey shook her head. "It's not a star. It wasn't there before."

"There's one over here too. It just flashed on and then almost blinked out." Frank craned his neck. "It's like a ring of smoke, but not quite."

"I see two more," Secretary of State Brent Baker said, his bald head pushed to the window.

"What are they, Nathan?" Katey sounded nervous.

"I don't know. If I didn't know better—" He swore and snapped up the handset next to his seat. "Colonel, this is the president. Get this bird on the ground now—*right now!*"

Before the pilot could comply, the craft's engine coughed, and the tail pitched right and then down. A loud tone poured from the cockpit area and filled the cabin. "WARNING, POWER LOSS. WARNING, POWER LOSS. WARNING, POWER—"

It ceased as fast as it had begun. Barlow heard the pilot order, "Autorotate." The lights in the cabin blinked out. "Brace yourselves! We're going down." Then came the words no one in an aircraft wants to hear: "Mayday, mayday, this is Marine One declaring an emergency. We have lost all power…"

If Barlow was right, the mayday was a waste of time. The radio would be as dead as the engine.

Barlow snapped his head around and looked at the rapidly approaching ground. He was no pilot, but he knew the helicopter had slowed too much for autorotation to work. There wasn't enough forward speed to drive the air through the rotors. The 20,000 pound craft was headed for a hard landing. Their only advantage was they had almost completed their descent. Only thirty feet or so remained. He hoped it was less than that.

The impact was twice as hard as Barlow imagined. Marine One hit the ground wheels down, bounced a few feet up, and then tilted to its right side. Barlow was too frightened to close his eyes. Before the window hit the ground a dozen feet from the helipad, he saw the rotor slice into the ground and shatter into innumerable sharp pieces.

His head bounced off the cabin wall, sending bolts of pain through his head and neck. For a moment he thought the blow had knocked his eyeballs from their sockets.

The gibbous moon shone through the windows on the other side of the cabin, casting an ivory glow on the face of his unconscious wife. "No. Dear God, no. No…" Blackness filled his eyes.

13

The Falling Sky

At Fort Meade, Colonel Jeremy Matisse had been ready to enter one of the nondescript buildings a hundred yards from the landing pad in the east parking lot. A soldier had been waiting in a Humvee a safe distance from the rotor blast. He saluted as General Holt, Jeremy, and Senator Ryan O'Tool approached the vehicle. O'Tool returned the salute and Jeremy had to resist the urge to remind the man that the salute was for the general and not him. To the sergeant's credit he held the salute until Holt returned it.

News that O'Tool would be accompanying them to Mount Weather had been discouraging. O'Tool was a powerful man in the senate, but to Jeremy he was mostly an annoyance. When the call to move to Mount Weather came through, it was revealed that heads from both houses of congress would be joining them. Since O'Tool was at USCYBERCOM, Holt was ordered by head of the Joint Chiefs to bring the senator along. In an impressive display of discipline, Holt simply replied, "Yes, sir."

"This is a bit of an adventure, isn't it, gentlemen?" O'Tool looked more like an eight-year-old headed to Disneyland than a ranking member of the senate in a global crisis. The man struggled with his harness. Jeremy had to help him before the UH-1N utility helicopter could lift off from Fort Meade.

"I don't see it that way." Holt kept his voice even and devoid of emotion. He was in full command mode. Jeremy knew the feeling.

"Oh, come on, General. I thought you military types loved conflict and action."

"We don't avoid it, Senator, but that doesn't mean we're blind to the dangers." Holt met O'Tool's eyes. "How long did you serve in the military?"

Holt already had that information. Jeremy figured his commander was making a point.

"Never had the privilege. I've chosen to serve my country through elective office." He looked to Jeremy. "When was the last time you were at Mount Weather?"

"I've never been. At least not the part we're going to."

"Really? Me either, but I have an excuse. Mount Weather keeps its cards close to the vest. Much of its budget is black ops. A lot of the money designated for FEMA feeds the underground facility. Frankly, it's morally wrong to keep the legislature out of the loop. We are the ones who sign off on your budget, you know."

"I do know that, Senator, but I can't help you." Jeremy glanced at Holt. The general's face was an emotionless mask. "That's above my rank."

"It's not above yours, is it, General?"

"As a matter of fact, it is. People with more stars than me deal with such matters. My teams create a budget for USCYBER-COM, and that's it. Mount Weather is need-to-know."

"You don't have a need to know?" O'Tool raised an eyebrow.

"I know about the site. I know its purpose. I know that when the president says I should get my fanny over there, it would be wise to go."

The flight from Fort Meade to Mount Weather was thankfully short. When the UH-1N touched down, the three exited. The rotors had slowed but still pushed enough of the January air to chill Jeremy.

A young sergeant waited until all were seated before cranking the Humvee's engine to life. They covered the distance to the center of the camp in short order. Jeremy exited first and waited for Holt to slip out. A grin brightened O'Tool's face.

"This place is cool," he said.

The sergeant led them to the door and had just placed his hand on the knob when their helicopter lifted off and another approached. In the moonlight, Jeremy could see the presidential seal on the side of the incoming chopper.

"POTUS is here."

"Ah, I beat the president." Why O'Tool found that something to boast about was beyond Jeremy.

"I assume he might have had a few things to deal with." Holt's words were colder.

"Hey, what's that?" O'Tool pointed to the sky.

Jeremy drew his eyes from Marine One and looked in the direction O'Tool indicated and saw a bright smudge. Then a flash and another smudge. His first thought was of an exploding comet, but that didn't make sense. More flashes of light, some leaving tiny points of illumination like glitter overhead.

Then he heard it. The sound of the helicopter's engines stopping. The sudden audio emptiness hurt Jeremy's ears. "Oh, dear God, no!"

First he glanced to the UH-1N that had just delivered them. It was falling, its impotent rotor turning with no power to provide lift. Next, Jeremy snapped his head back to Marine One. It was just twenty or thirty feet above grade and about a quarter mile from the landing pad.

Jeremy was on the move before his brain could sort out what his eyes were seeing. Instinct and stomach-churning fear drove him to action.

Holt's voice followed him. "Sergeant. Get the Senator below. Call for help. Do it now, soldier."

Marine One landed hard and bounced skyward, its frame bending in the middle. It tipped to the side like a capsized boat, sending the still-churning four-blade rotor into the small lawn that surrounded the H4 landing pad. The rotor fragmented, sending sharp shards of shrapnel zipping through the air. Jeremy hit the ground, covering his head with his hands and hoping a bit of rotor wouldn't impale him, pinning him to the ground like a bug in an entomologist's collection.

Something landed next to him. A few seconds later he saw the something was a someone. General Holt lay next to him and assumed the same protective position.

"You okay?" Jeremy pushed to his knees. Holt rolled to his side and touched the side of his face. There was blood.

"Superficial. Let's go." The general was on his feet before Jeremy. Once again the man, fifteen years his senior, amazed Jeremy.

They ran over the debris-laden lawn. Jeremy smelled aviation fuel. The helicopter's carcass lay on its side like an ancient dying creature. They slowed as they reached the craft.

Jeremy studied the shaft that ran from the engine to the rotor hub, trying to figure out how to use it as a step.

"Here."

Holt had placed his back to the roof of the helo and interlaced his fingers, forming a stirrup with his hands. Jeremy hesitated only half a moment before facing Holt and placing his boot in the general's hands. It made sense. Jeremy was younger and could move around in the tight confines of the cabin better than Holt.

"On three," Holt said.

Jeremy pressed down with his foot and straightened his leg as Holt lifted. It was enough. Jeremy struggled to what was now the roof and positioned himself to open the sliding door. It took three tries before he could pull it open. Something ignited in his back, and pain blazed up his spine. A problem for later days.

Summoning all his strength, he slid the door back far enough so it wouldn't close on its own. The moonlight was too weak to reveal much of the interior, but he could make out four bodies in the cabin.

He leaned in. "Mr. President?"

Nothing.

Jeremy's heart didn't know whether to beat more wildly or just stop.

"Status?" Holt called up.

"I see four individuals. All unconscious."

One of the bodies moved.

"I've got movement."

A small voice. Female. "Help us."

Jeremy looked around the ground and saw men and women running from several buildings. Where were the emergency vehicles? He didn't expect an air crash crew, but a base this size surely had its own fire department. Then he noticed that some of the personnel sprinting his way wore turnout gear and helmets. The pieces of the problem began to come together.

"I'm going in, General." Jeremy didn't wait for a response. He slowly lowered himself into the cabin, careful not to step on bodies.

There was new light. Jeremy was thankful until he realized the helicopter was burning.

· · · ·

President Nathan Barlow became aware of a strange presence near him. A man—tall, trim, and in a daily uniform. A moment later, he noticed he was lying on his side and his head hurt. A strange orange light surrounded him.

"Mr. Pres…Can you h…me?"

He didn't know the voice. Why was a stranger waking him? The shock dissolved in an instant, and the past few terrorizing moments washed forward in his mind.

"Katey? Katey!"

"I'm here, honey. Are you hurt?"

"Forget about me. Are *you* hurt?" He tried to move, but something was holding him in place. Then the orange and yellow glow caught his attention. "We're on fire."

"We have to move fast, Mr. President." The strange voice.

"Who are you?"

"Colonel Matisse. We can talk later."

The cabin rocked. Barlow looked up and saw a man in uniform looking back. "President first."

"No, my wife."

The colonel undid the lap belt holding Barlow in his seat. "Let's go, Mr. President. We don't have much time."

"I said take my wife first."

"Yes, sir, you did."

"That's an order."

"Yes, sir, I understand. Let me help you up." The man's voice was calm but weighted with urgency. "I don't have time to check you for injuries, sir. I apologize."

Barlow heard a grunt, then felt himself being lifted from the chair. Something was stabbing his side. He groaned.

"Raise your arms, sir." Matisse said.

Barlow did, and the pain almost made him black out. He heard sizzling, and the orange light dimmed some. From above, a pair of hands grabbed his wrists. A second later he was pulled from the cabin.

The moment the president's feet disappeared, Jeremy turned to Katey Barlow. She was conscious, and blood flowed from the right side of her head. "I'm sorry, ma'am, I'm going to have to move you."

"It's okay. I'm tired of this place anyway."

"Yes, ma'am. I don't much like it myself." He helped her to her feet. "I'm afraid I'm going to have to get a little personal." Before she could reply, Jeremy squatted and wrapped his arms around her thighs. "Arms up." He lifted, and the pain in his back flared. Her weight disappeared a moment later as Holt and whoever had joined him topside dragged her through the door.

He turned his attention to the remaining men. One he recognized as the secretary of state. He laid two fingers on the man's carotid. No pulse, at least that he could find. It didn't matter. He had to assume he was still alive. Try as he might, he couldn't rouse the man. He was dead weight.

"Coming down." Jeremy saw a pair of booted feet appear in the door. "Make room."

Jeremy moved back as much as he could. The rescuer was lowered, with the help of others he assumed, into the cabin.

More sizzling, less fire. Jeremy allowed himself to feel a moment of hope.

"What have we got?" The rescuer wore a fireman's turnout gear and helmet.

"This is the secretary of state. I can't find a pulse. I was just about to check on this guy." He pointed to the other man. The fireman fingered the neck of the living passenger. "Got a pulse. Strong. Okay, we take him first."

A rope dropped into the cabin. At least they wouldn't have to try to lift an unconscious man. The fireman knew his way around a rope and soon had a nonslip rescue loop tied around the victim. As those topside pulled the man up, the last of the orange light disappeared.

"Fire's out," Jeremy said.

"Maybe. Maybe not for long. All we have are fire extinguishers, and the engine is still hot. Fuel is still flowing, so I'd kinda like to get out of here."

"No argument from me."

The rope returned, this time with a rescue harness. "Someone up there is thinking." The secretary of state was limp. It took long moments before they were able to secure the harness and call for the team above to haul away.

"You're next, sir."

"I'll go last," Jeremy said.

"Please don't ask me to disobey an order, sir. This is a rescue, and I'm in charge down here. You can bust my chops later. We're not out of the woods yet."

Jeremy understood the point, and for the second time that day, he was letting someone boost him up. The air outside smelled of oil, fuel, and burning electrical wires. He stepped away from the door and knelt. When the rescuer's hands grabbed the doorframe, he helped pull the man to safety.

They leapt to the ground and put distance between them and the downed craft. Other men in firefighting coats and helmets held fire extinguishers—CO_2, dry chemical, and water. Once he had put fifty yards between him and the smoldering hunk of metal, he turned to see new flames licking up the side of the craft.

A flood of emotion, no longer corralled by danger, rose. What had gone wrong? Where were the emergency vehicles? He looked around and saw Holt approaching.

"You good, son?"

"Yes, sir. The pilots—"

"We got them out. Both are alive but unconscious. It was a hard hit."

Jeremy rubbed his face with both hands. "Why are there no emergency vehicles? I don't understand."

"They wouldn't start. The fire crew did an admirable job hustling out here on foot, carrying what gear they could."

"The vehicles wouldn't start?"

"Look up, Colonel."

Jeremy did and saw something he hadn't seen since a visit to Eielson Air Force Base near Fairbanks, Alaska—an aurora borealis. Ribbons of color painted the night sky. It took a second for Jeremy to make sense of what he was seeing. He pulled his cell phone from his pocket and turned it on.

Nothing.

"Oh, this is so bad."

Holt placed a hand on Jeremy's shoulder but said nothing.

▪▪▪▪

Lieutenant Commander William "Rocky" Rochester was flying at Angels 22—22,000 feet above the Atlantic—and banking left as he patrolled the three-mile limit of US territorial waters. He was one of several aircraft patrolling the skies. The country was on high alert, and a terrorist attack was assumed. His job was to intercept any unauthorized aircraft inbound and splash it if necessary. All commercial flights had been grounded, and civilian flights were diverted to the nearest airports. The only things in the air were either government-sanctioned flights, military aircraft, or possible threats.

He was outbound from the USS *Ronald Reagan*, which patrolled a hundred miles due east of Washington, DC. The night sky glittered with stars, and for a moment, Rocky wished this were a pleasure flight.

Rocky triggered his radio to report his position when the engines suddenly shut off and the heads-up display disappeared. The stubby-winged craft slowed, and the nose lowered.

He attempted to restart the engines, but they didn't respond. The craft was dead, something that should never happen. The F-22 slowed even more and then began to gain speed as the nose dipped more and gravity began its work. He triggered his microphone and attempted to call his ship. No response.

"Come on, come on." Again he tried to kick-start the Pratt and Whitney turbofan engines and got nothing. The $150 million craft was gliding to the dark ocean. Rocky worked the stick, but with no electricity, there was no computer assisted flying, no fly-by-wire.

It was one thing to lose engines, but to lose everything was impossible. There were too many redundancies. The control surfaces refused to respond. He had been in a bank at the time of the power outage, and the craft continued to turn.

His rate of descent increased. Rocky was determined to ride the craft as long as possible before bailing out.

He was thankful that his ejection seat was activated mechanically, not electrically. F-22s didn't float well.

Above him, flashes of light blinked from space. Below, a wide black ocean waited to receive him.

■ ■ ■ ■

Roni had finished another surgery when the lights went out again. She sat on a worn sofa in the doctors' lobby and sipped a black fluid someone called coffee. She had doubts. The nervous chatter of medical personnel and patients pressed through the door. Two other physicians were in the room with her. An ER doc sat in a chair with his head back, snoring softly. A surgeon, who Roni knew was a week from retirement and endless days in a motor coach plying the roadways of the US, rested his head on his arms like a first-grade student during rest time.

Roni had her eyes closed as well, but the sound of people grumbling interrupted her rest. She set the cup down and moved from the lounge.

"What's happening?" The nearly retired surgeon stood by her side.

"Lights are out again."

He shrugged. "They'll have the generator running again. Probably just ran out of gas."

Roni hoped he was right, but she had trouble stirring up some optimism. She moved down the hall to one of the exit doors.

She didn't like the look of the sky.

■ ■ ■ ■

It had taken Stanley two hours to work his way through downtown traffic and drive over the San Diego–Coronado Bridge. Royce had left before he had and made better time because most of her driving was down the I-5. Traffic was thick, but there were no intersections with dead traffic lights to deal with.

The elevators were out, so Stanley and Royce had walked up ten flights of stairs, the most exercise he'd had in a year. His legs still ached. They stood at the window, looking at the dark skyline of San Diego. The bay that separated Coronado from San Diego normally reflected the light of the high-rise towers and low-rise buildings. It was one of the most spectacular sights in the city. But tonight, only moonlight danced on the water. Every building was dark, including those in their condo complex—except their unit. Stanley insisted on keeping the lights off to avoid attracting attention.

"Good thing we left when we did." Stanley gave Royce a squeeze. "The bridge and the road up the Strand is blocked. Not a single car is moving."

"I don't understand." It was the third time Royce had said that in the last half hour. "Why do we have power when no one else does?"

Stanley turned to Donny's room. The soft glow of computer monitors served as night lights for the sleeping man-child. "I have no idea." He looked at Rosa sleeping on the sofa. "I'm glad she decided to stay. She'd be stuck in that mess out there. She's safer here, especially since her husband is on the road."

"Stanley," Royce whispered. "I'm scared. I'm really, really scared."

"Me too, sweetheart." He tightened his embrace.

14

Presidential Pain

Somebody tell me I'm wrong." Barlow had two busted ribs and a knot the size of a golf ball on the side of his head, and he had barely been rescued from a burning helicopter, but he still had a lot of energy—angry energy.

Jeremy and Holt stood next to the president's hospital bed in the below-ground facility of Mount Weather. "I wish we could, Mr. President," Holt said. "We believe your assessment to be correct."

"Star Wars satellites? I'd prefer to be wrong."

"With all due respect, sir, we wish you were wrong too." Holt kept his bandaged hands clasped in front of him. Both hands had been injured when he crawled his way to the top of the crashed craft, and they received further injury helping haul up the president and the rest of the passengers. The pilots came to just as the president's wife was being hauled out of the smoky cabin. They were able to help themselves out. The chief pilot was in a bed nearby, nursing a concussion and whiplash. The copilot had fared better but was still stiff and filled with aches and pains.

"Those couldn't have been our birds. Our EMPs are over China, Korea, and Russia." The president started to sit up but then winced and gave up on the idea. "Do we have word from NORAD about whose satellites those were?"

Holt didn't budge, but Jeremy could feel the tension. "We're having to make contact through off channels. The electromagnetic pulse knocked out all our communications satellites. The only radios that work are in this facility. NORAD is also a hardened facility, so we assume their electronics still work." The North American Aerospace Defense command's operation center was buried deep in Cheyenne Mountain, not far from Colorado Springs, Colorado.

"But with no working satellites or landlines, we're cut off. I assume ANR and CFB Winnipeg are out of touch."

"Yes, sir. No word from the Alaskan and Canadian regions."

"We have to be able to talk to them."

"We should have contact soon, Mr. President." A tall, slim woman entered the hospital area. Army Colonel Jill Sherwin was in charge of Mount Weather. Jeremy had never heard of her and assumed that was by plan.

"Where have you been?" the president snapped.

"Checking on the other helicopter that went down after dropping off the general and colonel. I've sent out a team to search the wreckage."

"Of course. I apologize for my attitude. I get testy after every brush with death." Sadness crossed the president's face. His secretary of state was dead, and he feared… "There's no way to know the status of the other inbound choppers?"

"Not yet, sir. I have communication with the search team, but that's only because our radios are stored down here. No above-ground radio is working. To be more accurate, nothing electrical is working aboveground. The squad has a manpack. Right now they make contact with a man topside who relays it to us. We're repairing our antennas. The pulse did a job on them."

"Have they reached the downed chopper?" Jeremy didn't want to hear the answer.

"Both pilot and copilot are dead."

There was a long pause. No one wanted to ask the next question. Barlow gave voice to it. "The VP?"

Sherwin was working hard to keep her Army composure. Jeremy felt sorry for the woman. This was, to his knowledge, the first time Mount Weather had been fully utilized, and it was all going wrong.

"I asked a question, Colonel."

Sherwin nodded. "Yes, sir. My apologies. We have no word about or from Marine Two or from the craft carrying the heads of congress and the senate. We hope for the best but assume the worst."

"Why do you assume the worst?" Holt asked.

"Well, sir, we know the time of departure, route, and cruising altitude of each craft. At the time of the event, all of them would be at travel altitude, which means that even the closest helo would be several hundred feet aboveground. It's possible that they could autorotate and come down a little slower." She shrugged. "We just don't know."

"I heard the pilot call for autorotation before we hit. It didn't do us much good."

Sherwin nodded. "Yes, sir. My understanding is that your forward speed was very slow as the pilots prepared to hover for landing. Autorotation requires forward motion so the air forces the rotors to turn. Not a gentle drop, but better than plummeting."

Barlow drew a hand across his face, a motion that made him wince. Jeremy understood—the strained muscle in his back was killing him.

"Let me see if I have this right: My secretary of state is dead, my chief of staff is still unconscious, the vice president and his crew are probably dead or dying in the midst of some wreckage, and all the key leaders of congress are in the same boat." He looked at Sherwin. "Should I assume the same is true for the craft carrying the Joint Chiefs of Staff and my cabinet?"

"I'm afraid so, Mr. President. We were getting direct information from radar operators at Langley AFB and other places until the EMP, so we know where each helicopter was and it's altitude at the time of the pulse. Survivability is close to zero, sir."

"When can we start sending and receiving messages, Colonel?"

Sherwin didn't hesitate. "Phase one, sir, is to fix the antennas. We are set to transmit on all military frequencies and in shortwave if need be, but we'll only be able to talk to bases like NORAD who have hardened communications facilities. Even FEMA's National Radio Station is out of communications, so we can't contact other military or first responders. I have no idea how long it will take them to get outside communications. Everything aboveground and in space is fried, sir. Communication is going to be limited for some time."

"Help me up." Again, the president tried to rise. No one moved to help. He slumped back on the bed. "Who's the commander in chief in this room?"

Jeremy helped Barlow up, letting the president's legs dangle over the edge of the bed. The man's face flushed but then quickly returned to its normal color.

"Anyone got a robe? I could use a pair of slippers too."

An Army physician crossed the ward. "Mr. President, you shouldn't—"

"Go away. That's an order."

"Sir—"

"You said my life wasn't in danger. I'm just banged up. I can handle the pain. I deal with congress all time, and I've survived that. Now leave me alone."

"Yes, sir." The doctor turned.

"Before you go, Major." Barlow waited for the man to turn. "Thank you. I owe you big-time."

"I'm here if you need me, sir. Please, no tennis."

Barlow screwed up his face. Jeremy couldn't imagine playing tennis with broken ribs. One of the nurses brought a robe and a pair of slippers to the president.

Jeremy had seen many secret things and secret places in his life. He had strolled hallways in the National Security Agency that few had walked. An underground lair didn't surprise him. The country had many such places, but he had never seen anything like this. It was a small town several stories below grade. Seeing a full-fledged hospital with an ER and operating theater had surprised him, and he thought he was beyond surprises. Although he had not received a full tour, he was pretty sure a few hundred people could live down there for many months, maybe even a few years.

Jeremy followed the president as the small entourage left the hospital behind and entered a wide corridor with an arched ceiling. General Holt was on Barlow's right, Colonel Sherwin on his left. Jeremy followed behind. The corridor was well lit, and Jeremy wondered about the power source. He guessed the generators were below grade with vents to the surface. Now wasn't the time to ask.

"Okay, folks, we are dealing with something beyond imagination here." The president seemed to gain strength with each step. "Before I left the White House, I invoked National Security

Presidential Directive 51 and Homeland Security Presidential Directive 20. We are now the government." He shook his head. "You know, conspiracy theorists think we keep a shadow government down here, people with the rank of cabinet members. Counterparts to those in Washington."

"A duplicate government," Holt said. "I'm aware of the folklore."

"At the moment, I wish it were true." The president drew a deep but careful breath. "When George W. Bush signed the presidential directives, he did so in the shadow of rising terrorism. In 2001 we learned that we are vulnerable to attack. What we've seen in the last day proves it again. Our enemies have struck—although I'm not sure which ones. But the electromagnetic pulse came from space-borne platforms, which limits the number of potential actors."

"Agreed, sir." Holt said.

Barlow turned to Sherwin. "I've only been here twice, and it's been more than a year since the last time. Remind me of the way to my office?"

"If I may, sir." Sherwin stopped at a blue phone hanging on the wall of the wide corridor and punched in a three-digit number. A few moments later, an Army staff sergeant arrived with an electric golf cart. The man slipped from the driver's seat and saluted.

"I've got this, Sergeant," Sherwin said. "Dismissed."

"Yes, ma'am." The soldier stepped to the side. Sherwin helped the president into the cart and then sat behind the wheel. She drove slowly as the whine of the electric motor echoed along the hard surfaces of the corridor. The corridor was wide enough to drive a pickup truck through. She made several turns and then entered a section of the complex that was unlike the Spartan wing they had left. Planters and trees flourished under grow lights recessed into the walls and ceiling. The smell of cherry blossoms in January caught Jeremy off guard.

A few minutes later they were in the presidential wing. It was not as ornate as Jeremy remembered seeing on his few trips to the White House. He had never been in the president's residence, but he imagined it followed the same basic interior design as the rest of the White House.

They entered a lobby replete with thickly padded leather chairs and warm, red oak side tables and coffee tables. Tiffany-style lamps were spaced around the area. A narrow hall led from one side of the room.

"Do you want to go to your residence or your private office, sir?" Sherwin asked.

"Private office."

"Yes, sir. We'll have to walk from here."

"I can manage, Colonel."

They exited the vehicle and walked through the lobby and down the hall. Two armed soldiers stood on either side of the hall. One held post halfway down the seventy-foot length.

"Shall I tell your wife you're here?" Sherwin had taken the president's arm again. His steps seemed a little less sure.

"Call her from the office, but I want you in on this meeting."

"Yes, Mr. President."

The president's subterranean private office was of CEO quality. Wide and well-appointed with an antique desk, the office looked almost identical to the Oval Office except for the shape of the room. The furnishings included two sofas with a flower print and three leather side chairs.

Barlow made for the largest leather side chair and lowered himself in. Perspiration speckled his brow. "Okay, that was more taxing than I expected."

"I'll call for the doctor," Sherwin said.

"No need. I just need to sit for a bit. Please, everyone, sit. We need to talk. Oh, and I need Senator O'Tool in here."

■ ■ ■ ■

"The way I see it, we have two overriding concerns. The first is maintaining a government. We have a legal responsibility to continue the government and its operations. Right now the government is me and Senator O'Tool here. One from the executive branch and one from the legislature isn't much."

"At least we're both elected, sir," O'Tool said. "That makes it constitutional, or close to constitutional."

"Agreed, but we need to get as many cabinet members here as we can ASAP. If it's true they're dead or incapacitated, we need to bring in the undersecretaries. Somehow, we have to get them here. Am I to understand that no vehicles are operating?" He looked to Sherwin.

"Nothing aboveground, sir. The pulse fried anything with a computer chip, including all modern cars. Not only that, the pulse was strong enough to send current through wires, damaging other electrical components. There are a few things still working, like emergency exit lights. I suspect that's because of their simplicity—just a battery, a sensor, and LCD bulbs."

"To be accurate," Jeremy said, "there were multiple pulses, not one."

"I want to come back to that," Barlow said. "But first, I want to know if we can get something in the air or, at very least, something rolling along the ground."

"We can try, sir, but early reports make it doubtful." Sherwin didn't sugarcoat things, something Jeremy appreciated.

Barlow frowned, but Jeremy couldn't tell if Sherwin's words or his own ribs caused the pain. "Do what you can. Use your resources, Colonel. You have several hundred people on the surface and down here. There's got to be a genius in the mix."

"Yes, sir."

"The other main concern is establishing communications with the military and the rest of the world. We also need to know what's going on in the streets. Any ideas how to make that happen?"

"The FEMA radio network is set up to make those connections, but their radios may be beyond repair."

"You have radios down here," Jeremy said. "Correct? I mean, you don't communicate with FEMAs equipment for security ops, right? And you mentioned shortwave."

Sherwin nodded. "That's an idea, Colonel. Of course, we can use our radios, but listeners will need working units as well. For now, the shortwave is our best, first choice. Also, radio is going to be line of sight and whatever we can skip off the ionosphere. Without satellites, we're limited."

"How widespread do you guess the damage is?" Barlow asked. He moved in his seat and winced again. Jeremy had been told the president had refused all but the most basic pain reliever. No doubt the man would love a shot of morphine.

The three military officers looked at each other. Holt answered. "We have no way of knowing until we get some intel, and that's going to be thin until the people out there can talk to the people in here."

"Best guess?" The president's tone was terse.

Holt sighed. "I think the country has been thrown back to the early 1900s. Worse in some ways. People then had lanterns they could light. The modern world is electricity dependent. I have no doubts every state is in chaos."

"So you see this as countrywide."

"Yes, sir."

Jeremy had to force himself to speak. Delivering bad news to a person of power was always difficult. There was a reason the ancients often killed the bearer of bad news. "I think it's global."

"Global!" Barlow fixed his gaze on Jeremy, and for a moment Jeremy felt like a candle in a pizza oven. "I didn't authorize the use of EMP weapons. I didn't have time."

"But they're up there, aren't they, sir?"

Barlow hesitated. "Not by my authorization."

"Sir…Forgive me, sir. I'm not looking for someone to blame. I…" Time to start over. "I suppose it is possible that the power outages and the EMP weapons are precursors to invasion and war. I don't deny that, but that explanation doesn't feel right."

"Feel right? I need more than a gut feeling, Colonel."

Neither Holt or Sherwin looked his way. "True, we can build a case that some country knocked out our power. Really, it doesn't even have to be another country. The digital age has made our country extremely vulnerable. I mean, General Holt and our team have made it our career to keep that from happening. True, China, Korea, and Russia have planted malware in our infrastructures. These things can spread over the Internet. That means a small group of people could bring a country's power down—a cadre of foreign corporations, anarchists, homegrown terrorists…It's a long list. But something is bothering me—"

The president raised a hand. "Wait. Doesn't the fact that EMP satellites were used prove we're dealing with a hostile foreign country?"

"No, sir. It doesn't."

"I've got to hear this." Barlow shifted again.

"Remember, sir, we're dealing with a worm, a computer program that can spread on its own."

"Like Stuxnet," Holt added.

"Exactly. Stuxnet spread from computer to computer and

network to network, searching for a specific kind of program that operated a specific kind of centrifuge used to refine uranium. It bypassed other systems. It was aimed at the Iranians, not the devices in the United States or friendly countries. That's why many analysts think the US was involved."

"If we were, I don't know about it, but then again, that was before my tenure." Barlow motioned to encourage Jeremy to continue.

"If the goal was to knock out just the grid in the US by means of electromagnetic pulse, then bringing down the power grid by infecting it with a worm is redundant. Let me ask something if I may, sir. If this is above my security clearance, just say so."

Barlow chuckled without humor. "Right now you guys are the only cabinet I have. Ask."

"Have the Chinese, Koreans, or Iranians mobilized their forces in any way to suggest they plan to attack us or one of our allies?"

"I get a security briefing every morning. As soon as we had the first blackout, I asked that very question. But be careful here. The goal may not be an invasion. Simply crippling us for a while could be the goal."

Jeremy shook his head. "Our country owes the Chinese boatloads of money, sir. The Russians are dependent on selling us oil, and their economy is too weak to be bothered with kicking us to the curb. Iran and Korea are led by madmen, so I can see that happening, but they don't have access to EMP satellites. I think we're looking at one problem. I think the worm—we're calling it Moriarity—made its way to the satellites over the communication networks between ground-based computers and space-borne ones."

"You know I can't rule out an act of war," Barlow said.

"I'm not suggesting you do, Mr. President. I'm just giving my opinion."

"Well, I guess that's why you're on the general's staff." Barlow rubbed his face.

O'Tool had been speechless since being summoned to the spontaneous meeting, something that surprised Jeremy. The man had been a motormouth since arriving at USCYBERCOM. He looked pale. Apparently this was more reality than he liked.

Barlow studied the man and then turned his attention to Jill Sherwin. "Colonel, please call the hospital and get an update on Frank."

She rose and moved to the desk, where a phone waited. The group sat in silence. Jeremy couldn't speak for the others, but he felt as if his internal organs had been scooped out with a melon baller.

Sherwin asked her questions, listened, and hung up. She returned to the seating area. "Sir, the doctor reports that Mr. Grundy is awake and alert and causing trouble because the doctor won't release him."

Somehow Barlow found the strength to smile though it lacked any evidence of joy. "That's Frank. We need to spring him before he hurts the medical staff." His gaze went distant. No one interrupted his thinking. No matter where he was, Barlow was the president of the country, even deep below the ground.

After a moment, Barlow spoke. "I am obligated to maintain a constitutional government no matter how extreme. For now, I have to assume that the VP, congressional leaders, cabinet members, and others are detained or dead. Therefore I am appointing an ad hoc government." He paused as if weighing his words.

Barlow took a deep breath and held it as he pushed to his feet. The pain was obvious. During high school, Jeremy had broken two ribs while playing football in the street. There was no such thing as a comfortable position in that condition. A simple sneeze could drive a strong man to his knees. The others rose with him.

"From this moment until I rescind this decision, or until we can constitute a viable government, the following shall be true." He looked at O'Tool. "Senator, you are now speaker of the house." He quickly raised his hand. "I know you're a member of the senate, but you served three terms in the lower house, and we need a bicameral legislature. Of course, you have no house to be speaker of, but this is the best we can do at this hour. Do you understand?"

"I do, Mr. President."

"Frank Grundy will be the acting VP." Barlow addressed O'Tool again. "Tell me you agree, Mr. Speaker."

"Um, sure. I mean…yes, sir. I agree."

"Good, that constitutes congressional approval." Another pause. "General Holt, you are now the secretary of defense and the new head of the Joint Chiefs of Staff and will serve in those capacities until I relieve you. Do you accept?"

Holt came to attention. "Yes, sir. I do."

Next he faced Jeremy. Jeremy's stomach went into free fall. "Colonel, I am giving you a field promotion to brigadier general. You will be the second member of the JCS. I don't know when you're eligible for promotion, so consider this a frocking. Is that okay with you, General Holt?"

"It is, sir." Frocking. Jeremy had seen it a few times—the awarding of the rights and insignia of higher rank to a member of the military who is not eligible for promotion.

"Sorry I don't have a star to pin on you, Jeremy. Do you accept this promotion?"

"I do, sir." Jeremy's heart quivered. He was uncertain what to think.

"Colonel Sherwin, you will remain base commander. I need you to get our communications up and running. I also need you to select some of your best people to serve in various positions. I'll let you know what those are when I have it figured out. One thing I need right away is an assistant. All of this has to be put into writing and prepared for signatures."

"Yes, sir."

Barlow rubbed the center of his chest and looked like a man with the worst case of indigestion ever. "We have just formed the most bizarre government in US history. God help us."

"Amen," Jeremy said.

15

Medical Chaos

Roni Matisse hustled down the hospital corridors toward the OR wing. Emergency lighting hanging from the ceiling and over the doors cast eye-stinging light. It was like facing an oncoming car with its bright lights on. The halls quickly filled with people, ambulatory patients, administrative staff, maintenance personnel, and workers from the cafeteria.

She pushed through them as fast as she could until she reached the waiting room just outside the double doors that opened to operating rooms.

"Excuse me." The voice was elderly and came over Roni's shoulder. Her first impulse was to ignore the person, but something in the voice made her stop.

"Yes?"

"Can you tell me what happened? What's going on?" The woman was short, bent at the shoulders, with gray hair peeking from beneath an out-of-style wig.

"No, ma'am. All I know is the generator quit. They should have it working again soon."

"But you're a doctor, right?" Her eyes were wet, and the glow of the battery powered lights made the woman look pale.

"Yes, but I don't know any more."

"Is my husband okay?"

"I don't know, ma'am. I don't think I treated your husband."

"He's in surgery. I'm worried. He fell and broke his arm. They're putting metal things in it."

Titanium screws and plates. It must have been a serious break. "I'm sorry, ma'am. I don't have any answers for you, and I have to go."

"But…"

Roni put her hands on the woman's shoulders. "Look, I know waiting is hard, especially on a day like this." *Had there been days like this?* "If I learn anything, I'll come tell you, but it could be a little while. Just wait here. Someone will talk to you as soon as possible."

The woman dabbed at her eyes with a tissue that looked as if it had endured a few hours of twisting. She moved away, feeling guilty with each step.

"His name is Jacob."

A sign on the doors read Hospital Personnel Only. Instinctively, Roni punched the large metal square on the wall to activate the automatic doors. Nothing happened. *I'm an idiot.* She took hold of the stainless steel handle and pulled the heavy door open. The corridor on the other side had the same eerie glow of emergency lights.

"Dr. Matisse." Surgical nurse Loren Grimm's expression matched her name. "Do you know what's going on?"

"I have an idea, but I can't be sure. All I really know is the generators went out."

"They'll be back up in a minute, right?"

"I hope so. Where am I needed?"

"We have three surgeries underway. We had four, but I just moved one to recovery before things went out again."

"What about the others?"

"OR-2 has an orthopedic surgery. Upper arm. They've been at that one for a while. My guess is they'll be closing soon. OR-3 is a trauma-induced abdominal aortic aneurysm. They went in about an hour or so ago. Or so I hear—I was occupied. OR-4 is a blocked intestine. OR-1 is empty."

"I'm going to gown up and see if I can help. You're going to have to do the same. First, see who needs what. I'll help where I'm needed most. Then pull in some nurses. We're going to need some extra hands even if they do nothing but hold a flashlight."

"I can't believe this is happening." Loren slipped on a surgical mask and a pair of sterile gloves.

Roni donned a fresh pair of scrubs and washed her hands as if preparing for a procedure. For all she knew, she was.

Loren appeared in the scrub area just as Roni had finished rinsing. As she dried, Loren pulled the first set of surgical gloves from their container.

"They want you in OR-3."

"The aorta?"

"Yes. Patient is a thirty-two-year-old male. He was one of the patients from the train accident. Began complaining of abdominal pain. CAT revealed an aneurism on the descending aorta. Apparently the injury weakened the vessel. The patient has a history of hypertension, so the condition may have been preexistent and aggravated by the accident."

"Initial injury?"

"Blunt trauma to chest. Xiphoid process cut the liver. First surgery went well. His postoperative complaints were attributed to the surgery. You know how crazy the place has been. No one thought there was a secondary cause."

All of this sounded familiar. Roni had been involved in similar surgeries. She couldn't blame the doctors. She would have assumed the same thing.

Loren continued. "A sonogram found the bulge on the artery."

Roni could picture the body's major artery with a bubble on the side. If the aneurysm gave way, the patient could be dead in minutes. "I assume Austin is the lead on this."

"Yes, Dr. Roth was the initial surgeon."

Roni felt bad for the patient. One surgery was grueling enough; two was something no patient should be asked to endure.

"I'll go see if he needs an extra pair of hands." Roni left the scrub room and entered OR-3. She was greeted with a loud, angry voice, tinted with fear.

"What is going on out there?" Blood covered the safety shield in front of the surgeon. The artery must have given way.

"I don't know for sure," Roni said, "and you don't want to know my guess."

Roth looked up. Even in the dim emergency light she could see the stress on the man's face. Charles Fulton was the anesthesiologist. Several nurses stood nearby, each focused on her task. One nurse held an emergency flashlight over the open belly of the patient. The emergency lights mounted to the walls created shadows increasing the odds of a mistake. Surgeons needed lots of light.

Roni stepped close. "What can I do?" The room reminded her how electronics-dependent surgery had become. The bank of monitors every anesthesiologist needed to monitor the status of a patient under general anesthesia was blank. No EKG, BP, body temperature, respiration, blood oxygen…nothing. A nurse worked a blood pressure cuff. Another worked an Ambu bag, forcing air into the patient's lungs.

"We're getting ready to hang another unit of blood. I got so much blood in here I can't see what's going on. Suction doesn't work. We could use an extra pair of hands in here. I need a clean field to close up the aorta."

She moved to the side of Roth and used some gauze to soak up the blood pooling around the abdominal organs. This kind of surgery was risky to begin with and nearly impossible in an OR with no power. A patient's only hope with a ruptured aorta was to already be on the operating table. The man had that going for him. Roth was a gifted surgeon. What he lacked in social skills, he made up for in surgery. If Roni ever needed surgery, she hoped Roth would be the doctor on the other end of the scalpel.

Five minutes further into the surgery, all of Roni's optimism evaporated.

"BP is dropping," the nurse said.

"Respiration is shallow and labored," Fulton announced. "We're losing him."

Twenty minutes later, he was gone.

Roth filled the OR with swearing worthy of a longshoreman and kicked over the instrument tray. "We can't operate like this. It's impossible. I feel like we're in the Civil War, amputating legs with rusty saws. This is the twenty-first century!"

He turned on Roni. "What happened out there?"

"Generators went off, and I think they're off for good."

"That can't be."

Roni didn't answer. She removed her bloody gloves and threw them in the hazardous waste bin.

"Where are you going?" Roth asked.

"To see if I'm needed in the other surgeries. If not, I'm going to CCU and see how they're faring."

"CCU…" The mention of the cardiac unit softened his tone. "That has to be a nightmare."

Roni paused at the doors. She was the head of trauma surgery, and they were looking to her for direction. She moved a few steps back into the theater. "I have no idea when power will be back online. It may be a long time. If so, we have our work cut out for us. I need everyone—surgeons, nurses, staff, everyone—to pitch in. Everything is dead. Something has taken out the electronics, and I mean everywhere. At least everywhere I looked. Make yourselves useful, people. Find a hole and fill it. Intensive care, ER, pediatrics, ICU…We're going to have to be creative. Really, really, creative."

■ ■ ■ ■

The early morning hours passed quickly. Roni had little time to do anything. The hospital administrator had put the facility on full emergency protocol shortly after the lights went out the first time. Every department had leaders, usually a doctor and the head nurse. They had trained for major accidents, earthquakes, hurricanes, and terrorist activity. But they had never planned on everything electrical being wiped out. There was no precedent for that. Some New Orleans hospitals had worked without power after hurricane Katrina and the subsequent flooding, but that hadn't turned out so well.

Every hour saw the death of a patient. With every hour the staff looked more like the cast from a cheap zombie movie. Missing sleep wasn't the issue. Medical professionals learned to function with little sleep. It was the stress that was hurting them. Modern medicine rode on a current of electricity that powered everything from digital thermometers to X-ray machines to CAT scanners, defibrillator paddles, and IV pumps.

The strangest and most disturbing events came at the expense of patients with pacemakers. Most died shortly after the electronics were fried. The lucky ones battled irregular heartbeats.

Refrigeration was gone, and while others were concerned about food spoilage, Roni wondered how long their fresh blood supply would last. Roth was right—medicine had been set back. The knowledge was there, but without tools they had been trained to use, most doctors were adrift. Lab work had been reduced to use most rudimentary assessments. Even the microscopes depended on power.

Over the last two hours she had moved from surgery to ICU, to CCU, to MICU, to the ER. The strangest and most noble thing she saw was a pair of paramedics pushing a gurney into the ER. Even in the January cold, the man and woman were sweating. Their ambulance had stopped three miles from the hospital. They had pushed the heart patient the full three miles. Sadly, it might have been a wasted effort.

Roni was not an overly emotional woman, but she felt a powerful urge to find a corner and cry.

16

This Is Crazy

This is crazy." Jeremy sat at one of the tables in the cafeteria.

Colonel Jill Sherwin had given him a quick tour of the facility, set up a conference room for them, and briefed them on the sit room and its operation. Two airmen manned the large facility. Jeremy guessed the place was twice the size of the one at NSA/USCYBERCOM and even the one at the White House. Of course, there was a reason for that. Mount Weather was meant to house the president, his cabinet, his staff, the Joint Chiefs of Staff, key congressional members, and their families during a nation-wide emergency. The situation room was equipped with the technology to gather information from every military base around the world, from FEMA operations around the country, and probably from a dozen other places that Jeremy was previously not cleared to know about. Most of that technology was useless now. Everything underground had power. Everything aboveground was as dead as stone.

Holt nodded. "You can say that again, General."

The title stabbed him. He had hoped to wear a star one day but not under these circumstances. "I don't think I can get used to that title, sir."

"You might as well. Down here there are only two generals." Holt sipped coffee and picked at a donut. Jeremy couldn't be certain, but he thought he might be the youngest general in modern military history.

Holt must have been reading his thoughts. "Teddy Roosevelt was the youngest president, but he got that distinction because McKinley was assassinated. Kinda takes the air out of the ego."

"I thought Kennedy was the youngest president."

"Nope." The voice came over Jeremy's left shoulder. O'Tool arrived with a tray of food. The cafeteria was close to empty, and that was fine with Jeremy. "Kennedy was the youngest elected president. TR was the youngest at the time he was sworn in." His tray held a pile of scrambled eggs, hash browns, four strips of bacon, and a bowl of grits. "This is crazy."

"I was just saying that."

"One president, one senator-congressman, and two generals."

"Don't forget the new VP."

"Right. I'll say this—Barlow is decisive in a time of trouble. That's a good thing." O'Tool dug into the eggs. "Man, these are good. You guys should get some."

"Maybe later," Jeremy said. "I've lost my appetite."

"Pity. They got a full kitchen back there. It looks like they could feed thousands."

"That's good for us but not for everyone out there."

"How long do you think it will take for things to get back to normal?" Another bite of food made it to O'Tool's mouth.

Holt looked at Jeremy. "It might be a long time, Mr. Speaker."

O'Tool smiled. "I like that title." He stopped chewing for a moment. "Okay, here's what I don't understand. Some satellites blew up and knocked out power all over the country. The EMP thing. Just how does that work?"

"Starfish Prime."

"Huh?" It was the only word O'Tool could get past his full mouth.

Holt's gaze lingered on O'Tool. "Ever heard of James Van Allen?"

"No. Should I...wait, the guy who discovered the Van Allen Belt?"

"That's him. Brilliant man. He's known for a few other things, including participating in a military and Atomic Energy Commission test. Starfish Prime sent a nuclear weapon into space, let it explode, and studied the results. There were several such tests—five, I think. In the late '50s there were other high-altitude tests. That was in early July of '62, and it was the first nuclear weapon exploded in space."

"I'm no scientist, but that doesn't sound wise."

"In retrospect, it probably wasn't, but in 1961, the Soviet Union announced it would resume nuclear testing. Starfish Prime, Operation Fishbowl, and other experiments provided scientific and engineering data and also told the Russians not to mess with us."

O'Tool had stopped shoveling food into his face, so Jeremy assumed the story had captured the senator's attention. "So we had EMP weapons back then?"

Holt shook his head. "Not really. The detonation knocked out about a third of the satellites in orbit. A few more went off-line later, including Telestar, the first telecommunications satellites. It also knocked out power in Hawaii, 900 miles away. Film of the event shows the explosion and the subsequent change in the sky's color. Did you notice the moon after the pulses?"

"No," O'Tool said. "I was hustled down here for my safety. Or so I was told."

"I saw it, General," Jeremy said. "The moon was bloodred. Pretty eerie. I get the chills just thinking of it."

"Me too. Those tests proved that high-altitude nuclear explosions could produce an electromagnetic pulse that could kill satellites and electrical grids. Starfish Prime went off 250 miles above the earth. That's about the same altitude the space shuttles used to fly, give or take a little."

"Okay, General, let me ask you something." O'Tool pushed his tray aside and rested his elbows on the table. "Did you know we had such weapons circling the planet?"

"There are close to 1000 operational satellites up there, Senator, and a whole bunch more inactive ones, assuming they're really inactive."

"What's that supposed to mean?"

"It means that some of those birds could have been dormant. NORAD can track anything in orbit larger than your fist, but they can't look inside the things."

"And keep in mind," Jeremy added, "that the EMP pulses didn't come from our birds."

"Generals, do we have EMP weapons in space over foreign countries?"

"I honestly can't say," Holt said.

"Can't or won't?" O'Tool was getting pushy.

Holt set his elbows on the table mirroring O'Tools position. It was an aggressive posture. "I don't know, Senator. I know lots of things—things above top secret—but I am not privy to everything. It's need-to-know for generals just like everyone else, including senators."

"Okay, let me ask it this way. Do you suspect that we have similar weapons to those that put us back in the dark ages?"

"I would be surprised if we didn't. This goes back fifty years and twelve presidential administrations. It goes back to

Eisenhower. For all I know, there are weapons up there that have been forgotten."

"Isn't that just swell? Crazy way to run a business."

"It's not a business, Senator," Holt said. "The military works in a rapidly changing world and is subject to elected officials. Policy often dictates military behavior. Eisenhower warned his successors to watch out for the military-industrial complex. He was right to make the warning, but it's a two-edged sword. Sometimes the military needs to beware the politicians."

"You don't like politicians, General?" Jeremy couldn't decide if O'Tool was hurt or angry.

"You misunderstand me. I don't dislike all politicians. I'm just saying that the military has to adapt to changes in the world and changes in its own government. It's worked for a very long time, but not always well. One president, like Reagan, wants space-borne weapons. In the age of ICBMs that made sense. It was the cold war. We needed to protect ourselves from the Soviet Union and the rising power of China. Today, our biggest concern doesn't come from technologically advanced superpowers. We haven't lost an American life to China, Russia, or Korea for a long time. We've lost thousands to terrorists using very untechnical means."

Holt leaned back. "My point, Senator is this. Conventional weapons can be grounded and stuffed in a hanger. Troops can be called home. But space-borne weapons are a little more difficult to deal with, especially those with nuclear warheads. It wouldn't be wise to bring them crashing back to earth chock-full of radioactive material. I can tell you this. We know the Russians and Chinese have put military birds in space. It appears that many of them were EMP weapons. I'm assuming we've done the same. Not this administration. For all I know, those platforms could be twenty years old."

"And if so," Jeremy said, "then their onboard computer systems would be well out of date and subject to viruses and worms. Which may explain what happened here."

"So, if I have this right, scores of these EMP weapons have been flying around up there for, what, decades?"

"That's true for some. There may be newer ones," Holt said.

"Okay, bottom line this for me, gentlemen. How far down the toilet are we?"

Holt and Jeremy exchanged glances. Holt delivered the message. "Further than I thought possible."

"Peachy. Just peachy." O'Tool stood. "Do either of you have any good news?"

Jeremy couldn't come up with any.

■ ■ ■ ■

After O'Tool left, Holt rose, refilled their coffee cups, and returned to the table. "I want to ask you to do something, Jeremy."

"Name it, sir." Jeremy sipped the coffee.

"Something should be said about Secretary of State Baker."

"You mean like at a memorial service?" Jeremy hadn't seen that coming.

"Yes. The body is in cold storage. They have a morgue associated with the hospital. I know his family would want to take care of these things, but..." His gaze drew distant. Jeremy let him have a moment. "Look, we don't know how long it will take for things to play out. If travel can be resumed, I imagine they will bring the family in. That's how this is supposed to work. The president, VP, cabinet, joint chiefs, and leading congressional members and their families are supposed to hole up to make sure the government continues. I can't imagine the president telling Baker's family they're no longer welcome. Anyway, someone needs to offer some spiritual words, and you know I'm no good at that."

"I'm not a pastor, General, but I will do what I can. I don't imagine they have a chaplain stationed here."

"I doubt it. We'll bring it up the next time we speak to the president. I think Baker was a Presbyterian or something like that. You being a Christian and all…well, I thought you might know what to say."

"Yes, sir, I can come up with something. I didn't bring my Bible. I didn't anticipate the day's events."

Holt chuckled. "If you had, you'd be a prophet, and I think that outranks me."

Jill Sherwin stepped to the table and came to attention.

"As you were, Colonel."

"Thank you, sir. If the generals have a moment, I have something to show you."

Holt tilted his head an inch. "Am I going to like it?"

"Yes, sir. It's a car. And it runs."

17

The Red Moon Above

Jeremy and Holt rode to the surface in one of Sherwin's electric carts. Although it had been less than a day, Jeremy felt he had been underground for weeks. Of course, he hadn't slept, he had eaten very little, he was overwhelmed with the situation, and he was worried about Roni. None of those things helped.

The January air was crisp, and a sharp breeze blew from the north. He wondered if bad weather was on the way. That's all they would need. The setting moon hung a few degrees over the horizon, still red, still ominous. Bright streaks of white cut the obsidian night.

The sound of running engines hung in the thick, cold air. "You got the generators up here working?"

"No, sir," Sherwin said. "We store several portable generators below grade for emergencies. I had them brought up here to power the portable work lights. Asking my men to repair the antennas by flashlight seemed a bit much."

"A bit?"

"They're resilient and dedicated." She stood a little straighter, like any officer proud of her charges. "If I asked them to work by candlelight, they'd do it without complaint. Of course, if more of the space bombs go off, the generators are toast."

Jeremy heard another motor. Its pitch was different from those of the portable generators. He stepped from the cart the moment Sherwin slowed it to a stop. In front of them was a classic VW bug. It was running. Next to it stood a man who couldn't be more than an inch taller than the minimum 58-inch height requirement to serve in the military. The man came to attention, his spine straight and eyes fixed straight ahead. Since Holt was the senior officer present, Jeremy let him put the man at ease.

"This is Staff Sergeant Joel Tate. His assignment is generator maintenance. He's proficient in diesel and gas generators as well as other things. He's also a bit of a gearhead with a useful hobby. He rebuilds old cars."

"I'm interested in hearing what you have to say, Staff Sergeant," Holt said.

"Yes, sir. Of course, sir. I was just…The idea came to me…I mean…" He looked as if he lost the ability to breathe. Jeremy assumed the young man had never stood before so many officers at once, two with the rank of general.

"Inhale," Sherwin ordered. The man did. "Now focus."

"Yes, ma'am."

"Better?" Sherwin studied her soldier.

"Yes, ma'am. I guess I'm a little off my game."

"We all are, son," Holt said. "Tell me about your car."

"Yes, sir. This is a 1967 Volkswagen Beetle. It has a 1500 cc engine. It belonged to my grandfather. I've been restoring it for several years. It's a hobby. Fixing old cars, I mean." He smiled, a man in love with autos. Jeremy could appreciate that, although he preferred CPUs and keyboards. "The colonel briefed us on the problem. The EMP pulse, I mean. That got me thinking. I figured that my old bug might be the easiest thing to fix."

"It was affected?" Jeremy asked.

"Yes, sir, it was, but not to the same extent. The electrical took a beating. The pulse burned out the fuses and fried some of the wiring, including the battery cables, the ignition wires, and a few others."

"But it's running," Holt said.

"Yes, sir. That's the beauty. Modern cars and trucks have computer chips and sensors and the like. They're complicated. Not these old cars. These were built in the day when a man could—excuse me, Colonel—when a person could gap the points with a matchbook cover and adjust the timing by ear. I found a bunch of wire that wasn't connected to anything, so the sudden current didn't hurt it. I was able to rewire the ignition and a few other things to make the engine run. I bypassed the fuses with some metal slugs I cut down in the shop. I had to do that by hand, so it took a while, but I was able to jump the fuses that ran to the engine. I'll need to cut down a few more if we want lights and radio."

"What about the spark plug wires?" Jeremy asked.

"I stole them from our supply room."

Jeremy blinked a few times. "You keep Volkswagen parts in the shop?"

"No, sir, but we do keep some for the gas generators and some for the big diesel units. I, um…improvised."

Jeremy didn't ask how. He wasn't sure he'd understand. "And the battery?"

"The one in my car was rendered inoperable, but those in the storage weren't. They're not connected to anything, therefore no current flow. No current flow, no damage. We have several 12-volt batteries that are used to replace bad units in the electric carts. In '67, Volkswagen switched to 12-volt systems. So we're golden."

"What about the other vehicles on the lots?" Holt asked.

"I think we can get a few of them running. Not the radios. That's a completely different animal. We'll have to be creative with some of the wiring. The real problem is bypassing computer systems in the vehicles. The older the engine, the better. The new vehicles will require new chips, or we'll need to rework the whole electrical system."

"Can that be done?" Jeremy stepped closer to the idling vehicle and wondered when he had last seen anything so beautiful.

The sergeant shuffled his feet. "I wish I had more good news for you, sirs, and maybe I will. It's going to take a long time to get anywhere near normal around here."

"Or anywhere." Jeremy turned to Holt. "What do you think, sir?"

"I think I want to shake this man's hand."

Jeremy turned his attention skyward again. More white hot streaks scratched the black sky.

"Meteor shower, sir?" It was Jill Sherwin.

"I don't think so, Colonel." He watched another light cross the sky. "The stars will fall from the sky, and the heavenly bodies will be shaken."

"Excuse me, sir?"

"Something from the Gospel of Mark, Colonel. The Bible."

■ ■ ■ ■

Roni Matisse had managed a ninety-minute nap, but her mind wouldn't let her rest. It sent one bizarre dream after another bouncing around her mind. Her subconscious was taking out the trash by creating a train of nonsensical dreams. In one, she was performing surgery while traveling on an airline. A female flight attendant was cranky because the operating table kept her from moving the goody cart through the aisle. To make matters worse, Roni was operating on the pilot and was losing him.

In another dream she wandered a distant field, lost and alone. Above her a red moon flicked on and off as if a child were playing with a light switch. When the moon was off, the stygian black kept her from moving. When it was on, she could see only the green field awash in bloodred light.

An hour and a half of that had been enough. She might have been sleeping, but she wasn't resting. Her nap ended an hour or two before sunrise, and she left the tiny office she had used for a bedroom, scrunched down in a side chair. Next time, she decided, she'd abscond with a hospital pillow and a blanket and make the floor her bed. Hopefully everything would be back to normal soon.

Not one part of her believed that.

She wandered the hospital, helping where she could, and then made her way up the four-story stairway onto the roof. She was not alone. Several hospital staff had staked off areas to smoke or to be alone with their thoughts.

One was more sociable. Dr. August Pickett, the hospital administrator, was a stout man with an intelligent, black face. Harvard trained, he was one of the smartest physicians Roni had ever met. His fifty-five years had been good to him. His short, tight hair was going gray, making him look even more distinguished. He had come to the hospital from a position in San Francisco and had proven himself as adept at administration as he had in cardiac surgery. He still scrubbed in from time to time.

"Doctor." His voice was a rich bass, smooth, and his words came easily. "I want to thank you for your work. You've gone above and beyond the call of duty."

"Thank you. I heard you helped in pediatrics and ob/gyn."

He raised an eyebrow. "I don't know how much help I was in

the latter. I haven't delivered a baby in twenty years. Fortunately, we had enough people to cover the few cases we had here. Mostly I helped the nurses and physician's assistants. I assisted in a couple of surgeries. Mostly I patrolled the CCU."

"Not many administrators would do that."

"I don't know about that. We all have to pull together until this is all over."

"Over. That's a great word." She looked up and watched the falling stars. "Normally, seeing a falling star would bring joy. Doesn't feel that way."

"I don't think they're meteors."

"What else would it be?"

"Space debris. Did you see the flashes in the sky?"

Roni nodded. "What's that got to do…" It hit her. "You mean something from space did this? Like a comet or something else?"

"I don't know about such things." Pickett pinched the bridge of his nose. He looked as weary as she felt. Her primary concerned had been trauma surgeries. He had the whole hospital to worry about. "I know my way around the human body, but anything above the roof of this building is foreign to me. I don't even like to fly."

Her mind shuffled possibilities, and she didn't like any of them. Terrorist attack, war, aliens in spaceships, and the one nagging fear she hadn't wanted to talk about. "Jeremy would know more about this."

"Is he at home?"

"No, he's…" she paused. "He's up north. Working."

"He's military, right? Sorry, I can't keep up with all the doctors and nurses we have. Throw in their spouses and kids, and I get lost."

"Yes. Air Force. He's in computers." Saying Jeremy was in computers was like saying van Gogh liked art.

There were questions in his eyes, but he didn't ask them. Instead, he turned his attention to the cityscape. "It's quiet now, but if this goes on for more than a day, things will get out of hand." He stepped closer to the parapet that rimmed the building. "Power outages are never good, but in cities with large areas of low-income housing, it gets bad. I've seen it before. Two days, there will be looting and injuries. Three days, there will be deaths. The National Guard will be called in, assuming anyone has a way of calling them in, but I suspect that much of their work will be protecting government buildings. Pity the mom-and-pop shop."

"And here I thought you were the eternal optimist." She moved to his side. "Do you think it will get that bad?"

He looked at the sky again. "My gut tells me yes."

"How often is your gut right?"

"It has a pretty good record."

"Any word when the generators might be online again?" She folded her arms. The lab coat did little to ward off the chill of the wee hours.

"Our building manager has had a look at them. He says they're all but destroyed. They're not coming back online anytime soon."

"How will we function?" An ache spread through her.

"Function? Not well, I'm afraid." He lowered his head and looked at his shoes. "Some of our doctors and nurses are here and can't get home, and some are home and can't get here. We have a hospital that looks twenty-first century, but at the moment it's early twentieth at best. The staff is worn to the bone. I'm setting up shifts so people can get rest, but that means splitting the staff so only a portion of what we have will be caring for patients."

He let the words hang in the cold air, and then he continued. "My father used to say, 'Son, do what you can, when you can, where you are. It's all you can do.' That's all we can do. That and pray."

"My husband would agree with that." She regretted the comment. Such things usually led to an unwanted discussion about faith in the family.

Pickett raised his head. "He sounds like a good man, this husband of yours."

Her ache turned to warmth. "Yes. Yes, he is. I wish he were here." She wished it more than she let on. Roni had always been independent, but Jeremy's strong arms would be welcome.

After a moment, Pickett said, "Do you hear it, Doctor?"

She listened, straining her ears to locate whatever noise he had in mind. "I'm afraid not. What should I be hearing?"

"Silence." He raised a hand. "I know, a person can't hear silence. At least that's what we're told. But I hear the emptiness. No engine noises, no trash trucks, no street sweepers, no sirens, no lowrider with a booming bass. Nothing. What did Simon and Garfunkel sing? 'The Sounds of Silence'? Before tonight, I didn't understand the title. They should have told us silence was so frightening."

"We'll get through this, Dr. Pickett. We have a great staff. They'll make miracles happen."

"That's what we need. A miracle." He turned to her. "Thanks for letting me vent a little. Time for me to lift my chin and get back to work."

He walked away, and if Roni didn't know better, she would have said the man was three inches shorter from the weight on his shoulders.

Roni turned her back on the black and quiet city and walked to the stairway. There was someone she wanted to check on.

■ ■ ■ ■

Roni found Cody Broadway where she had left him in ICU, on a bed surrounded by medical machines that had nothing to do with him and that wouldn't work even if they had been needed. The room was dark, lit only by the light from the emergency lamps mounted near the exits. Cody's room was as far from the light as any cubicle in the space could be, so what little glow pushed through the glass divider that separated the room from the nurses' station did minimal good. Even so, Roni was glad it was there. Feeling her way around the ICU wasn't her idea of fun.

She passed the nursing staff and doctors, who looked wan from lack of light. She suspected the stress of keeping patients comfortable without electricity had also drained the color from their faces.

Before heading to Cody's room, Roni stepped beside Padma. The woman had the slight, narrow appearance of East Indian women, but it seemed to Roni that her friend had lost fifteen pounds in the few hours since she dropped Cody off.

"How's it going, Padma?"

"How do you think?" The response felt like sandpaper on skin. Padma closed her eyes. "Sorry. I'm…I'm a little…"

"On edge? Yeah, I know the feeling. They didn't teach this in med school."

Padma conjured a smile, but Roni focused on the moisture in the woman's eyes. "All our emergency training seems inadequate in the face of the real thing."

Instead of speaking, Roni pulled the woman into her arms for a moment. At first, Padma resisted, her shoulders and spine stiff, but then she melted and allowed Roni to hold her. They parted a moment later.

"Thanks," Padma said.

"Yeah? Who said that was for you?"

Padma grinned. This one looked genuine. "How are you holding up?"

"Fine. Great. Swell. Peachy. Okay, I'm ready to find a dark corner and curl up. Fortunately there are plenty of those."

"If you find one that will hold both of us, let me know." Padma took a ragged breath, and Roni grew more concerned. The strongest, least flappable people in a hospital were found in the ER, the ICU, and pediatrics. Padma's shakiness wasn't good. "You here to see the boy?"

"Yes. How is he?"

Padma shrugged. "Haven't been able to check on him. I look in there every time I walk by. He seems fine. Quiet."

"Thanks." Roni patted the woman on the shoulder and then moved to Cody's room.

The boy lay on his side, staring at the pale green wall. He didn't move when she entered, but his eyelids flickered.

"Hi, Cody." Roni spoke softly. "How come you're not asleep?" She knew the answer. What boy could sleep after all he had been through?

"I dunno."

"You okay?"

He shrugged. "I guess."

Roni stood at the foot of his bed as doctors did with patients. She had assumed "the posture"—authoritative, confident, knowledgeable, in control, but still exuding a measure of care. Force of habit. She pulled the visitors chair—a wide, yellow, faux-leather, midcentury-looking thing—to the side of the bed.

"Sorry I haven't been by sooner. It's been a crazy night."

"Yeah. Crazy." He didn't look at her.

She reached through the side rail and touched his hand. He didn't respond. "Things will get better, Cody. I know things are bad right now, and I know you're hurting. Things will get better."

"No it won't. My mom is gone. My dad's been gone. I'm alone."

A tear pooled where the corner of his eye and the bridge of his nose met.

Roni felt her eyes burning, and she plumbed the depths of her mind, looking for something to say. The standard line, "We did everything we could and used all our skill and resources to save your mother," just didn't cut it.

"Cody, I wish things were different. I wish what happened to you hadn't happened. It stinks, and I know you're hurting. What son wouldn't hurt? You have a right to be angry—"

"I'm not mad."

"I am. I'm angry that a good kid like you has to go through this. Life isn't fair, and there's nothing I can say that will make it all right. I'm sorry, Cody. I really am."

"What's going to happen to me?"

She feared the question. "A social worker will come talk to you whenever he or she can get here. Do you know what a social worker is?"

"No."

"It's someone with special training to deal with things doctors can't."

"They'll take me away. I won't see my friends anymore. They'll put me in an orphanage, and everyone will forget about me."

Her first inclination was to disagree, to say, "No, that's not going to happen," but he was right about some things.

"I don't think they'll put you in an orphanage, Cody."

"Then what?"

"I imagine that social services will take you to a family, a special family. They call it foster care. There are mothers and fathers waiting to take you in and give you a home and a safe place to be."

"I don't want to live with another family."

"Cody, you can't live on your own. You're not old enough."

He sniffed and squeezed his eyes shut. The tears found a way out. A moment later he dissolved into sobs. Roni stood, lowered the side rail and sat on the bed. Less than a second passed before she pulled the boy into her arms as abysmal sorrow poured from his body.

"I...I want to stay with you."

Not possible. I don't know anything about rearing children. Even if this whole thing blows over tomorrow, I can't take on a new responsibility. No way. Not possible.

"Please don't send me away."

Roni's heart chipped, then cracked, and finally shattered. She added her tears to his.

18

Ain't Nuthin' Right

Jeremy felt like a corked bottle floating on a wide, churning sea. Reports were trickling in from military bases with communication equipment protected from EMP attack. Early reports had cleared up a few things. Early evidence indicated that Jeremy and General Holt had been right. The EMP pulses had come from satellites at various orbits above the earth. The first contact made from Mount Weather was with NORAD. They tracked everything that moved above the planet. Some of the satellites had been in space for several decades and declared retired by their parent government.

The fact that the pulses occurred in sequence instead of all at once indicated planning. A few of the satellites had eventually been identified. What puzzled Jeremy was that no one country was responsible. Some had been Chinese, some Russian, some Israeli, and sadly, many were American.

One thing was clear. If the president was to be believed, and Jeremy had no reason to doubt him, the US had not ordered the activation of their space-burst satellites. They had gone off on their own, helping take down the Eurasian grid.

To make dark times even darker, non–Star Wars–style satellites had self-destructed. Those with emergency destruct devices
installed to keep them out of the hands of the enemy or to destroy
them should they start to fall to earth had blown themselves
to pieces. Those that lacked explosives to do the work simply
stopped talking to their earthbound handlers, most likely victims of the EMP pulses or a computer virus that shredded their
electronic brains.

The world was without power and without satellite communications. Military birds had become multimillion-dollar paper-
weights, coursing through space and waiting until their decaying
orbits gave in to their fiery deaths in the atmosphere.

Jeremy spent the night and early morning hours wondering
how such a thing could be done. His body craved sleep, but his
mind refused to allow it. There were thoughts to think and speculations to be made.

His computer had been wiped by the pulse, obliterating the
information he needed to analyze the worm as he planned to do.
He would have to find a way to retrieve that information from
the NSA building at Fort Meade. President Barlow had made getting the information to Jeremy a priority, but it would be hours
before he could have the material he needed.

The military had been crippled but not paralyzed. The possibility of an EMP attack had been considered for decades. No
one could be certain about the effects such an attack would have
on the country, but the computer models had been close. What
wasn't known was what an entire wave of such attacks would do,
or what would happen if a rogue worm had first infected the
computers of the world.

Now they knew, and the answer wasn't pretty.

Still, military paranoia had proven its value. Many aircraft and
vehicles, including those thought to be "hardened," were out of

commission, but some of the new craft remained useful or could be easily repaired. The question was, was the attack over? Were more powerful satellites still up there waiting to launch a new attack, maybe with some new twist in the force or pattern?

Barlow had decided to risk enough helicopters to search for downed aircraft carrying cabinet members and congressional leaders. They found several but no survivors.

The VP was dead, as were most members of the president's cabinet. Still, some had made it to Mount Weather, and the president was assigning new positions as fast as he could. The government would continue but as a shadow of what it had been.

President Barlow declared a national emergency, and the military swung into action but far more slowly and with less effect than anyone could imagine. Efforts were being made to get communication aircraft up and doing the work previously assigned to satellites. Only aircraft stored below grade had a chance of doing their work. Even hardened aircraft, previously thought to be immune, were hamstrung. They would fly again, but only after some serious work.

Jeremy walked from the underground facility to stare at a night sky formerly hidden by light pollution. Stars twinkled from light-years away, immune to the plight of seven billion people on a small blue orb in the corner of the galaxy. He saw other lights. Not stars, but what he assumed were fragments of scores of EMP satellites and clouds of radioactive material.

The red glow neared the horizon. The faux aurora borealis continued to dance with the solar wind. Bits of satellite streaked through the sky, turning to superheated dust on the way. How odd that the sight should look beautiful.

He gazed southwest to DC and wondered about Roni. The distance between them never seemed so great, even when he served overseas and she remained in the US to further her medical career.

The first congressional leaders and undersecretaries who were being ushered in to replace their deceased bosses arrived with their families. Soon, he thought, Roni would be sent for. He determined to take her in his arms and never let go.

The sky came alive again with more EMP bursts.

Falling skies.

Blood moon.

"Blessed Jesus, what have we done?"

■ ■ ■ ■

"Can't sleep?"

"No." Royce Elton lay beside her husband, staring through the dark of their room. Her eyes tried to focus but had no object to capture their gaze.

"It's almost dawn. You should sleep." Stanley rolled to his side. She could feel his gaze even though she knew he couldn't see her.

"So should you."

"It's different with me. I'm a man."

"What's that supposed to mean?"

He chuckled. "I have no idea. I'm too sleepy to be coherent, but I can't do more than nod off for a few moments."

"Since you're a man, maybe you can tell me what's going to happen next."

"Beats me, hon." He pushed up in the bed. "I don't understand any of this. Everything is out everywhere."

"Not here." She sounded more desperate than she wanted, but her usual emotional shields had weakened. "I've been thinking about that since we went to bed. I think we're the only unit in the complex with power."

She felt her husband rise from the bed. The descending moon cast a red hue through the windows. Royce had stood at that window before coming to bed, and all she could see were the dim shapes of the skyline. Every streetlamp in San Diego was out. No boats sailed the bay. Dark upon dark. Layers of black. Royce had an uneasy feeling that the darkness was oozing through her pores and polluting her soul.

He pushed back the curtains. Every curtain in the condo had been closed, and Stanley limited the lights being used. He said he didn't want to invite unwanted questions. It made sense to Royce. She had more than enough unwanted questions swirling in her mind already.

"I'm a pretty smart guy, don't you think?" Stanley stood with his back to her. "I mean, I'm no genius, but I'm no mental lightweight."

"I've always thought you were brilliant."

"Then why can't I figure this out?" He turned. "I mean…Look, this is impossible. I've been lying awake in that bed all night, wondering how we could be the only people in the city with power. I checked the other units on this floor and the two floors below us. I can see the courtyard and most of the other buildings in the complex. The Navy yard has generators, but there isn't a single light. It's…"

"It's what?"

"Never mind. I'm just a little creeped out."

"Everyone is. What were you going to say?"

He returned to the bed. "My imagination is getting the best of me."

"Say it."

He sighed. "I was going to say something stupid. I was going to say that it feels—unholy."

Royce didn't respond. She felt the same thing.

A soft sound came from the living room. Royce tipped her head to direct an ear toward the door. Nothing. "I thought I heard something. Maybe Rosa is up. I know she starts her day early."

"We might as well join her. I'm tired of lying in bed." He slipped on his robe, looking like a three-dimensional silhouette. "I could use some coffee, and since we're the only one in the building who can brew anything, we owe it to ourselves. Coming?"

"Yes. I want to check on Donny anyway."

She pulled on a silk robe, tied it close, and wiggled her toes into a pair of slippers. Stanley preferred to prance around in bare feet, but Royce's feet demanded some protection. The habit began in childhood and stayed with her through the following decades.

As usual, Stanley let her go through the door first. Always the gentleman, even before sunrise. Royce's slippers padded quietly across the carpeted floor and on the wood flooring of the living room.

Royce stopped midstep, gasped, and put a hand to her mouth.

"Watch it—" Stanley cut off his comment. He had seen what caught her attention. Royce took a step back and reached for Stanley, grasping the lapel of his robe.

Windows ran the length of the space from floor to ceiling, so the living room was slightly lighter than the bedroom but cast in the same reddish light. On the sofa, Rosa snored lightly. Near the windows rested Donny's wheelchair. It was empty.

Donny stood by the window, his nose only inches from the glass.

On the other side of the glass, ten stories above the ground, was a dim figure. All black. A shadow, lacking substance and definitive shape.

The shadow face turned their direction. Royce was certain she saw a smile. And then it was gone.

Stanley was beside Donny before Royce could take two steps. The sound of his bare feet pounding the floor woke Rosa. "What's wrong?" She saw Donny standing and gasped.

Their son was capable of standing, walking, and even running, but aside from leaving his chair to slip into bed or sit on the toilet, he almost never did.

"Son, are you okay? What are you doing out here?"

Donny didn't say anything.

Royce moved to her son's side. "Baby, what's wrong?" Her heart slammed her sternum like a wrecking ball. She gazed at the ground, half expecting to see a body lying there. She saw nothing.

She looked to Stanley. "Did you…I mean…"

"I saw it. I wish I hadn't."

Donny stared through the glass at something only he could see. "Shadow, shadow on my right. Shadow, shadow on my left. Shadow, shadow everywhere. Shadow has all the might."

For the first time since he had been a toddler, Royce saw her son cry.

■ ■ ■ ■

They were everywhere. Black wisps. They floated in the air, drifting on unseen currents. They walked black streets. They sat on lampposts and stood on the hoods of parked cars. They skipped across the water of the bay, their feet not breaking the surface. Hundreds of them. Thousands of them. Each moment brought more. Empty eye sockets. Tongueless mouths.

Donny could see them, smell them, hear them.

"Shadow, shadow in the air. Shadow, shadow on the ground. Shadow, shadow on me…in me…around me…"

In a single motion, the army of shadow beings turned and faced him. Donny could see the blank faces of even the most distant. Countless empty eyes, countless soulless things that haunted him. Things that knew his name…and knew where he slept.

* * * *

Jeremy hadn't slept much since arriving at the underground facility. A strange bed in a strange place in very strange world conspired against him. Added to that were his concern for Roni and the constant pressure to nail down the source of the digital worm that had brought so much trouble. He had other duties as well—helping with rebuilding communications and adding his two cents to the military challenges facing the president and his handful of advisors. He hoped more leaders would arrive. Being part of the two-officer Joint Chiefs of Staff was ludicrous, but he knew the president's goal was to have as full a government as possible in the situation regardless of how ridiculous it might appear on paper.

One other thing kept him awake this night. At 0900, he was to lead a short memorial service for a man he didn't know. Jeremy reminded himself that he was no minister. He was a man of faith, a churchgoer, a student of the Bible…but to stand in front of a group and offer words of comfort frightened him.

He found a Bible in a room used as a library. The people who designed Mount Weather had thought of everything. The book room was filled with novels and history books. He found several translations of the Bible and religious books covering every major belief system. It made sense. The place was meant to hold members of congress and perhaps other dignitaries, people who would hold a wide spectrum of beliefs.

He thumbed through the New Testament, looking for verses to use as a text and making notes on a legal pad. He recalled some verses used by ministers at funerals he had attended. Psalm 23 would be read. It was familiar even to nonchurchgoers and contained perhaps the most comforting words in the Bible—at least in this context.

He found verses in 1 Corinthians 15 about the resurrection of the saints. Was Secretary Baker a saint? A believer of any kind? He didn't know. He had seen the man on the evening news but had never exchanged a word with him. As a colonel in the Air Force, Jeremy carried some weight with the lower ranks, but he was just one of hundreds of colonels. Even his newly minted rank of general was a contrivance. His specialty wasn't in an area that brought a lot of attention. To most he was just a computer jockey.

He thought of other funerals he had attended, and he realized he didn't usually pay much attention to the officiants' words. This didn't surprise him. People who mourned were likely to think of their loss. Somber moments tended to shut the ears and open the heart. He wondered if anyone would remember what he said.

Sometime after 0200, Jeremy crawled into his bed and prayed that God would help him say the right things.

Then the guilt came.

The world was inverted. People were suffering and would suffer more in the days ahead. He was safe, warm, fed…and yet he worried about not stumbling over himself.

Jeremy decided to pray for the family of Secretary of State Baker instead. It seemed a more noble prayer.

▪ ▪ ▪ ▪

At 0900, Jeremy stepped to a thin metal lectern in the common area of the underground facility and gazed at fewer than fifty people who formed the congregation. Some were FEMA people assigned to the building above, others were military, and a few others were part of the team that kept Mount Weather at the ready.

"We gather for the somber and important duty of saying goodbye to a patriot, a man who gave himself to the service of our country and died while serving in one of our nation's most important roles. Some here knew him well; others knew him by name and position only…"

The crowd faced Jeremy. The president wiped away a tear.

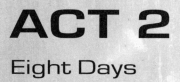

ACT 2

Eight Days

19

Chaos Theory

Jeremy knew nothing about space-time dilation except from the science-fiction stories he read from time to time, and he doubted he could trust those to explain why the past week flew by yet seemed to move so slowly. Sheltered below grade, he was losing his ability to track time. In the evening hours, the lights in the public areas dimmed to simulate twilight, but there was never any true darkness. If Jeremy wanted that, he had to lock himself away in his room and turn off the lights. He found little comfort there.

His was one of the few private rooms available. The president had a suite of course, a set of rooms that included an office, bedroom, bathroom, living room, and kitchenette. Jeremy's place was like a large dorm room. The VP's suite had been given to Frank Grundy. The other suites went to speaker of the house—a role filled by Senator Ryan O'Tool until a few key congress members and senators were located and brought to Mount Weather. O'Tool became as much of a president pro tempore as a man could be with only ten senators.

During the first few days, people were trying to get intel on what had happened and what was going on above grade. Forming a working government on the fly had proved daunting. Jeremy's admiration for President Nathan Barlow grew by the hour. The man made decisions like a machine, quickly assimilating the sparse information coming his way and adjusting his thinking accordingly.

Intelligence was coming in, gathered by military personnel on the ground and in the air. Communication was difficult, but the radios and vehicles that had been sequestered below grade were pressed into use. Jeremy had long known that the military and the national government were awash in paranoia. It turned out to be a good thing. Several air bases around the country, including Edwards Air Force Base in California's Mojave Desert, maintained underground hangers and garages.

Still, the EMP blasts had done more damage than anyone thought possible. Hardening technology was designed to protect delicate avionics, computers, and communications, but it could never be fully tested. That would require tests with airburst nuclear explosions, which treaties would not allow.

The scope of the EMP pulses had been a surprise. No one knew if it was possible to harden electrical systems against wave upon wave of pulses from space. The present fear was that once the hardened aircraft and vehicles were out of their bunkers, more pulses might occur. A devious mind would think of such things, which meant that such a scenario was possible. For that reason, only a few military helicopters were exposed during the first few days, and those were used to search for key government personnel.

By midweek, several Air Force E-3 Sentry AWACS—airborne warning and control systems—were in the air, serving as communication relay stations. They were more limited than satellites, but they enabled some communications between military stations and what government remained. At least they were no

longer depending on line-of-sight radio or shortwave radio signals skipping off the ionosphere. The system had holes in it, but
it was better than nothing. Jeremy shared the president's fear that
the AWACS could be brought down by more EMPs. Every action
had some risk.

On day three—the president had begun counting the passage of time as days since the power outage, which he dubbed the
Event—Jeremy received some of the software and computers he
needed to complete his work. His work area had not been in a
hardened part of USCYBERCOM, so much of the information
he had gathered after the Moriarty worm appeared was lost, but
the backup files were kept safe in the NSA data center. His team
had created a set of computers for Jeremy to use. What Jeremy
needed was the server bank tucked away at Fort Meade, but for
now he had to stay put. Fortunately, Fort Meade was close enough
for radio communication. At least he had that going for him.

The long metal table in the situation room at Mount Weather
looked as if it could endure a direct hit by a bunker buster. Like
every sit room Jeremy had seen, this one had several video monitors. Most were dark. The largest monitor was mounted to a
wall at the far end of the rectangular room. At the end of the
table stood an Army major who looked as if he hadn't slept in a
month. His red eyes made him look as if he had been on a two-
week bender and had just sobered up ten minutes before stepping into the room.

Major Mark Gilbert had the posture of a man born under a
pallet of bricks. He straightened his spine several times during his
presentation, but it never seemed to last. Jeremy didn't know the
man, but he was sure he had seen his share of action. An Army
Ranger tab was on his sleeve. This was no ordinary soldier. He
had endured in training what few could and had earned the pres-
tigious tab. Something had bent him.

"Mr. President, our domestic intel is limited. We have some teams in the streets, mostly National Guard. Our regular units are on alert and protecting ground assets. We've done flyovers of several major cities: DC, New York, Chicago, Dallas–Fort Worth, Los Angeles, Denver, and San Francisco. Our assumption was that urban areas will be the hardest hit by the lack of power and transportation."

"Was your assumption correct?" Barlow grimaced as he moved in his seat. The busted ribs had to hurt.

"Yes, Mr. President. We're seeing rapid growth in crime, violence, and looting. There are reports from every major city we've contacted. Of course, every mayor is asking for military assistance. They're expecting things to get worse." He paused before pushing a button on a small remote he held in his hand. "This is New York."

The image of fires burning in Manhattan filled the screen. The video image skipped from scene to scene. In each one, people had gathered in the streets, at times facing off with police in riot gear.

Gilbert continued, activating the remote every few moments. The city changed, but the activity did not. "We're fortunate that it's January. In the northern cities like New York and Chicago, the cold has kept people indoors. Of course, there's a down side to that."

"Heating?" the president ventured.

"Yes, sir. Many of the residents in those cities heat their homes with oil. Most have set in a supply, but that will run out soon enough. When it does…" He didn't bother to finish. "In the South, where the climate is generally warmer, most homes are warmed with forced-air units that run on natural gas. We have yet to determine when that will run out or how long the gas company can keep things flowing without power. Of course, there's no power to run heat pumps or fans, but clearly, their time is limited."

"What's being looted?" Holt asked.

"That's the strange part, sir. Most of the damage has been stores with big-box items: televisions, computers, and the like."

"You're kidding, right?" Barlow seemed stunned. "Those things won't work. Why would anyone steal a fried television set?"

Gilbert pursed his lips. "It's hard to say, sir. My guess is that those prone to looting aren't the sharpest crayons in the box. Or they assume everything will be fixed soon."

"Grocery stores?" Jeremy asked.

"Some, but not many. I imagine that will increase once people realize the power may be off for a long time. Of course, I hope I'm wrong about that."

"You're not." The comment came from a man in a pair of tan slacks and a white polo shirt. He looked ready to head to the golf course. Dr. Wade Rouse was the director of the Federal Emergency Management Administration. He had been handpicked by Barlow because of his expertise in disaster mitigation (he taught at CalTech) and his no-nonsense thinking. Always polite, always focused, he had been described as a force of nature. FEMA had image problems. Barlow came into office determined to change that, and he needed someone who could sweet-talk members of congress with kind words or intimidate them with his intellect. In any gathering, someone thinks he or she is the smartest in the room. In Dr. Rouse's case, he was.

"May I?" He had no need to ask. FEMA would have to deal with much of the fallout. He may have been the second-most stressed man in the room.

"It's why we pay you the big bucks, Dr. Rouse," Barlow said. A few in the group offered polite chortles.

"Thank you, Mr. President. The study of group and individual dynamics during a crisis is detailed and long. I'll spare you my dissertation, but here is what I believe we can expect."

An open notebook rested on the table in front of Rouse, but he never looked at it. He spoke from memory.

"As the video footage shows, crowds are massing and the rioting has begun. This is to be expected, as is the increase in frequency. We're just a few days into what may be a protracted energy outage. People are frightened, and that can cause normally sane people to commit major…indiscretions. The problem will grow worse. Food will be the issue. Looting televisions makes sense at first, but soon people will become concerned about feeding their children. Our citizens are not prone to plan for disaster, no matter how many public service announcements we run. It's human nature to forget the last disaster and assume no others will occur. New Orleans has suffered for almost ten years because people eventually quit caring. That includes previous administrations. When the wind stops blowing, people start forgetting."

"You don't have a very high opinion of the American citizen," Barlow said.

"I know too much to think differently, Mr. President. This is my specialty. It is why you brought me onboard. When you did, I only asked one thing."

Barlow nodded. "The right to speak freely to those higher up…I believe you called it the power curve."

"Yes, sir. I'm exercising that right now. The worst part of this disaster may be ahead of us."

"From more EMP pulses and the worm?" Holt shot Jeremy a glance.

"I can't speak to that, General. That's out of my wheelhouse. But our greatest enemy is our own citizenry. Other countries will face the same problem. The first couple of days, I assumed an invasion was immanent, but then I learned the whole world suffered from the same problem. No doubt they thought *we* were invading."

"Give us a bullet list, Dr. Rouse." Again, Barlow shifted in his seat. The padding in the chair couldn't make the president comfortable. Watching the commander-in-chief squirm made Jeremy think of his own back and shoulder. No real damage, but that didn't mean he was without pain.

Rouse tapped the table with the back end of his pen and contemplated his next words. "Riots in the cities will increase. The larger the city; the greater the danger. Riots usually begin in late afternoon and last into the night. I believe these will begin soon because the city streets are dark. However, there is still enough moonlight to encourage such activity. There will be fires. Cars and buildings. Grocery stores and restaurants will be targeted—first mom-and-pop shops and then the megastores. People have to eat, and city dwellers don't grow and store crops. Most can get by for a week. After that…" He raised his hands as if in surrender. "Much of the food will be close to spoiling. Meat has been sitting in powerless refrigeration units.

"Divisions will occur along racial and socioeconomic lines—"

"Wait," General Holt said. "I like to think we're beyond that."

"I like to think the same thing, General," Rouse replied. "But research indicates we're not. The poor will resent the rich and assume they have stores of food and will be the first to get power."

"That's ridiculous," Barlow snapped.

"Of course it is, but people in stress turn on others. Some noble souls will try to help, but they will be overrun by others."

Vice President Frank Grundy shook his head. "I can't believe that of our citizens." His face was bruised, and his neck was still so stiff from his injuries he had to turn his body to make eye contact with those around the table.

"I find no joy in this, Mr. Vice President, but it is what it is." Rouse let the words hang in the air.

"Somalia. Rwanda." Jeremy whispered the words.

"What was that, General?" Barlow fixed his gaze on Jeremy.

"Sorry, sir. I mentioned Somalia and Rwanda."

"Meaning?"

Jeremy straightened and cleared his throat. He might have the rank of general, but aside from Major Gilbert, he was the low man on the totem pole. "Rwanda was once led by the Germans. When they pulled out, they left a leadership vacuum. The violence between the Hutus and Tutsis in the mid-1990s left a million or so people dead, many killed by machetes. The interesting thing from our perspective is that the violence was not racial. Hutu and Tutsi are both black. It was tribal. Somalia remains a country with no functional government. It is run by warlords."

"Warlords who capitalized on famine," Rouse interjected.

Grundy wasn't convinced. "Those are third-world countries—"

"It makes no difference, Mr. Vice President." Rouse's words were firm. Jeremy doubted if a bulldozer could move the guy off an opinion. "And it's not just the general citizenry." He looked at Barlow. "There is an eighty-five percent chance that the military will fragment."

"Meaning?" Barlow pressed.

"Some units of the military may take it upon themselves to mark off a territory."

Holt huffed. "American warlords? Not possible."

"I hope you're right, General. I really do. For the first time in my life, I've started wishing I were wrong." He looked away but continued speaking. "The next area of concern will be health issues. Without power, sewage can't be processed properly. Much of it will be funneled into oceans and lakes. Clean water may become a problem. Almost all utilities manage water with electric pumps controlled by computers. Some things could be done manually if the utility workers show up. But they may not if they fear for the safety of their families.

"Police effectiveness will be diminished. Radio operation is out. Patrol cars don't work. What are they to do with people they arrest? Many police stations have holding cells with no windows and steel doors. People could die in those. Even the facilities with bars instead of solid doors will face overcrowding. Has anyone thought about the prisons?"

No one spoke.

Rouse continued. "There are nearly three million people incarcerated in US prisons and jails. For every 100,000 people in the country, 700 are incarcerated. Prisons are without power. The cells are locked shut. I assume officials can open individual cells manually, but what do you do with the prisoners? How do you feed them? How do guards communicate?"

Jeremy hadn't thought of that. He wondered what else he hadn't thought of.

"Regions with enclaves of survivalists and anarchists will be particularly dangerous. Survivalists have been preparing for just this kind of emergency, and they're armed, which means they can take what they want from others. In the cities, gangs and criminal mobs will have power equal to the police, maybe greater. Do you want me to carry on?"

"Is FEMA prepared for this?" Barlow's face suggested he already knew the answer.

The director of FEMA didn't hesitate. "No, sir. Not by a long shot. We have stores of food, but not for 315 million people. We have some generators, but they weren't hardened. We have a lot of work to do to get those things running. My best guess is that only a quarter of my staff and field workers are available."

"You're guessing?" Grundy furrowed his brow.

"Yes, Mr. Vice President. We all are. I can't communicate with my office in DC, Security, or our ten regional directors."

The president's eyes traced those around the table. "Monica

will be in soon. We found her at her office. Not much she could do there, but she wouldn't leave the helm. Maybe she has some Homeland Security info for us." He took a deep breath. "Do you have suggestions for us, Dr. Rouse?"

"Yes, but I imagine you've already considered them, and if not—well, I don't think you're going to like them."

"I don't like any of this," Barlow admitted.

Rouse pursed his lips. "First, the obvious. I recommend doing whatever is necessary to protect the strategic oil reserves and the fuel reserves at our military bases. It will take a fair amount of fuel to keep generators running once they've been repaired. And once this is over—if it ever is—it will be some time before oil production and transportation are back online.

"Next, thought will need to be given to protecting food reserves and farmland. For the first time in history, our farmers could be in danger from hungry hordes. Most will be safe for a while because many farms are somewhat isolated and transportation is limited.

"Then…" Rouse took deep breath and exhaled. "I also think you need to prioritize areas and cities vital to recovery and write off the rest."

"I don't think I like where you're headed with that." Barlow's words were cold.

"I don't either, Mr. President, but emergency personnel know they can't save everyone. It's fine to want to, but it can't be done. Survival and recovery of the country is at the top of the list. Let's not fool ourselves. People have died, and many more will die. There isn't a thing we can do about that, but we *can* save many. We need to designate areas as camps for refugees fleeing crime-riddled neighborhoods, places where we can protect people."

"You know about the conspiracy theories that say your

organization has concentration camps for US citizens." Grundy's gaze was steady.

"Yes I do, Mr. Vice President. The claims are bunk. We have staging areas for our workers, and that's it. We need a presidential order and a directive to the military to allow us to use large buildings—office buildings, college campuses, sports arenas, anything and everything where we can put people for their safety and where we can feed them. We can't go door-to-door to every home and apartment. Once we have enough vehicles working, we can start transporting any who are willing to go with us. But…" For Rouse to pause wasn't a good sign.

"Just say it, Dr. Rouse."

"We need to start with areas populated by well-educated people, food suppliers, and workers who can get things done."

"And those who don't fit those categories?" Grundy pressed.

Rouse simply shook his head.

Barlow inched forward in his seat. "You're asking me to designate certain populations as more important than others. We don't do that in this country."

"Sir…" His face reddened. A moment later he slammed his notebook shut. His next words came out rapid-fire. "I don't enjoy this, Mr. President. I'm facing an impossible situation. It's the Wild West out there. In a few days we have gone from being a world power to being a third-world country. Money is meaningless. No banks are operating. No ATMs work. Babies are crying for milk, and I can't do anything about it. All I have is limited information and research that barely applies. I'm open for ideas. Anyone think they have a better feel for this than I do?"

Grundy started to speak, but Barlow put a hand on his arm. Silence followed the outburst.

A moment later, Rouse said, "I apologize, sir. I guess I'm a little stressed."

"You're doing a great job, Wade." Barlow spoke like a father. "We're all dealing with things beyond our worst nightmares. I can't argue with anything you said. You've helped clarify things for me. This is chaos theory at its worst."

Something occurred to Jeremy. "Dr. Rouse, I haven't seen your family here. As a cabinet member you have a right—"

"They're dead." The man stared at his closed notebook.

"Wade…" Barlow began. "I hadn't heard. I—"

"They were on an airliner. My wife was flying back from London. She had the girls with her. They were already in the air over the Atlantic when the order to ground all craft went out. The first wave of EMP pulses hit before the plane could turn back. They never arrived." He stood. "I need a moment, Mr. President."

"Of course, Dr. Rouse."

20

Roni's Choice

Only the most life-threatening conditions warranted surgery. Still, there were too many of those. Some surgeries could be delayed. Even cancer surgeries, except those of the skin, had to be postponed. Appendixes, however, cared nothing about the lack of electricity. Neither did stab and gunshot wounds. Those operations were performed under battery-powered light. Key vital signs were monitored the old-fashioned way: Blood pressure was monitored with manual sphygmomanometers and stethoscopes. EKG monitors were replaced with two fingers on the carotid artery. When possible, surgeries were done under spinal anesthesia and other chemical means.

The greatest weight fell on the anesthesiologists, who had to sedate and monitor patients. Scalpels worked with or without power. Electrocauterization was out. Small-vessel bleeding had to be handled in other ways. IVs dripped fluid without help of pumps. Roni was beginning to feel like a field surgeon during World War I.

Her last patient had come through fine, but Roni and her team felt as if they had just finished a marathon. Surgery had become an entirely new experience.

She stripped off her gloves and surgical gown and exited the OR. Dr. August Pickett waited for her. With him were three uniformed men. US Army.

"Did the surgery go well?" Pickett smiled. It seemed fabricated.

"Not the way I like to do business, but he should be fine. Who are your friends?"

"They haven't said. They just asked for you."

Roni's heart stumbled as if it forgot its natural rhythm. She assumed this had to do with Jeremy, but she didn't know if the news was good or bad.

A young man with sergeant stripes asked, "Are you Dr. Roni Matisse?"

"I am."

"Would you please tell us your husband's name?"

"Colonel Jeremy Matisse, United States Air Force."

The young man nodded. "And where is he stationed?"

"I don't know where he is now. Normally he works out of Fort Meade."

"Very good, ma'am. I know I sound overly cautious, but do you have ID?"

"You could have started with that and skipped the questions," Roni said.

He offered a patronizing smile. "No ma'am, I couldn't."

"I have my hospital ID. My driver's license is in my locker. Don't have much use for it this week."

"No ma'am, of course not. Hospital identification will be fine."

She showed the plastic laminated ID with her picture and name.

"Thank you, ma'am."

"How is my husband?" She had resisted asking the question as long as she could.

"He is well and has asked that we bring you to his location."

"Which is?"

"I'm afraid I can't say," the sergeant said as he glanced at Pickett.

"I don't understand. How do you plan to get me there?" Roni took back her ID.

"We have a vehicle, ma'am. Some military vehicles are still working."

She didn't ask how. She was sure he wouldn't say.

"If you'll follow me."

He turned and took two steps. Roni didn't move. Her mind, however, hit top gear.

The soldier turned. "Ma'am?"

"Hang on, Sergeant. Give me a sec."

"My orders were to bring you right away."

"I get that. Sit tight for a second." She studied the shine of the corridor floor.

Pickett stepped closer. "You should go, Roni. We'll get by."

"I know." She felt as if she were wearing concrete pants. Thoughts buzzed like bees in a jar. "I have a boy with me."

The sergeant retraced his steps. "Excuse me, ma'am? I was told you didn't have children."

"We don't. It's…" *How to explain this.* "The social system in the area has failed. I can't send the boy to foster care."

"You didn't tell me this, Roni." Pickett looked to be somewhere between peeved and puzzled.

She smiled as sweetly as she could. "That's because I've been keeping it a secret from you." Pickett didn't return the smile. "Look, the kid lost his mother when this all started, and his father was a cop who had been killed in the line of duty. He has no family. Social services is dead in the water, and sending him to some home that has no power and rotting food in the refrigerator would be cruel. And…he's kind of grown attached to me."

"And you to him, it sounds like," Pickett said.

"I suppose. I haven't thought about it that way. Not until now."

"Ma'am, my orders are to find you and deliver you to the general."

"General? I told you my husband is a colonel."

"Not anymore, ma'am." He looked at Pickett. "Doctor, will the boy be safe here in the hospital?"

"As safe as any of us are. Most of us can't get home. We have others in the children's ward—"

"Forget it." Roni raised her gaze. "I can't leave the hospital. I won't leave the boy."

The sergeant smiled. "The general mentioned you might say that. I'm under orders to ask you to reconsider, ma'am."

"Tell my husband there is nothing I want more than to be with him, but I can't leave now. We've already lost too many doctors and nurses. I refuse to leave patients on their beds. I can't. I wouldn't be able to face myself when all of this is over."

"Understood, ma'am." The sergeant held out his hand, and one of the other soldiers handed him an envelope. "He asked me to give this to you if you refused to accompany us." He passed the missive to her. Her name had been written on the envelope—in Jeremy's hand. Her heart skipped, and she wanted to hug it like a junior-high girl with her first love note.

"Thank you."

"You're welcome, ma'am." The sergeant looked around the corridor. "I see your generator is out."

"Yes," Pickett said. "The wiring is destroyed, and we think something happened to the mechanics."

"That's possible," the sergeant said. "A lot of generators, especially those tied to computer systems, received greater damage. If you'll show us to the generator, we'll take a look at it. The corporal specializes in such things."

"That would be wonderful."

"It was General Matisse's idea. He figured Dr. Matisse would refuse our invitation. He also knew you could use a little help."

"The whole city needs help."

"Yes, sir, but we are limited in what we can do." The sergeant turned to Roni. "I imagine we'll be here a few hours, ma'am. If you change your mind…"

"Thank you, Sergeant." Roni turned and moved to her office as fast as she could. It wouldn't do for the others to see her cry.

■■■■

Roni vacillated between fury at herself and calm assurance that she'd made the right decision. The hospital needed her. She didn't come to medicine for the money or prestige; she wanted to help people, to make them whole and well. So her decision was correct. Still, it just felt utterly wrong. She had just turned down the opportunity to ride out the situation with her husband. She didn't know where he was, but she assumed his setting was better than hers. He wouldn't have sent for her otherwise.

Leaning back in her desk chair, she stared at the envelope on the desk. It was plain white, no letterhead printing, inexpensive stock. In the return address spot were a pair of initials: JM. Her name and nothing more appeared in the address area of the envelope. No clues as to Jeremy's location. At least he was alive— something she didn't know until the men in uniform showed up.

She took the envelope in hand again, feeling its texture. The back flap was sealed. The correspondence was meant just for her. A personal note. It took another full minute for her to call up enough courage to open the letter. She removed a letter-sized piece of paper. Like the envelope, it was unremarkable. It had the feel of copier paper, not fine stationary. It was folded in thirds.

An inner voice said, *It's not too late. They're working on the generator. You still have time to change your mind. To see Jeremy. To hold him. To inhale his scent. To know that whatever happens will happen while you two are together.* The voice appealed to her heart and to her mind. The words made perfect sense.

"No." She spoke to an empty room.

A knock on the door jarred her. She jumped as if her chair had been wired. "Come in."

August Pickett swung the door open, entered, and closed it behind him. He sat in a chair next to her desk. The chair wasn't much to look at. Few people entered her office. She used the room to fill out forms, read e-mail, and review notes about pending surgeries. She took occasional breaks here between surgeries. The space was functional but had the decor of a limestone cave.

Pickett fixed his gaze on Roni like a father scrutinizing a teenager. "You okay?"

"Sure. Fine."

"That's good…good." A brief pause. "Just one more question—are you nuts?"

"Some have thought so." The question hurt, but she didn't let on.

"I've just joined their ranks. You should go. We can get by without you."

Roni kept silent.

"Dr. Matisse…Roni, the hospital was here before us and will be here long after we're gone. We can manage without you."

"You know how to make a girl feel special."

"You know what I'm saying. Go. Go to your husband. He may need you. I know you need him."

"I can't, Dr. Pickett. I may not be the keystone that keeps everything going, but we need every pair of hands we can get. We're short of doctors and nurses. Some are leaving to walk home. I can't blame them for that, but I can't be one of them. I've done three surgeries since sunup, and we have a backlog of patients. We have them doubled up in rooms and lining the halls."

"I'm aware of that, Roni. I'm the hospital administrator."

"And I'm the head of trauma surgery."

Picket pulled at his ear. His lips tightened. "What if I relieve you of your position? Will you go then?"

"No. I'll walk to the next hospital and offer my services. I'm pretty sure they'd take me up on it."

"You are the most stubborn woman I've ever met." His jaw tightened.

"Thank you."

"Don't get glib with me, Doctor. I'm trying to help you."

She softened her tone. Roni respected the hospital administrator. He was a man of science, a fine doctor, and a superior executive. He also had a soft heart. When tragedy struck one of the hospital staff, Pickett was there. He attended every funeral and visited every hospitalized doctor, nurse, and janitor. "And I'm trying to help the people who come to the hospital."

She set the letter down and turned her chair so they could talk face-to-face. "Look," she said. "I know it's not fashionable for doctors to take ethical oaths these days. Many med schools have done away with the Hippocratic Oath, but I take such things seriously. We have damaged people here, and more are probably on the way. This is going to get worse before it gets better."

"You can't know that, Roni."

"It's a pretty good guess. Look outside at the strange colors and falling stars. I know they're not stars, but you know what I mean. Anyway, something has gone really wrong. This isn't just a failure of the power grid. If it lasts long, we will have a lot of injured people coming in."

"I can still do surgery."

"I know. I'm putting you on the rotation list. If the soldiers get the generator running, we can do more than do-or-die surgeries. And we need to prepare for the generator to go out again. Getting fuel for it will become an issue soon."

"You know that much about generators?"

"No, sir, but I'm almost as smart as I am stubborn."

He huffed. "That makes you a genius. Let me ask this: Is it the boy? Would you leave if you hadn't bonded to this kid?"

That stopped Roni. She didn't have an answer. Was it Cody and not her ideals keeping her planted in the hospital? "I don't know."

"You asked if the boy could go with you, didn't you?"

She had. "It was just a question."

"Questions reveal our thoughts. You want to go. You should go."

Roni leaned back. "You really want me to leave, knowing you'll have one fewer surgeon?"

"Yes."

"Liar."

Pickett sighed. "Okay, you got me. Of course I want you to stay, but I believe you *should* go. Now get out of here."

"I'm afraid you're stuck with me."

Pickett rose and headed for the door. "Stubborn. Bullheaded. Intractable." He opened the door, stopped, and fired one parting shot. "Thank you, Roni."

Once again, tears rose. Roni hated being emotional. She seldom wept, but the stress and strain were eroding her emotional foundation. She picked up the letter and turned to read from the light of the window.

Then she wept again.

21

An Idea

Jeremy jogged the concrete floors of the underground facility of Mount Weather. It was a slow jog, a thoughtful jog, meant more to jostle the mind and work out problems than to work up a sweat. The pale artificial light gave the place an otherworldly feel. The place would be brighter with Roni. Every place was brighter with her, but she had made the decision he knew she would make.

He worried about her. Here he was safe. Soldiers guarded the facility inside and out. Blast doors were closed. Here he had food, power, warmth, a bed…but no wife. Roni was in the thick of things. She was in a city already known for having one of the highest crime rates in the country, confined to a hospital with glass doors and few security guards, if any. He wanted to protect her, but he couldn't do it living like a mole in a burrow.

Something else had been eating at him. He spent most of his time trying to do two things. First, he worked on defeating the Moriarty worm. It made no sense to get computers up and running just to have them downed the first time they connected to a network. Second, he had been assigned to oversee plans to create a workable communications system between heads of state in different countries. It was proving to be an impossible task. Even if they came up with a plan, they had no way of sharing that with the Russians, Chinese, or any other country. Most communication between countries was done by satellite relay.

One avenue remained open: oceanic communications cables. The first underwater cable had been laid in 1850. Optical fibers were used now, replacing less dependable copper. In 2010, every continent had been connected, including Antarctica. The problem rested with the telecommunication equipment at the ends of the cables. They were knocked out like all the other electronics in the world. Unless the equipment was deep underground or hardened in other ways, it was little more than a dust collector. Jeremy pushed ahead on the assumption that other countries would have the same idea.

He also had another idea, and today he was fleshing it out with each stride. Two miles into the jog, he decided to air the concept. He altered course and stode to a side conference room assigned to the Joint Chiefs of Staff. In the previous twelve hours, the key players of JCS—most of whom had been key aides to the original JCS—had arrived by various means and immediately set up shop. The president relieved Holt and Jeremy of the temporary JCS standing, making Jeremy a happy man. He had felt out of his depth. General Holt remained part of the group as an advisor.

The door to the conference room was closed. Jeremy took a moment to slow his heart and ease his breathing before giving a hard knock, just as he learned at the Air Force Academy.

"Enter." The voice was gruff.

Jeremy stepped in. Seated around an oak conference table sat the chairman, the vice chairman, the chief of staff of the Army, the chief of naval operations, the commandant of the Marine Corps, and the chief of staff of the Air Force, all recently appointed to those positions by the president. General Holt sat to one side. A couple of stars didn't make one a big wig with this group.

"What is it, General?" Admiral Archie Radcliffe, the new chairman, was Navy through and through.

"Submarines."

"Excuse me?"

"Sir, in our meeting with the president this morning you said all ships were disabled and those in transit were adrift."

"Correct. Nav is out, electronics are out. Only mechanical controls work. The nuclear reactors shut down as designed."

"But the subs spend almost all their time underwater, right?"

"Yes. They're nuclear powered. They can stay down as long as they want, but we can't contact them."

"We don't need to, Admiral. They'll try to contact us and won't be able to. What do they do in a case like that?"

"They assume a war and try to assess the global situation."

"Which they can't do, because there are no communications. They're equipped to monitor communications of other navies, right?"

Radcliffe thought for a moment. "Yes, but that may just drive them deeper, unless…"

"There will be no engine noises from surface ships. No aircraft carriers, warships, cruise ships, or even fishing boats. Would they assume that an attack would render every ship useless?"

"No. If they feared a nuclear exchange, they would sample the air for radioactivity. If they don't find anything…"

"Would they return to base?"

"Possibly. Likely."

Jeremy smiled for the first time in days. "Then we have a way to send envoys."

"You expect me to send a boomer or fast attack into a hostile foreign port?"

"Maybe. I'd start with a friendly port. Travel on the surface. Fly a flag. Approach with an open hand. Their vessels are going to be out of commission too—except their subs."

"The goal being?"

"Communication, sir. It will be easier to defuse the situation face-to-face, and we can exchange information about rebooting the digital world."

"I think he's onto something, Admiral," Holt said.

"Maybe. We'll talk about it. Thank you, General Matisse."

Jeremy slipped from the room and hoped he was right.

••••

The letter was handwritten. The words bore no indication of haste. It was a letter written after much thought and soul searching. Each line was equidistant from the one above it. The margins narrow. It was a letter written by a man of detail, focus, intelligence, and love. Roni recognized the script as her husband's. The cursive was tight and lacked flair. It was the handwriting of a punctilious man. Jeremy had the neatest handwriting Roni had ever seen. She had adopted the rushed script that had become the joke and hallmark of physicians in the US. Every loop, descender, and ascender reminded her of the careful, cautious, dedicated man she married. So different they were, so connected nonetheless.

An ache grew in her, spreading from the hot center of her gut to the tips of her fingers and toes. She missed him more than she thought humanly possible. They had been separated for longer periods, but the world had been normal then, not like it was now.

It took Roni several moments to focus beyond the appearance of the words to their meaning. She read the letter for the fourth time since receiving it.

My Dear Roni,

I gave orders that this letter be given to you in the event that you chose to stay at the hospital. I figured you'd be there and not at home. I'm no good at predicting the future, but I know the love of my life. I suppose dynamite couldn't budge you. This disappoints me, but it is a selfish disappointment. I am never happy when we're separated, but this is by far the worst. I can't even pick up a phone and hear your voice. I imagine your work has been demanding beyond words. I hope you are finding time to rest and eat. The hospital and your patients are blessed to have you.

I am safe and busy helping get things up and running again. Things are just as Rex said they would be.

Rex. Their code word. Not long after they married and Jeremy began earning higher ranks and more responsibility in digital warfare defense, he said there might be times when he would be called in to work on things he couldn't talk about or go to a place he couldn't discuss. "Should that happen, I'll phone or send word and use the word *Rex* in conversation. It means that I might be gone for a few days and not to worry."

"Why would I worry?" she deadpanned.

"You wound me." He laughed. Now, as she continued reading, she wished she hadn't joked about it.

I worry about you and pray for you every time you come to mind, and you come to mind every few minutes. Please know this: I love you now and forever. As I consider everything our marriage has been, my only sorrow has been that I have not been able to adequately explain my love for Jesus and my need of Him. He has been the steel in my spine since high school. My faith has made me what I am and freed me to love you even more. You've been patient with me, never mocking, but also never accepting.

Roni, I do not wish to bring more pressure into your life or start a theological discussion. I just ask [Here the even spacing of the words faltered] you to consider all we've discussed over the years of our marriage. When I look at what has happened to the world, I'm reminded of many things in the Bible—things too long to discuss in this letter, but you've heard me speak of them before.

Roni, you are the beat of my heart. I love you more today than when we married, something I thought was impossible. I want the best for you: safety and comfort. Over the years we've had discussions and playful banter, but I need you to consider the matter seriously.

Remember, kid, distance may put miles between our bodies, but not our hearts.

All my love,
Jeremy

An emotional stew boiled in her. She felt the warmth of his love as if he were standing in the room; she also felt the cold chill of his concern. Something had Jeremy worried, something beyond the catastrophic events surrounding them. What was he seeing that she couldn't?

A soft knock on her door pulled Roni's attention from the letter. She quickly folded it again. "Come in."

The door opened slowly, and Cody's face appeared between the jamb and door.

"Hey, you. Where have you been?"

He left the door open as he walked in. "I've been playing in the children's wing."

"Did you have fun?"

He shrugged. The kid was big on shrugging. "I guess. People up there are unhappy."

"The patients?"

"Them too. I meant the doctors and nurses. They look scared."

Roni pushed back from the desk and patted the seat Pickett had been sitting on a few minutes before. Cody climbed in, his feet dangling a foot above the floor. "It's a scary time, Cody, and the doctors and nurses are tired. They've been working for a long time. Most haven't seen their families for days."

"How come?"

"They live too far away, and the cars don't work anymore."

"How come?"

"Well, I don't know for sure. Something has happened that makes anything with a computer chip or electronics quit working."

"Like the lights?"

"Yes, like the lights."

He studied her for a moment. "You're sad too, aren't you?"

"I'm fine."

"You've been crying. I can tell. Your eyes are all puffy and stuff, just like my mommy's when she would cry. You know…after my daddy…"

"Yes, I know." She smiled. "Okay, you got me. I've been crying, but I'm okay now." She stood. "Let's go see if there's any food in the cafeteria. If not, we'll steal a soda."

"Okay. I like the cheese and crackers."

"Okay, we'll steal some of those too."

As they walked from the office and down the corridor toward the cafeteria, the lights came on.

"God bless the US Army," Roni said. For some reason, the phrase "God bless" warmed her.

Twenty minutes later, Roni was back in the OR, working on the first of six patients assigned to her. This was why she stayed, she reminded herself. These patients needed her.

A small voice in the back of her head said, *And you need Jeremy*.

••••

Jeremy took a bite of a tuna sandwich as he sat alone at a table in the cafeteria. The president entered, and everyone in the space stood. Barlow put them at ease. He wasn't alone. With him were his wife and two adult children and grandchildren. The latter had arrived only an hour before. The kids seemed fascinated with the underground facility, and Barlow seemed to enjoy giving the tour. The president, however, looked wan and thinner. He waved off any inquirers about his health. "I'm fine. Just feeling the weight of it all."

Jeremy wasn't so certain.

The sight of the president's family made Jeremy think of Roni, something he did frequently.

He worried about her constantly.

ACT 3

Eight Weeks

22

Placing Blame

Military technicians had taken two weeks to get communication working through undersea cables. The president had issued a state of emergency, and the military used it to commandeer communications facilities and anything else they needed. Jeremy had led one of the teams working on the transatlantic cable. He lacked the expertise needed to cobble together the necessary parts to make what he thought of as transmitters, devices that could send signals through fiber optics. He did, however, have the knowledge to rebuild the computers necessary to make the system work. It was no walk in the park, and Jeremy had never had to be so creative. Just finding motherboards that didn't look as if they had spent a couple of hours in a microwave proved daunting.

He received help from FEMA, which made sheltered equipment available. General Holt oversaw the rebuilding of a military network. Much of it had been hardened—yet one more reason to be thankful for paranoia—but powering the system proved more difficult. The military had not been paranoid enough. Still, things began to fall together.

By the middle of the third week, EMN—a new acronym Holt coined for the Emergency Military Network—was functioning with some success. The network was an adjunct to Slipper, which was still being rebuilt. The JCS and the president had communications with several key military installations, including NORAD. Their equipment was already underground, as were those in other locations dedicated to continuity of government. Every new connection was a reason for celebration.

The number of airworthy craft was limited, but there were enough to overfly many urban areas. Teams of military personnel were sent to debrief state governors and mayors of major cities. They returned with troubling reports and bleak forecasts.

Jeremy sat at a computer, checking and double-checking the safety of the EMN. Terminals could be connected only to previously approved servers. No computer or server touched the Internet. Moriarty dwelled there, waiting for the next opening.

"We ready?" Holt stepped into Jeremy's office.

"Yes, sir. Any minute now. I'm transferring connections to the sit room."

"Good. The president wants you there in case something goes wrong with the connection."

"Yes, sir. Things have been stable for several hours. I've been chatting with my Russian counterpart."

"How are they doing over there?" Holt moved to the terminal. An image of an empty room was on the computer monitor.

"Not good, General. Not good at all."

"Anything the president should know before the video conference?"

"Many things, sir. Way too many things."

Holt's lips formed a line. "Let's go. I want us to be in the room when POTUS gets there."

"Yes, sir."

....

The sit room seemed too large for the few people in it. Barlow entered with Vice President Grundy. No one else.

"We good to go, Jeremy?"

"Yes, Mr. President. The camera is ready to go."

"Microphone?"

"On the table, sir. The techs tell me they'll be able to hear you just fine."

"I'm not sure I want to hear him." He moved to the long table. "My regular seat good enough?"

"Yes, sir."

Barlow and Grundy sat. "Okay, let's get this over with."

The large monitor on the far wall lit up, revealing the Russian version of the sit room. It was dim, as if lit from battery-powered lights that flickered. In a moment, a short, thin man entered and sat in a chair. Two other men entered with him. All looked as if they had just finished eating a large bowl of lemons.

"Mr. President," Barlow said.

Bogdan Arturovich Vysotsky greeted Barlow with a string of obscenities, all in English. The tirade continued for a full minute. Jeremy tried not to stare, but he couldn't keep from looking at his president. The man sat in his chair, unmoving at first, and then began to study his fingernails as if bored.

Vysotsky continued to spew venom, and Barlow let him. Finally the Russian president had to stop for air.

"Impressive, Bogdan Arturovich. You may have used every

English swear word in existence. Did I detect a few Russian slurs in there as well? Yes? How cosmopolitan of you."

On the monitor, a translator began to relay the message when Barlow slapped his hand on the conference table. He hit it with enough force to move the microphone an inch. "No! No translator! You just proved you can handle English as well as any longshoreman. I assume you can speak and understand more civil terms."

Vysotsky leaned forward as if intending to climb through the camera and throttle the president. He stabbed a finger at the lens. "This is your fault, Barlow. The streets of my country are littered with the bodies of our great citizens. They starve to death. They freeze to death. They turn on each other and on their government. All because of your American aggressiveness."

"You don't believe that, Bogdan. We didn't attack you."

"It was your EMP satellites that have crippled us. Yours and the Chinese—"

"And it was yours that knocked us off the grid. Do you think we would do this to ourselves?"

"We had to retaliate."

Barlow didn't blink. "Retaliation, eh? Is that what you're going with, Bogdan? Really? Retaliation? For a politician, you are a lousy liar. You didn't retaliate. Those satellites went off because of a computer worm. I'm sure your people have already told you that."

"Yours shouldn't have been there in the first place."

"And neither should yours!" Barlow bellowed the words. "But they were, and now we are where we are."

"You're safe in your Mount Weather—"

"And you in your Mount Yamantaw. So what? Every major nation has a facility like this, and it's a good thing, or we wouldn't be involved in this pleasant conversation. Now, maybe we do away with the posturing and get down to business."

More curses flowed over the cable. The image faltered and

slipped out of focus before returning to normal. Jeremy had warned the president about this. The EMP satellites were nuclear and left a great deal of radiation circling the planet, radiation that still played havoc with electronic devices.

"Stow the language, Bogdan. You can't intimidate me. I work with the most frightening things on the planet—politicians."

Jeremy thought he saw the Russian president fight back a grin.

Bogdan motioned for the translator to leave. The moment the door closed, Bogdan leaned over the desk as if attempting to whisper in the president's ear. "So, do we blame the Chinese?"

Barlow grinned. "I wish we could, Mr. President, but they know the lay of the land. They're next on my call list. They may be worse off than we are with that huge population."

"It is true. I have already exchanged words with them. Their winter is as harsh as our Russian ones. They do not have food reserves enough to feed their billions."

"We don't have reserves enough to feed our hundreds of millions. India must also be suffering."

Bogdan nodded, his face a canvass of sadness. "Yes, we have been getting reports."

"I was hoping you were." Barlow looked distant for a moment and then snapped back to the moment. "Mr. President, it is important we keep in contact. I am told that your people had the same idea to use the undersea cables. I commend you."

He shrugged. "What else is there?"

"True. Bogdan Arturovich..." The president had returned to using the Russian's patronymic. "The time has come to put away national rivalries. Our countries will recover, but it will take a long time, maybe more years than you and I have left. We just don't know. I do know that the blame game won't work. Our losses will be severe. The worst is ahead of us, I'm afraid, and we still have to track down the real culprit."

"What is your plan, Mr. President?"

"My father used to say that a man walking across the country would fare better if he focused on his next step and not his final one."

"He sounds like a wise man."

"He was, Bogdan. He was, and so are you. Your country needs you, and the world needs your country. Let's work together."

"That won't be easy, Mr. President. Most of our leaders blame you."

"I can imagine."

"The Chinese blame you. So do the North Koreans, or so I hear. The French are a little put out too. Is that the right phrase? Put out?"

"It is. Can you convince the Chinese to work with us?"

"No one convinces the Chinese. We must convince them to convince themselves."

"Will you try?"

Bogdan scratched his scalp, mussing his gray hair. "I will try, Nathan, but their anger is acute. Honestly, I'm not sure many countries will follow your lead." He hesitated and then added, "Nor will they follow mine. I fear I have burned too many bridges."

"We have to try."

Bogdan nodded. "Many leaders will use this opportunity to seize more power. Not everyone is as understanding as I."

That made Barlow laugh. Bogdan joined him.

"So that you know, I am sending technicians by submarine to some of our allies. We hope to expand our makeshift communication."

"Submarines. An excellent idea."

"You've done the same thing, haven't you?"

"Of course."

"I never know if I can trust you, Bogdan."

Another chuckle. "That's the way Russian politics works, Nathan." He looked straight into the camera. "You can trust me, Nathan. You can trust me, even if no one else does."

23

Liam Burr

Liam Burr studied himself in the mirror and still liked what he saw. Five feet eleven, trim and fit, coal-black hair without a strand of gray, dark and intelligent eyes, olive skin, a distinctive chin and nose. His appearance turned the heads of men and women alike. The gaze of the women lingered. At thirty-eight, he carried himself with the aplomb of a man twenty years his senior and the humor and zest for life of a man fifteen years his junior. Young women ached for him; older women dreamed of him. To call him movie-star handsome fell short of the mark.

He placed a red tie over the buttons of his white dress shirt and examined it in the mirror like a jeweler counting facets on a diamond. He didn't feel red today. He tried a brown tie with the image of books stitched into the fabric. Too casual. Next came a cobalt-blue tie with no pattern. The same color as the background of the flag of the European Union. Strong. Bold. Businesslike. A tie fitting a leader in the ever-tightening band of member states.

Burr represented Italy and had done so for the past six years. It took only two years to secure a position of influence among the twenty-seven member states. He moved through the halls of the three political centers of Brussels, Luxembourg, and Strasbourg with ease, making friends and sealing supporters for his causes. He granted favor upon favor, year after year, until the bulk of the key leadership owed him. Some owed him mere courtesy; others owed him much more. Those who didn't owe him for some favor still showed deference. Rumor was he had dirt on almost everyone. The rumor was true.

Politicians around the world came to agreement by debate, mutual benefit, or fear of exposure. The formula stretched back to the ancient Greeks, and the principle had not changed in the twenty-first century. Politics was human chess. Push the right piece at the right time, and one's opponent was on the defensive. To date, Liam had never had to throw open his "vault of secrets," as his enemies called it. Liam's raised eyebrow usually sufficed.

As much as Liam liked women, he loved power and money more. He had plenty of both, but he longed for more of the former.

He slipped the blue tie around his neck and under his collar, tying a Windsor knot with practiced ease. Right the first time. It was one of the many games he played. Having to retie a necktie was a failure of concentration and execution. Liam hated failure of any kind. He didn't tolerate it in himself or anyone else.

"Benito!" His voice was clear and strong.

Two seconds later, Benito Moretti entered—a stout man with the shape of a German beer keg. "Yes, signore."

"My coat, please." Liam watched Benito take a moment to analyze his boss's attire. Dark pants, no pinstripes, white shirt, blue tie. Without hesitation he disappeared into the large walk-in closet and emerged with just the right coat—a Valentino. Liam liked to test Benito. He had several suits of the same color, the cheapest of the lot costing 2500 euros—$3500 US—and kept the suit coats and trousers on separate hangers. It took a practiced eye to discern the subtle differences between the Valentino and the Caraceni. Not that those numbers mattered now. The price of a suit in a society with no power and a rapidly depleting source of food no longer impressed anyone. Still, Liam liked to look good. Just because others struggled with the basic needs didn't mean he had to. Besides, looking good was part of his personality and image. In his world, the man with the expensive suit held power over the man in the cheap rags.

"Is the car ready, Benito?"

"It is, sir."

"The Rolls?"

"Yes, sir. I'm still trying to get the other cars working. Fortunately, we maintain spare parts for the Phantom II."

"They are difficult to come by, Benito. I've been buying parts where I can find them." He thought about the rusted corpses of the other Phantom IIs sitting inside his twenty-car garage. Liam was no mechanic, but he loved vintage vehicles, and he could afford the best wrench monkeys in Italy. By today's standards, the electrical system of the Phantom was simple. No computer chips in 1931.

"I have replaced most of the electronics, and the car starts and runs as it used to."

"But..."

"The electromagnetic pulse burned out the filaments in the bulbs. We must travel by day or when the moon is up."

"You've done well, Benito."

"I have taken too long, sir. Pietro could have done better and faster."

Pietro was the full-time mechanic in Liam's employ. He had not been able to return to the estate since the outages. For all

Liam knew, the local mobsters or the Roman city government had pressed the poor man into repairing their vehicles. Cosa Nostra or politicians. In Liam's mind, they were often the same thing.

"You are too hard on yourself, Benito. You have proven your value to me many times, but never more than these past two months. You have remained faithful to me during this difficult time."

"I have no family, sir, and it is my honor to be of service to you."

Benito lived on the estate just outside Rome. He was more than a butler; he was also in charge of Liam's safety. His skills had been put to use in the Vatican guard until he knocked one of his superiors to the hard surface of Saint Peter's square. Liam rescued him from a prison term by calling in a few minor favors. Benito proved grateful, and Liam paid him three times what he had been making before. He made a salary normally reserved for upper executives. Liam learned early on that money could buy loyalty.

"I take it you were able to get fuel."

"Yes, sir. I had to rig a hand pump, but it worked just fine."

"I trust you've taken precautions for additional fuel."

"Yes, sir. We should have no problem reaching Strasbourg. We will have to find fuel once there."

"That won't be a problem, Benito."

"I have prepared several days of food. Fortunately, we still have Alda to feed us. I'm afraid my cooking would be substandard."

Alda was the cook. She and her daughter lived on the premises. "The drive is only ten or twelve hours. Why plan for several days?"

"We don't know what awaits us along the way, sir. If the roads are blocked or we have mechanical trouble, we might be stranded for a time."

"Of course."

"Forgive me for saying so, signore, but you look weary. Did you have another bad night?"

Liam buttoned his coat to make sure it hung on his frame correctly. "Yes."

"The same dreams?"

Liam turned from the mirror and from Benito. "They don't seem like dreams. They are so real."

"The same people?"

He stepped to an antique mahogany dresser with a marble top and gold-plated drawer pulls. "*People* is not the right word. They are...monsters."

The image of eyeless, human-shaped shadow creatures stabbed his brain. This time they had come at 3:25 a.m. The morning before at 2:13. The time before that at 2:31. In each instance, one shadow figure hovered over his bed, staring at him through orbless eyes. Each time he awoke, the beast would be a few inches closer. He had tried sleeping in a different room. The mansion had twelve bedrooms to choose from, but the creatures always found him.

Closing his eyes did not make them go away. It was as though his eyelids had grown transparent. Regardless of how tightly he slammed his lids shut, he could still see through them. Once he had covered his face with a pillow; another time he used his arm. Still he saw them. Staring. Hovering. Oozing closer and closer with each night that passed.

The first night, he fled from his bedroom, sprinting over the threshold, down the curved, sweeping stairway, and out the front door.

They were there in the moonlight, in the air, hovering over his mansion, over the estate like black ghosts. And each one stared at him.

At him.

Him.

■ ■ ■ ■

Things at the hospital had improved, but the rest of DC had grown worse. A small cadre of soldiers had kept the generator going and delivered fuel. Roni had learned from one of the soldiers that the president had been working with governors and the mayors of major cities, allocating fuel to high-need facilities like hospitals, police and fire stations, and key government buildings. She also learned that the help was limited.

"I passed several empty hospitals on the way here," the sergeant had said.

"How do you know they were empty?"

"The windows were broken, and there was evidence of fire."

"Looters?"

"That'd be my guess. Some people are looking for meds, others for food. Druggies have been cut off from their sources. Their providers can't move around like they used to. It's not safe out there—not even for drug dealers."

"They can't all be stoners and addicts."

"I saw a woman coming out of one of the hospitals. She was wearing an apron." He chuckled but it was abbreviated. Roni didn't need years of medical school to recognize a weary man. "It was like she stepped out of the *Donna Rollins Show*."

"*Donna Rollins?*" Roni thought for a moment. "*Donna Reed?* The old television show?"

"Yeah, that's it. *Donna Reed*. That show was old before I was born."

"Just to be clear, Sergeant, it was old before *I* was born."

"Yes, ma'am. Of course. My grandmother used to watch reruns. I saw them when I spent time over there. Anyway, I couldn't figure why a housewife would be looting a hospital. Then it hit me—she had a sick kid or husband or something. Needed meds."

"We get a lot of people asking for meds we no longer have. Why would she be wearing an apron?"

"Crazy, ma'am. There are a lot of crazy people out there, and I mean that literally. Bug-nuts. I've been in a couple of neighborhoods, and it's like a zombie apocalypse."

"How's your family, Sergeant?"

He cut his eyes away. "I don't know, Doc. They live in Wyoming. I can't get a hold of them."

Roni recalled the conversation as she poured another cup of coffee. A night that included four straight hours of sleep was a luxury. Everything was a challenge. Elective surgeries were ended the first day of the crisis. Now weeks into the Event, only the most severe cases went into the ER. Some of those were police officers shot while on duty. Meds were running short. Harris Memorial had been declared one of the "keep open" hospitals in the city. Patients from other facilities found ways to get there. The place was full, the meds few, and desertion by medical staff was on the increase—less than she anticipated but more than she hoped.

She couldn't blame them. Most of the day, Roni wished she could walk to her home in College Park. It took all her willpower not to drop Jeremy's name and new rank of general and get one of the few operating vehicles to take her home.

Logic won out. There was nothing at home for her. She had possessions, but she couldn't use them here and had no way to protect them. She had visions of her lovely little home in shambles or burned to the ground. She didn't know the facts, so her mind filled in the scene in the most garish, frightening way.

The weather had turned. Eight inches of snow had fallen the previous night. Travel had already been nearly impossible except on foot and bicycle. Now it was worse.

She wondered how many people were freezing in their homes. How many would suffer frostbite and not be able to get medical help? Her sense of powerlessness intensified.

Roni walked up the stairs to the pediatric wing to check on

Cody. He was playing in one of the activity areas with a boy about his age. The boy was bald, and Roni wondered how much chemical therapy was left for the cancer patients. She doubted it was much. A brief vision of the children's ward filled with small corpses raced across her mind, and she did her best to exorcise it. She was a doctor, trained to face the truth regardless of how difficult. She had grown weary of that.

She poked her head in the room. Cody and the boy looked at her. Cody smiled, but his playmate didn't. Dark skin circled his eyes. He looked gaunt, thinner than he should, weaker than was right. The cancer had its food source.

"You okay, Cody?"

"Yes. Are you okay?"

The question made her smile. Lately, Cody had begun showing concern for Roni's health. No doubt he was seeing what she refused to acknowledge. "Yep. I'm good. I'm going to the doctor's lounge for a bit and then to the cafeteria. You know how to find me, right?"

It was a useless question. Cody moved around the facility like he owned the place.

Roni went to one of the lounges. The door was left unmarked in an effort to give doctors a place to rest from the constant pressures of hospital medicine. The place was empty.

She sat, removed Jeremy's letter, and read it again. She had quit counting the number of times she had read the missive at twenty-five. His handwriting comforted her, and his unfaltering concern for her soul was endearing. Still, she wasn't ready to adopt a belief in God. The more she saw, the less she believed.

Where was God in all of this? That young cancer patient playing with Cody could use a God. Cody could have used a little help from the Almighty before his mother and father were killed. Millions were hungry. She rethought that. She had learned that the problem was global. In that case, the better part of seven billion were hurting. How could Jeremy's God allow that?

She folded the letter and clutched it to her chest. Over the years, she had accepted the incongruity of their relationship and never felt his faith was artificial or contrivance. It was as much a part of her husband as his skin. Although she knew it made him a better man, it wasn't something she could adopt. It just didn't make sense.

But then again, what did?

24

Donny Boy

Stanley Elton had always considered himself a resourceful man, intelligent, insightful. He had gone head-to-head with the IRS, financial lawyers, district attorneys, and others who tried to bring down a client. To date, none had succeeded. Part of that was due to his long-lasting commitment to never take on a client with shady business practices. For him, the first principle of accounting was "Never do books for crooks."

Years of hard work and a superior education equipped him for life in the high end of the business world, but an MBA couldn't prepare him for what he and his family now faced.

He sat on the sofa and stared west over the ocean. The sun had burned off the morning clouds, revealing a cerulean sky through which white-and-gray California gulls rode air currents as they searched for food. Their smaller brethren, California least terns, provided competition. Before the Event, the gulls had grown lazy, able to find food from garbage on the beach or in landfills. But there was less of that now. The birds had to hunt the shore the way they had been designed to do. The gulls, the terns, the brown pelicans, the ocean, and the fish that swam in it went about their business as if nothing had changed.

But things had changed.

Stanley was a wealthy man, used to getting what he wanted by handing over a plastic credit card and knowing he could pay off the balance each month. But now there were no credit card companies. No machines to process transactions. No functional ATMs. No operational banks. His millions no longer existed. Being an accountant, he knew more about banking than most. Paper money was an anachronism. He seldom carried more than a hundred dollars in his wallet, and that only for the rare times he couldn't pay for something with a plastic card. His money was kept in zeros and ones, a binary representation of everything he built over two decades of work.

The money was gone, at least for now. It disappeared when the world's power went out and its digital records were erased. Such information was kept in computer server farms around the country. Very few electronics survived whatever happened, so he doubted that those servers had been secure enough to keep such information safe. Big banks promised such security, but he knew enough bank CEOs not to believe the promises.

So what if they were right? What good was money now? He couldn't access it, and even if he could, people who had what he needed—food—no longer needed money. In only a few weeks, people had quit trading money and started bartering.

Still, he was better off than most. For reasons he had been unable to uncover, his condo still had power, something he kept secret. Stanley couldn't explain it and didn't want to answer questions. He struggled to be thankful for electricity, but he couldn't shake the feeling that it was...unnatural.

He had other concerns. Donny's behavior had changed. He spent less time in the wheelchair. He paced in his room. He paced in the living room, pausing only to eat oatmeal and whatever else Royce could get down the boy. Of the four—Royce insisted that Rosa stay with them until things settled and her husband could find a way to cross the country back to their home—only Donny ate three times a day. The rest rationed their food.

On the second day of the blackout, Stanley became concerned about food. He and Royce were busy professionals, so they tended to buy food in bulk to cut down on trips to the store. All perishable food they kept frozen. Dry and canned goods they used sparingly.

They did their best to keep a low profile. Cooking created aromas that could attract attention. Like many in the building, they used barbecues to cook meat even though their stove worked.

First they ate anything that could not be frozen—mostly fruit and vegetables. Rosa made large pots of stew before the vegetables and potatoes went south. The stew could be frozen and left in the freezer. Stanley didn't know why his appliances still worked, but that didn't keep him from using the freezer.

By the second week, people began knocking on doors of the condos, begging for food and medicine. Stanley opened the door only once. A man charged in, knocking Stanley to the floor. He carried an ugly-looking knife stained with a dark substance Stanley assumed was blood.

"Give me food or I'll kill you." His eyes were wild. He looked ferocious and scared.

Stanley raised a hand as the man leaned over him. Then came a thud, a snap, a cry of pain. The man stumbled to the side, his back arched. Rosa stood next to him with an upright vacuum cleaner in her hand. She lifted the heavy device again and swung it in a wide arch, catching the intruder square in the chest.

The man screamed again and scrambled out the door. Rosa slammed it shut and shouted something in Spanish. Stanley had no idea what she was saying, but he got the idea it was something that wasn't uttered in polite company.

Royce sprinted to Stanley's side. "Are you all right?" The color had gone from her face.

"Yes. Caught me off guard." Stanley looked to Rosa, who had locked the door and was leaning against it. Her hands shook, and the rest of her body began to follow suit. The vacuum cleaner, slightly bent, lay on the floor.

"I think I broke it." Rosa melted into tears.

Stanley took her in his arms. It was the first time he could remember touching her. He let her cry against his chest for a moment before looking up and seeing Donny standing on the threshold of his bedroom. Most of the time, Donny was oblivious to events occurring around him. Not so now. He looked crushed.

"Oatmeal…"

He wasn't asking for food. His tone said what his limited vocabulary could not.

The days oozed into weeks, and Stanley grew more concerned. The streets of Coronado were silent and littered with abandoned cars. At night the San Diego skyline was little more than dark shapes. Each day seemed to bring a new fire somewhere in the city. The bridge saw only foot traffic and people on bicycles. Occasionally, Stanley saw an ocean kayaker paddling near the shore, not to enjoy a day on the water but to reach a destination. Sailboats occasionally moved through the channel and under the bridge, heading to places Stanley couldn't imagine. Some sailed out of the bay, others sailed in. Maybe the recreational sailors just felt safer on the water than in the city. He couldn't blame them.

Along Coronado's jetties, scores of people lined up to fish in hopes of bringing home dinner. Those with boats moored in the harbor fished from the side. Only sailboats and rowboats moved along the waters.

Stanley wondered how long it would be before he was standing with them and fishing for his family.

Donny was his biggest concern. Communication with his son had always been just one step away from impossible, and that hadn't changed. Donny had never paid much attention to his parents except when he needed to be dressed or fed. Stanley assumed that Donny's inability to bond was part of his condition. But shortly after the outages, Donny had changed. He no longer spent his days at the computer doing whatever it was he did. Three days into the Event, Stanley walked into Donny's room and found it in disarray. The blankets and sheets had been stripped from the bed and spread over the computer monitors. The computers hadn't been turned on since.

Stanley continued to watch the gulls and for a moment admired their freedom and simple life. For them, life went on. They knew how to survive. He wasn't sure he did.

25

Eli Shade

Liam Burr arrived in Brussels and directed Benito Moretti to drive straight to the Espace Léopold, a complex of contemporary buildings that housed the European parliament, a legislative chamber of the European Union. After twelve hours in the car dodging pedestrians and abandoned vehicles, Liam wanted nothing more than a warm bath and a long nap, things he would normally get at his apartment a few miles from his office. They drove by that building, but looters had been there before them.

No matter. He had a spacious office with everything he needed. What he didn't have, he was certain Benito could find. Best not to be traveling the streets with the city in this condition. Liam understood human nature, and that knowledge told him that he needed to be on his guard.

To navigate the city, Bento had to be creative. Cars and delivery vehicles rested in the lanes of the *Rue de la Loi* and other streets around the complex. Any truck or van that looked like it might carry food had been ripped open. A few had been burned.

They passed several restaurants along *Rue Stevin*. All were closed and exhibited signs of forced entry.

"It looks like a war zone, sir." Benito sounded troubled.

Liam sat in the backseat; Benito sat behind the wheel of the right-hand-drive vehicle. "It does, my friend. In times of crisis, people descend to the lowest level. Self-preservation becomes a priority, even if it means taking the property and lives of others. Desperation brings out the basest qualities."

"I'd like to think it would bring out the best."

"Has that been your experience, Benito? I don't think so."

Benito slumped his shoulders as he worked the Rolls through the streets. "No, sir, it hasn't. I'm an optimist most of the time."

"And now?"

"As the Americans say, 'Not so much.'"

"Life has a way of making pessimists of us all."

Benito cocked his head as if thinking. "Have you given up on humanity, sir? No optimism at all?"

The question made Liam smile. Benito could be quick tempered and rough. Pity the man who crossed him, but like a crème-filled candy, he had a soft center. "Not at all. We are in desperate times, but the end has not come. We will rise from all of this. We will rebuild a better world and punish those responsible for so much carnage."

"Dropping bombs on the city would have done less damage."

Liam agreed. "They turned the citizens of the world against their own governments and neighbors. It is a more cruel choice."

"Yes, sir. I agree." Benito pulled onto the *Rue Archimède*, their brief tour over.

The grounds of the European Commission, normally bustling, looked abandoned. Evidence of looters was widespread, but the buildings were largely undamaged, no doubt the result of security and soldiers stationed to protect EU assets.

Benito pulled to the front entrance of the mid-rise and stopped the Rolls, exited the driver's seat, and opened the door for Liam, who thanked him. Liam always thanked the help.

"I'll park the car after I'm sure you're safe in your office."

"No need, my friend. I'm sure I can manage."

"Yes, I am sure you can." Benito closed the car door with just enough force to make certain it latched. One didn't slam the door of a 1931 Rolls Royce.

"You're going with me anyway?"

"Yes, sir."

Liam smiled. Benito had a temper that had brought him trouble several times, but he had never raised his voice to Liam. When safety was an issue, Benito could be more stubborn than his boss.

The lobby of the building showed signs of intrusion. Once immaculate, the place bore scars of disrespect. Someone had taken a knife to the furnishings and walls. A circle encompassing a stylized "A" had been spray painted on one of the walls. Anarchists—people who believed the best government was no government. Liam wondered if that opinion had softened in recent weeks. It was easy to be critical of leaders when one had a full stomach and warm home. If any good came out of all this, it might be a new appreciation for government and business leaders who made the contemporary world contemporary.

Benito walked in front of Liam, his attention fixed on every cubbyhole, hall, and dark place where someone might hide. They rounded the corner of the lobby and entered a wide hallway that led to the first-floor offices when a soft sound caught Liam's attention.

It caught Benito's too. The stocky man spun and seized the shirt of a tall man behind them. Before Liam could speak, Benito had the man on his back. Weapons were drawn and a single command given: "Halt!" The word was spoken in French.

Liam looked down the hall and saw three uniformed soldiers of the Belgian Army. A dark anger washed over Benito's face before he realized what he was seeing.

"Help the man up, Benito." Liam turned his attention to the highest-ranking member of the contingent, a baby-faced sublieutenant. "My apologies." He raised his hands. "I'm going to reach into my suit coat pocket for identification. I would be grateful if you didn't shoot me." He smiled and slowly removed a calf-leather wallet and opened it, revealing his EU identification.

The sublieutenant stepped close enough to retrieve the ID but only after he motioned Benito to stand next to the wall. After a moment, the man handed it back. "I am sorry for the interruption, Signore Burr. Things have been…stressful."

"On the contrary, Sublieutenant. It is I who should apologize. My friend provides for my protection. I'm afraid your man surprised us. We would have called ahead but…" He shrugged.

"I understand, monsieur. As you can tell, we've had a few problems here. Anarchists mostly."

"I commend you for staying with your post." Liam moved to the man whom Benito had felled. "You are brave and loyal men. When life gets back to normal, I will remember your service. I feel safer knowing you are here."

"You are too kind, monsieur."

Liam watched the man's chest swell. "I suppose the only way to the fourth floor is by the stairs?"

"The executive elevator is working. It's electric. Army engineers were able to rebuild the drive motor. The diesel generator provides enough power to run it. It is not as fast as it used to be, and at times the ride can be uncertain."

"Uncertain?"

"It lacks smoothness." The young man smiled.

"It sounds like an experience that shouldn't be missed."

Liam took his leave and moved to the executive elevator. Once the doors closed, Benito apologized.

"Nonsense, my friend. The imbecile should not have crept up behind us as he did. You were in the right, and I appreciate the way you handled things."

"Thank you, sir."

The elevator ride was slow and the speed of the cab inconsistent. Liam made a note to take the stairs next time. The more people who showed up, the more the generator would be taxed. Liam didn't like confining spaces.

Liam's office on the fourth floor looked unscathed. He found a handwritten note on his desk—a list of commissioners already in the building. There weren't many. He didn't expect a full house. It would be days before others could get here. Some would be unable to figure out a means of travel. Some wouldn't bother to try. The realization made Liam smile. Fewer people meant fewer problems.

Benito excused himself to park the car. Liam removed his coat and hung it on an old-growth Honduras mahogany coat rack that was forty years older than he and walked to the window. From nearly fifty feet above grade, he could better see parts of the city. It reminded him of World War II photos of Europe. There was less damage, but Brussels, like Rome, London, and every other city, looked anemic.

"Not the view one expects, is it?"

Liam jumped and spun. Standing in the doorway was a dark-skinned man dressed in black, an ebony fedora on his head and cocked an inch to the right. His eyes were two chunks of anthracite. Thin lips almost devoid of color tipped up at the ends, giving the impression the man had forgotten how to smile.

"Who are you?"

The man in black entered without invitation, removing his hat. His long-sleeve shirt, trousers, and shoes were coal black. "I apologize if I startled you." He spoke in Italian but in a fashion that made Liam think it was not his first language. He could detect no accent. The man stepped to the sitting area of the office, a space marked off by a large Persian rug and a pair of custom sofas crafted after the style of French Empire settees. A matching pair of chairs completed the collection.

"You have a well-appointed office, signore." The man pointed to a painting hanging from one of the walls. "Is that a Renoir?" He rose and moved to the painting of a woman in a cobalt blue dress with a bustle. "*The Parisian*, if I'm not mistaken. 1874." He turned and stared at Liam. His gaze made Liam's heart stumble. "Isn't this supposed to be in the National Museum of Wales?"

"It's a copy."

"Is that so?" The man turned back to the painting and leaned close. "A copy, is it? Yes, of course. I'd say the same thing."

"I believe I asked your name." Liam tried to sound authoritative, in charge. He wasn't as convincing as he wished. He tried to calculate when Benito would return.

"Yes, I believe you did." He paused. "Why does an Italian surround himself with so much French…stuff?"

"Since you refuse to show me the basic courtesy of your name, I'm going to have to ask you to leave." He walked to his desk and picked up the phone.

The man laughed. "Are the phones working now?"

"The intercom should. It's low voltage, and as you can tell by the overhead lights, we have a generator."

"So you do." The man looked up, and the lights went out. "Had, Signore Burr. Had a generator."

"How…how did you know the generator would go out?"

"A small trick, signore." He paused. "Sit." It was an order not a request.

Liam did.

"My name is Eli Shade."

"Eli Shade."

"For now that name will do."

"What do you want, Signore Shade?"

"You, sir. I have come to collect your help."

Odd wording. "I'm afraid I'm rather busy, the world being the way it is. I'm sure you may have noticed."

"Noticed? I did more than notice. I caused it."

Liam leaned back in the chair. He was dealing with a madman. "I see. That's not something I would go around telling people. I imagine there are a great many people who would like to get their hands on you."

"Would you be one of them?"

Liam rolled his response around in his mind before speaking. "If I believed for a moment that you caused all this, then yes. I'd wrap my hands around your throat."

"Ah, I knew I chose wisely. I've noticed that the more gentlemanly a man is, the more violence he harbors. Do you agree?"

"Perhaps. I've not given it any thought."

"Now you're lying to me, Burr. It is never wise to lie to me."

"And why is that?"

"I am many things, Burr, far more than your tiny brain can understand, but patient I am not. I also have an enormous ego, just like you. I have a compulsion to protect it."

"I grow weary of this, Shade. It's time for you to leave." Liam stood.

So did Shade.

Something took hold of Liam's shirt, lifting him two feet off the floor. The something was a shadow, one vaguely shaped like a human except larger by a third.

"What—"

The shadow carried him toward the window, slowly at first. A glance terrified Liam. Instead of a view of Brussels, he saw a curtain of shadowy shapes—eyeless faces and hollow mouths pressed to the glass in a single, undulating mass. Black, ill-defined hands pressed through the tempered glass pane. Fingers crooked. Reaching, grasping, clawing.

"No—" His voice failed him. He screamed but heard only silence.

The hands touched him, pulling at his flesh.

Centimeter by centimeter he neared the wall of glass. Hands pulled at his ears, fingered his open mouth, clawed at his eyes.

"No. Please. God, no!"

"You don't believe in God, Burr." Shade's voice. In his ears, in his brain. The words tunneled through the soft tissue between his ears like worms boring through soft dirt.

Liam was outside, hovering fifty feet above the hard concrete surface below. Then he began to rise. Slowly at first, like a child's runaway balloon, then faster, like a plane and then a rocket. The air grew cold and thin. The earth receded.

Liam had flown many times to many countries. The window seat had always been his choice. He enjoyed looking down on the earth as he flew over it. He knew what thirty-five thousand feet looked like.

The air was too thin to breathe. Frost crystalized on his skin and then the surface of his eyeballs. He gulped for air like a fish left to die on a dock. His body began to spasm. He managed to mouth one word. "Please."

The last image Liam saw before his eyeballs frosted over was a nearly faceless image of the man who had been in his office.

"If you insist," Shade said.

He let go.

■ ■ ■ ■

The door to Liam's office opened and closed. He heard the lock being set. The cold on the outside was gone, replaced by the relative warmth of his office. The cold still on the inside leaked out.

His vision began to clear. He looked at the windows that moments before had been covered by hideous creatures. Thankfully, the creatures were gone. He felt the Persian rug beneath him.

Then he saw a pair of feet in expensive dress shoes. A pair of gray slacks rose from the shoes. Liam didn't move. A hand gently slapped him on the cheek. "Mr. Burr."

Mister? American accent.

"Are you with me, sir?"

"Who…"

"My name is Fred Pierce, sir, and we need to talk."

"I'm…alive."

"True, but you may not be happy about that later. Here, let me help you to the sofa. It's got to be more comfortable than the floor." He helped Liam up.

"Where is…I mean…"

"Shade? Who knows. He comes and goes as he sees fit."

"We must call for help."

Pierce shook his head. "I don't advise that. Just because Shade isn't here doesn't mean he's oblivious to what we do."

"You know about him? You've seen him?"

"Seen him? Yes, you could say that. I've seen more of him than I care to mention. When you're ready and able to talk, I'll fill you in."

"Are you with him?"

"Like you, I've been chosen. In some ways, Liam, I am your new best friend, like it or not."

Pierce was average height, average build, average brown hair, average blue eyes, average middle age. Nothing about him was distinctive. He smiled.

The man frightened Liam.

26

Things to Come

Jeremy walked the halls of the Mount Weather facility. Next to him strolled President Nathan Barlow. The man moved slower, his shoulders drooped, and his skin seemed to sag and was a full shade paler than when they first arrived.

"It's impertinent of me to ask, Mr. President, but how are you holding up?"

"I'm fine, Jeremy. Tired. Stressed. I'm still well enough to irritate my wife."

"Good to hear, sir. There are not many higher callings."

Barlow chuckled. "They'll put that on my tombstone: President Nathan Barlow, United States president, New York senator, history professor, wife irritator."

Jeremy smiled. The man might look like death warmed over, but he still had a sense of humor.

"I've been talking to my advisors one-on-one. I've been president long enough to know that a certain amount of gamesmanship goes on when you get too many people in the room. I have an order for you, but first, tell me about your progress."

"As I mentioned in our group meeting yesterday, sir, we've made little progress on finding the source of the worm. We have more communication now but not nearly enough. Our biggest problem is that so many of the computers that were affected by the worm were wiped clean by the EMP pulses."

"Like blowing up a building after committing a crime. A harsh way to get rid of evidence."

"That's a good metaphor, sir."

"But you have some information. You said it was like Stuxnet." He motioned to a bench in the common area. Several workers stared at them, but none approached. They sat. "Jeremy, it's just you and me right now. This stays between us. Did we do this to ourselves?"

"No, sir. The source of Stuxnet is still undetermined, although I suspect Israel…" He looked at the president. "Sir, are you saying we had something to do with Stuxnet?"

"That happened under another administration. Believe it or not, the president doesn't get every bit of information, but yes, I believe that we had a hand in it—and let me answer the question you're too polite to ask. Yes, if the opportunity came my way to knock out the Iranian nuclear refinement centers without sending a single armed man over the border, I would take it. Without hesitation. So I ask again. Did we do this to ourselves? Did we plant a worm that turned on us?"

"No, sir. I can't see how. The effect is too wide and over too many systems. We didn't do this to ourselves."

"Then who did it to us?"

"I wish I could tell you. I'm taking a new approach, sir. I've learned all I can—and when I say 'I', I also mean my team, limited as it is. Now I'm trying to create a scenario in which I could replicate the problem. Each failure tells me what doesn't work."

"You're trying to unleash another digital worm? Another Moriarty?"

"Not release it, sir. The computer and communications infrastructure is too damaged even if I wanted to do so. No, I'm trying to figure out what has to be done for the worm to be successful. I know the power outage was meant to reboot computer systems. And it's not enough to just destroy computers and the power grid. Moriarty destroyed our ability to fix the damage."

The president took several deep breaths and then closed his eyes. "Ever see the movie *Things to Come*?"

Jeremy shook his head and then asked, "As in the H.G. Wells novel?"

Barlow grinned. "I had you pegged as a sci-fi type. Yes, the movie was based on the Wells novel. I'm not surprised you haven't seen it. It was made before you were born." He chortled. "For that matter, it was made before *I* was born. 1936. Raymond Massey."

"Was it a good movie?"

Barlow shrugged. "I suppose. For the time. Good is subjective. I thought it was boring. The story covers an entire century and predicts a world war in 1940. They got that part pretty much right. They weren't even close on 1970, and who knows if they'll be correct about 2036. In the movie, the war left the world desolate. People lived in burned-out, bombed-out buildings. Local leaders—the roughest and toughest people in the area—took control, making those around them little more than servants."

"I think I know where you're going with this, sir."

"The movie and the book were off on the year, but they got the social decay right." Barlow's gaze grew distant. "I got word this morning…the White House has been destroyed."

"No."

"I'm afraid so. A mob, probably starved out of their minds, stormed the place. Since I'm here, security was lighter than it would have been normally. The mob killed the few capitol police on duty."

"Horrible. How bad is it?"

"Looted and burned to the ground."

Jeremy closed his eyes and tried not to imagine the image. The effort was futile. His mind painted a bleak picture of the great building lying in ruin and dead security men unmoving on the ground. "It doesn't seem possible."

"Not the first time, General. During the War of 1812, the British occupied the capital in August of that year. British General Robert Ross called for the burning of all public buildings. Almost every building of the government came down, including the White House. To his credit, his men were only allowed to torch government buildings. In that sense, he saved the city from complete destruction."

Barlow took a ragged breath. Jeremy heard a slight rattle. "It's one thing to see the place burned by a foreign force, but to have our own citizens do it…I'm stunned. At the same time, I'm not surprised. We don't have a great track record for dealing with natural disasters. We tend to throw money at the problem. Money is worthless now. So is gold. All the gold dealers who talked people into investing were wrong. No one cares. What is the father of three going to do with a gold nugget? Buy food? What would the seller need it for? A joke. A horrible, soul-grinding joke."

He drew a finger under his eye. "A courier brought film of the place burning." He shook his head. "Film, mind you. Not digital tape. Not many digital cameras working. A few, but not enough. I have no idea how they got the thing developed."

"Can troops be sent in?"

"Why? It's too late, General. The place is a smoldering mess. To protect some of these places, troops might have to fire on desperate citizens. This isn't a bunch of malcontents or protestors;

they're desperate, pitiful people. I can't imagine giving the order to fire on a crowd like that. Can you?"

"No, sir."

"Some things are improving. I guess I should be thankful for that. Your submarine idea was a good one. The Russians, Chinese, and British have pressed their subs into service. Setting them up as radio relays was brilliant, Jeremy. Inspired. So was the advice to have only a portion on the surface at one time." Jeremy had come up with the idea of a chain of submarines relaying radio messages over the ocean.

"There could still be satellites up there waiting to go off. I doubt it, Mr. President, but I can't see exposing the few working assets we have."

"With the subs spaced over the oceans and AWACs flying over the continent, we're getting pretty good radio coverage. Not good enough, but at least our bases can talk to each other. Well, some of them can. The cable connections continue to hold with major countries."

"Every step forward is something to be thankful for."

Barlow nodded. "Are you praying for us, Jeremy?"

Jeremy blinked and cocked his head. "Sir?"

"You're probably the most spiritual man in the mountain. I sensed that when you performed the memorial service for Baker. I don't think I ever thanked you for that. If I haven't, then thank you."

"I am happy to help any way I can."

"Good. Now answer the question."

"Yes, sir. I pray for our country and I pray for you. Daily."

"Good," Barlow said softly. "Very good." He seemed lost in thought. A moment later, "I have been too. God hasn't heard from me very often, so He may not be taking my calls."

"I'm sure you have His ear, sir."

"If things don't improve soon, many of our people are going to be living like they did in the first century. Water treatment plants are off-line, and so are sewage plants. Medicines have run out, and producing new ones is impossible without all the tech we've come to depend on. What was the life expectancy back then?"

"Much of it depended on what one did for a living. Priests and scholars often lived longer than those in farming and trades. Call it forty or so."

Barlow thought for a few moments. "Jeremy, I've been a marginal Christian all my life. Like many politicians, it served me to speak of my belief in God and my commitment to Christ. Somehow, that seems inadequate now."

"It sounds like your thinking has changed, sir."

"I suppose it has. Well, not my thinking, but the way I look at faith." He looked Jeremy square in the eye. "I know American history back and forth, but I know very little about biblical history or the Bible for that matter. Does the Bible describe what we're going through?"

Another surprise question. "Yes, sir. It does. The more I know, the more I've come to believe that this might be in keeping with biblical prophecy."

"When you get back, I want to hear about it."

"Get back, sir?"

Barlow took another deep breath. More rattles. His skin paled. "I've…I've made a car available to you and a driver too. Go get your wife. And the boy. They…they tell me there's a boy somehow involved. Bring them both."

"Sir, the boy is not family—"

"Enough of that noise, General. Bring them both, and if anyone complains, send them to me." He grimaced.

"Sir, are you okay?"

Nathan Barlow groaned. Raised his right hand to his chest. "Oh, no…"

The president of the United States slipped from the bench and fell to the floor.

••••

Liam Burr watched the sunset. Normally he would pause to appreciate the beauty of the daily event, but his mind could concentrate only on what had taken place a short time ago. Had it been real? It must have been. The man calling himself Fred Pierce sat in one of the French chairs, his legs crossed, staring at Liam.

"Who are you?"

"I've already told you, Mr. Burr, my name is Fred Pierce."

"I didn't ask your name. I asked who you are." Liam sat up. The room began to spin.

"You'll want to take it easy, sir. You've had quite the fright."

"That's one way of putting it. What a dream. I must have passed out and—"

"No, sir. It was no dream. You have been called to change the world. Of course, as I understand it, you already had that on your agenda. It's why you were chosen."

"Chosen? I must admit, I didn't like the recruitment technique."

"I don't imagine you did, but you need to take this seriously. Shade is not a being to mess with."

"Odd choice of words." Liam rubbed his eyes, hoping they would clear. They hurt from the frost that had coated them… how long ago? The sun was setting. He had been out for at least two hours.

"Odd? I suppose, but would you call Shade a man? No, siree. He's much more than that."

"Where is Benito? Where is my aide?"

"Dead, I suspect. That's how Shade works."

"No. I don't believe that. Benito doesn't die easily…" After what he just experienced the statement seemed foolish. "I have to find him."

"You won't. If Shade follows course, your man is nowhere to be found. Don't ask. I have no idea. I've just seen his work before."

The thought of Benito lying dead in some snowy field tugged at his normally icy heart. "Back to the question, Pierce. Who are you and what do you have to do with me?"

"I'm your new assistant. I'm here to help you achieve your goals—well, achieve Eli Shade's goals. I specialize in communication, speech writing…that sort of thing. My job is to make you lovable and trustworthy."

"And to make sure I cooperate."

"No. Shade will do that. I'm just a humble wordsmith, among other things."

"What things."

"I'm pretty good with technology. That doesn't matter now. What does matter is that you understand what has just happened."

"Enlighten me."

"Sure." Pierce leaned back in the chair and recrossed his legs. "You are dead to all your previous plans. Give up any idea of calling the shots. Sorry, does my American colloquialism confuse you?"

"I speak English and understand American."

"Cute. My point is that you are now in the employ of Eli Shade. Cooperate, and you'll have more wealth and power than you thought possible. Refuse, and Shade will make you sorry for it. Trust me on this."

"You've experienced this?"

"You don't want to know."

Liam leaned forward, resting his arms on his knees. "I must be dreaming. Things like this don't happen in the real world."

"Look out the window."

Liam did.

The shadow faces were back, so many of them he couldn't see the sky behind them. He shot to his feet and backed to the wall. "I—I've lost my mind. This can't be. No, I refuse to believe it."

Pierce sighed loudly like a parent making a point and rose. He walked to the office door, unlocked it, and flung it open. "Look."

"No. I can't."

"LOOK!"

When Liam refused to budge, Pierce took three long steps his direction, seized the front of his shirt and pulled him to the door. Liam was helpless to resist.

They were there. Eyeless but seeing. They filled the doorway and the hall outside. Gravity had no power on them. Some hovered upside down like tethered astronauts or sideways like lizards clinging to the wall.

"No. I refuse to believe."

Pierce moved Liam closer.

"Please, no more. I believe. I believe. No closer, please."

Pierce released Liam and closed the door, twisting the lock. "You should probably sit down again. You look a little pale. Not that I blame you. I soiled myself the first time."

"You're not one of them?"

"I'm one of you, if you catch my drift. I'm just a little more adaptive than you. You'll get used to the idea. You won't like it, but you'll get used to it."

"What's to become of us?"

Pierce shrugged. "As I understand it, fame, fortune, and world domination. After that, I don't know. Sooner or later we die, but that's true for everyone. What matters now is surviving one more day. Right?"

Liam gave a slight, slow nod.

"Okay, you're the boss. Or about to be the boss. I'll take care of my part; you take care of yours. I'm the behind-the-scenes guy. Your new advisor, aide, whatever. Make up a title. The important thing is that you appear in control of everything."

The lights brightened. Pierce raised an eyebrow. "And so it begins. The building now has power."

"How?"

"I have no idea. I gave up trying to figure that out. Here's what I know. Do as you're told, and you see the sunrise. Don't, and you'll be taking a dirt nap."

"You American's have a way with words. Not a good way. Just a way."

"I can open the door again."

"NO—please don't."

Pierce smiled, but Liam saw no real joy in it. Deep in the man's eyes, he saw terror.

27

The President Needs a Friend

To Jeremy's surprise, the facility doctor and nurses didn't take the president to the infirmary but to his apartment. He noticed that medical staff loaded the president on a gurney, covered him from foot to chin with a white sheet, and covered his eyes with a towel. It took a moment to realize they were doing their best to conceal his identity.

"We'll take care of it from here, General." The doctor said the words as if they were an order. The medic tried to sound in control, but majors seldom gave orders to generals, even new generals.

"I stay with him. At least for now."

The doctor said nothing, but his expression made a speech.

They covered the distance from the common area to the president's suite in short order. They didn't run. That would bring more attention. Instead, they walked at a brisk pace.

Katey Barlow waited with the door open. She looked ghostly: eyes red, face pale, tremulous hand to her lips. She stepped aside as the medical team entered. A muffled, "I'm fine, baby," came from the man on the gurney.

"You'd better be." Her words were saturated with tears.

Jeremy followed the medical team to the bedroom door and stopped at the threshold. He knew his limits. Inside the room was a simple bed, a pair of nightstands and—to Jeremy's surprise—an oxygen bottle, heart monitor, and an IV stand. A table to the side held several instruments, including something that looked like an EKG machine.

It made sense. The facility was meant to house hundreds, including the president. Electronic medical equipment had survived in the hardened structure. Jeremy couldn't imagine doing this kind of medical work without the proper instruments. Then he thought of Roni. She had done plenty of that.

He heard a sniff behind him and turned to see Katey standing in the middle of the small living room. "He's talking. That has to be good."

"He always talks. He jokes that after he dies he'll still be making speeches."

"Here, sit. The doctor will let us know what's going on soon. I'll stay with you."

She sat. "I've called the kids. They'll be here any minute. They'll want to know what happened."

As she finished the sentence, there came a knock on the door. "I'll get it." The president's two children waited on the other side of the threshold. Teddy Barlow was two inches taller than his father but had more resemblance than difference. He looked as his father must have in his early thirties. Abigail Barlow-Tate was shorter than her mother and looked half the weight. At first, Jeremy thought he was looking at a teenage girl, but then he saw the lines around the woman's eyes and mouth. He stepped aside. The two went to their mother's side. She hugged them both.

Jeremy closed the door and took a seat in a side chair.

"They're in there with Dad now." Katey sniffed, nodding at

the closed bedroom door. "I don't know how bad it is. General Matisse was with him."

He inched forward on the seat and told what little he knew.

"He just collapsed?" Teddy looked like a man who couldn't decide between anger and heartbreaking sobs.

"Yes, sir. We were walking and talking. We sat on a bench in the common area. He said, 'Oh, no,' and then fell forward. I broke his fall and sent for the doctor."

"He was…I mean…" Abigail's lip trembled.

"Yes. He was alive and semiconscious. By the time the doctor arrived he was fully awake again."

"Was he…is he in pain?" Teddy pressed.

"Some, and he was breathing on his own. I can't tell you what's wrong." He looked at Katey. "I assume you know more than me."

Katey nodded. "Yes, he's been having—"

"Mom! You know Dad told us not to talk about this with anyone."

"Don't 'Mom' me. General Matisse is one of your father's advisors. Besides, he was there when your father needed him." She faced Jeremy. "You may have saved his life for a second time."

"I just called for help and tried to make him comfortable. That's all I could do. My wife is the doctor in the family."

"Nathan told me. Still, I think you have a right to know. The president has been having heart problems. He denied it for a long time. Symptoms developed after his last annual physical. He kept them to himself. All of this stress has made things worse."

"Is that why there's medical equipment in the bedroom?" Jeremy pushed back in the chair and spoke softly.

"Yes. He doesn't want people in the compound to know. He thinks it would undermine his leadership. The key medical staff knows and the vice president. Oh, and the chairman of the Joint Chiefs."

"I see." Jeremy had suspected as much. He had even discussed it with General Holt.

"General…may I call you Jeremy? Rank seems so unimportant at a time like this."

"Of course, ma'am."

"I…I don't know how to ask this. You did a wonderful job at Secretary Baker's memorial service, and General Holt tells us you are a spiritual man. I…"

"You're asking me to pray for the president?"

Tears trickled down her face. "Yes. Yes, I am."

....

The living room filled with more people. The first to arrive was Frank Grundy. The VP looked three shades paler than the last time Jeremy had seen him and more haggard than when Jeremy helped pull him from the helicopter crash that nearly killed the then chief of staff. He hesitated at the doorway, and his eyebrows twisted in confusion.

Jeremy stood as Grundy entered. "Mr. Vice President. They got word to you?"

"Word?" He took two steps into the room and froze. "I'm here to talk to the president…What happened?"

Katey glanced at Jeremy. "The president has experienced a medical episode."

"What's that mean? A medical episode?"

"He collapsed." Jeremy filled him in. "Mrs. Barlow was just telling me that he's been unwell for some time but keeping it secret."

"That I knew." Grundy looked stressed when he came in. He looked worse now.

Another knock. This time the VP opened the door. Admiral

Archie Radcliffe, head of the JCS gave the same puzzled look as Grundy. They exchanged glances. Grundy faced Jeremy. "You're with me, General." He pushed past Radcliffe. The two men followed in his wake. Grundy stopped midstep and turned to speak through the still-open door. "I'll be back in a few minutes, Katey. I just have to have a short meeting. I promise. I'll be right back."

Jeremy caught sight of her nodding. Then he closed the door.

Grundy led the two military men to the seating area where Jeremy had received his impromptu promotion from Barlow. He didn't sit, which meant Radcliffe didn't sit, which meant Jeremy remained on his feet.

"Is he still able to lead?" Grundy's words were short and sharp.

Jeremy's first urge was to shrug but that didn't seem appropriate. "He was unconscious for a few moments."

"What constitutes a few moments." Radcliffe snapped the question.

"Less than a minute, sir. When he came to, he was confused. That passed in seconds. He asked to be helped up, but I refused. I sent for help and kept him still."

"Did he seem like himself? Intellectually, I mean."

"I believe so. His sentences were complete and clear. He seemed aware of his surroundings."

"Good. Good." Grundy exchanged another glance with Radcliffe.

"General Matisse—Jeremy—I know you're not a doctor, but give me your best guess. Was it his heart? What's your gut tell you?"

"That'd be my guess. I'm not sure it was a typical heart attack. Maybe arrhythmia? I hesitate to say even that much."

"I understand."

Jeremy decided to risk a question. "This may be above my clearance, but if you didn't know about this, why are you here?"

"He didn't answer his office phone and there's been…an event."

"More EMPs?"

"No."

Jeremy got the idea. Once the real Joint Chiefs had made it to Mount Weather, he had been relieved of that responsibility. It felt like Christmas. "I see you two have some things to talk over. Unless you need me, I'll excuse myself. I promised to sit with the family for a while."

The vice president cleared his throat. It was enough to freeze him in his tracks. "What I'm about to tell you is above top secret and doesn't fall in your service area, but I'm going to need advice. By that, I mean the president is going to need it."

"We all need it," Radcliffe said.

Jeremy's blood chilled. This sounded bad.

"Syria has launched a missile attack on Israel." Grundy looked like a man sipping acid for lunch. "Admiral Radcliffe and I were called to the communications area to receive the coded message. That's why we didn't know about the president."

"How bad is it?" Jeremy wished the men would sit. He could use a chair.

"Too early to tell," Radcliffe said. "Intel on the ground has relayed some information to one of our subs in the Mediterranean. The sub's radar picked up the missiles while they were airborne. Info is in short supply. We can't do flyovers. The satellites we use to monitor the area…well, you know. CIA has been in touch with their contacts in Mossad. We know that Tel Aviv and Haifa have been hit, as well as some smaller cities. We assume that the Syrians are using Iranian Fajr-3 and Fajr-5 missiles. There's a good chance Tel Aviv was hit with a Zilzah-2. That beast carries a thousand-pound warhead."

"Early reports from the ground indicate several buildings were hit. The Syrians used their old trick of sending missiles with ball bearings in the warhead. Increased casualties." The VP finally sat. Discussing the attack seemed to wear him down. "This wasn't an attack to shake up their neighbors or to make a point with Israel. The more I know, the more I believe it is the beginning of war."

"But why?" Jeremy lowered himself into a chair. His stomach roiled. His heart pounded like an airplane piston.

"You want my guess?" Radcliffe said. "Israel has always been quick to punish aggression against them. They have the best technology and intelligence in the area, but that's all gone. The loss of power and computers and nearly everything else has hamstrung them. They're more vulnerable than ever before. But that leaves us with a question, General Matisse."

Jeremy stared at Radcliffe. "You want to know how Syria could have missiles ready to fly and onboard guidance able to hit their targets."

"Precisely. You got an answer for me?" Radcliffe's gaze bored into Jeremy.

"They would have had to keep the missiles, or at least the electronics, in a hardened area. Or they found a way to rebuild their electrical systems faster than we can." He paused. "No, Admiral Radcliffe, I don't have an answer for you. If you asked me if this was possible I would have told you no."

"And you would have been wrong." Radcliffe crossed his arms.

"Yes, sir. I would have been wrong."

"If I asked if Iran could launch missiles on their own, would you tell me no?"

Jeremy straightened. "I don't know what to tell you, sir. General Holt and I studied this at length, and we were both convinced that what you describe couldn't happen."

"He's still at Fort Meade?" the VP asked.

"Yes. The president sent him to oversee the reconstruction of our computer network. The NSA database is still good. It's kept underground, but our analysis software took a beating, as did the computers that run it. He has people working around the clock, rebuilding whatever they can."

Grundy rubbed his face as if doing so would wipe away his memories. "This is the one thing the president and I have never agreed upon. I've always thought we backed Israel too much, and he said we didn't back her enough."

Radcliffe pressed his lips into a line. Jeremy imagined gears turning in the man's big head. "You know, sir, you may be the one calling the shots."

"The president isn't dead, Admiral."

"Of course, sir. I know that, but if what Jeremy is telling us is even close to accurate, he might be incapable of making the tough decisions."

Grundy took in a deep, noisy inhalation. His chest expanded. "If it comes to that, I'm ready, but I will not write the president off until I have to. Understood?"

Radcliffe dipped his head an inch. "Understood, sir, but it's my job to keep the decision makers apprised of all military options. I take that obligation seriously."

"What military options do you see? Mobilizing forces is a little more difficult these days."

"True," Radcliffe said, "but we have a sub in the vicinity. We could put cruise missiles where they would do the most good."

Grundy shook his head. "Israel has three Dolphin-class diesel-electrical boats, and they just received two more AIP Dolphin-class boats. They can launch their own cruise missiles."

"Yes, sir, assuming that none of them were in port or surfaced to recharge batteries. Much of the sub fleet is not AIP."

"I hate to show my Air Force ignorance of Navy things, but what is AIP?"

"Air Independent Propulsion," Radcliffe said. "Nuclear subs

can stay down for months. They make their own oxygen and water. They come to port only for provisions. Diesel-electric boats run on engines on the surface and electric motors beneath the waves. Their submerged time is limited. AIP allows non-nuclear subs to stay submerged longer."

"Do we know how many of their subs might have been vulnerable when the EMP pulses went off?"

"Not exactly. The Navy keeps track of those things, but much of that information was lost. CIA might have some idea, but I think we'll know soon enough."

"How so?" Grundy squirmed.

"All we have to do is count the number of cruise missiles slamming Syria." Radcliffe seemed to enjoy the taste the statement left in his mouth. "Lots of destruction means their subs are all safe. No missiles, then…well, you get the idea."

"Gentlemen?"

Jeremy turned to see Teddy Barlow approaching. "My father wishes to see you."

They stood. Jeremy addressed Grundy. "I wish I had a better answer for you, Mr. Vice President. I really do." He started to walk away.

"General Matisse. My father asked to see you also."

Jeremy blinked several times and then looked at Grundy and Radcliffe. There was nothing to say. Jeremy became the caboose in the train of power walking to the president's apartment.

28

Jonesin'

Eight weeks after the lights went out, Roni's world was still a mess. She had a few advantages on the rest of the people in the city—the rest of the people in the world. The hospital's generators had become a priority in the city. Dedicated doctors from other hospitals who had found their way to Harris Memorial had brought mixed messages. The bad news: All but a few of the hospitals had been boarded up. Doctors, nurses, techs, and support staff walked away to care for their own families. The military, police, and fire moved many patients to the few hospitals like Harris Memorial that could still function, albeit at reduced efficiency.

There were stories of great courage and sacrifice, as well as horrible tales of patients left to die in their beds, neglected by the only people who could help them. One new arrival mentioned paramedics who had walked from the firehouse to the hospital to care for as many as they could. Their training, while extensive in trauma, was limited. Still they did what they could. In her own hospital, heroes rose. Ambulatory patients picked up the slack created by missing nurses and volunteers. Some work they couldn't do, but they could empty bedpans, make beds, or just sit and visit those in worse shape than they.

Jose Lopez was one such hero. Recuperating from surgery that removed cancer and a good bit of his stomach, he began to make rounds as soon as he was able to walk. At first, he just went from room to room and offered to pray for any who would let him. Those who blamed God for the crisis often swore at him. Especially those who had lost loved ones. He never walked out. He listened. He nodded. He wept with them. If they allowed it, he read aloud from their favorite books. He never took offense. Jose found a way to make the most depressed person laugh. He had even drawn a few guffaws from Roni, who had begun her own war with depression.

Jose spent part of his days doing menial work, including mopping vomit from the floors or helping run the laundry. Shamed at her own stereotyping, Roni wondered if the Hispanic did this kind of work for a living. Turns out, he held a PhD in civil engineering. "I wish I had specialized in mechanical or electrical engineering. I would be more useful. Not much need for what I do."

"You do plenty, Jose. You have the superpower of humility."

"I never thought of it that way. Mostly, I want to do what Jesus would do in this building."

Roni had just smiled, but the words grew roots in her mind. She might have been able to dismiss it as naive religious talk, but the words of Jeremy's letter kept them alive.

Still, she might have compartmentalized the Jesus-talk, chained it in the dungeon of her mind, had Dr. Clarence Southwell not come on the scene. Dr. Southwell was a tall man with a bald head, a semicircle of white hair that reached from ear to ear, white skin that indicated he spent more time indoors than out, and a thousand-watt smile. He moved through the hospital as if it were his second home.

In some ways, it was.

Southwell was the lead pastor of a megachurch not far from the hospital. Roni had heard of it. They advertised on television, showing images of a large sanctuary filled with happy people lifting their hands and singing upbeat songs. In the ads, Southwell was well dressed and dapper, wearing natty blazers and casual slacks. He spoke with a smooth, steady pace, seasoned with a hint of a Southern accent.

He came to help around the hospital nearly every day, walking six miles each way. The walk was dangerous and often grueling. He carried food with him, handing it out as he went. More than once he had been robbed. Twice he had arrived with cuts and bruises on his face and neck.

"You're lucky to be alive," Roni told him as she helped out in the ER.

"Blessed, Doctor. I'm blessed."

"If you say so. I'm afraid one of these days they're going to kill you."

He shook his head. "Probably not. They want the food. If they kill me, they won't be able to rob me in the future." He laughed. Roni would have cursed.

She gently placed a butterfly bandage over the cut on his forehead. There was little she could do for his black eye. "Why do you do it?"

"Do what? Pass out food?"

"You spend—what, two or three hours walking here and run the risk of being pounded to the ground coming and going."

Southwell shrugged. "It needs to be done. I can do it. My church shares from the limited supply of food. The least I can do is try to put it in the hands of people."

"Where is the food coming from?"

"The government provides some of it. It's not much. At first it was produce from storage areas, and then it became canned goods. Then MREs. Now we're seeing C-rations."

"What's the difference?"

"MRE means 'meals ready to eat.' They're prepared packages of food used by the military. The older ones were called C-rations. They have a long shelf life. They don't make C-rations anymore, but there are still some in military and FEMA storage areas."

"So, the fact that they're using C-rations means they're running out of the newer stuff?"

"Probably. The only people getting fresh food are high-priority institutions like hospitals and key military facilities."

Roni had stepped away, newly depressed. "What you do is noble, Pastor, but I'm going to advise you to stop. One of these beatings is going to go too far, and all your good intentions will be for nothing."

"Good work is never for nothing, Doctor. Through time, Christians have been persecuted and beaten for many things. They crucified Jesus—what are a few bruises compared to that?"

"I'm not worried about bruises, Pastor. I'm concerned about a crushed skull."

"I have a Baptist head. It's hard to crush."

"Funny as that is, you need to stop. The work you do in the hospital is appreciated, but I fear for your life."

"We're all dying, Doctor. No one gets out of this life alive. If I'm going to die, I'd like to do so while doing something worthwhile, something with eternal value."

"Do you still carry your driver's license?"

"Um, yes. Out of habit. Why?"

"May I see it?"

Southwell gazed into her eyes as if he might find her thoughts there. He shifted on the exam table and removed a well-worn wallet. He extracted his license and handed it to her. Just as she thought.

"It says here you weigh 250 pounds. I'm guessing you weigh 180 now."

"I've trimmed up some. All that walking, you know."

"When was the last time you ate?"

"Last night. I had supper."

"Supper, huh? MRE?"

"Yes. Most of one."

"You shared your meal?"

"I don't need much."

"You need more than you're getting. You can't help others if you don't help yourself."

He slipped from the table, wobbled for a moment, and then steadied himself. "I'll keep that in mind."

"You should rest for a while. How's your pain level?"

"I'm fine."

"Ministers shouldn't lie, Pastor. How's your pain level?"

"I've got a headache, but nothing too bad."

"I'll give you a pain reliever—"

"Save it, Doc. There are those who need it more than me."

He was right, of course. His pain was minor compared to some, and the supply of meds was diminishing despite FEMAs efforts to keep operating hospitals supplied. Rationing was the policy. Use only what must be used. Nothing more.

"We're going to hold another worship service in about an hour. I would love to see you there."

"I'm afraid I'm a little busy." Three weeks earlier, Southwell had started a church service for any who could attend. He visited those who couldn't. The small hospital chapel filled the first week. They moved the service to the large lobby at the front of the hospital. Once, Roni had walked by and saw the place filled wall to wall with patients and medical staff. The room was cluttered with wheelchairs and gurneys. She hesitated for a few moments to take in the scene.

Jeremy once told her the sick were attracted to Jesus. They came in hope of healing. "Of course they do," she had said. "Who wouldn't want to be well? Unfortunately, I don't see much miraculous healing going on these days."

Jeremy explained that Jesus had a greater ministry, but He did heal wherever He went. Roni had been feeling argumentative that day and quipped, "I guess Jesus is a homebody these days. Not doing much travel and healing."

The words had hurt her husband. She saw it on his face and immediately wished she could take them back. She apologized, and he forgave her. He always forgave her. Forgiving herself had been the challenge. That hadn't changed over the years.

"You're always going to be busy, Doctor. Always. This is the kind of thing one makes time for."

"Thank you for the invitation." Roni walked from the cubicle.

....

The music from Southwell's service rolled down the halls. It was sweet and uplifting. Once again, the staff had set him up in the large lobby of the first floor. The ER had settled, and her services were no longer needed. Roni set out to find Cody. The weeks had brought them closer together than she imagined possible, especially under the circumstances. She was often busy for hours at a time, and Cody was left to entertain himself. He proved adept at that, dividing his time between reading and playing with the children in the pediatric ward. No child was allowed outside without several adults supervising. The madness of the city continued to grow.

Cody was nowhere to be found. She checked all the usual spots: her office, the children's ward and playroom, and the cafeteria. No Cody. She asked around. No one had seen him. Not prone to anxiety, Roni found herself in a wrestling match with her imagination.

Having checked the surgical waiting area and the doctor's lounge, where he sometimes waited for her, she trotted down the stairwell and back to the first floor again. Cody liked crowds, maybe…

Roni moved to the lobby. As before, the place was jammed. She arrived as Southwell was leading prayer. The congregation of medical personnel and patients held hands, forming an unbroken chain of human contact. Those strapped on gurneys held the hands of those in wheelchairs who held the hands of those standing or sitting nearby.

The room was quiet, a tableau of reverence, of the wounded worshipping with the wounded; the damaged with the nearly whole. Here and there, IV stands stood like narrow chrome soldiers watching over the crowd.

The scene broke Roni's heart. She was used to seeing the broken and bloodied on her operating table. Doctors developed calloused hearts and cataracts that allowed them to see only the work they needed to do, not the human whom the body parts comprised. It was self-defense. Madness waited for those who cared too much.

She scanned the group and saw Cody by the wall. Like the others, he had bowed his head. Why was he here? Something new to see? The opportunity to be with others in her absence? At least he was safe. Along the wall stood Jose, his hands folded, his head down. She could see his lips move in silent prayer.

The quietude ended with the baritone voice of Dr. Southwell. Roni bowed her head out of respect for the man and the patchwork congregation.

"Our heavenly Father, we thank You for this day of life and for Your love. We come before You with hearts filled with gratitude for all that You've provided—"

Really? He's lost seventy pounds for lack of food. What provision?

"We are also thankful that in these difficult times we have You as our foundation and our continued strength. In our weakness Lord, You have made us strong. In this darkness, You have given us the light of Your Son, Jesus Christ."

He paused and took a breath and then continued. "This day, O Lord, many will leave this world. We pray that You will welcome them into eternal life. Father, we are not blind to the great need around us. Help us help others and thereby help ourselves. Father, we remain confused but acknowledge that You remain at life's helm, Your mighty hand on the tiller. We remain confident in Your love."

Roni felt like a Peeping Tom spying on the private activities of others. She was an outsider crashing their party.

"We pray for the doctors, nurses, and hospital staff who continue to make great personal sacrifice for our benefit. Bless their minds, hearts, and hands. We are thankful for them. Father, we also pray—"

"Nobody move!"

The voice was loud, harsh, and laced with fear and anger. Roni snapped her head up and opened her eyes. A man in dirty clothes marched toward the crowd. He held a gun in a trembling hand. His black hair was matted and wild, his eyes wide and tinged with yellow, his gaunt face robed in a scraggly beard.

He moved the gun from side to side as if looking for just the right target. Roni started for Cody. An eardrum-splitting crack filled the space, and the wall next to her seemed to explode. A hole existed where once plaster had been. Several in the group screamed.

"I said don't move." The man spewed obscenities.

Like all doctors, Roni had done a rotation in the psych ward as part of her medical training. She had seen crazy before, and this was it. She had also seen drug-induced psychosis. She had no doubt this man was in severe withdrawal.

"Take it easy, son." The voice was familiar. Dr. August Pickett, the hospital administrator stood. "How can I help you?"

"Wh—who are you? You a cop?"

Pickett smiled. "No, son. I'm not a cop. I'm the hospital administrator. I'm the guy you want to talk to."

"I'm not your son. Stop calling me your son!"

"Okay. My bad. What do you want me to call you?" Pickett kept his tone even and friendly.

"Nuthin'. Don't call me nuthin'."

"Very well. Let me guess. You want drugs. Right? Opiates maybe? I hear it's hard to score on the street these days."

"I don't care what you hear. Just get me the stuff."

"Sure. Come with me. I'll take you to the pharmacy. I'm sure we have something that will help you."

"No. I'm staying here. Go get it. Get it all. I want everything. I don't want to have to come back."

"If you come with me, you can show me what you want. I'm not very good at guessing." A waver in his voice betrayed his fear.

Pickett was trying to put distance between the gunman and the others. That much was clear. Roni let her eyes drift to Cody. His eyes were wide, and even from a half dozen paces away, she could see the poor kid tremble.

The gunman fidgeted more, his eyes dancing around the room. "You heard me, and—" His gaze fell on Cody.

"No," Roni whispered and took a step forward, but before she completed the stride, the strung-out attacker sprinted to the boy.

"Lemme go! Lemme go!"

"Stop." Roni moved forward as did several others, Southwell included.

"Don't you do it. Don't even think it or I'll put a bullet in the kid's brain." He pressed the gun to the back of Cody's head, just above the spine. He pushed hard enough to drive Cody's head down. He whimpered. "Shut up, kid, or I'll kill you right where you stand."

"You don't need him." Southwell's voice was calm and smooth. "You got me. You don't need to hurt the kid." He started toward the two.

He cocked the gun and Southwell stopped in his tracks.

"Hey, pal." Pickett got the wild man's attention again. "I'm going. Just don't hurt the kid or anyone else. I'll get you what you want. What you need. I just have to run to the pharmacy. I'll bring all the narcotics I can grab. You can choose what you want."

"I want it all."

"Great, you can have it. I'm going down that hall right now. Just chill. It will take me a few minutes."

"You'd better come back. I mean it, man. And if I see one uniform, I spread the kid's brains all over the place. You hear me? Then I start shooting everyone. I got me another clip. I can take you all out."

"No problem, pal. I'm going. I promise. I'll be right back. Okay? I'll be back." Pickett turned and started for the junction of the lobby and hall.

"Lemme go. Lemme go!" Cody struggled.

"Shut up, kid. Please…" The man closed his eyes. "Please… just…SHUT UP!"

He was losing it. Drugs had eaten holes in the man's brain.

Roni had seen it before. He wasn't rational because he couldn't be. Fear, anger, and a serious jonesing for high-octane drugs. The adrenaline coursing through his veins wasn't helping.

"Cody, stand still. Just be still."

Cody tried to look up, but the business end of the handgun kept his movement to an inch or two. Roni could see the tears dripping from his eyes.

"Son—" Southwell started.

"I ain't your son. I ain't nobody's son." He lifted the gun from Cody's head and pointed it at the reverend. "You stay back—"

Cody pulled away and ran along the wall toward Roni.

"Cody!" Roni was moving before she finished the first syllable.

The gunman redirected the weapon.

"No!" Roni screamed.

"No!" Southwell's voice.

A shot. Loud. Another. Muffled. Then another.

Screams. Panic.

Roni scooped Cody into her arms and turned her back to the sound of gunfire.

There were no more shots, just a command. "Get a gurney. Stat."

Roni turned to see a struggle on the floor. One of the male nurses, a former Navy medic, rose. He held the gun and with a practiced motion ejected the clip and cleared the chamber.

"We have a man down." Someone shouted.

Roni stopped. Nurse Padma, Roni's friend from ICU, moved to her side. Her olive skin had paled. "Is he okay?"

Roni set Cody down and looked him over, turning him so she could see the back of his head. She found a red spot where the weapon had pressed against his skull. "He's fine, aren't you, boy?" She ran a hand through his hair. "You were so brave. So very brave."

Roni hugged him hard and fought the tears. She failed.

"We're losing him." The voice was familiar, but Roni didn't bother to guess who it might be. She was just thankful Cody was safe. She didn't care if the gunman was hurt. He deserved what he got—

What made her think it was the gunman? She stood and turned her attention to the front of the room. Two of the burlier male nurses had the attacker pinned against the wall, his feet several inches off the floor. Something was missing.

No, *someone*.

"Padma, take Cody. Get him away from here."

"I've got him. Come on, cowboy. Let's get out of the way."

Roni pushed to the front. Two doctors and an ER nurse were repositioning Dr. Clarence Southwell's body on the floor as blood pooled beneath him. His pale skin chalky, his eyes open.

"Pastor?" Roni worked around to the minister's head. Dr. Charles Fulton of the ER had ripped the man's shirt open. Three entrance wounds dotted Southwell's torso. One about the middle of the ribcage on the left, one two inches above the navel, another one an inch to the right of the sternum. Frothy blood poured from the chest wound. More blood pooled in Southwell's mouth. She turned his head to the side to clear his airway.

Fulton looked up. He didn't speak. He didn't need to—his face said the unspoken word. *Hopeless*.

Southwell coughed and did his best to look into Roni's face. "The boy?"

"Safe. Fine. Thanks to you." One of her tears fell on his face. She wiped it away. "You're going to be fine."

He smiled. "Doctors…shouldn't lie." Her words from a dying man.

"Thank you, Pastor. You saved him."

"Praise God." The word came with a gurgle.

He raised a blood-saturated hand and touched her face. "An eternal difference, Doctor. That's what matters…"

The light left his eyes; the color drained from his face. For the first time in her medical career, Roni thought she saw a soul leave a body.

29

The President's Bedside

The president's bedroom was not as Spartan as Jeremy first thought. Someone had even thought to hang art on the concrete walls—prints from early American history. Perhaps the decorator wanted the occupant to remember that the country had been through hard times before. A line of presidential portraits occupied one wall: Washington, Lincoln, Teddy Roosevelt, Woodrow Wilson, FDR, Truman, Johnson, and both Bushes. It took a moment for Jeremy to interpret the unspoken message: Revolutionary War, Civil War, Spanish-American War, WWI, WWII, Korea, Vietnam, Gulf War, Iraq/Afghanistan. Why else would the president be in the facility had war not broken out? Turns out there was another reason, although war seemed to be creeping over the horizon.

Barlow had regained some of his color. He sat up in bed, a stack of pillows behind him. He wore pajamas. Apparently he felt well enough to change.

"Before you ask, I'm fine. I'm alert. I'm able to carry on."

"That's good to hear, Mr. President," Grundy said. He sounded sincere. Jeremy would hate to be calling the shots. "You had us worried."

"I have an irregular heart rate, and my heart has lost a step or two. When things settle, I'll have a surgical tune-up, but we're a long way away from that."

"Can they do that here?" Grundy was starting to resemble a deflating balloon.

"I suppose they could in an emergency, but it wouldn't be ideal. Of course, there are no ideal places for heart surgery these days." Barlow looked at Jeremy. "Maybe your wife would like to see a side of the president no one else has—the inside." He smiled. It was weak.

"She's a trauma surgeon, sir, not a cardiologist. If you get hit by a car, however, she's your girl." Jeremy returned the smile.

"I think I'll pass." Barlow adjusted the nasal cannula delivering oxygen to him. He stared at Grundy. "Let's hear it, Frank. You look worse than I feel."

"I'm trying to look sympathetic, but I can only manage pathetic."

"Leave pathetic to me. What's happened?"

Grundy hesitated. "Have the doctors—"

"So help me, Frank, if you don't start talking, I'm going to have my wife come in here and slap you around."

"Yes, sir. Sorry, sir." He took a deep breath. "Syria has launched a missile attack on Israel." He repeated the report he had given Jeremy a short time before.

Barlow leaned his head back on the pillows and stared at the ceiling. "How?"

Radcliffe chose to answer. "We don't know, sir. It's possible that they had their missiles in a hardened silo or storage facility."

"They hit targets?"

"Yes, sir. Tel Aviv for one. Haifa for another."

"Haifa. We have a Navy presence there. Did we lose assets in the attack?"

Radcliffe nodded. "I have people looking into that, Mr. President."

The president moved his gaze from the ceiling to the men in his bedroom. "So their guidance system was working?"

Grundy and Radcliffe looked at Jeremy. "Yes, sir. I've not seen flight tracks. I understand that one of our subs was monitoring the area and caught the attack on radar. They might be able to tell us if the missiles auto corrected during flight. If so—"

"Then the Syrians have found a way to get their electronics to work. I was led to believe that part of the world was dark like everywhere else."

"Yes, sir," Jeremy said. "That was my understanding too."

Barlow thought for a moment. "Has Israel retaliated?"

"Not yet, sir," Radcliffe said. "They've had enough time to do so. We think their systems are still down."

"The Syrians' *should* still be down." Barlow grimaced but in a manner different than Jeremy had seen before. This time it was the news that gave him pain. "What I wouldn't give for a spy satellite." Then a thought hit him, and his face paled. "The missiles—tell me they were conventional and not nuclear."

"Syria doesn't have nuclear warheads, sir," Grundy said.

"Iran does. They bought some, and they've built a few with stolen uranium. Only a handful of people know that."

Jeremy hadn't been one of the handful. The news shocked him.

"They're taking advantage of Israel's weakness." Barlow pulled at his lower lip, thinking. "Admiral Radcliffe, what can we do to protect Israel?"

Radcliffe looked at the floor. "Not much, sir. Our sub has

a limited supply of Tomahawks onboard. We could rain down some pain on Syria, and I think we should before they get any more ideas."

"I disagree with the admiral." Grundy took one step closer to the bed. "Our workable munitions are in short supply. Launching an attack from the sub would make it a target. As it is, she's spending more time near the surface than we like so we can monitor the area, and that's pretty limited. We're great with electronic surveillance, but there are very few electronics to surveil."

"Apparently the Syrians have more than we assumed."

"Yes, sir, but even that isn't certain. A missile is primarily a mechanical device. It can fly without guidance. Maybe they got lucky."

"Not likely," Radcliffe said. "They hit key cities. Sure, a few hit smaller towns. At least that's what the people on the ground are telling us. As you can imagine, news from the ground is slow. A spare radio from the sub was transferred to one of our ships in the Haifa port. There's been no word."

"We have to assume that one or more of our ships have been struck. That makes this an attack on the United States."

"What is our field readiness, Admiral?" Barlow looked at Radcliffe.

"There or in general, sir?"

"There."

"Not good. We have some communication through rebuilt radios, but that is limited. Moving troops is still slow. We have some transportation up and running, but we don't have enough to move a large number of soldiers. We have very few working naval vessels. The same can be said for the enemy."

"Except that some apparently can fire missiles. What else can they do?"

"I have no answers to that question, sir. Not yet." Radcliffe gave no indication of what Jeremy assumed was churning beneath his skin.

"What a way to run a country." Barlow frowned. "Burrowed underground, limited intel, hamstrung by distance, and over-whelmed with the suffering of our citizens." He thought for a moment. "Keep me appraised. I want info as soon as you get it. No sitting around assessing whether it's worth my time. It is, no matter how small. Understood?"

"Yes, sir." Radcliffe straightened. "What shall I tell our sub?"

"Tell them to sit tight. They are free to defend themselves."

"What about Israel, sir?"

Barlow's tone softened. "She's on her own. God forgive me, but she's on her own. We can't help her. Lobbing cruise missiles at Syria might come back to haunt us. For now we wait. Dismissed."

"Sir—" Radcliffe began.

"I said, dismissed."

"Yes, sir."

Jeremy turned to walk from the room.

"Not you, Jeremy. I need a word."

■■■■

Jeremy caught Radcliffe and Grundy glancing at him through the corner of their eyes.

Barlow motioned to a side chair on the other side of the room. "Pull up a seat, General."

"Yes, sir." He pulled the chair to the side of the bed.

"My wife tells me you were a great comfort to her and the kids." He smiled. "Kids…they haven't been kids for a long time. Old habit I guess. Nothing makes a father more proud than seeing his children become adults. Nothing makes a man sadder."

"I didn't do much, sir. Just sat with them."

"Katey tells me you told them what happened and then prayed for me at her request."

"That's true, sir. I was happy to do so. I'm still praying for you."

"That's good to hear. I could use some help from the Almighty. I guess God helps those who help themselves. Isn't that what the Bible says?"

"No, sir. That's from an old Greek proverb. I think Ben Franklin used it in *Poor Richard's Almanac*. It's not in the Bible. The sentiment is accurate, though."

Barlow chuckled. It sounded like a cough. "Great. Heart attack, missiles hitting Israel, and now I display my biblical ignorance."

"Many people make that mistake."

Barlow settled his gaze on Jeremy. Jeremy saw a sadness in the man's eyes. "How long have you been a Christian, Jeremy?"

"I became serious about faith in college, but it began before that."

"How serious?"

"It's very important to me, sir. It's the center of my being."

"Your wife. She a believer too?"

Jeremy developed a pain in his heart. "No, sir. She's not."

"Really, I thought…Never mind. Her science get in the way?"

Jeremy shook his head. "I don't think that's it, Mr. President. She's a very independent woman. Very focused. It makes her a great surgeon. Don't get me wrong. I love her with every fiber of my being. I'm less a man without her."

"Still, it has to hurt."

"Yes, sir, it does. A lot."

Barlow shifted in the bed and let out a little groan as he did. He quickly waved Jeremy off. "My back is stiff. Don't grow older, Jeremy. It's not for sissies."

"I'll try not to, sir."

"I asked you to stay for two reasons. First, thank you for all you've done. I'm glad you were there when I keeled over. Not a time to be alone if you catch my drift. Second, I have a question for you, but I'm not sure how to ask."

"Just say it, sir."

"Are you one of those Christians who take the Bible literally?"

"Yes, sir, but I need to explain that."

"I'm not going anywhere."

Jeremy tried to order his thoughts. "That word *literal* gets a bad rap. I believe the Bible says what God intends it to say. I also believe God inspired it. *Inspired* is another word that needs explanation. It comes from a Greek word meaning 'God breathed.' That is, content from the Bible originates with God, who then used humans to write what He wanted recorded. That content includes history, poetry, sermons, and a lot more. It uses metaphor and even a little bit of fiction."

"Fiction? You're kidding."

"I should say, instructive fiction. Jesus told parables. A parable is a tiny story that conveys a spiritual truth. It is an ancient teaching tool. So when we say the Bible is meant to be taken literally, we mean we interpret it the way it was intended. For example, there's a verse in the psalms that reads, 'He will cover you with his feathers, and under his wings you will find refuge.' The author is using descriptive language. He's not saying God is covered in feathers. When I read a verse like that, I recognize the writer is using poetic devices. Still, I can take the truth literally. God is the One we turn to in times of stress."

"So it's all subject to interpretation?"

"Some things are, sir, but most of the Bible is very straightforward. When it tells us there was a man named Moses, I believe there was a man named Moses."

"And the miracles?"

"I believe those are historical events, sir."

"Good. We could use a few miracles these days. As I mentioned before I took a header, I haven't been a spiritual man, and what I don't know surpasses what I do know, but I understand enough about the Bible to know some think it predicts the future. Do you believe that?"

"Yes, sir…well, let me back up. The Bible doesn't predict the future. The future is known to God, and He has revealed it to us."

"I don't follow."

"I'm not explaining it well. Let me say it this way: The prophecies in the Bible tell us what is going to take place because God has decided to do those things. In a sense, we're reading history that has yet to happen. All unfulfilled prophecy has to do with Christ's second coming and the events leading up to it and following it."

"And you believe all this? You believe that what was written in the first century applies to the twenty-first?"

"I do, sir. Some of the prophecies are in the Old Testament, so they're older than two thousand years."

"Maybe I'm too pragmatic, Jeremy. Some would consider you superstitious or delusional."

"Do I seem that way to you, sir?"

Barlow pursed his lips. "No. You seem like a pretty sharp guy."

"Thank you, sir."

"Still, today's intellectuals might think otherwise. Faith is for the ignorant. Their words, not mine."

"Sir, I…" Jeremy decided to leave the sentence unfinished.

"Carry on, General."

"I'd rather not, sir. I fear I'll be misunderstood. I'm not as arrogant as I was about to sound."

Barlow narrowed his eyes. "How about if I make it an order."

"Yes, sir. I was going to say…man, this sounds bad…I have an IQ of 145, graduated from the Air Force Academy at the top of my class, and earned two graduate degrees, including a PhD in computer science. I am many things, sir, but stupid isn't one of them."

Barlow laughed. "That's how I like to hear a man talk. Okay, *Dr.* Matisse, tell me this. Do you think all that has happened is part of your Bible?"

The words in Jeremy's head began to zip around like hummingbirds in a hurricane. Images came to his mind: the bloodred moon, fragments of destroyed satellites falling to earth like stars… "Immediately after the distress of those days the sun will be darkened, and the moon will not give its light; the stars will fall from the sky, and the heavenly bodies will be shaken."

"A Bible verse?"

"Yes, sir. Matthew 24:29. I'm also thinking about one of the Old Testament verses I mentioned: Joel 2:30-31. 'I will show wonders in the heavens and on the earth, blood and fire and billows of smoke. The sun will be turned into darkness and the moon to blood before the coming of the great and dreadful day of the Lord.'"

"You have it memorized?"

Jeremy nodded. "I've been reading it a lot lately."

"So it seems. Well, red moon and falling stars I get, but the sun is still shining. Can I expect that to blink out soon?"

"I don't know, sir. Other people know a lot more than I do about these issues. I'm not a prophecy expert. I'm just a run-of-the-mill Christian."

"With an IQ of 145 and a couple graduate degrees."

He felt his face warm. "I wish you hadn't made me reveal that. Now my humble image is tarnished."

Barlow grinned. "Your secret is safe with me, General. One last question. Okay, two. First, does your Bible say what role America plays in all this?"

Jeremy's heart sank. "No."

"It doesn't? The most powerful country in the world, and we have no role to play in these events?"

Jeremy leaned forward to rest his elbows on his knees. "Sir... according to some scholars, America is powerless in the last days. If not powerless, then otherwise busy."

"We're not a player?"

"Again, this isn't my field—"

"Stop hedging your comments, Jeremy. I need the straight skinny."

"The Bible lists several countries involved in the last days. It uses different names, but most scholars recognize Russia, China, and a European conglomerate."

"The European Union? Are you serious?"

"The conservative scholars think the symbolism in the book of Revelation refers to what we call the European Union. Ten leaders from Europe."

"There are more than ten members states of the EU."

It took a moment for Jeremy to conjure up the courage to speak the next words. "There *were*, sir. I might be all wet here, but it wouldn't surprise me if ten nations took leadership for the continent."

"They couldn't keep that up for long."

"That's the point, sir. If this is the end times, they don't have to. They don't have much time."

"We haven't had contact with the EU, but we do have cable to England. I wonder if they've heard anything."

Barlow fell silent and closed his eyes. Jeremy watched the man's chest rise and fall. Certain the president was still breathing, Jeremy rose, returned the chair to where he found it, and started for the door.

"Jeremy?"

He turned. "Yes, sir."

"Earlier I gave you an order. I give it again. Go get your wife."

"Yes, sir."

"And General…thanks."

30

Lunch

Jeremy had been "housebound" for more than two months. General Holt had left the Mount Weather facility to oversee the USCYBERCOM reconstruction. Jeremy had wanted to go with him, but in the early weeks, his team had arrived and moved into the underground complex to determine the origin and distribution of the Moriarty worm. Uprooting everything again was considered counterproductive.

Much of Jeremy's work had been limited by communication problems. Bit by bit, SIPRNet, or Slipper, was replacing the temporary EMN. The military equivalent of the Internet eventually connected every key military base, the Department of Defense, and scores of other high-priority locations. Many of the server locations were hardened and were largely unharmed. Power had been the key problem. Still, the power surges and EM pulses had crippled the system for weeks. Getting the computers online and chatting again had been a priority and had consumed much of Jeremy's and his team's time. Tracing the flow of the digital collapse was impossible without some of those systems online or the ability to speak to those who had been tracing the activity before the pulses knocked the world back a century or two.

Communication remained a problem. The military, government, and general population had become packet dependent—addicted to immediate communication. Why shouldn't they be? What happened was thought to be impossible. The military had long known that airburst nuclear warheads could be used to knock out power and communications, but it could only be done in limited areas. An enemy or terrorist might be able to knock New York off-line, but not the whole country. Scores of space-borne EMP weapons going off almost simultaneously was beyond the thinking of even the most paranoid. Jeremy realized that one could not be too paranoid in the twenty-first century.

Power to civilian areas was slim. A few older hydroelectric plants could be run with some efficiency without the benefit of computers. It had been done a century before; it could be done again. Unfortunately, there weren't enough of those to make much of a difference.

The president and FEMA had done herculean work getting gas and diesel to key facilities like military, fire, police, hospitals, and industrial plants. The latter were brought online based on their ability to help solve the crisis. New computer chips were manufactured as quickly as possible. Most of that work had previously been done by computer-controlled robots, so new approaches had to be created.

Progress was slow, but it was progress.

The president had also directed the Strategic Petroleum Reserve to allocate some of its 780 million barrels to relief and military efforts. The reserve held enough oil to meet the needs of the country for 30 days at previous usage. Of course, that assumed the delivery system of pipelines, trucks, and trains were operating. They weren't. Not at first.

Slowly, trucks were rewired. Old trucks, which had no need for computer chips in their engines, were the first to hit the roads again. Oil was sent to areas of the country facing the most severe weather. The president had placed the country under martial law, granting him the freedom to remove freedom. Oil stored in privately held energy companies was seized and pressed into use. Semitrucks owned by individuals were commandeered. Posse Comitatus laws were brought to bear, and where they did not provide enough legal power to the military and FEMA, the new congress passed additional laws from deep within Mount Weather. Senator O'Tool had quit being a mouthy pain in the fanny and had become an able leader. He had taken a while to learn that he wasn't the center of the universe.

Roads had been cleared, sometimes by soldiers and locals pushing cars to the side. As road-grading equipment was jury-rigged to run again, cars were pushed aside with no thought to damage. All that mattered was making roads passable again.

Also among the first to get help were farms, dairies, orchards, and food processors. When possible, local police, sheriffs, and the National Guard were used to guard food supplies. Locals pitched in to help gather winter crops by hand. They were guaranteed a share of the food.

News of these operations reached Mount Weather in various ways. Some came through local military bases; some came by messenger.

Rural areas fared better than others. Hunting, fishing, and farming were second nature to these people. Like the survivalists hidden in the woods and backcountry, rural folks could last much longer without outside help.

Those in the cities…Jeremy didn't like to think about it.

. . . .

"How long do you think this will last, sir?"

Jeremy sat in the passenger seat of a Humvee, one of the few that had been successfully rewired. The soldier asking the question looked too young to shave and glanced at him through red, runny eyes.

"How long have you been making this run, Corporal?"

"I don't know, sir. It's all kinda run together. Seems like a couple years." He steered around the carcass of a bus that had been pushed to the barricade that kept northbound traffic away from southbound on the Baltimore-Washington Parkway. He tagged the sentence with, "Not that I'm complaining, sir. I mean…"

"No need to explain. I've done my share of complaining."

"Yes, sir. I mean…"

"Relax. I'm not going to bite you. Your service is appreciated. Got family?"

"Yes, sir. Mississippi."

"Have you heard from them?" Another military vehicle honked its horn as it traveled north to Maryland.

"No, sir."

"At least it's a warm state."

"Yes, sir."

Jeremy hadn't answered the young soldier's question. He didn't have an answer and said so. "I wish I could tell you more."

"Understood, sir. I know everyone is doing what they can." He kept his eyes forward. "Will the general be staying long?"

"No. The president is a tough boss. He wants me back ASAP."

"Yes, sir. How is he? The president, I mean."

His hesitation lasted only a moment. The president's health

was a state secret. "He's still giving orders." Jeremy smiled, making light of his comment.

"I heard—"

"Don't finish that, Corporal. You're likely to hear a lot of things, much of it false."

"Yes, sir. Understood."

Downtown DC looked like London during World War II—burned cars and buildings, trash piled in the streets, buildings with broken windows, and the smell of sewers. People wandered the freeway, looking in cars. Jeremy couldn't imagine what they searched for. Any food would have spoiled long ago.

"They're looking for things like candy bars." The corporal seemed to be a mind reader. "Sometimes they find something useful like lighters or even weapons. Kinda looks like a zombie movie, doesn't it?"

"Do you get used to seeing this?" Jeremy felt ill.

"No, sir. Whenever I see it here, I go back to the barracks and dream about it."

Jeremy had many times read Bible passages about the end times. God's wrath falling on humanity. Was that what he was seeing now? The president had asked him if they were in the last days. He said no, but he believed they were on the threshold. This was not what pastors and scholars called the tribulation—seven years of ever-increasing trouble for humanity. His study had led him to believe that the church, or Christians around the world, would be taken from the world before God poured out judgment. He was still here, so he had to assume the tribulation had not started.

Of course, there were good people who believed the church would go through some or all of the tribulation. For the first time in his life, he hoped they were correct. Not because he wanted to see events unfold but because he didn't want Roni to have to go through the pending ordeal alone.

He thought of the letter he had sent. Had it achieved anything?

"Pull over."

"Excuse me, sir?"

"I said pull over. There." He pointed to a woman with two children. Their faces were dirty.

"It's not safe—"

"Do it."

The corporal did as ordered, but Jeremy could see he didn't like it. The man's eyes scanned the area as if expecting wolves to come out of the abandoned cars lining the side of the parkway.

The woman backed away.

"We're not going to hurt you." Jeremy slipped from the Humvee.

The woman looked too old to be mother to the children. Her face was drawn and pale; her eyes looked as if they had gone from blue to gray, life having stolen what had once sparkled there.

As Jeremy opened his door, the woman pulled the children away. She didn't run. Instead, she kept her eyes on Jeremy, like a stray dog uncertain whether to fight or flee. She pushed the children behind her, imposing her body between them and Jeremy.

"Wait. I'm not here to hurt you." Jeremy's words were firm yet gentle.

The woman took another step back. Her face was worn and revealed her age. She was the children's grandmother, not their mother.

"I have something for you. Just stay there. "He opened the rear door and reached in. In the back was a field pack. He opened it and removed several packages of crackers and processed meat. He held them out for the woman to see. "This is for you."

The woman stopped her retreat. Jeremy looked at the food and the rest of his lunch. Not knowing what they would find on the trip, he had packed more than needed. The woman's eyes widened.

"My name is Jeremy. This is for you and the children." He put the food back in the rucksack and held it out. The woman kept her distance. Jeremy guessed the little girl was no older than five, although it was hard to tell through the dirty coat and hood she wore. The other child, a boy, looked to be a year older. Both peeked around the legs of the woman.

"It's food. There's bottled water too." Jeremy took two steps from the vehicle, set the sack on the ground, and backed away.

The woman eyed the bag, and then her already wide eyes widened further. A moment before, he had seen hunger in her orbs; now he saw fear. She looked to his right. He traced her gaze but had only turned his head a few inches when something hard and cold stopped him. Through the corner of his eye he saw a bearded man with a shotgun. The barrel was pressed into Jeremy's ear.

"What else you got, soldier boy?" The voice was gruff and angry and stunk of rotting gums.

"Put the gun down, pal. You don't want to do this."

"Don't I? Really? That's what you got for me? I don't want to do this?" The gunman leaned more of his weight into the gun, pushing Jeremy's head to the side. "You guys have been useless. I used to look up to men in uniform. That was before they brought the world to an end."

"We didn't cause this."

"Yeah? Well, I think you did."

Jeremy tried to figure his next move. He wore a sidearm—an M9A1 nine millimeter—but it was holstered to his hip, and any motion for it might cause the gunman to detach Jeremy's head from his shoulders.

"Look, pal. I was just trying to give the woman and kids a little something to eat."

"I had kids. I had a wife. They knew hunger too. Where were you then?"

"I'm sorry for your loss, but—"

"Shut up. I'm hungry too."

"Good." A familiar voice. The corporal. The pressure of the barrel against Jeremy's head lessened. "You hungry, pal? I got a copper-jacketed nine millimeter slug you can chew on. Of course, that might be hard to do once I shoot your face off."

"Jus'…jus' take it easy, sir." The man lowered the shotgun. "I didn't mean nothing by it."

"If you wouldn't mind, General."

Jeremy got the message and took the shotgun. He emptied it of its cartridges and pocketed them. Fury, hot and impulsive, flooded Jeremy, who took the weapon, raised it over his head and brought it down like a club on the road. He repeated the action until the stock broke away and the barrel bent. He tossed it to the side. He then turned to the man. "Hands on the car."

"Look. I'm sorry. I'm just hungry—"

Jeremy grabbed the man's coat and turned him toward the Humvee. A quick search revealed a .38 police special. It looked old and worn. "I think I'll keep this."

"So now you're gonna steal from me."

"I think it's better for all concerned." Jeremy saw the woman and her children were still nearby. Good. "You got him?"

"He won't try anything, sir. I'm not that lucky."

Jeremy stepped to the rucksack, picked it up and walked to the woman. This time, she held her ground. "Please take this. It isn't much, but it might help some." He reached in the bag and removed a sandwich sealed in thick plastic. The woman took the sack.

"Thank you."

"I hope it helps." He squatted to be eye-to-eye with the

children. They looked like waifs plucked from a Dickens tale. He felt tears rise. "You guys stay strong. Things are getting better." He wondered if he had just lied.

Jeremy marched back to the assailant and shoved the sandwich in the man's chest. "Don't choke on it."

The woman and children were moving from the parkway and into a copse of trees. Once out of sight, Jeremy said, "Let him go, Corporal."

"Yes, sir." The soldier stared at the gunman for a few long moments. "Leave. In fact, you should run."

The man did.

Back in the Humvee, the corporal asked. "You okay?"

"Yes. Thanks. I seem to owe you my life."

The corporal laughed. "You owe me more than that. You gave away my lunch too, sir."

●●●●

The streets leading to Roni's hospital reminded Jeremy of several depressing movies he had seen. Real life was worse than imagination. The main building of Harris Memorial looked in good shape, unlike the office buildings and restaurants just a block away.

Two military vehicles stood at the front of the building. Several National Guard soldiers patrolled the parking lot and walkways around the structure. They came to attention the moment Jeremy exited the vehicle. He returned their salutes. "Carry on." It took all his willpower not to sprint through the doors and start calling Roni's name. It wouldn't be seemly for a general to do, not that he much cared about that.

The lobby furnishings had been rearranged. Chairs were lined up like those in a theater or a church. As he walked through the lobby, he noticed that many of the chairs sat askew. Then he noticed a dark stain on the floor. His heart tripped. He moved down the main hall toward the ER in back. He knew one of the doctors' lounges was there. He'd start with the ER, move to the lounge, jog up the stairs to Roni's office, and if need be, camp out in the surgical wing.

He got lucky. Roni walked down one of the halls and through the intersection of the corridors. A blond boy was with her. He was eating what Jeremy assumed was canned tangerines. She glanced his way and continued on. He started to call out when she returned to the corridor intersection. She stared and stood motionless as if the sight of him had petrified her.

She was thinner.

He took another stride toward her.

Her hair was shiny with oil and in need of a good shampoo.

Another stride.

There were bags under her eyes, and her shoulders slumped as if she had been carrying bags of concrete for the last two months.

Two more steps.

Her skin was pale and her cheeks sunken.

She looked beautiful.

"Hey, good looking, come here often?"

Her lip quivered. "Hey, sailor."

"Sailor? No need to be insulting."

She took one step his direction and then ran into his arms. He held her tight, unable to believe she was in his embrace again.

They both wept.

In a crazy world, in a dark city, in a violent environment, Jeremy felt better than he had in his life.

••••

Then a small voice. A boy's voice. A voice with a sob in it. A voice Roni had come to know so well.

"Are you going to take Roni away from me?"

The last thing Roni wanted to do was pull away from her husband. She would be happy to die right on the spot, right at that moment. Still she released Jeremy.

"And who is this young man?" Jeremy dropped to a knee.

"This is Cody," Roni said. "Cody, this is my husband, Colonel—General Matisse."

"Just Jeremy to you, Cody." Jeremy held out a hand. "It is a pleasure to meet you." Cody shook hands but his face showed his fear. "I hear you've been taking care of my wife. Thank you."

"You're going to take her away, aren't you? Everybody leaves me."

Roni looked into Jeremy's eyes, and then he turned back to Cody. "I've come to take both of you away. That is, if you'll come with us."

"I can go?" He brightened.

"Roni sent a letter to me. Just between you and me, pal, I think you might be stuck with her. Or I suppose you and I could take off and leave her behind."

"Fat chance of that," Roni snapped. She missed sparring with her husband.

Jeremy rose and put his arm around Roni. "No objections, Dr. Matisse. I have a plan and a presidential order. Let's find the hospital administrator, and then we have some catching up to do.

He took her hand. It was as if she had been reborn.

■ ■ ■ ■

"The plan is simple, Dr. Pickett. We have more vehicles operating now. The military and emergency vehicles get priority on parts. Our mechanics are creating new ways to get vehicles rolling again. It's a slow process, but we're making progress." Jeremy sat at a cafeteria table. Cody wanted to sit next to him. It reminded Roni of the boy's need for a father figure.

"Wait," Roni said. "I can't leave the hospital in the lurch—"

Pickett raised a hand. "You can and you will, Dr. Matisse. No one has given more than you. You've saved countless lives, but things are better now. Not good, I know, but what the general suggests will work. If the military can transport doctors to and from the hospital, we can run shifts."

"That's the idea." Jeremy took Roni's hand. "I can arrange for trips back here. Where we're going is some distance but still workable."

"I don't know…" Roni said.

Pickett sided with Jeremy, something Jeremy appreciated and needed. It was going to take two men to move one woman. "Dr. Matisse…Roni…listen to me, and listen closely. This isn't just about you. It's not just about the hospital or patients." He looked at Cody. "This is no place for Cody. True, he's safer here than out there, but it sounds like you'll be going to a safer place. I don't have to remind you what happened—"

"No, you don't." She cut her eyes to Jeremy.

His eyes narrowed. "What happened?"

"I'll tell you later."

He raised an eyebrow. "You can count on that."

"I can make this work," Pickett said. "I just got word that the government has helped get another hospital back online. Roni, don't make me take away your surgery privileges. Just go. I'll work out a schedule so you can cover a few days a week. That will give the other surgeons time off."

"But—"

"Good. It's decided." Pickett stood. "I checked the schedule. You have no surgeries. Anything that comes through ER we can handle. Now get out of here." He walked away.

Jeremy was impressed. "The man knows his mind."

"You really have a presidential order for this?"

"Yes, and he's not the kind of guy one argues with." Jeremy mussed Cody's hair. "Come on, Champ. You're not going to believe where I'm taking you."

■■■■

When President Barlow opened his eyes, he saw the frowning face of Franklin Grundy. "I'm glad I don't have to see that face every time I wake up."

"Sorry to disturb you, Mr. President. I know the doctor gave you orders to rest."

"And I gave orders to be kept in the loop." He pushed up in the bed. Katey stood at the bedroom door, her hand raised to her lips.

"Israel retaliated. Four submarine-launched cruise missiles. All targets were in Syria. We think they used Gabriel 4LRs. They wouldn't even have to surface."

"We guessed they would respond with SLCMs. Damages?"

"Unknown. Without our spy birds and contact with operatives in country, we can do little more than make estimates from trajectory. All sites were military."

"Which is a shade kinder than Syria was with them."

"Yes, sir. If I were Syria, I wouldn't depend on such restraint."

Barlow reached for a glass of water next to his bed. Grundy handed it to him. He drank half the contents and handed it back. "I suppose we should be thankful the power outage has made war a little more difficult."

"That leads me to the bad news, sir."

"I thought the missile attack was bad enough."

"Yes, sir. Of course." He paused. "Cities in Syria are coming back online. Somehow they have power again."

"How?"

"No one knows, sir."

"Israel?"

"Dark as before."

"Not good. Not good." Barlow rubbed the center of his chest.

ACT 4
Eight Months

31

Meetings

General Holt stepped into Jeremy's office. He had aged several years in the last eight months. Still robust. Still strong. Still in possession of a steel-trap mind, but the strain had taken a toll. He spent much of his time at Fort Meade helping rebuild Slipper—the secret Internet protocol router network for the military. Jeremy was confined to overseeing the security of Mount Weather's computer systems and tracking down the Moriarty worm. With more and more military bases and radar instillations online and other communications following, he had been able to make some headway but not nearly enough. He could demonstrate that the malignant, self-writing program had started on the West Coast, probably Southern California.

"I have a message for you, Jeremy."

"Since when did you become a messenger boy?"

Holt took a chair near one of the several computers in Jeremy's workstation. "I'm doing a lot of work I never imagined I'd be doing."

"I hear that. How are things at USCYBERCOM?"

"Moving along. Most of our systems have been rebuilt and

some of our specialty software reconstructed. To tell the truth, I thought we were better protected than we were. We took a much bigger hit. If someone had asked me if all this could happen, I would have wagered my stars that it couldn't, and you know how much I love my stars."

"I do know that. I've grown fond of my one star."

"You wear it well." He leaned back. "Know anyone in San Diego?"

"Not really. Been there a few times. I know a great pizza place."

"Good, because I'm going to ask the president to send you on a little trip if he can spare an aircraft."

Jeremy understood the comment. Some aircraft were operating—mostly those kept in hardened centers in Nebraska, California, and Alaska—but getting other craft off the ground was proving difficult and time consuming. A little rewiring could get a bi-plane airborne, but most modern aircraft were fly-by-wire. The controls were operated with computer assistance. In the first few weeks, a few aircraft had been pulled from museums. Jeremy knew several World War II fighter planes, like the Corsair 4AU, had been used to patrol the skies. Even getting those in the air required herculean efforts, and pilots often flew without full instrumentation.

"What's in San Diego?"

"North Island Naval Air Station for one. You got an e-mail through Slipper. Someone hacked the system to send you a love note—of sorts."

"Someone hacked the system? Again?"

Holt nodded. "Kinda embarrassing, isn't it?"

"I need the parameters of the hack—"

Holt waved him off. "We're working on that. Right now, I'm concerned why someone singled you out for this message. Any ideas?"

"Sir, I don't even know what the message is."

"It's short, Jeremy. Just one word: *Oatmeal*."

. . . .

Liam Burr looked out the window of his Brussels office and saw lights. Street lights. Office lights. Traffic lights. Headlights and taillights of cars that could not run a few months ago. People strolled the streets again. Repairs were made to damaged buildings. The city looked as it did this time last year—except for the hovering shadow figures drifting on the night currents.

"Warms the heart, doesn't it, Mr. Burr?"

Liam turned to see Fred Pierce. He hated the man. He also feared him. During his university days, Liam learned to play poker from an exchange student. He also learned some of the terminology. Pierce was a man with an ace up his sleeve. He said the right things, kowtowed at the appropriate times, and made suggestions that were too much like orders.

"It does. I don't understand it."

"Neither do I. Well, not completely. I'm sure our friends had something to do with it." He stepped to Liam's side and joined him in his city gazing. "At least the citizens are not asking questions."

"They should. I would."

"Yes, sir, but you are several levels smarter than they are. Most people in the world will not question a benefit. They just take it and believe it's all free."

Liam studied the man next to him. "And you, Pierce? Are you smarter than they?" He nodded at the scene out his window.

"I like to think so. I'm pretty sure it's one reason I'm here and not out there." He turned and took a seat on the sofa in the sitting area. "I've spent a lot of years convincing people they need something one of my clients has: shampoo, sport shoes, weight-loss drinks, and clothing. When I became a political consultant, I found the work to be the same. I sell my service to the politician, and then I sell his or her ideas to the voters. People respond the same." He chuckled. "You know, I used to believe the old maxim, 'You are the message.' Ever heard that?"

"I have. You don't believe it?"

"To an extent, but it's largely false. The message is the message. The person is just baggage. Take someone running for president. If he wears a nice suit and doesn't vomit on himself while on camera, people will listen to him. If he has money to run a decent campaign, he stands a chance of getting elected. It's not just American politics. Let's face it, people don't vote for the most qualified, they vote for the least offensive. I can give you a list of politicians who are not smart enough to find their way out of a revolving door."

"No need." Liam put his hands behind his back and turned to Pierce. "So now you're saying I'm stupid?"

Pierce grinned. "No, sir. You're the exception that proves the fact. In fact, I believe you are the smartest man I've ever met."

"Even smarter than you?"

"By far, Mr. Burr, by far. I'm not brilliant; I'm skilled. There's a difference. Also, I sacrificed my conscience on the altar of income. Forgive me, but so have you—no, wait. That isn't quite right. You already had more money than a man can spend. You sacrificed your soul on the altar of power."

A caldron of fury boiled in Liam's gut. "You may wish to watch yourself, Signore Pierce."

"Sometimes honesty is offensive, Mr. Burr. I am what I am because I am brutally honest with myself. I manipulate everyone but myself. It is how I survive. And just to be clear, I fear only two things: failure and that thing in the black hat and coat. He really scares me." A second later. "He scares you too, but that's not why you do what you do."

"Is that so?"

"It is. You know he can bring you more power than you ever imagined. You will become the most powerful man in the world, and I will be the one trumpeting your arrival. I can't do what you do. It's not in me. I don't have the smarts. But you can't do what I do. You don't have the skill. Together, we will change the world, and maybe Shade will let us survive. Maybe."

Liam wearied of the conversation. He didn't want to argue. He knew he would lose. "Are they ready?"

Pierce stood. "Yes, sir. The other nine members of the New European Union are waiting for you."

．．．．

The conference room was well lit and warm. Tablet computers rested in front of the EU members. Unlike most of the rest of the world, Belgium, Italy, Central Asia, Germany, the Netherlands, Turkey, Denmark, Russia, Iran, and Luxembourg were back in the twenty-first century. Half of the members were not part of the old EU. The addition of Iran, Central Asia, and Russia were inconceivable before the Event, but—at least in Liam's mind—the EU needed broader horizons. Some had taken to calling the group the Northern United Treaty Organization. The moniker had been first coined by Pierce. "Easier to sell, and it shows a change has been made," he had said. NUTO was the organizing and governing force for much of Europe and Asia. Every day their influence grew, partly because they were the first to be back online in communications, manufacturing, and food distribution. People thrived wherever NUTO sank its roots. No one knew how, but countries whose leader associated with the group came online faster than those who didn't. NUTO citizens found life returning to normal; non-NUTO countries continued to suffer from hunger, disease, and anarchy.

"In America, business leaders say people change when it hurts too much to stay the same." Pierce had sounded proud of the advice and stated it as a proverb proven by centuries of experience. "Do you know when most people quit smoking?" He had asked Liam in a private meeting. "When they're diagnosed with cancer. Fear of death is a powerful motivator."

Individually they were not the mightiest countries, but together they formed a formidable unit. Their mysteriously regained electrical, digital, and communications systems melded them into a unified global player. They could produce goods and food while other countries struggled to do so.

Liam walked into the room like a battleship pulling into port—powerful, unstoppable. He looked around the table at the six men, three women, and their aides.

Liam sat at the head of the table as newly elected president of the NUTO.

"I trust everyone is well," he said in English. He flashed his best winning smile and received polite smiles in return. "I wish to address the idea presented in my brief sent to you last week. Did everyone receive the document?"

Everyone in the group had.

"Very well, with your permission I will summarize, and then we can discuss." Liam didn't need their permission and didn't wait for it. "We are fortunate to be ahead of the rest of the world in our recovery. While most of the world still struggles to return to normal, we are largely there. Still, we have challenges. My country and yours have lost a great deal of data. Processing paperwork from several billion people is impossible. Anyone can claim to be anyone else. We can create New Euros for banks based on recovered records, but most of those records were erased by the aggressive acts of the US and Israel."

He let the last phrase hang in the air. Computer security experts from several countries had noticed bits of code similar enough to the Stuxnet attack of 2010 that took out so many Iranian centrifuges used to process uranium, code that qualified as a digital fingerprint despite denials by the US and Israel. No one on the continent believed them, certainly not Iran.

"The damage they caused will take years to clear up. Sadly, we cannot unwind the clock. We must deal with what is before us. We owe it to our citizens—to the world. A civilized world operates on information. Banks must be able to distinguish their customers from those claiming to be customers. What is to prevent an unscrupulous person from taking the identity of someone else? What would keep someone from claiming to be me or you? Nothing, my friends. Nothing. We must find a way to identify our citizens quickly and accurately."

"And you think this RFID chip will help us achieve all of that?" The Russian representative was a brutish man in appearance, a Neanderthal in a suit, but his mind was as sharp as any Liam had encountered.

"I do. Many people have photo IDs, but those are easy to fabricate. We're already receiving many reports of false identification cards and documents. Of course, that is secondary to the fact that bank records, health records, and just about everything else has been destroyed. Only paper remains. We need a system that will help government, business, banks, medical institutions, schools, and the like get back up to speed quickly. A simple implanting of a radio frequency identification chip under the skin of the hand will facilitate secure business and make certain everyone receives only their share. This way we have a unified set of records. Every purchase, doctor's visit, and government handout will be recorded on the chip, which can be read with a simple device and uploaded to our new servers."

"People might object," the Chinese representative said.

"Yes, some might. That is their choice. Soon, I believe, they will see that this is best for all of humankind. The needs are great. Even now, people are taking unfair advantage of food distribution, collecting multiple times from different distribution facilities and hoarding. This problem will be eased as more and more stores open with food for purchase. Paying with debit cards and checks is still not possible, and frankly, I don't think we should return to those days. The European Union brought a single currency to its member states. Now we have new members. Imagine the work involved in converting Russian or Chinese currency to the Euro or some other standard.

"Will some consider this an infringement of their right to privacy?" Liam continued. "Certainly, but all of us in this room know there is no innate right to privacy. This is for the greater good. He looked at the Chinese representative, a small man with a big ego. "How many people died from starvation in your country?"

He hesitated before saying, "We are still assessing the problem. In the outlying regions, many died because of the cold. Those in agricultural areas did better. The cities...half a billion maybe. India was worse."

"That is the problem. There are too many people. Governments and aid organizations must be able to work quickly. This is the best way."

"Manufacturing will take some time," said the Belgian. She was petite but known to have a bite.

"A good observation, but I have a surprise for you. There are hundreds of millions of chips just waiting to be used." Liam enjoyed their confused looks. "A company in North Korea already has a stockpile of the tiny chips. This is not a new idea. It has been talked about in many countries."

"They will make the chips available to us?" the Chinese rep asked.

"Yes, they will. They were starving even before things went dark. They are in a difficult way. We have what they need." A dark figure appeared at the back of the conference room. Liam stared for a moment. No one else saw Eli Shade.

Shade was smiling.

32

Donny

Jeremy had seen many aircraft in his career and flown on several, but this was his first time in the rear seat of a USAF F-15E. He had been told the fighter was one of several sequestered in underground hangers. The military couldn't house all aircraft in hardened, below-grade facilities, but they knew enough to keep some underground. This F-15 had been sheltered in Nebraska. Jeremy was thankful for forward-thinking paranoids.

He had traveled by car to Thurgood Marshall International Airport near Fort Meade, a civilian airport pressed into service. Not that commercial planes were flying these days. The trip across the country passed quickly once Jeremy adjusted to the small confines of the cockpit and the gut-turning takeoff. Thankfully, the pilot showed no desire to give Jeremy the ride of his life. Being a general had its perks.

There had been almost no conversation on the trip. The pilot, an Air Force captain, looked weary. Jeremy didn't need to ask. Men like him had been on constant duty since the Event. They had seen too much.

From the air, Coronado looked like a vacation spot. Jeremy was pretty sure the view from the ground was less spectacular. As the F-15 banked for approach, Jeremy saw a bay full of small boats. "What's with the boats, Captain?"

The answer came through Jeremy's helmet speakers. "Fishing, General. A lot of people along the coast have taken up fishing to eat. A few of the commercial fishing boats are operating, but most are still out of commission. Not enough parts to go around."

Jeremy had done his research on San Diego. In some ways, it had fared better than most megacities. The eighth-largest metropolis in the country, it was populated by people in every financial strata and from almost every country in the world. Its mild climate made it one of the most survivable cities. It had one other advantage: It was a military town, and bases were the first to receive power. The Navy operated several bases in the county. San Diego was Navy country.

But they also had their own set of challenges. Population for one and minimal agriculture near the city for another.

North Island Naval Air Base had been one of the busiest of the military installations and had made progress in getting planes into the air. Navy personnel moved around the buildings and aircraft. Most of the aircraft looked as if they hadn't been moved in nearly a year. They hadn't.

A sailor in a Humvee waited near the taxiway. The pilot rolled the aircraft from the runway to the tarmac and stopped near a fuel truck. It was good to see more vehicles in operation, disheartening to consider how many gathered dust. Mechanical and electrical supplies trickled in to most bases according to their perceived importance to national security, relief work, and proximity to the warehouses. Some factories were producing parts but at a limited rate. Those in the first areas to receive power had to rebuild much of their equipment, and ironically, they depended on other factories that made the parts.

The man by the Humvee came to attention as Jeremy approached, brought up a salute, and held it until Jeremy responded in like kind. "General, I'm Petty Officer First Class Irwin Dupont. I have been assigned to drive you to your location." Jeremy noticed the man had a sidearm strapped to his hip. He glanced around the field and saw every sailor was packing. He understood. He still wore one when he went into DC to see his wife.

Jeremy retrieved a piece of paper from the flight suit he had been required to wear. "Know how to find this place?"

The petty officer took the note, studied it, and then handed it back. "Yes, sir. High cotton."

The comment raised Jeremy's eyebrow.

"Sorry, sir. Something my mother used to say. It's in the high-rent district."

"I thought all of Coronado was…high cotton."

"Yes, sir, it's just that some areas are more high-rent than others. This is top-of-the-line digs, sir."

"Give me a minute to get out of this suit, and then we'll go see how the other half live."

Dupont gave a sad smile. "Lately, sir, the other half have been living like everyone else."

"Understood, Petty Officer. I haven't forgotten."

▪ ▪ ▪ ▪

"I bet they have quite a view." Jeremy craned his neck to see the upper floor of the tower. "Do you know which building they're in?"

"Yes, sir." He pointed at the ten-story structure. "Each building has its own address."

"Okay. I'll be back as soon as I can."

"Begging the general's pardon, but my orders are to escort you and provide protection."

"I'll be fine."

"Sir, please don't make me choose between an Air Force general and a Navy admiral."

Jeremy chuckled. "I think I know how that would turn out."

"Yes, sir. The admiral has two stars."

"Figures. Let's go."

Jeremy was surprised to see the power on in the building and said so.

"The whole city came online when the base did. That's true for areas around the other bases. The rest of San Diego is still hit and miss."

"So the elevator must be working. Good. I'd hate for you to have to carry me up ten flights of stairs."

"The general looks pretty fit. I doubt you'd need my help."

"Who said anything about needing help?" He pushed the elevator call button. As he waited, he could see damage done to the lobby and windows.

"Things got rough," Irwin said.

"You should see DC."

A few minutes later they exited the elevator and stood before the door to the condo from which the e-mail to Jeremy had originated. Irwin knocked. Hard.

"Who is it?" A male voice.

"Mr. Elton? My name is Jeremy Matisse. I'm with the Air Force."

"Air Force? How do you know my name?"

"Open the door, sir, and I'll be happy to explain."

There was a pause. "What is this about?"

Petty Officer Irwin raised his voice. "Please, sir. The general needs to speak with you."

"General? Okay, hang on."

Jeremy listened as Stanly Elton unlatched several locks. The door opened an inch. "Identification."

Jeremy pulled his military ID from his pocket. "I'm for real, Mr. Elton."

The man opened the door. "Come in." He sounded abashed. "Sorry. I'm afraid I've become overly cautious."

"Understandable." Jeremy stepped into the condo. It was neat and clean. For some reason, he expected to see a mess. "Are you Stanley Elton?"

"I am." He motioned to a place behind Jeremy. "This is my wife, Dr. Royce Elton." He nodded in the direction of a middle-aged Hispanic woman. "This is Rosa. She is a friend of ours." The woman looked frightened.

"Doctor?" he said to Royce.

The woman wore clothes designed for a slightly heavier woman. There were dark circles under her eyes. The woman gazed at the sidearms the men carried. She looked frightened too. "PhD. I'm a geneticist."

"Ah. I married a doctor. A surgeon." Jeremy smiled. He looked around the space. Well appointed, well furnished. A view of the bay out one window, a view of the ocean out the other. This was the domicile of the rich. Then he saw an empty electric wheelchair. His gaze lingered. Few things drew attention like an empty wheelchair.

"My son's," Elton said. "He's in his room."

A sense of relief ran through Jeremy.

Elton continued. "He doesn't need the wheelchair. In fact, he hasn't touched it in months." He paused. "It's a long story."

"Mr. Elton, do you have a computer on the premises?"

"Yes. Several of them. Actually, my son has them. I don't use computers at home. I get enough of that at work…*got* enough of that at work."

"May I ask what you do, sir?"

"I was an accountant. Not much need for that now. My wife teaches at UCSD. Not much use for that either." He glanced at his wife. "I suppose I should offer you a seat, but I'd like to know why you're here."

"We received an e-mail from this location. It was addressed to me."

"I don't see how that's possible, General. I haven't sent any e-mails. We've…the building has had power for only a few weeks, and we don't have access to the Internet. I guess the servers were wiped out or something."

Jeremy noticed the man's self-editing. "This didn't come over the Internet. It came over a secure military network. Most people don't know it exists."

"I don't know anything about it. How could I access a secret military network?"

"That's one of my questions. To send this message, someone had to hack into the system. Trust me, that's almost impossible."

"I can't help you, General. I can operate the basics of a computer, and I'm really good with accounting software, but that's it."

"Yet you have several computers in your home."

"True, but they're not for me. They belong to my son."

"Could he have sent the e-mail?"

Elton said no. "He's…he's special."

Jeremy cocked his head.

Elton broke eye contact. "Donny is not like other people. He's an adult, but he's more of a child. He barely speaks and seldom makes sense."

"That might explain it."

Elton looked at Jeremy again. "What's that mean?"

"The message had only one word: *Oatmeal*."

Dr. Royce Elton gasped.

. . . .

Roni Matisse finished her shift in the Mount Weather medical facility. Sitting on the sidelines while at Mount Weather was out of the question. Since college, her life had been spent on the edge. She seldom worked to exhaustion, but she always stayed busy. Even on her days off from the hospital she felt the need to do something constructive. After only a few days at the facility, she asked for medical privileges. The staff was glad to have her. She made frequent trips back to DC as promised but spent half her time in the underground facility. Although the facility had a fully functioning operating room, it was seldom used. Roni had assisted with two appendectomies and one gallbladder removal. There had been several injuries, mostly among FEMA workers on the surface. For the most part, medicine in the facility was undemanding.

Her work at Harris Memorial continued to be challenging. As more hospitals came online in DC, the flow of ER and surgical patients decreased. Medications were still in short supply and had to be used judiciously.

Adjusting to the small apartment and life under artificial light proved easier than Roni thought possible. Cody loved it. He played with the children of congressmen and senators, high-ranking military personnel, and rank-and-file soldiers. Only a child would find adventure in this, but if pressed, Roni would admit the experience was pretty cool. Still, she never forgot what was happening not far from the secret compound. People suffered. Things were better, but they were not good for those who still struggled to get by on too little food and very little technology. She wondered if things would ever return to the previous normal. She didn't like thinking about it.

As Roni walked from the hospital to their apartment, she caught sight of Senator Ryan O'Tool sprinting her way. His eyes settled on her, and he adjusted his course.

"Dr. Matisse, I need you. I mean, *we* need you."

"Settle down, Senator. What's the problem?"

"The president has collapsed."

Her spine fused and her knees went weak. "Where is he?"

"The sitting area outside his apartment. You know where that is, right?"

She did. Jeremy took great pride in introducing her to the president. They first met in the space O'Tool mentioned. Roni and O'Tool immediately started running back that direction as they talked. "Tell me what happened."

"We were discussing recent intel on the Israel-Syria problem. We were also wrestling with the new EU—"

"Cut to the chase, Senator. Tell me exactly what happened to the president."

"He was talking…he grimaced…he clutched at his chest, moaned, and fell from his chair. I think he hit his head too."

Roni stopped and faced O'Tool. "Here's what you're going to do, Senator. Get to the hospital and tell the first person you see…" No, that wouldn't do. Word would spread. "Ask for the shift doctor and tell him I sent you. Then you say this: 'President down. Possible heart. Crash cart. Stat.' Then tell them where to go. Got it?"

"Shift doctor. Down. Heart. Crash cart. Stat."

"Go. Go now."

One second later, Roni was on the run again. She prayed with each step, something she couldn't recall doing before.

■ ■ ■ ■

Donny sat in front of several computer monitors, his hands in his lap. He did nothing more than stare.

"This is Donny," Royce said. "Donny? There's someone here to meet you." He didn't respond.

Jeremy expected a young teenager but instead saw a thin twenty-something with uncombed hair. He sat like a statue, eyes fixed on scrolling code that meant nothing to anyone but him.

"He's off-planet." Royce looked embarrassed by her comment. "It's a phrase we use when Donny isn't responding. He seems to block out everything around him."

"Does he just stare at the monitors?"

"No, usually he's pounding on one of the keyboards." Stanley moved past Jeremy and stepped to his son's side. "Sometimes he types all night. Well, he used to. I mean, once we lost power…"

"Tell him, Stanley," Royce said. It wasn't a suggestion.

Stanley looked at Jeremy and Irwin. "You won't believe me."

"I've seen a great deal, Mr. Elton. I can pretty much believe anything."

Stanley looked at his son. "We didn't lose power when everyone else did. I mean, eight months ago. My office went dark. The whole city went dark. So did every condo in this complex. Every unit but ours."

"You need to explain that," Jeremy said.

"I wish I could, but I can't. We kept it secret of course. You can imagine the danger we faced if everyone on Coronado learned we had power when they didn't. That kept us going for a long time, but then a while back, it just quit. It came back on when everyone else's in Coronado did. I understand we have the Navy to thank for that."

"There are countless people to thank, including those who got the portion of the grid that feeds this area up and running." Jeremy moved closer to the monitors. "Are you telling me he wrote this code?"

"He's a savant," Royce said. "He's incapable of caring for himself. His communication is limited to a few words, and *oatmeal* is his favorite. He uses it for everything. Like other savants, he's extremely gifted in one area but incapable of dealing with normal activities."

"Oatmeal," Donny said, parroting the word.

"Does he know what he's doing?"

Royce shrugged. "That's hard to say. Some savants do what they do without thought. It's instinct to them. Donny is only happy in front of a computer." A moment later, "He gave it up for a while. After everything went south. Covered up the monitors with blankets and sheets. A day or two ago, he picked it up again."

"Except he never did surf the Net. He writes this gibberish." Stanley ran his hand over Donny's head.

"I don't think it's gibberish, Mr. Elton." Jeremy's stomach flipped. He turned to Donny. "Hi. Donny. My name is General Jeremy Matisse. I got your message."

Donny blinked, turned his attention to Jeremy, and began to weep. "Shadow, shadow on my right. Shadow, shadow on my left. Shadow, shadow everywhere. Shadow has all the might."

He sobbed.

•••••

Roni rounded the corner that led to the presidential wing and to the large meeting area outside his apartment. A security agent started to stop her when a voice bellowed through the area: "Let her in." The voice belonged to a man she had only met once since coming to Mount Weather, Vice President Franklin Grundy.

She sprinted around chairs and sofas. President Barlow lay on his back. A large contusion grew over his right eye. Roni dropped to her knees. "How long has he been out?"

Grundy answered. "Four minutes. I looked at my watch."

"Has he been unconscious the whole time?"

"Yes."

She searched for a pulse. "The head wound. From the fall?"

"Yes."

Roni looked up. Admiral Radcliffe and Secretary of State Baker stood next to Grundy. She returned her gaze to the man on the floor. His skin was pale and his eyes at half-mast. She found no pulse, and he wasn't breathing. "Who knows CPR?"

No one spoke, so Roni did. "Get down here, Admiral."

He didn't hesitate. "Tell me what to do."

Roni tilted the president's head back and pulled open his mouth. She ran a finger over his tongue, searching for vomitus. She leaned forward and placed her open mouth over his and forced three breaths down his trachea. His chest rose and fell. "I'm going to do compressions. Every time I say 'five,' you breathe for him. Don't be shy about it."

"Yes, ma'am."

Roni ripped open Barlow's shirt, not to make compressions easier but to save time when the crash cart arrived. She put one hand over the other, placed the heel of her hand on the president's sternum, arched forward and pushed. "One, two, three, four, five..." She paused a second to let Barlow's lungs fill and then started compressions again.

She was sweating by the time the medics arrived. She called for an airway, an Ambu bag, and the defibrillator.

The medical staff worked with practiced precision. Roni heard a gasp and then, "Oh, dear God, no." She didn't look. She didn't have time, but she had no doubt the president's wife had arrived.

They loaded Barlow on a gurney. Roni climbed on the wheeled stretcher, straddled the president's body, and continued CPR.

Twenty minutes later, in the medical complex, Roni declared the president dead with the full agreement of the head physician. Katey dissolved into tears. Her son and daughter had arrived. Their tears joined hers. The area where they had worked on the president was limited to only those working to save his life. Security took charge of the location. The family and advisors waited in a side room. Admiral Radcliffe took the news like a military man, with all his emotions locked down. He turned to Grundy. "Any orders, Mr. President?"

"Yes. Someone get me a chair."

33

Jeremy, Donny, and Shade

Jeremy held Donny for several moments, letting him weep on his shoulder. He wasn't sure what had triggered the sudden outburst, but it was heartfelt. The sobs came and went. Just when Jeremy thought Donny was regaining composure, he would descend into despair again.

"Is he normally like this?" Jeremy turned his head enough to see Royce. Tears wet her face.

"No. He didn't even cry as a baby."

"How does he know you, General?" Stanley kept his voice low.

"I have no idea. Nor can I imagine how he could hack the military network." He pushed Donny away so he could look in his eyes. "Hey, buddy. Feeling better?"

Donny didn't speak. His lip quivered and he looked as frightened as any man Jeremy had ever seen. "Does he understand me?"

"He understands a few things, but we're never quite sure what. He so seldom responds beyond a few words.

Jeremy put a hand on Donny's shoulder. "Hey, pal. How about it? Do you understand me."

No response.

"May I look at your computers?"

Donny shot to his feet and stepped to the side, making room for Jeremy to sit.

"Thank you." Jeremy took the seat. It felt warm.

Donny ran from the room. His mother followed. A moment later, Jeremy heard an electric whine. Stanley and Irwin stepped aside as Donny drove his electric wheelchair into the room. He maneuvered like a NASCAR driver and pulled next to Jeremy. His eyes were still red, but he now showed a new enthusiasm. "Oatmeal."

"Oatmeal indeed." Jeremy set his hand on the keyboard. It was sticky, and he might have pulled back if the streaming code hadn't pulled him in. "This may take a few minutes."

"Just a few, sir?" Irwin asked.

"Days." He looked at Donny. "I'm betting Donny here understands more than we give him credit for." Jeremy pushed the keyboard toward the savant.

Donny looked at it and then at Jeremy. He giggled.

Jeremy chuckled then said, "Stuxnet."

A few moments later, Donny had scrolled through the code and stopped. Jeremy recognized several lines. They were similar to the famous code but not identical. Material had been added.

"A question, sir," Irwin said.

"Let's hear it."

"Shouldn't these computers have been wiped clean like all the other computers in the world?"

"Yes."

"But they weren't. Why?"

"I don't know," Jeremy said. "Something is beyond weird."

"Shadow, shadow." Donny uttered the words softly, his gaze directed at Irwin. Was he answering the question?

Jeremy pointed at the center monitor. "Shadow?"

Donny put his fingers over the keyboard but then hesitated. His hands shook until his fingers touched the keys. Tap. Tap. Tap. The lines of code scrolled and then stopped. Donny pointed to the center of the screen. "Shadow. Shadow. Shadow."

Jeremy leaned closer. Amid the symbols and programming language were two words: Eli Shade. Jeremy muttered the words. Donny shuddered.

"What's an Eli Shade?" Stanley asked.

"It's a name." Jeremy leaned back in the chair. "Hackers and people who write viruses and digital worms are often arrogant. They like to include a signature in the code. It's always a pseudonym."

"Why would they do that, sir?" Irwin moved closer to look over Jeremy's shoulder.

"It's digital graffiti, a way of bragging without signing your identity." He studied the name. "I don't recognize it. Eli Shade. Odd name. Shade...shadow...I wonder if this is what Donny means by *shadow*." He tapped his chin with a finger. "Why Eli? Eli is a variation of a Hebrew name: El—one of the names of God." Jeremy wondered if Israel had been behind this as many assumed they were Stuxnet. Of course, that had never been proved.

Jeremy began to think aloud. "Eli Shade. Eli Shadow. El is often translated *ascended*. Name of God. God's Shadow? Who would call himself God's Shadow?" He didn't expect an answer. He didn't have one. He did, however, have a feeling.

A very, very bad feeling.

▪▪▪▪

Jeremy studied the file. It was as elegant as it was ingenious. "I need to compare this to other captured infections. Most were wiped out when the EM pulse hit. I assume that was the idea." Jeremy was thinking aloud.

"Sir, are you saying someone in this family is responsible for everything that's gone on? For the outages? The end of technology? The starvation and riots and—"

"Stow that, sailor. Am I clear?"

"Crystal, sir."

"Good." Jeremy turned to Royce. "Ma'am, does your son travel?"

....

Eli Shade knew how to make an entrance. Liam had to give him credit for that. The thing liked to appear behind Liam and clear his throat. Liam always jumped. Shade always laughed. This time, however, he dropped the theatrics and merely manifested in the middle of Liam's office, a few feet from where Pierce sat. Pierce squealed, jumped up, and backpedaled.

"One of these days you're going to give me a heart attack." Pierce patted his chest.

"It won't be your heart that kills you, Mr. Pierce." Shade's voice seemed deeper, darker, more ominous.

Pierce opened his mouth as if ready to ask what the comment meant but then decided against it. A moment later, another shadow figure appeared at Shade's side. Shade looked mostly human, but this creature didn't. Empty eyes, gaping mouth. Pierce took two more steps back.

Liam took the lead. "To what do I owe this pleasure?"

"I have something to share with you, Mr. Burr. We need to talk." Shade smiled.

Liam stood. "Very well." He rounded his desk where he had been sitting. "Will the seating area be adequate?"

"No. I'll meet you on the roof."

"The roof?" Liam said.

Shade and his sidekick disappeared.

"This is new," Pierce said. "Why the roof?"

"I'll let you ask him that." Liam donned his suit coat and started for the office door.

A gentle wind blew from the west, sending invisible fingers through Liam's hair. At least he hoped it was the wind. He had seen too many invisible things over the past eight months. The thought chilled him.

Shade and his friend were waiting for the two. Shade's face was difficult to read—it wasn't quite human enough. Liam and Pierce crossed the concrete roof to the parapet. The hum of the ventilation system provided the evening's night music.

"The roof, Signore Shade? I'm puzzled." Liam sounded calmer than he felt.

"We're taking a little trip. This is easier than dragging you through a pane of glass." Shade's grin was sardonic.

"I appreciate that. Where are we—"

Shade was on him in a moment. Before Liam could draw a breath he was airborne, held in the clutches of the ghoul. He wanted to scream but held his voice. Pierce didn't.

The streets of Brussels scrolled beneath him. The hour was late, but the city was still busy. Citizens continued to enjoy the return of food and power. He had no idea of their speed. Wind whipped around his head, but Liam had learned he could not trust his senses when Shade was around. He was helpless and decided passivity as his best course of action. When a man can't do what he wants, it is sometimes wise to do nothing.

The city gave way to dark rolling hills, countryside Liam didn't recognize. He turned his gaze and saw a small mountain in the near distance. He guessed that was their destination.

He was right.

Shade set him down gently on the apex of the mountain. Liam felt grass beneath his feet. The mountain couldn't be very tall if grass could grow on its peak—assuming the mountain existed at all.

"Better than our last flight, Signore Burr?" Shade asked.

"Much better. Thank you."

"I have a different point to make this time."

Liam could hardly wait.

Pierce and his escort settled next to Liam.

Shade placed his hands behind his back. "I appreciate your willingness to meet with me on such short notice."

You must be kidding.

Shade glanced over his shoulder at Liam as if he had heard the thought. "We are making fine progress, thanks to you two. You have done admirable work and have saved countless lives, but more work remains. Many are still dying from lack of food and safe water. Chaos covers most of the planet. For the world to heal, things must change."

"Much has already changed," Liam said. "I take it you have some specific...suggestions."

"I do." Shade turned to Liam. "I offer you the world." He made a gesture, and the lights of a thousand cities pushed away the darkness of the valleys below. Lights twinkled like diamonds in a jewelry case—yellow, white, gold. The valleys looked encrusted with gems.

"The world?" Liam had to work to get the words out. The vision before him was stunning.

"The world needs a new leader. A single leader." Shade moved closer to Liam. "There are more than 190 countries in the world, Liam, each with its own leader, each with its own idea of how people should live. Some cooperate with others, but most don't. Fear, jealousy, border disputes, food distribution, water, and one hundred thirteen other factors lead to wars and rumors of wars."

"One hundred and thirteen—"

"Do you doubt me, Signore Burr?"

"No. Of course not. The number is new to me, that's all."

"I know the facts, Liam. Better than you. I have made a study of humanity for…well, a very long time." Shade again turned his attention to the horizon of jewels. "You humans work from the wrong motives. You emphasize the individual instead of the entire fabric of human existence. The French dislike the British; the British hate the French. African nations war with each other. Criminals form alliances to attack the very society that makes their existence possible. In good years, 30,000 people, mostly children, die of starvation. More die from bad water or lack of simple medicine, and the world is fine with that. No one cares. Your race acts like cattle in a herd, fish in a school, birds in a flock, caring only for what happens that day. The future is a mere philosophical construct at best, an afterthought at worst. Do you agree?"

Liam thought it best to do so. "Yes."

"What your world needs is a leader. A single leader. You have seen what happens when a global crisis occurs. Countries immediately blame others. Cooperation ceases. Each turns to its leaders, believing they will provide the answer when in reality they are children playing with dynamite. Children. Yes, a good metaphor."

Shade stepped to Liam's side and put his arm around his shoulders. It felt cold. "Children cannot survive on their own. They need the strength and wisdom of their parents. That is what this world needs—a parent. You, my human friend, are that parent, that father."

"Parent to the world? NUTO is difficult enough to manage."

"And it is that kind of tiny thinking that keeps the world on the eve of destruction. Have I not given you food when you were hungry?"

"Yes. You've been very kind."

"Have I not given you riches far beyond what anyone can imagine?"

That was true. Liam had no need for more wealth, but he had been willing to take it.

"Yes."

"Have I not given you great power?"

"Indeed you have."

"And why have I done these things? Because, my friend, you have done everything I ask. You have followed me, and I have given you food and power. Now I offer all the cities of the world." He squeezed Liam's shoulder hard enough to make the joint hurt. "You follow me, and the world will follow you. You can be the savior of this planet."

"There will be resistance," Liam said.

"Of course. There always is. I will help you deal with that. I will show you what you need to do. I will deal with your enemies. I will make you messiah to the world."

"May I ask what you get out of all this?" Liam asked.

"Satisfaction, my dear Liam, satisfaction." He gazed skyward. "There's someone I want to hurt."

Liam couldn't raise the courage to ask who that might be.

"Liam Burr, I have brought you to this high mountain to show you the world I offer. All you must do is follow me. Will you do so?"

Liam looked around him. The sight was beautiful and the offer compelling. The world could benefit from a single leader, one who could put an end to the troubles. One willing to bring every country into line. If not him, then Shade would cast him off like a sandwich wrapper and choose someone else. The loss would be too great.

He raised his head. "Yes, Mr. Shade. I accept."

Shade smiled. It was frightening. "Mr. Pierce will be by your side. He will be the Aaron to your Moses."

"Yes, sir."

"Don't underestimate him, Mr. Burr. Every messiah needs a prophet."

■ ■ ■.■

Jeremy made arrangements for an aircraft that could accommodate the Elton family, Rosa, and all of Donny's computers. Because Rosa was Donny's nurse, Jeremy thought it best to bring her. He promised to do his best to locate her husband. Rosa said she hadn't heard from him in eight months and feared the worse. He had been transporting canned goods to Atlanta when the lights went out.

To his parents' surprise, Donny didn't resist when Jeremy started to dismantle the computer setups. In fact, he looked pleased.

The C-23 Sherpa, a small prop-driven transport aircraft, was comfortable but slower than the fighter jet. With a range of a little more than 700 miles, the craft had to refuel several times on its journey across the country. Happy to have a plane that could still fly, Jeremy made no complaints. They wouldn't arrive in Maryland until the wee hours. Jeremy had planned to sleep on the flight, but sleep wouldn't come. Donny, however, slept the sleep of the heroic.

In the dark thirty-seat cabin, Stanley asked the question Jeremy knew he would. "General, are we really to blame for what happened in the world? Have people suffered and died because of us?"

It took a moment before Jeremy could answer. "I don't know, Mr. Elton. The early form of the worm is on Donny's computers.

His computers and your condo were not affected. That looks suspicious."

"But Donny isn't capable of doing such a thing. He doesn't see the world the way we do." Royce had been in tears most of the day.

"Perhaps that's the problem, Mrs. Elton. He didn't know what he was doing. Still…something doesn't ring true. I wonder if someone used him and his genius. Maybe gave him the Stuxnet worm and let him play with it."

"I've never heard of Stuxnet, and neither my wife nor I are capable of writing such a complex piece of software."

They could be lying, Jeremy thought, but for some reason he believed them. He wondered about the name he found in the code. Eli Shade…a hacker's nickname? Each time he thought of it he felt disquiet.

"What will happen to us?" Royce asked.

"I've set up a place for you to stay at Fort Meade. USCYBER-COM is located there, as is the NSA. They're going to want to go over the code line by line, and that will take some time, even for a team. It's extremely complicated."

"So we're prisoners?"

"You'll be staying on base in one of the officer homes for visiting dignitaries, not a prison cell."

"Are we free to leave at will?" Stanley pushed.

Jeremy hated saying it. "No. But I'll make sure you're comfortable, and you will not have to worry about food."

"I suppose that's good," Royce said.

"Look, I don't know how this will work out. It's not up to me. Just continue to be honest and straightforward."

"Do we need a lawyer?" Stanley asked.

"That's a good question. Are there still attorneys?"

The flight continued with little conversation.

■ ■ ■ ■

Jeremy was travel weary and glad to be back home even though home was deep below Mount Weather. Now that Roni was with him most days, *home* seemed the right word. With Roni and now Cody, a tent in the desert was home. He was looking forward to a hug, a kiss, and a bit of sleep before reporting to the president.

Roni waited outside their small apartment. Her eyes hinted at a story she didn't want to tell.

"It's early, even for a doctor," Jeremy said. He retrieved his hug and kiss. "I assume Cody is in bed."

"Yes, sleeping like a rock."

"He may be the smartest of us all. You're not going to believe what I uncovered in San Diego."

Roni smiled and it looked as if the act took effort. "We need to talk, babe."

He didn't like the sound of her voice. "What's wrong?"

"It's the president." She poured out the story like a faucet streaming water.

The news was a punch to Jeremy's middle. The months had brought the president and Jeremy close. He doubled over, propping himself up with his hands on his knees. He fought the urge to vomit and the almost irresistible desire to curl up on the floor and weep. Instead he straightened, took a deep breath, put his arm around his wife, and entered their apartment, the day's success a distant memory.

EPILOGUE

Jeremy and Roni stepped from their officer's home at Fort Meade. After spending slightly more than a year living below grade, returning to a house, small as it was and situated on a military base, was a pleasure. They decided to stay at Fort Meade for several reasons. First, Jeremy's work with USCYBERCOM was still much more than a nine-to-five job. He didn't keep track of the hours he worked. He didn't have time. Second, their home in College Park had suffered extensive damage from looters. Much of DC was still unsafe. Jeremy couldn't focus if he had to worry about Roni and Cody's safety. As it was, every time Roni went to DC to do hospital rounds and surgery, he had to release her into the hands of God. Fortunately, the military provided security for the facility, and Roni always traveled with two armed soldiers. The same was true for other doctors who still needed transportation from home to the hospital and back.

The air this morning was sweet and cool. January had come around again and with it a more stable world, at least in appearance. Communications between countries had improved, which was good for the most part. Still, disturbing reports from central

Europe trickled through. The members of NUTO thrived more than their counterparts in almost unbelievable ways.

President Grundy had taken the reins of leadership in a steel grip. He was no Barlow, but he didn't lack for confidence and focus. He made his goal clear: Bring the United States back to its previous glory. Jeremy wondered if that was possible.

President Barlow's body had been treated in the small mortuary in Mount Weather and kept in a simple coffin stored in a cold room. He was buried in Arlington Cemetery on Christmas Day. The service had been recorded and would be broadcast when enough television stations were functioning again.

Radio and newspapers became more important because they took less work to resurrect. They were nothing like they were before the Event, but it was a start.

The Eltons lived on base. Few knew their connection to the Event. Donny was proving useful. Though he seldom spoke, he made his ideas clear in programming language. With his help, Slipper became even more secure, as did networked computers. In the years ahead, the rebuilding of the Internet might rest on the man-boy's work. It took a team of six to decipher what he wrote. That team included Jeremy.

Roni stepped on the porch. She held a mug of coffee. "Beautiful day. The sky is so blue."

"That's because air travel is still limited. Less pollutants in the air."

"I suppose, or the sky could just be pretty because it wants to be."

"Why, Dr. Matisse, you're still a hopeless romantic."

"Someone's got to do it." She took a sip. "Cody is getting his shoes on. He'll be out in a moment."

"I've got to get that kid to stop calling me General. It's respectful and I appreciate it, but it doesn't seem right."

"You could ask him to call you something else, like Dad."

"Dad?" He chuckled. "You think he'd go for that?"

Roni nodded. "I think so. Why don't you ask him?"

"I think I will." Jeremy's smile faded. He looked into the distance, over the buildings and roads that made up Fort Meade.

Roni took his hand. "What's wrong?"

"Nothing. Just thinking."

"Nothing, eh? I'm a doctor and a woman. You can't lie to me. Spill it."

He shrugged. "Just thinking about the future."

"That always depresses you. You know, most people think the worst is over."

Jeremy shook his head. "People are still dying because of this thing, and the more I know about the changes in the world, the more I think the worst is yet to come."

"More Bible prophecy?"

He nodded. "The Bible doesn't tell us everything, but it tells us enough. There is more darkness on the horizon. Something is going on. Something in the spiritual world I don't understand."

"I wish we could believe it was all just the work of an innocent savant."

"Me too—"

The front door opened and closed with a bang. Cody burst on the scene like an artillery shell. "Come on or we'll be late for chapel."

"That sounded like an order, General."

"I believe it was, Doctor." Jeremy took Roni's mug and set it on a small table next to one of the porch chairs. He picked up two Bibles, handed Roni's to her, and offered his arm. She took it as they stepped from the porch.

A few steps into the short walk, Jeremy called to Cody, who was making his way along the sidewalk by leaping over every crack and joint in the concrete. "Hey, kid, I've got a question for you…"

. . . .

Dr. Sean Scotcher returned to his small, cluttered office in the Center for Disease Control in Atlanta, found a recent biomedical journal, and threw it on the floor. "Shot down again. What's wrong with me? I must be hideous."

He wasn't hideous. Short, sure. Pencil thin, okay. Balding more than a thirty-two-year-old man should be, admittedly. But none of those are horrible, so why did yet one more woman politely tell him to get lost when he asked her out? He didn't understand. What he lacked in some areas, he made up for in brains.

To make things worse, there were few women to pick from. Only the most-needed scientists, researchers, and administrators were allowed in the facility. Theirs was one of the few that received immediate attention when the power went out. Rightly so. Confined in the building were strains of the most deadly viruses, spores, and bacteria known to humanity. Ebola and its variants, altered malaria, dengue fever, military-grade anthrax, and a hundred more. Just one mistake or one unhappy employee could unleash invisible murderers. Millions would die.

Precautions had been taken to make sure such a thing could never happen. That was before the events of this last year.

At night, Scotcher fabricated tales of a man who released a plague on the world. It was just a way to pass the lonely hours. Maybe he would write a novel or movie script. Hollywood liked a good tale of destruction by disease. Boy, could he teach them a few things. Of course, no one was publishing books or making movies anymore. Maybe someday.

The door to his office creaked open.

"Go away. I'm busy."

It opened anyway, and an odd-looking man in a black coat and hat entered. "I'm sorry to bother you, Dr. Scotcher. My name is Eli Shade, and I wonder if I might have a word with you."

Reader Questions

1. Jeremy is a Christian man married to an unbelieving wife, yet they have a happy marriage. What qualities did they exhibit that made this possible?

2. Although not a person of faith, Dr. Roni Matisse goes to great trouble to help the patients who come to her hospital, even to the point of refusing an opportunity to leave for a safer place. What makes her so giving?

3. Before the Event, life was good for Jeremy and Roni. After the lights go out, each is challenged to be something they never expected. What challenges did they face? How did they face them? What sacrifices did they make?

4. Cody is a ten-year-old boy who has lost everything. As a doctor, Roni has seen such things before. Why does she bond with Cody?

5. Cody changes Roni in subtle ways. How did his arrival in her life alter her?

6. Roni's view of Christians is changed by the actions of several people, including her husband, Dr. Southwell (a Baptist preacher), and Jose (a Christian patient). How did they exemplify the gospel?

7. Donny Elton is a savant, extremely gifted in one area of life yet unable to care for himself. His disorder, which empowers him but also brings about great damage, changes the world forever. Was he just a tool of Eli Shade ? Why would God allow such a thing to take place? Is Donny guilty?

8. Eli Shade is unlike any other antagonist, yet he is familiar in many ways. Whom does he remind you of?

9. Jeremy faces the fact that something is going on he can't explain. All his knowledge about computers and digital warfare isn't enough to explain all that he sees. In the book, he never gets the answers he wants. Is this true to our life experiences? Do you have questions that go unanswered?

10. This story doesn't end "happily ever after." It is meant to replicate life. What do you think happens after this?

11. Jeremy makes clear that he is no prophecy expert, but he knows a great deal. Nonetheless, we get the idea that things are unfolding a little differently that he guessed they would. Is that likely with our understanding of prophecy? Are there things we don't know? What questions about the end times do you have? Do you think we humans have it all figured out, or are there still mysteries about the days to come?

12. In your view, who is Liam Burr?

13. Who is Fred Pierce?

A Word from the Authors

During a radio interview recently, one of us was asked what, beyond the obvious, is the difference between fiction and nonfiction. The answer? Nonfiction is education; fiction is exploration. In this book, we describe events that might fit the biblical narrative about the days leading to the end times. What is presented is the outcome of a series of what-if questions. That is how fiction works. It is not meant to replace scholarly works on the subject but to put a face on what might happen.

Our goal is to entertain in a way that prompts you to wonder and think. With a topic like this, entertainment is not the ultimate goal. We hope that this work will whet your appetite for the prophetic material of the Bible. Much of God's plan about the future is still hidden, and we have tried to respect that. What is presented here is a creative scenario of what could happen, not what will. Only God knows those details.

Thank you for reading, and may God bless you.

Dr. Mark Hitchcock
Alton Gansky

THE MAYAN APOCALYPSE (A NOVEL)

The self-proclaimed Mayan descendant Robert Quetzal, media guru to the vulnerable, has taken Mayan prophecy claims to the extreme. Not only does he teach the end of the earth will come on December 21, 2012, he also offers a way out—for a price.

Andrew Morgan, a wealthy oil executive who has lost his family in a plane crash, is mad at God. Devastated by the tragedy, he puts his faith in Robert Quetzal and the ancient Mayan predictions. In his quest for answers, he meets Lisa Campbell, a smart, intuitive journalist researching the Mayan calendar. Lisa thinks the 2012 theories are nonsense and doesn't hesitate to say so. Morgan dismisses her when he learns she is a Christian.

As December 21, 2012 draws closer, a meteorite impact in Arizona, a volcanic eruption in Mexico, and the threat of an asteroid on a collision course with the earth escalate fears. Are these indicators of a global collapse? Will anyone survive? Does the Bible have the answers? Or has fate destined everyone to a holocaust from which there is no escape?

To learn more about Harvest House books and
to read sample chapters, log on to our website:

www.harvesthousepublishers.com

HARVEST HOUSE PUBLISHERS
EUGENE, OREGON